A Very Merry NANNY

VERY MERRY BOOK TWO

LYRA PARISH

OFFICIAL PLAYLIST

- Lie to Girls - Sabrina Carpenter
- My Kink is Karma - Chappell Roan
- us. - Gracie Abrams, Taylor Swift
- All I Want for Christmas Is You - Mariah Carey
- Indifferent - Megan Moroney
- Risk - Gracie Abrams
- Good Luck, Babe! - Chappell Roan
- champagne problems - Taylor Swift
- Winter Things - Ariana Grande
- this is what slow dancing feels like - JVKE
- Do It for Me - Rosenfeld
- Christmas Tree Farm - Taylor Swift
- Mastermind - Taylor Swift

LISTEN TO THIS PLAYLIST ON SPOTIFY:
https://bit.ly/averymerrynannyplaylist

Dedicated to those who love a grumpy, introverted hero with a daddy voice. Mm.

*What if I told you none of it was accidental
And the first night that you saw me,
nothing was gonna stop me?*

—*TAYLOR SWIFT, MASTERMIND*

CHAPTER 1

EMMA

"That tickles." I giggle as Asher Banks playfully kisses along my neck and jaw.

He knows my rules—the ones I established two years ago after a disastrous breakup that changed my outlook on love. For me, flirting is as far as it goes.

No one pays us any mind as we slip into the shadows at my best friend's party. Billie told me Asher wasn't invited, but here he is, looking like a snack and smelling like a bad decision.

His broad shoulders and thick brown hair shield my expression from the prying eyes of the guests.

"You're so damn pretty, Em, and still a pro at playing hard to get," he whispers, his voice gravelly, capturing my full attention.

Hooking up with him would be fun—I'd definitely enjoy it —but it would come with a world of regrets.

"You're a flirt," I reply, but it's deeper than that. Asher wants something I'll never give him—my heart.

He deserves someone who can commit and love him in ways I can't. This gorgeous man needs a devoted partner who

1

can bear him an heir to inherit the family's riches. That's not me.

"Don't let my date see you," I warn as he twirls a lock of my dark red hair between his fingers.

Everyone knows I'm not attending this party alone; the world learned that when the paparazzi with their long zoom lenses chased me around New York and snapped pictures of me with my date.

Tonight's headlines read:

It's official! Emma Manchester has a different man every month.

It only took a couple of hours for me to be labeled a billionaire whore who pumps and dumps men. I love that for me—especially since I haven't been intimate with anyone since my ex. It's all just ridiculous rumors.

"So tell me, Em. Did you give the poor bastard your rules?" His tone holds playful amusement.

"Every man I date gets the rundown. Yes, even your *brother*."

Honesty is key, and I won't pretend when it comes to love or dating. I physically can't; it makes me sick.

Asher crosses his arms over his broad chest, studying me intently. "It's been months, and I've still got it bad for you."

"All fuck boys say that about the pretty things they can't have." I meet his gaze, confident he's just playing games.

I could have him if I wanted, even for a night. To be clear, I don't. That's why I ended it over the summer.

"I don't think I can handle you being with him," he admits.

I try to ease his jealousy. "I'm not into your brother. We're friends, just like us."

He lets out a relieved breath. "And he was made aware?"

The two of them are highly competitive.

"Yes," I confirm. "Before we arrived."

"Ah. Well, I hope you find what you're looking for, Emma. You can always change your mind about me." He smirks.

"I don't do second chances, Ash."

"Rule number three. I haven't forgotten, but I also know there are exceptions to every rule."

As the string quartet in the corner of the penthouse shifts to a more upbeat song, the atmosphere in the room transforms.

Silence hangs heavily between us, and I know I need to walk away before I do something I might regret. "I should go."

"Maybe you should stay."

"Ash."

I'm convinced that the blue-eyed billionaires have placed bets on who can win me over like a trophy. Many have tried, but they all face the same fate: being dumped by me.

Billie believes I'm their karma—the one who always gets away—having broken so many hearts without a hint of remorse. Strangely, my reputation hasn't deterred anyone; if anything, it seems to have encouraged them. I've become a challenge.

Asher tilts my chin upward. "I'd settle down for you, Em."

He wears the same expression he had the night I told him it was over. He was falling too hard, and I... wasn't.

"Save it for someone who can reciprocate."

"Having part of you is enough," he mutters.

"No." I shake my head. "You deserve better."

"You think better than you exists?"

"I believe there's someone better for you than me."

"Ah. That's where you're wrong."

"Didn't your parents teach you not to play with broken toys? Someone always gets hurt, even if you're careful. It's the sharp edges you don't see, Ash." I force a smile as I look into his honey-colored eyes. "It was great seeing you again."

"Em," he says, pulling me back to him. "I want you to be happy."

"Me too," I murmur, seeing straight through him.

Everything about Asher fits my type—tall, handsome, intelligent, a bit of an asshole—but there's no spark. Not even a flicker.

After our first kiss, I felt nothing. I thought I would.

Ash had rented an art exhibit for us to privately enjoy the sculptures of one of my favorite artists. We strolled through the rooms, appreciating the playful works with their pop culture references. The lights were low, the mood was right, and the wine was flowing. The night was both romantic and thought-provoking.

Before we left, Ash pressed his perfect lips against mine in the foyer. When we pulled away, he asked if I had felt it. By the look on his face, I could tell he had.

I didn't. That was the moment I realized I might be broken and may never experience butterflies again.

"I'm really sorry," I say, recalling how I hurt him. I can never apologize enough.

"Stop apologizing," he responds gently. "You made me realize what I was missing."

As I take in his physique, noticing the outline in his jeans, I briefly contemplate the idea of a fling. The white button-up clings to his chiseled body. "Stop testing me," I warn. "Rule number 3."

"Busted, I suppose. Guess your rules are unbreakable."

His words make me chuckle. These players always think they can fool me, but I block their advances at every turn.

"Tempting as ever, Ash. One day, you'll thank me."

Our eyes meet, and we share a silent conversation before he grins. "Emma fucking Manchester. Always a pleasure," he says, wrapping his arm around me and giving me a gentle squeeze.

"Put some respect on my name."

"Always," he replies, and I break away from him. "Still a firecracker."

I laugh and shake my head. "Still a flirty bastard."

I make my way to the golden-glowing champagne fountain at the center of the room and pour myself two glasses—both for me.

Billie's parties never disappoint, and the hors d'oeuvres are divine. A celebrity chef has prepared mini beef Wellingtons, truffle risotto arancini, and oysters on the half shell. Expensive alcohol flows like a river as the string quartet transitions to a Taylor Swift song.

I catch Ash's gaze and playfully roll my eyes as he winks at me.

Just as I turn the corner, I nearly collide with Billie. Her jet-black hair is pulled back, and her blue eyes sparkle, framed by a smile from her vibrant red lips.

"I've been searching for you all night," I tell her.

"Here I am. Also, I didn't know you were still playing games with the Banks brothers."

My best friend has a magnetic, black cat energy and only tolerates a select few humans. I'm fortunate to be one of her closest confidants. She trusts fewer than five people on the planet.

"That's only because your brothers wouldn't give me the time of day," I retort.

Easton and Weston are as sexy as sin, but they're also nine years older than me. They've adopted me as their youngest sister and friend-zoned me long ago.

She sips from her crystal glass, the contents a light brown liquid. "The question still stands—when will Emma Manchester stop being a maneater?"

"Soon, I hope, but I've accepted that this might be my reality. Maybe I'll be single forever."

"You and me both."

"It's exhausting. I just want to feel something. Anything." I sigh. "I'm convinced I'm broken," I whisper.

"Nah. I think you're just bored. You have a buffet of men to choose from in the city; it's too easy for you. Monotony has always been your enemy, Emma. Think about it—you need a man who doesn't want you more than you want him. When have you ever had that?"

Never.

"Sometimes I hate how well you know me." I down one of my glasses. A server takes it from me as I sip from the other. "Almond champagne from Italy?" I ask.

"I had it flown in for us because it's our favorite."

"Billie!" a high-pitched voice calls, and I turn to see Harper Alexander approaching. "And Emma!"

She wraps me in a tight hug. I haven't seen her in months. "What are we discussing?" she asks, glancing between us.

"Champagne," I reply, eager to divert the conversation from my relationship failures.

"We were talking about Emma's love life," Billie interjects, refusing to change the subject.

I groan. "The lack of."

"It's like nothing has changed in twenty years," Harper laughs. "But Christmas is coming. Maybe you'll find love under the mistletoe."

I nearly choke on my champagne. "It would take a miracle."

She laughs, playfully bumping against me. Once I regain my breath, I follow Billie's gaze to Asher.

"I thought you weren't inviting him," I say.

"I didn't," she replies, glaring at Harper.

"It was me," Harper singsongs. "Asher's an asset."

"Asher's an ass," Billie retorts.

I clear my throat. "You two would be perfect together. You're compatible. Plus, you can't stop eye-fucking him."

"Give me a break," Billie scoffs.

"You're doing it right now," Harper points out.

Billie's brows crease, and I speak before she can deny it.

"I've missed you both. A lot. Is there anything I should be updated on?"

"Other than our siblings finding love?" Harper shakes her head. "No."

"I love that for them," Billie replies.

This summer, I traveled nonstop and returned to the city last week, but I'm already ready to leave again. It's like I can't sit still; I can't settle down.

"Can we take a picture?" I ask, sliding my phone out of the handbag that once belonged to Marilyn Monroe. I couldn't resist carrying it, even if the internet is outraged by my perceived disrespect.

I stand between Harper and Billie, holding my phone upright but struggling to find the right angle.

Harper offers to help.

"Smile pretty," she says, pressing the button and capturing several shots of us in slightly different poses. I quickly scroll through the photos and find one where my eyes are closed and I'm making kissy lips. They're making silly faces, too.

"This is my favorite one," I announce.

"If you post that, people might think I'm fun," Billie mutters before laughing. The world has labeled her the serious one who never smiles.

I have thousands of pictures from over the years to prove them wrong, but she leans into the 'bad bitch' rumors, and it has become part of her personality. Harper and I know the truth, though.

I finish my second glass of champagne while scanning the room, recognizing so many familiar faces and old friends.

"If we were characters in Sex & the City, who would I be?"

It's a question I ask every few years.

"Carrie," they say in unison.

I inhale. "Still?"

Billie lifts an eyebrow. "You're a great friend who's always worried about your love life."

"I think the three of us are Carrie. Uh, who's that with your brother?" My eyes lock on Weston Calloway.

Billie turns. "Oh, that's his new girlfriend. They haven't officially announced their relationship yet, but you can see it written all over his face. He has the same look Easton has now that he's found the love of his life."

"Wow. I never thought I'd see Weston look at someone the way you look at Asher Banks."

"And to think I believed you'd drop that conversation," she replies. "I was wrong."

"Sorry, it's the alcohol. You know how it makes me too truthful. But you're right; he's in love with her," I whisper, seeing it so clearly.

Billie smiles. "He looks happy."

"I'm jealous," I admit reluctantly. "Everyone seems to be finding love but me."

"I knew this would happen," Harper says.

Our eyes meet. "Of course you did."

Recently, she predicted her brother's entire relationship, down to where he'd marry his wife.

At the time, he was single and angry at the world. She has also predicted a few of our other friends' engagements. Unfortunately, I've never sparked her Spidey senses, and she's never given me a cupid love reading.

Billie, on the other hand, has had several.

I reach for her hand, and she takes it. "Sense anything this time?"

"You're complicated. I don't feel any energy."

"Sounds like a premonition for my entire love life." I laugh because if I don't, I'll end up crying.

She lets go. "I'm sorry."

"It's me, not you," I jokingly say as my phone buzzes.

I glance down and see it's my sister, Claire. She's four years older than me, and while I consider us very close, I haven't spoken to her in almost two weeks and haven't seen her in months.

"Why did you make that face?" Harper asks. She's too perceptive.

"Nothing."

"Thinking about Hudson?" Billie asks, respecting my boundaries as I respected hers about Ash.

I met Hudson Jolly the day his brother proposed to my sister. The chemistry we shared sometimes haunts me.

"Who?" I ask, but she knows better.

Hudson is the kind of man who breaks hearts for a living. Flawlessly handsome with dark brown hair and striking green eyes, his scowl brings me to my knees. He's broody and even more unavailable than I am.

I considered staying in Texas to make him my special project in July, but I ultimately decided to leave.

Billie clears her throat, and I notice both she and Harper are staring at me.

"Huh?" I glance between them.

"You were thinking about that guy," Billie states.

"That's ridiculous. We met once and exchanged a few words. Nothing more." My phone continues to ring. "I have to take this. She'll fly into the city and kick my ass if I ignore her again."

"Good luck," Billie says.

"The patio is quieter," Harper suggests, pointing toward the sliding doors. I quickly slip outside and answer. "Claire. Hi!"

"Well?" she asks expectantly.

"Well, what?" The booze has kicked in. *Great.*

"What time will you be here tomorrow? You never replied to my texts."

I let out a nervous laugh.

She gasps. "You forgot about my Halloween party, didn't you?"

I force a smile. She has an uncanny knack for knowing, regardless of the distance or how we communicate. "Don't worry, I'll be there."

"And you have a costume?"

"I have a closet full. See you tomorrow around eight, right?"

"Okay." She doesn't sound convinced. "I've missed you, Em."

"Missed you too! How's Jake?"

Jake, or JJ, is the wonderful man who proposed to my sister. He loves her deeply, and their relationship makes me want to believe in love. Sometimes, I envy what she found on that desolate country road in the middle of nowhere.

I glance at the New York skyline, watching the city lights twinkle like stars until my vision blurs.

"He's great. Happy. Super busy because tree season kicks off on Monday. I can't wait for you to see his costume. Oh, by the way, Hudson is coming," she adds casually.

"And?"

"Nothing. Just a passing thought."

I clear my throat, remembering the connection we shared the first time our eyes met. "He's emotionally unavailable. I'm not into repairing broken hearts."

She laughs. "His heart isn't broken. It's frozen. Just like yours."

I remember the day I met him and his adorable son, Colby. Months have passed, and yet that man still haunts my thoughts. Maybe my fantasies, too.

"Anyway, I've gotta go. See you tomorrow," I say.

"Before nine," she reminds me.

"Okay, okay. Until then. Love you! Bye!"

The call ends, and I head back inside, grabbing a third glass. The alcohol starts to rush through me.

"Everything okay?" Billie asks as I approach them.

"Yeah. I have to be in Merryville tomorrow night for my

10

sister's party that I forgot about. Shit, I hope I can get a flight to El Paso on such short notice."

Although I could use my father's resources, I refuse to ask for help.

Everything I have I've earned, and I take pride in that. Some would argue I'm not self-made, but I'd argue that being a Manchester has done me no favors. It's only made life harder.

"You should purchase a private jet," Billie suggests.

I laugh and shake my head. "Why, when I have two besties who will let me borrow theirs?"

"Touché," Harper replies. She and Billie own a luxury fashion company and built a billion-dollar brand from scratch, just like me.

As I glance over Billie's shoulder, I notice my date flirting with Dove Weatherly.

"Wow, they look perfect together," I gasp.

Harper glances at them and nods.

Dyson's fingers brush against Dove's as they stand close. She laughs at whatever he says.

"Looks like my plan worked after all. Even earlier than I predicted. Great."

"You played matchmaker tonight?" Billie asks.

I shoot her a wink. It's one of my things. Women tend to gravitate toward the men I date. "Why not?"

"You're an angry little cupid," Billie snickers. "Don't forget about my New Year's Eve party."

"I promised to be there. Wouldn't miss it for the world." I prefer to stay flexible with my schedule and love the unpredictability of life. I crave it. However, if I commit to my besties, I do not ditch them. *Ever.* "I should probably head home."

Billie wraps me in a tight hug, then Harper does the same.

Harper meets my gaze. "I think you're moving into a new era, my friend."

"Is that a prediction?" I ask.

She grins widely, not denying it.

"I'll keep you updated on what happens in Texas," I say, aware that I need to pack and figure out what costume to wear.

"You better," Billie warns. "We'll see you in two months."

"I might be back before then."

Billie smirks. "Claire will convince you to stay longer. Guaranteed."

After another hug, I stroll across the room toward Dyson.

When our eyes meet, I point to the door and wave goodbye. He glances over at Dove before smiling back at me. It's a silent thank you that resonates loud and clear. While I may struggle to find love for myself, I excel at helping others.

As I ride the elevator down to the ground floor, I contemplate life.

The next man I commit to will be someone I can spend the rest of my life with; there are no exceptions to this rule.

I might remain single forever.

CHAPTER 2

HUDSON

Colby screams at the top of his lungs, throwing a tantrum in his Batman costume. His face is bright red, and his lips are swollen.

"Mimi is taking you trick-or-treating tonight. You love the parade," I remind my son in the calmest voice I can muster. He turns five in a month and has been struggling to adjust to preschool and new schedules.

When he melts down, I let him express his feelings for as long as he needs. I've read countless parenting books and joined various forums, determined to provide him with every ounce of support I can.

As his cries continue, I sit on the floor, crisscrossing my legs beside him.

"Wow, Bee! Your Batman costume is awesome. Look at that symbol on your chest!" I point to it.

I'm good at refocusing his attention, a superpower he doesn't recognize.

He takes a ragged breath and sniffles as tears stream down his cheeks. "It's a bat."

"Oh really?"

13

He nods as I trace the outline of the symbol with my finger.

For months, I worried that I had done something wrong as a parent. My mom explained that she went through a similar phase with me at my son's age. She handled it differently, enrolling me in extracurricular activities, which worked because my issues stemmed from the adjustment of becoming a big brother. I know how fortunate I am to have been raised by supportive parents who attended every talent show, luncheon, and football game. They're amazing grandparents, too.

Many of Colby's challenges are rooted in feelings of abandonment, which is why I constantly remind him that I'm not going anywhere.

I still worry that I'm not doing a good job as a dad. Perhaps I always will.

From what I gather, no one really knows how to raise kids; they simply figure it out as they go. Honestly, that thought is terrifying, too.

"Hands down, you've got the coolest Batman costume I've ever seen," I tell him. "In my entire life. And I'm old."

"Really?" He blinks, wiping the tears from his face.

"Dude, yes, really." I squeeze the padded muscles on his arms. "Flex for me."

He lifts his arms and strikes a pose.

"Your turn," he says.

I mimic him, peeling up my shirt to show my bicep.

"Nice, dad."

I grin. "Ready for candy?"

"What kind?" he asks.

"All of them. Which ones do you want?"

"Snickers! And Tootsie Rolls!"

"Yum. Will you share?"

"Yes!"

He's a sweet kid with a big heart who loves to give.

14

In August, I spoke with his pediatrician about the meltdowns and have been practicing my approach. Redirecting his attention is the only thing that works when he's spiraling. It requires my undivided attention and softly spoken words.

Suddenly, there's a knock at the door, and Colby bolts toward it as the knob turns. The pads of his feet pound against the wooden floor as my mom enters.

Her brows furrow. "Honey, you good?"

"Perfect," I reply with a smile.

"Mimi!" Colby laughs and stretches his arms wide. My mom lifts him onto her hip, showering him with compliments and kisses.

"Baby, you're getting so heavy," she groans. He may not even be five yet, but he's already taller than many kids his age; it's the Jolly genes at work. He'll hit six feet before he's fourteen.

Everyone thinks he's older than he is, but he doesn't turn five until December 1st.

"Ready to go, Batman?" Mom asks.

He nods eagerly, like going trick or treating was his plan. If my mother had shown up ten minutes earlier, the night would have been canceled. Her timing is always perfect.

"Put your boots on, please," I tell him.

He slides down from my mom's arms and dashes to his room.

Mom watches me as I stand.

"Another meltdown?"

"Only the second one this week. It's progress, at least."

She offers me a small smile. "You look tired, son."

"I'll catch up on sleep later."

"How about I bring Colby back to you after dinner tomorrow? That'll give you some extra time to get organized before Monday."

"Yeah, that would be great."

"Have a good night," she adds with a brow lifted.

"Have a good night, Ma."

"At least try to have fun?"

"I'm gonna have the best time," I respond, my tone dripping with sarcasm. Honestly, I'm tempted to skip it altogether.

Mom tilts her head. "Who're you trying to fool?"

"Myself. I'd rather stay home, binge on slasher films, enjoy a few beers, and hit the hay before midnight."

"You can do that any day of the week. And who knows? Maybe you'll meet someone."

I exhale heavily. "Mom."

"It would be nice to see you happy again."

"I *am* happy."

She raises a brow, unconvinced.

"I am," I assert. "I have everything I need. You're starting to sound like Mawmaw. No one in Merryville has caught my eye, and I don't have time to waste dating random women."

Before she can respond, Colby races past us and bolts outside.

"Wait, his candy bucket!" I grab it from the kitchen table and hand it to her.

"See you tomorrow," she says, waving goodbye. "He'll be good and sugared up for you."

"Lucky me. Thanks again, Mom." I stand back, watching him climb into the booster seat in the back of her SUV.

"I love you, Bee," I say.

Colby leans forward, slipping his mask over his eyes. "Love you, Dad."

"Be good for Mimi, okay?"

He nods and gives me a thumbs-up. Soon, they're out of sight, heading down the gravel road.

My house resembles my childhood home, where my parents still live. The layout is ideal, even if it feels too spacious for just Colby and me. I once envisioned a different life and dreamed of having a large family.

Once upstairs, I consider texting Jake and canceling. But then I remembered the promise made to him, so I'll suck it up and go. Begrudgingly.

My costume, a near-perfect replica, took months to assemble. I had the chest plate and armor custom-made, the gloves hand-sewn, and my boots shipped all the way from Europe. It wasn't cheap, but I'm guaranteed to have the best costume in the room.

After getting dressed, I grab my helmet and leave. As long as I show up and make my presence known, I'll fulfill my promise. I'll stay at least one hour. My brother might be disappointed, but at least I kept my word.

I take the four-wheeler through the forest that separates our houses. The sun has already set, and my headlights illuminate the path ahead.

A chill washes over me, and I'm grateful for the layers of my costume, even though they're not quite enough. I plan to spend most of my time by the bonfire anyway.

Jake's cabin comes into view. The warm lights make the windows glow in the dark. Cars are parked along his driveway and fill the pasture beside his house.

People stream in and out of the house. As soon as I walk inside, Claire approaches me with a grin. She's dressed as Little Red Riding Hood; her hair is styled in tight curls. The engagement ring on her finger sparkles under the fairy lights strung overhead.

I wrap my arm around her, and she snuggles in too close for comfort.

"Claire?" Jake calls out. When I turn my head, I see he's also dressed as a Mandalorian. Claire immediately steps away from me, wide-eyed.

I shake my head and lift my helmet.

She playfully slaps my chest. "Asshole."

Jake chuckles. "Nice costume."

"How did you know?" I ask.

"I wasn't told about the Mando party," Lucas chimes in. He's my annoying little brother, but I love him. At thirty-two, he works with me and Jake on the farm, and the three of us have always been close.

"This wasn't planned," I explain. "I kept my costume a secret to avoid exactly this."

"Well, I did the same," Jake adds.

Claire stands in front of us. "The more I drink, the harder it'll be to tell you apart."

"I doubt he'll leave your side again," I say.

Jake wraps his arm around his Little Red. "Damn right."

More people arrive, and Claire welcomes them with gelatin shots. Jake hands me a flask, and I take two big swigs.

"Ew. What is this?" I ask, handing it back.

"Moonshine."

"Did you make it in the toilet?"

"Nah, my garage. I've been practicing."

"Gross. Warn me next time before you give me some nasty stuff. I'm not your test subject."

He leads me into the kitchen, gesturing to the purple liquid in a cauldron. "This punch is great, but it'll knock you on your ass, so be careful."

I fill a plastic cup to the brim and down it in one go.

"Damn. You gettin' lit tonight?"

"I'm only staying for an hour."

He removes his helmet completely. "No."

"Yes. I promised I'd be here. I never promised I'd stay all night."

Everyone thought my reclusiveness was just a phase and that I would eventually return to my old self: easygoing and even fun. But being abandoned with a newborn son during the holidays changed me. Now, I prefer solitude.

Jake refills my empty glass and hands it back to me. "Tonight, you're having fun."

"What's that?" I smirk, downing the drink.

He flips his cape over his shoulder. "I have a feeling things are about to change for you."

"Oh really? Did you consult your crystal ball?" The passion punch makes my cheeks flush and tingle.

Jake chuckles. "I'll bet you."

I shouldn't entertain the idea, but it seems like easy money. "Give me the terms."

"I bet you'll have a girlfriend by midnight on New Year's Eve."

Laughter escapes me. "Is it considered cheating if I have control over my situation?"

He shakes his head. "Nah. When you find your person, nothing will stop you from being with her—not even a thousand bucks," Jake says.

"Double it," I counter.

"Triple it," he retorts. "Three thousand dollars."

He offers his hand, and I grip it firmly. "You're so fuckin' stupid."

"Can't wait for you to eat those words. Also, I expect to be paid before Valentine's Day."

"Ah. Cocky too. But the same goes for me. Payment is due before February 14th."

"Deal," Jake confirms, and we shake on it.

I can't remember the last time I did anything besides be a dad. And I have no plans to change my routine. I almost feel guilty, but he made the bet, not me.

"Just so you don't try to weasel out of paying me: you believe I'll find love before New Year's Day?"

"Yup. That's right," he replies.

"You're way too confident." I narrow my eyes. "You don't actually have a crystal ball, do you?"

"Nah. Just a hunch," he says, as he scans the crowd for his fiancée.

The world fades away as I adjust my helmet. When the DJ cranks up the music inside, I slip outside to where it's quieter. A shiver runs up my spine as the cool breeze envelops me.

The sound of tires crunching on gravel captures my attention. Moments later, a BMW pulls into the property and parks in the field. When a pink Power Ranger steps out of the vehicle, I can't help but laugh. It takes some serious guts to wear full spandex like that.

She checks her phone, the screen lighting up their masked face in the dark. I keep my eyes on her until she slips inside the house.

Jake's best friend Hank, dressed as Woody from *Toy Story*, approaches me. "Who's that? I didn't recognize the car."

"Not sure," I respond. "Can't place the body type either."

"I think I'm gonna go find out."

"Good luck with that."

Hank walks away, and I move to a seat by the fire. When I lift my head, I see Hank approaching the pink Power Ranger. The costume leaves little to the imagination, and I doubt it's providing much warmth.

Hank says something, and his laughter echoes across the yard. From her body language, it's clear she's bored. After a few more seconds, she breaks away from him.

I stare at the flames as they dance toward the star-filled sky. I'm mesmerized by the sight as she sits beside me on the oversized log. Her presence is unnerving, and I've never been so grateful that my face is obscured from view. She pulls out her phone and types something furiously, then locks it.

"Didn't I just see you inside?" she finally asks.

That voice.

It's familiar.

I shrug.

"How have things been? Claire loves it here and has

begged me to stay during the holidays. Maybe I'll flip a coin," she tells me.

I give a thumbs-up, my heart pounding in my chest.

It's Emma—Claire's flirty and much younger sister.

I met her on the Fourth of July when Jake proposed.

Emma considered staying but left after just one day.

I had no idea she'd be here.

"Where's Hudson?" she asks. "Claire said he was out here."

I wish I could see her pretty face, the one I've been following on social media as she traveled around in her campervan alone these past few months. I should walk away, but against my better judgment, I turn toward her and remove my helmet.

She gasps. "Oh, um. You and Jake have the same costume?"

"By accident, trust me."

She reaches into the tool belt of her costume and drops something into my gloved palm.

"I got Colby a dinosaur. If he still likes them."

The T-Rex wears silly shoes and has a toothy grin. I try to hold back my grin but fail. "Thank you for this. I'm sure he'll love it."

Emma briefly met Colby, and he immediately fell in love with her. That was when I knew she needed to stay far away from me.

She removes her mask, revealing her dark red hair in braids. "You're welcome. Now I wish I had gotten you one, too." She smirks as she stands. "Anyway, it was nice seeing you again."

As she walks away, I realize I'm genuinely smiling.

It's been a long time since a woman has had that effect on me.

Shit.

CHAPTER 3

EMMA

I step inside the house, my heart racing. That man is...*breathtaking*. I can't remember the last time someone stirred such a physical reaction in me with just one look.

I spot my sister and pull her away from JJ's side, where he's playing beer pong with friends.

"What's up?" she asks.

"You didn't tell me Hudson has the same costume as Jake," I whisper-hiss.

"Oh, shit. Whoops." She giggles, already a bit tipsy. "I honestly forgot. I've had several shots since then."

"I thought he was Jake," I explain. "I almost embarrassed myself."

"I did the same thing." She hiccups. "Did you give him the T-Rex?"

I nod.

"And?"

"He smiled and thanked me."

"He actually smiled? Not a sarcastic one?"

"It was genuine, Claire."

In that moment, I saw him—the essence of who he truly is.

My sister studies me as I swallow the lump in my throat.

"You and Hudson," she muses, considering the idea.

"Don't start that. No matchmaking. You know I have rules."

She playfully rolls her eyes. "Rule number one: Mutual attraction is required. You find him attractive, don't you?"

"Claire. *Come on.*"

"Rule number two: No leading anyone on. If there's no spark after the first kiss, it's over."

"Are we really doing this here?" I whisper, relieved she's keeping her voice down.

I glance around the room, but no one is paying us any attention.

"Rule number three: No second chances. Rule number four: No sex unless a future is possible. Rule number five: Every interested party must know the rules before the first date."

"You remember," I say begrudgingly.

"Great! So when will you share your rules with Hudson?"

The group playing beer pong yells, pulling our attention away. Jake high-fives Lucas, and they banter with their opponents, clearly celebrating a win.

Claire turns her focus back to me. "Have you thought about my offer? You promised you'd tell me tonight. Pretty, pretty, please stay for the holidays."

Something deep inside me insists that I should stay, and I've never ignored my intuition when it's this strong. Even if I regretted it later, there was always a good reason, even if it involved a hard lesson. But this feels different—like it's one of the most important decisions of my life. I have to be in Merryville for the holidays.

"There is one tiny thing, though," Claire says. "I rented my house on Candy Cane Lane. But you can always stay in our spare room. It doubles as my office, but the couch folds into a comfy bed. Jake will be working most of the season, so it'll mostly be just us. Well, when I'm not at the snow globe shop."

"I'd stay here with you?"

She nods. "I doubt the inn in town has any availability. Booking a room this late in the season would be a miracle. They're already booking for next year."

I take a deep breath. "I don't want to impose. You recently got engaged and should enjoy time with your soon-to-be husband before the wedding."

As if summoned by our conversation, Jake walks over and asks, "What are you two chatting about?"

"Emma is staying with us for the holidays and dating your brother," Claire replies, emptying her cup.

"Which brother?" he inquires.

"Hudson. Obviously," Claire tells him, prompting a hearty laugh from Jake.

"Why is that funny?" I ask, feeling slightly offended. "I could date your brother if I wanted to."

"I appreciate your confidence," he chuckles. "But I'm not so sure about that."

I scoff. "This sounds like a challenge."

"Oh, winning him over would be the challenge of a lifetime. I don't think you understand, Em," he says, glancing at Claire before looking back at me. "I just don't want you to get hurt. Hudson's undateable."

"I don't want to date him," I insist.

"Happy to hear that. Now, about you staying until New Year's."

"No, I didn't agree to that. I have to be at Billie's party. However, I'll be here a few weeks, though," I clarify, and Claire pouts.

"Well, there's plenty of room here, or you can stay at my parents' or grandma's house. I promise they'd host you like you were at a bed and breakfast. There's also a small cabin in the backyard with electricity, heat, a tiny fridge, bathroom, and shower. It's currently filled with Christmas decorations, but we have time to tidy it up. We'd love to host you for the holidays. We'll figure out all the details," Jake offers, his kindness shining through.

A wide smile spreads across my face as I think about it. If I were back in New York, I'd be alone. I might even stress bake. "Okay."

"Does that mean you're officially staying?" Claire's eyes sparkle with excitement.

"I guess. But only through Thanksgiving."

She pulls me into a tight hug, and Jake squeezes us both. It feels right. I can't remember the last time I spent the holidays with Claire; she was always too busy. Last year was the first time she took a vacation in a decade, and a month later, she quit her job.

My sister laughs, and I adore the sound. "This wasn't on my BINGO card this season."

I can see her happiness, which makes me happy, too.

"Just to confirm, you're both absolutely sure I won't be a bother?" I glance between them.

Jake removes his helmet, and I meet the same green eyes as Hudson's. It's a Jolly thing; every one of the Jolly brothers has eyes the color of Christmas trees.

I understand why my sister fell in love with him. He's kind and caring—just a genuinely nice guy.

"I'll be working from dawn 'till dusk almost every night, rotating weekends off. I'm sure Claire and Tinsel would love your company."

Tinsel is Jake's thirteen-year-old senior cat who hates everyone. When I asked to see her earlier, Claire told me she was locked in her bedroom. That cat rules the roost—Jake's words, not mine.

My sister grows giddy. "We're making gingerbread cookies weekly. Jake keeps the dough prepped in the fridge."

"Ooh! Can I help decorate the cabin, too?" I ask excitedly. That was my favorite holiday tradition as a kid.

"From floor to ceiling. A tree in every room," Claire confirms.

"It's going to look like Christmas threw up in here, and you're going to love it, Em," Jake laughs, his Texas twang becoming thicker the more he drinks.

"I hope I do. I wished for holiday cheer. I could use some magic this season." The words spill out just as Hudson enters. I lock eyes with him and resolve that every Halloween for the rest of my life will involve wearing a full face mask. Going incognito feels incredible.

Earlier, when he smiled at me, the world around me melted away, and I had to escape. I felt a sizzle beneath the surface. It might have been a flicker in the dark, but the spark was undeniable.

Maybe I'm not dead inside.

Maybe Billie was right, and I need a man who doesn't want to collect me like a trophy. But I have no idea what he wants. He's closed off. His defenses seem far too high for me to overcome.

Hudson Jolly is the challenge. For once, it's not me. As I think about him, my breath hitches, and I place my hand over my heart.

"Are you okay?" Claire asks.

"Yeah, I had a burst of adrenaline."

Her brows knit together, and she turns her head to look at Hudson.

"Emma," she whispers, already aware of the cause.

"Don't," I say, unsure how to process this feeling that I've desperately yearned for. Emotions almost overwhelm me, and I feel foolish. Or maybe I'm just drunk.

Hudson grabs a bottle of tequila and heads back outside. As he leaves, he sucks the air from the room.

Claire and Jake are chatting about s'mores, but I'm too

lost in my head, tangled in thoughts of Hudson, still caught in the grip of the Mandalorian costume that has me entangled.

"Right, Emma?" Claire's voice jerks me back to reality. I wasn't listening to anything they said, just lost in thoughts of him.

Why him?

"I think I need some fresh air," I say, approaching the door before she can respond.

I lean against the porch railing, letting the cool air fill my lungs as the sweet scent of roasted marshmallows waft through the night. A couple sways slowly in front of the fire while laughter and chatter drift from those gathered on logs. Everyone looks so content, free from worry. And then there's me, the girl carrying the weight of the world on her shoulders.

As I turn my body, I spot Hudson sitting quietly on the porch swing, gazing into the darkness. He glows orange beneath the pumpkin lights sporadically hung overhead. His helmet rests beside him as he takes a swig from the bottle he grabbed earlier.

As a child, I would freeze in uncomfortable situations. My mom would have me count down from five and pretend I was a rocket ship soaring into space. At blast-off, we would take action. To this day, when facing difficult moments, I use that same principle.

After five seconds, I head in his direction, removing my mask. If I can see his face, I want him to see mine.

Music fills the silence, and I can't quite place the song— something about a truck and cheating, perhaps? Shaking my head, I slide onto the swing next to him. His jaw tightens, making me wonder if I have a similar effect on him. Am I just imagining it?

"May I?"

He hands me the bottle, and I take two large gulps. As I swallow, I cough. "Ew."

My throat burns as the liquid settles in my stomach. I tilt the bottle to read the label.

"Careful," he warns, but I don't think his concern is for the tequila. The smile he had earlier has vanished.

I take another drink, bracing myself for the burn, and then pass the bottle back.

"I get your costume," I say, pausing for him to fill the silence. He doesn't respond. "A bounty hunter who protects the child. You were trying to be clever, but there's a deeper meaning behind it. Don't you know a Mando should never remove his helmet? Too dangerous."

Does he realize I saw the *real* him earlier? That he let his guard down, if only for a moment?

I catch a smile playing on his lips. Regardless of whether he admits it, I know I'm right.

We pass the bottle back and forth. I want him to speak, to engage in conversation with me.

"Are you shy?" I ask.

"No." That's all he says for the next ten minutes. I don't find the silence uncomfortable; it's intriguing.

"Then why don't you talk much?"

He turns to face me. "I have nothing to say."

I swallow the lump forming in my throat. I've never had to work so hard to chat with someone.

"Do you want me to go away? Or do you want me to stay?"

He shrugs, not caring about who I am or what I've done.

"Hate to break it to you, but I'm into the grumpy act."

He hands me the tequila, and our fingers brush briefly. An electric spark shoots through me; I think he feels it too. Hudson studies my lips as I memorize his. We linger too long, and I glance away.

I lean back on the swing, my vision blurring slightly as I stare up at the stars. One streaks across the sky, leaving a glittery trail behind.

"Make a wish," I tell him. A smile spreads across my lips as I close my eyes. He doesn't react.

"What did you wish for?" I ask.

No response.

"You can't tell me, or it won't come true. And I want it to," I say, knowing I wished for a chance to get to know him.

"It's always the quiet ones," I add, shaking my head and practically talking to myself.

Hudson finally chuckles.

"Ah, so you know how to laugh. Good to know."

His expression darkens, and I swallow hard. "Would you like to dance with me?" I ask.

"I don't dance."

I stand on wobbly feet, and my boot gets caught on a loose board. As I stumble, his strong hands catch me, preventing my fall. His striking green eyes study me as his hands settle at my waist.

"My hero," I whisper.

His dark hair is a tangled mess. "You're stubborn."

I laugh, wrapping my arms around his neck. He's tense. "Relax."

The slow song continues, and I inhale the woodsy scent of his cologne while we dance under the lights. The beat changes, and he gently spins me around, pulling me closer.

"You lied about dancing."

"I never said I couldn't," he mutters.

"What are you so afraid of?"

He smirks, as if he can read my mind. *Can he?*

"You should stay away from me," he warns.

I fixate on his full bottom lip. "That's usually my line."

"I'm serious," he insists.

"I don't like it when people tell me what to do," I reply matter-of-factly as he twists me around.

Rebellion urges me to act. I could easily capture his lips, given how close his heated mouth is to mine. For a brief moment, I imagine the taste of tequila lingering on his tongue.

"Emma." My name falls from his lips in a low growl. I love the way it sounds. "Don't do this."

"I'm staying for the holidays," I confess.

"Of course you are." He carries an air of cockiness as if he breaks hearts for a living.

Even though Hudson weakens me, I strive to find my confidence. The attraction, mixed with unspoken words and sexual tension, is overwhelming—too intense, too dangerous.

He's right. I should keep my distance. The stronger the desire, the deeper the heartbreak.

"You're doing it again," I say.

"Doing what?" he asks, raising his brows.

"Sending mixed signals."

"I'm not," he replies, looking unimpressed.

"Look, I'm immune to the fuckboy rules. You pretend you're not interested, throw out a warning that I should stay away, and then move into the ignoring phase, even though it drives you crazy to think I could be with someone else. It's how the chase always begins. We don't have to do this." I step closer, studying him, my lips hovering just an inch from his.

"We do." He leans in, and my breathing grows ragged with anticipation.

"I have rules," he whispers, his warm breath brushing against my cheeks.

"I do too." I swallow hard as his bottom lip barely grazes mine. When his scruff brushes against my jaw, I'm mushy putty in his hands and he knows it. A buzzing feeling builds deep inside me, awakening the butterflies I thought had gone dormant.

Fuck. Fuck. Fuck.

I want to kiss him. I *need* to know if...

My fingers weave through his hair, and I'm milliseconds away from discovering if he is the man I've been searching for.

"I can't do this," he murmurs, gripping the fabric of my costume tightly. His words contradict his body, which betrays him. It's a battle no one wins.

"Why?" I whisper just as a throat clears behind us.

I glance over my shoulder to find JJ standing with his arms crossed.

"What are you two doing?" he sings, glancing between us. I feel like a teenager again, caught fooling around in the dark.

I place my hands on my hips and stand a little taller. "You didn't warn me that your brother was a player, Jake. A fucking pro at the game."

"Really?" Jake seems surprised.

"Yes." I turn back to Hudson. "I can't imagine how many hearts you've broken."

"You first." He licks his kissable lips.

JJ tilts his head. "Hudson has a reputation."

"And?" I ask.

"They used to call him 'Hudson the Heartbreaker,'" he explains.

"Oh, perfect. This will be fun," I reply.

Hudson scowls.

I rebuttal his expression. "I love a challenge."

JJ laughs. "This is the best thing I've heard all night. I can't wait for Valentine's Day. I'm going to be rich."

Hudson shakes his head at his brother.

"You'll be begging for me, just like the rest of them," I tell him.

"Don't think so, sweetheart. I beg for no one." His eyes sweep over my body. "Not even you."

Hudson walks off the porch, helmet and tequila in hand.

Jake turns to me. "You really think he's a player?"

"Top tier." I watch Hudson stare at the flames, seemingly unfazed. Maybe he has no fucks to give, but I want to find out.

"He said he doesn't dance," I mutter.

"He hasn't danced with anyone in over five years." Jake pauses. "It was a thing he had with his ex."

"Who?" I ask.

"Him and his ex."

"Ah," I say, curious about what happened, but I know that in time, Hudson will reveal all his secrets without me having to ask.

"You should go easy on him," Jake warns. "Claire told me they call you Maneater Manchester."

"I don't go easy on anyone." I grab my mask and slip it over my head. "The best way out is always through."

"You can't fix him, Em," Jake says.

"I don't want to," I say. I want him just how he is.

CHAPTER 4

HUDSON

As I swallow down the awful tequila, someone sits beside me on the log.

"Can I have some of that?" my youngest brother, Lucas, asks. We share more similarities than differences.

I pass him the bottle, and he takes a generous swig. He wipes his mouth with the back of his hand, careful not to smudge his Dr. Phil mustache. "Disgusting."

"I'm numb to it," I confess as Emma follows Jake inside.

"Wait." His eyes widen. "Are you drunk?"

"Probably."

"Wow. I haven't seen you like this since..."

He trails off, and he doesn't need to say more. That unspoken name lingers. *Meredith.*

"Sorry," Lucas says quickly. "Not trying to bring up the past."

"Don't worry about it."

Lucas lifts the bottle to his lips again. "It does grow on you."

I chuckle. "Yep."

We both turn our attention back to the fire. Fresh logs crackle and pop, sending sparks into the night sky.

"Who were you talking to a few minutes ago?" he asks.

"Claire's sister, Emma." She's thirty, younger than my thirty-nine, and much closer to Lucas's age than mine. Just another reason for her to steer clear of me, despite her magnetic pull.

"Is she back? Is she single this time?" He takes another sip from the bottle.

"We didn't discuss relationship statuses."

"My bad. Thought you had, seeing as you were five seconds away from devouring her face."

I shoot him a glare. "I wasn't."

"Oh, come on. A whole group of us sat here and watched a love story unfold. Ask Sammy."

Sam, my brother's best friend, turns our way.

"Did you see Hudson almost kiss that woman?" Lucas asks.

"Oh yeah," Sam replies, taking a sip of beer.

"It was nothing," I insist.

"Really?" Lucas challenges. "So, you'd be okay if I asked her out?"

"Sure. She seems fun. Your type," I admit.

"And age," he says, patting my back.

"I'm not sure you can handle a woman like her, though."

He laughs. "I guess we'll see. I still owe her a thank you for posting about the farm last year. Got so many thirsty women in my DMs."

I almost forgot about the flood of attention her shout-out brought us. If it weren't for Emma, the farm's Instagram wouldn't have blown up, giving me something else to focus on this year. I'll always be grateful for that.

As I glance back towards the house, I catch a glimpse of Emma through the front window. She's laughing, and I find myself curious about who she's talking to.

"I think I need some water," I announce, standing.

"You're not fooling me," Lucas says.

I ignore him and head back inside. My eyes immediately seek out Emma, who's chatting with Hank. Again. It looks like he hasn't given up on her after all.

Emma glances my way, but I continue forward, feeling the alcohol coursing through my veins.

My phone buzzes, and I pull it from my pocket. Mom has texted me several pictures of Colby in costume. The last photo shows a huge pile of candy scattered with empty wrappers. I lean against the kitchen counter as I type a response.

HUDSON

Thank you! Looks like he had a great time.

MOM

We all did! I love that we can share this with him. Thank you, sweetie!

HUDSON

Every Halloween belongs to you.

MOM

Deal. Are you having fun?

HUDSON

Yeah, but I'm about to head home.

MOM

Great! See you tomorrow.

HUDSON

Good night! Send my love.

MOM

Good night. I will.

My parents are the only ones I trust to keep Colby overnight, and even then, I worry. Some days, he's the only reason I keep going. My son is my everything. The thoughts ground me as I set my helmet on the counter and chug a bottle of water.

"Thirsty?" Emma whispers beside me, her brown eyes sparkling.

"Do you always try this hard?" I ask.

"You think this is trying?" she snorts.

"It's *something*."

A beautiful smirk forms on her lips.

Her eyes scan my body. "You enjoy the attention."

"Stop projecting," I say.

One of her brows raises as she studies me. "What did you say earlier? You don't beg?"

I glance at her. "You remembered? How thoughtful."

I'm intentionally being an ass, but it doesn't seem to faze her.

"You will."

"You're a cocky little thing."

She moves closer, making my heart skip a beat. "I thrive on challenges. And you, Hudson Jolly, will be my greatest one yet."

"Already turned on by me? You might have broken a record." I study her. "I've warned you, but you're too damn stubborn to listen."

"You have no idea," she says, pressing her back against the counter. "Now tell me about your rules."

Jake walks over to the fridge and pulls out a tray of gelatin shots. "Have two. Both of you."

"I'm good. I'm about to leave," I explain.

"Fuck that." He pushes the jiggly squares toward me.

"Fine." I take two and pop them in my mouth at the same time as Emma. We swoosh them around then swallow.

"I suppose you're still single," she says. "Or are you just playing hard to get because you're with someone?"

Ah, there it is.

I scan the room and see countless women I've turned

down over the years. There are more here than I'd like to admit.

I don't respond.

"I have a feeling you're not the type to flirt if you're in a relationship."

"Flirt?" I deadpan.

She playfully licks her lips, then narrows her eyes. The silent exchange continues.

"Emma," a deep voice calls.

"Hi Lucas," she replies sweetly. "You're baby Jolly, right?"

"You can call me baby anytime you want," he retorts.

This is the kind of banter Emma is used to, but she won't get that from me.

"Are you single?" he asks, and I roll my eyes. But I'd be lying if I said I wasn't curious about her answer.

"For now," she says, but I know Emma better than she thinks. I've read countless rumors about her online, and there's a kernel of truth among them. Emma dates because she hasn't found a man who can make her happy yet. She's still searching.

"Can I get you a drink?" Lucas asks, wasting no time.

"I'd love that." She's trying to make me jealous.

Lucas fills two glasses with punch, adding extra vodka. He hands one to her, and she watches me over the rim as she drinks.

Rather than being an audience to their awkward flirtation, I walk away. I might regret walking away from her tomorrow, but for now, I care about nothing—that's the tequila talking.

As I move toward the front door, Claire grabs my cape and pulls me closer. "Where do you think you're going? The fun is about to start."

"Home," I explain.

"You're playing Pangea with us." She takes my arm and drags me to the small crowd gathered around the coffee table.

In the center, a flattened pizza box has names written on it, each enclosed in large circles.

"Add yours," Claire says, handing me a permanent marker.

"I don't want to play."

She huffs in response. Jake snatches the marker from my hand and writes it for me.

"The two of you are disgustingly meant for each other," I say. "Both annoying and don't know how to take no for an answer."

Jake laughs, wrapping his arm around Claire and kissing her forehead.

Seconds later, Emma writes her name too. The sweet scent of her perfume drives me crazy, and I instinctively move away from her.

"Anyone else?" Claire yells over the music. Seventeen names fill the board.

I clear my throat. "Please explain the rules. I want to know what I've been peer pressured into."

"I was getting to it," she replies in her corporate tone.

Claire tosses her brown hair over her shoulder. "We'll flip a coin. If it lands on the circle around your name, you have to drink. If it lands on a blank spot, you get to add a rule to the board."

"And we can write anything we want?" Lucas inquires mischievously, glancing at Emma.

"Anything," Emma confirms with a nod. "Just make sure it's general, you know."

Our eyes meet, and I'm determined to hold her gaze until she looks away. She doesn't. Instead, Emma takes a sip of her drink, an eyebrow raised. This woman is like a tiger, stalking her prey. She has no idea what she's getting into with my emotional unavailability, and no amount of warning will deter her. She's like a moth drawn to a flame. I will burn her alive.

"Anyone have any questions?" Claire asks, bringing me back to the moment.

I grab the whiskey bottle from the counter. If I need to crash on Jake's couch, so be it.

Emma continues to stare at me, but I refuse to get caught in her gaze again and keep my focus forward. Each time her eyes land on me, my heart pounds harder, and it shouldn't.

It can't.

Claire pulls a quarter from the red pouch on her waist and hands it to her sister. "Guest of honor."

Emma grins, flips the coin, and we all watch as it lands on a blank space. She grabs the marker and scribbles something, but it's upside down.

"What did you add?" Lucas asks.

"Kiss someone in the room," Emma replies. "An easy one for couples."

She's cunning, already plotting her mischief, and I see right through it.

"An easy one for me, too," Lucas tells her.

I roll my eyes.

She heads to the kitchen for more punch and returns to my side.

"Now, who's playing dirty?" I ask.

"Not yet, but you'll know when that statement is true."

"Mm. Just don't do something you'll regret."

"Never."

We don't exchange another word.

The quarter spirals through the air, landing in various circles and blank spaces. My name is hit twice, and Emma's name appears the same number of times.

I flick the quarter upward, and it comes to rest on Lucas's name. He takes a drink before Emma tosses it again. Almost in slow motion, it lands in the 'kiss someone in the room' circle.

"Oh," JJ says. "Who's the lucky person?"

39

Emma scans the room before slowly turning to face me.

"Seriously?" I ask, knowing she would do this but hoping she wouldn't. "Lucas is waiting for you."

"I didn't choose Lucas," she mutters.

"It's the rules!" Claire chimes in.

Emma stands on her tiptoes, places her hand on my cheek, and gently slides her lips across mine with her eyes closed. As much as I want to reciprocate, I hold back.

When she realizes I'm motionless beneath her touch, she pulls away, brows furrowed.

Everyone stares at us before the attention awkwardly shifts to the pizza box.

"Cheap shots get you nowhere," I say, crossing my arms over my chest, needing to get the fuck out of here.

"I'll remember that." She smirks.

We continue playing for the next hour, and after what happened with Emma, no one else even dares to kiss me, thankfully. The locals know I'm not the one, and I guess Emma does now, too.

When the clock strikes midnight, most people have left. It's just me, Emma, Jake, and Claire. Jake is munching on a cold slice of pizza while I lean back in my chair, feeling lightheaded.

"You're not driving home," Jake says, smacking loudly.

"I'm about to walk," I reply, exhaustion creeping in.

"You can sleep on the couch," my brother offers.

Claire yawns and Jake takes her hand as he stands.

"You two will be okay in here?" he asks, grinning.

"Yeah."

He turns his focus back to Claire, tucking a strand of hair behind her ear. "Let's go to sleep, my love."

"Okay," she responds.

My brother scoops her up in his arms and carries her down the hallway.

"Good night," she calls to us, and a minute later, it's just Emma and me.

"You'll regret not kissing me back earlier," she warns.

"Still salty," I reply with a sarcastic laugh. Maybe it's the alcohol, but a part of me already regrets it. "You're used to your boy toys doing whatever you want."

She narrows her eyes, and I sense that I may have offended her.

"Ah, I hit a nerve. I'm not like anyone you've ever met before, sweetheart. If you say jump, I won't. I do whatever the hell I want." I brush my fingertips across her cheek. "Not even a pretty face can change that."

Emma bites her lip, contemplating. "We'll see."

I step away from her and grab my helmet from the counter. Staying here would be a mistake, especially in this state.

"Good luck," I tell her as I twist the knob. "You'll need it."

CHAPTER 5

EMMA

"Good morning," Claire says as I reach the end of the hallway that leads to the open-concept kitchen and living room. The two spaces flow seamlessly into one another, and I can easily imagine how cozy it becomes when the fireplace is roaring.

"This place is beautiful," I reply, still half-asleep.

"Jake designed and built it himself." She tucks a few strands of her freshly washed hair behind her ear.

"Jake of all trades," I remark.

She laughs. "Hungover?"

"Nah. Thankfully, your future hubby made sure I drank plenty of water last night. He's like the big brother I've always wanted." I twist my hair into a low bun, still wavy from yesterday's French braids. "You're lucky. I'm not sure I would've believed a man like him existed if I hadn't seen it for myself."

"Same," she agrees. Meeting Jake last year was her Christmas miracle.

As I walk past the couch, I spot Tinsel stretched out from one cushion to another. Her fluffy gray fur sticks out in all directions, and I wonder if she's as soft as she looks. Around her neck is a collar with a jingle bell attached. "Aww. You're even cuter in person."

"Be careful. She'll hiss if you startle her while napping," Claire warns.

I settle into a stool across from her in the kitchen. Claire hands me a steaming cup of coffee, and I inhale the rich scent of chocolate and hazelnut. I'm glad a part of her is still snobby when it comes to coffee, especially since I wouldn't know how to survive in Merryville without high-quality brews, even if it's too hot to drink right now.

As I wait impatiently, I glance around, surprised to find no trace of last night's party. "How did you clean up so quickly?"

When I went to bed, the beer pong table still dominated the dining room, and every flat surface was cluttered with bottles and empty cups. The hardwood floor was sticky from spills.

"Jake took care of it before I woke up."

My jaw nearly drops.

"And he even brought me breakfast in bed." She begins pouring herself a fresh mug.

"Pfft. I don't think I can be any more jealous."

She chuckles, and after a few silent seconds, she clears her throat. "I heard you and Hudson kissed last night."

I cock my head, hoping my cheeks don't betray me. Just hearing his name makes my body tingle. "That sounds like a small-town rumor."

She blows gently on her coffee. "We both know there's usually some truth behind every rumor."

"It didn't happen," I assert, watching the steam dance above my mug. It feels like sweet torture waiting for my caffeine fix. "It was just booze-induced flirting, that's all. You know how I get."

I'm convinced that the terrible alcohol we consumed too quickly is to blame. But then I recall how close our lips were—

I almost moved forward a millimeter and did what I've now been accused of.

A part of me wishes I had. The thought is unsettling because I've never regretted not kissing someone before; it's usually the other way around.

"He rejected me. You saw it happen," I say, trying not to get too caught up in thoughts about a man who doesn't care about me.

"You didn't kiss on the porch?" She narrows her eyes.

"No. Jake assumed." I chuckle, remembering how he was the one who interrupted us. With a simple clearing of his throat, we were jolted back to reality. If I had kissed Hudson and felt something, the night would have ended differently.

"Jake said he saw—"

"I promise you it didn't happen. I gave Hudson the chance, but he turned me down. Twice. He's the king of playing hard to get."

Claire knows I can spot a player from a mile away—even the sneaky ones.

She tilts her head, as if recalling various memories of him. "No way."

"You've never picked up on those fuckboy vibes from him? Just look at him! He could ask any woman to fall to her knees, and they would."

Claire bursts into laughter, shaking her head. "I think you've got him all wrong."

"Your future hubby said his nickname is Hudson the Heartbreaker. There's only one way to earn a nickname like that."

I wonder how many hearts he's broken over the years. I bet he has a higher tally than I do.

Her brows furrow. "He hasn't dated anyone in years."

I study her. "Because he pushes everyone away. It's his MO, and it works for him."

"Until you," Claire says.

44

"I've noticed he doesn't talk much. Why is that?"

Claire grabs some ice cubes from the freezer and drops them into my mug before doing the same for herself. "He doesn't open up to strangers."

"But I'm your sister! I should get a pass."

She snort-laughs. "It took Jake proposing before Hudson believed I wouldn't leave. Over six months."

"Wow." That saddens me because it means his issues run deeper than I thought.

"He has trust issues," she says.

"No kidding. He told me to stay away from him. Should I? Be honest with me."

"I don't want you to get hurt, Em. But I also don't want you to destroy him. Hudson is a good guy. A great dad. He's just..."

"Unavailable," I finish her sentence.

"Exactly. He's a green flag who thinks he's red. When it comes to love, he's a Scrooge. A Grinch. He's really smart, Em, but also extremely private." Her tone shifts to a warning. "In the game of chess—"

"You always have to stay two steps ahead of your opponent. I know," I say, interrupting.

In the world of CEOs, my sister is cutthroat—a true nightmare. Even though she isn't that person anymore, she could be in an instant. Reading and understanding people is one of her superpowers.

"Shit," she whispers. "I hope you two don't destroy each other."

She watches me, concern etched on her face, and I give her a small smile. "I'm not going to date Hudson. You have nothing to worry about. I won't break your future brother-in-law's heart."

"Why don't I believe you?"

"Pretty sure that man is unbreakable." I stare out at the meadow, likely filled with wildlife in the early mornings. The tall windows let in ample sunlight, and the room glows brightly.

Claire clears her throat. "Not that I'm a relationship specialist or anything, but I believe the right partner could change everything."

"I hope he finds her," I reply, recognizing how love can heal deeply rooted wounds. Part of me longs to be the woman who rescues him, but more importantly, I want to discover what I'm missing too. That's why I've searched so fervently and unapologetically. Finding love feels like the ultimate treasure hunt, driven solely by emotion.

"What if you are the one for him?" Claire asks.

"I don't know." I keep my emotions in check as I reminisce about last night. I can't shake the thrill I felt when our eyes met. His perfect lips were so close, and our warm breaths mingled together. The gorgeous Grinch had complete control, and what's frightening is that I was completely okay with it. That never happens.

I wonder if he knows he's gotten under my skin. I hope I'm buried under his.

Claire grabs eggs from a basket on the counter and pulls a slab of bacon from the fridge. "Enough about that. How long will you be staying?"

She skillfully shifts the conversation, effortlessly taking charge. I appreciate her efforts, as my brain hasn't fully woken up yet.

"I'm not sure," I admit. "But I can promise I'll be here for your birthday."

"That's only three weeks away."

My sister was born on Thanksgiving over thirty years ago. Every Turkey Day, whether it was her actual birthday or not, we'd celebrate with cake and watch the parade from our father's penthouse in Times Square. It became a silly family tradition, and we've never missed a year—this will be the first time.

"At least stay through Christmas. It's the most magical time of year in Merryville. You'll get to experience the Winter Solstice Festival and the tree lighting ceremony too."

"Maybe," I smile, recalling how incredible she said it was.

After Maddox and I broke up, I chose to live more spontaneously. Now, I don't stay in one place or with one person long enough for it to matter. I'm not running from anything, but no one has sparked my desire to settle down. Maybe no one ever will.

Yet, if Claire could find love, given how resistant she was to it, perhaps I could too.

"Do you miss your old life?" I ask.

"No," she replies without hesitation. "Working for Dad felt like wearing leggings that are a size too small. Sure, you can pull them up, but you shouldn't keep them on long-term."

I didn't expect that from her, and I burst into laughter. "I'm genuinely happy for you."

Claire was the second in command at Manchester Enterprises, our family's hotel chain, slated to take over when our father retired. But after meeting Jake Jolly last winter, her life transformed.

Now, she runs a thriving snow globe shop in downtown Merryville, showcasing her custom designs. No amount of money could ever replace what she found here: love and passion.

Claire discovered what she had been missing— overwhelming support, understanding, and the feeling of being known and appreciated for who she truly is.

"You know that seventy-five percent of people who visit Merryville during the holiday season end up moving here? Seventy-five percent, Em."

I laugh because my sister has always had a knack for memorizing facts. It's one of her many quirks, and I love that about her. "So, what's your plan? Have me stay here during Christmas, hoping I'll move?"

She giggles. "I can only hope."

As she cooks for me, my thoughts drift back to Hudson.

The more he drank, the more he spoke, but it still wasn't enough. I want to know him better, even though I probably shouldn't. If he wants me to stay away, I should respect that. But I don't believe him. His words say one thing, but his emerald-green eyes tell a different story.

Claire slides a plate across the bar top, bringing me back from my daydream. My eggs are cooked perfectly, and the bacon is arranged beneath them to form a smiley face—a nostalgic touch. Our mom used to make this for us and called it our happy breakfast.

I chuckle as old memories resurface. "Start the day with a smile. I miss Mom."

"I do too. She'd be proud of you, Em," Claire says as she hands me a fork.

"She'd be proud of you too." I cut into my eggs, trying to push the memories away. "Well?"

The yellow yolk spills out. "You've still got it."

Eggs are one of the few things my sister can cook, and I appreciate them all the more as my stomach growls in anticipation.

Just as I take a bite, Jake walks in, carrying an armful of chopped wood. He stacks it neatly by the fireplace. "Mornin', Em."

"Good morning! Is it supposed to rain today? It looks cloudy out there."

"Nah, just overcast. A storm's coming in on Thursday, and we'll get a cold snap over the weekend," he explains, removing his leather gloves. "Perfect fireplace weather."

Once he's done, Jake heads into the kitchen. As soon as he gets near Claire, he wraps his arms around her and kisses her cheek.

"You two are adorable," I say. "Grossly adorable."

Jake whispers something in her ear, just loud enough for her to hear, and she giggles in response.

"Stop, that tickles!" she laughs as he continues to pepper kisses along her neck.

"I really shouldn't stay here during the holi—"

"You're good," Jake interrupts. "It would be an honor. I get to spend the rest of my life with my CeCe."

Claire loops her fingers in the belt loops of his faded jeans, looking up at him like he's her savior. In a way, he is. "I love you, babe."

"Love you more," he replies.

I take a bite of bacon as Jake moves to the fridge to pour himself a massive glass of orange juice.

"I'm heading to the store later to stock up for the weekend. The roads are supposed to be pretty bad. Need anything?"

"A box of condoms," I blurt out, raising an eyebrow.

"What size?" he asks, tilting his head.

"XXL."

"She's testing you," Claire explains. "He has no limits. Nothing, and I mean absolutely nothing, phases him. I've already tried."

Jake downs his glass. "She's right. With brothers like Hudson and Lucas, I've experienced it all."

"Pity." I scoop the rest of the eggs into my mouth.

"You can always try," he suggests.

As Jake chats about the weather, I finish eating. "What do people in Merryville do for fun?"

"Hiking, horseback riding, crafts, crocheting, farming. There's a book club that meets on Thursdays. I guess there's a little bit of everything. But it's the season for holiday events. The sign-ups for the cookie contest just opened up. Judging is the first weekend of December."

"You shouldn't have told her that," Claire warns. "But

Emma is only staying until my birthday. She won't be around."

"It's after that," he confirms.

A wide smile spreads across my lips. "Hmm."

My sister grows giddy with excitement. "You'll stay until the contest?"

"I can imagine it now: City girl turns Christmas cookie queen."

"Do you bake?" Jake asks, pouring himself some coffee.

"A little," I reply, scrunching my nose.

"And you're considering entering a highly competitive baking contest? They might eat you alive, Em," he says, genuinely concerned.

"She's being humble, Jake," my sister interjects. "She used to bake a lot."

"I've also burnt my fair share of cookies."

"Well, everyone gets a participation ribbon," Jake reassures me.

I make a face. "And what does the winner get?"

He gives me a half-smile. "A gold trophy and your name in the Christmas Cookie Hall of Fame."

"It's official, I'm entering," I announce.

"You're serious?" he asks, raising an eyebrow.

Claire shakes her head.

"As serious as a heart attack. It will give me something to focus on while I'm here. Now I need to prove to you that I can win."

"It will be a challenge," he cautions.

"My favorite."

"Now, I just need you to commit to staying through the New Year!" Claire claps her hands together. Her excitement is contagious. "It's happening. I can feel it."

"Not happening," I say.

Jake clears his throat. "If you're serious, go down to city hall first thing tomorrow and pick up a registration form. It will come with a packet of rules. Then, while you're in town, stop by Glenda's Café and get the pumpkin pancakes with cream cheese for breakfast. You'll thank me later."

"Writing this down," I say, unlocking my phone to take a note.

"I have a feeling it's going to be an unforgettable Christmas," Claire adds, glancing at Jake.

"Can't wait," I respond as I stand and stretch.

"She's never leaving," Jake says to my sister.

"I know," Claire shrugs.

She's hopeful, and I don't want to burst her bubble. I'm unsure whether I could live in a small town like this, but for Claire, I would try. I love my sister. She's one of my best friends, always providing a reality check and keeping my interests at heart.

As I gaze outside, contemplating what the future may hold, I notice an opening in the woods. "Is that a trail?"

"Yeah. It's a three-mile loop that connects to both my brother's and my parents' houses. It makes it easier to navigate around the farm, especially when it's packed with tourists. Last year, we decided to create it to help us get around more efficiently. It's a lovely little hike, particularly if you enjoy being in the woods. Plus, it's almost impossible to get lost."

"I can't wait!" I exclaim. "I'm going to check it out now."

"You should. Take a jacket; the temperatures are dropping."

I head to my room, where I've been sleeping on the fold-out couch. My suitcase lies open on the floor, its contents strewn about. My Power Ranger spandex is discarded where I peeled it off.

After dressing, I walk through the living room, where Claire and Jake are lounging on the couch with Tinsel.

"If you need anything, call me, okay?" Claire says.

"She'll be fine," Jake assures her.

Claire makes a face. "She can be clumsy sometimes."

"Pfft. Don't reveal all my secrets!" I say as I step out through the patio door and cross the backyard. A footpath leads directly to the trail.

The crunchy leaves snap beneath my feet, and a breeze carries the scent of winter. A pleasant shiver runs through me as I enter the woods.

Change is in the air—I can feel it deep within. As I inhale the fresh air, I wonder if Claire is onto something. Maybe there is magic in Merryville. I have nothing to lose and everything to gain.

CHAPTER 6

HUDSON

Temperatures are steadily dropping due to a cold front sweeping from the Rockies into Texas. This weekend, they're expected to dip into the thirties, and I couldn't be more excited. The transition from autumn to winter is my favorite time of year when the crunchy leaves turn to ash and the world grows quiet.

I've learned to embrace silence, a concept Emma Manchester would never understand.

I lift the ax above my head and bring the blade down onto the thick trunk. After several swings, the wood finally cracks and splits. I adjust one side and continue chopping it into smaller, more manageable logs.

The town often loses power during the season due to ice build-up on the lines. Now that I have more than just myself to consider, I stay prepared just in case.

My son is the sole reason I'll spend my only day off working myself to the bone. The last thing I want is for Colby to be cold because of my negligence. I've learned to put his needs above mine without hesitation.

While I have a generator that powers only the fridge and water pump, I plan to upgrade it to run the entire house eventually. However, that's quite an expense, and I've been saving for Colby's college.

I fill the wheelbarrow with wood and push it toward the storage shed. It's heavy, but I prefer to overload it and make fewer trips. The soreness in my muscles reminds me that I'm alive.

Sunlight peeks through the clouds, and suddenly Emma bursts into my thoughts with her red hair and captivating brown eyes. Frustration surges within me. I can't deal with her. Since the moment I first laid eyes on her in July, she has felt like poison in my veins. Getting too close would be a disaster, especially after last night when I almost kissed her.

It was a near miss, and I'm grateful to Jake for stopping it. He didn't respond to my thanks.

Part of me wanted to say screw it and press my lips against hers, but I chose to listen to the angel on my shoulder instead of the devil whispering in my ear. I cannot cross that line with Emma "Maneater" Manchester.

Yes, I know about her nickname. The entire internet knows. And while she's incredibly tempting, acting on that desire would be disastrous for both of us.

This season, I don't have time for any distractions.

With the farm short-staffed this winter, I face more work than usual. Lisa, one of the clerks who helped wrap gifts for the shop, is on maternity leave, one of my cousins can only stick around for half the season, and Colby's recent anxiety about being away from me complicates things further. My to-do list feels endless.

Now, with Emma here for a while, I worry about how to keep her at arm's length. My heart is too cold for her, and I doubt she can ignite it, even though she radiates warmth.

I can't deny the spark when our fingers brushed against each other. It wasn't supposed to mean anything to her, but I could see the surprise in her eyes and on her face. For a fleeting moment, I imagined spending a lifetime with her.

I close my eyes, forcing those thoughts away. Emma is just a distraction, wrapped in a beautifully stubborn package. Though she isn't good for me—or for Colby—she occupies the forefront of my mind, urging me to take a chance on her.

"No," I growl, refocusing on my chopping area.

Just as I reach for the ax, my phone vibrates on the ground where I left it. As I approach, I see it's a call from Donna, Colby's nanny.

She cares for him from noon until sunset, Monday through Friday. I drive him to pre-K in the mornings, and she picks him up from school. While she isn't cheap, I've felt at ease this season knowing Colby is in good hands while I prepare the farm. Easing the stress that has burdened me for years is invaluable.

I bend down to answer. "Hudson."

"Hi. Um. I don't know how to say this," she mumbles, her voice tentative and uncharacteristic.

"Okay." My brow furrows. This isn't a good sign. Donna has never hesitated to speak her mind.

Alarm bells ring as I brace for the worst. Just when I think life can't possibly get any more complicated, it always does. My trauma prevents me from ever feeling entirely comfortable, and I hope that one day I'll look back on this time in my life and feel proud that I survived it. Because if I can get through this, I can endure anything.

She clears her throat. "I was offered another job, and I accepted. I'm moving tomorrow."

"Excuse me?" I stare at the dark clouds rolling in, speechless.

It's a metaphor for my life: A brief glimpse of sunlight followed by overcast skies.

"I'm so sorry, Hudson. I love Colby and appreciate everything you've done for me, but I was offered a live-in position with a family in San Antonio. It's a salary I can't refuse, and after my divorce, you know how badly I need this."

I want to be upset, but Donna warned me she was searching for a permanent position when I hired her. I just thought I had more time and hoped she'd stay in Merryville until January, when the season ends.

Two more months—that's all I needed.

"I'm really sorry," she repeats, emphasizing how much she loves Colby. "I wish I could say goodbye. Maybe we can FaceTime?"

"Maybe."

In less than twenty-four hours, I'll be working from sunrise to sundown until December 23rd, rotating weekends off. The Seasons Greeting ceremony, which kicks off our season, starts before Colby is released from school. I have no idea what I'll do.

"I appreciate your help. Congratulations," I tell her, too shocked to say anything more.

"Thanks for understanding."

That's the last thing she says before the call ends. I stare at my phone, wanting to hurl it into the forest surrounding my house.

"Fuck," I mutter, my voice echoing through the trees. Taking the hard road is exhausting, even if it's the only path I've ever known.

"You good?" I hear from behind me, pulling my attention back to reality.

As Lucas approaches, I grip my phone so tightly my fingers ache. He must be headed to Jake's.

"What's going on?" he asks.

I huff. "Donna took another nanny job in San Antonio and is moving."

"When?"

"Tomorrow."

"That's utter bullshit," he says, his jaw clenched.

Lucas knows how hard I've struggled to juggle everything

this past year. I keep telling myself it could be worse. Right? But this feels strangely like rock-bottom.

"No one is available to pick Colby up from school tomorrow. Maybe I'll keep him home and pray he doesn't get cranky."

"What about Claire?" Lucas asks.

"No." I glance away from my brother. "I hate this."

Lucas offers a sad smile. "If you keep Colby home from school, maybe we can convince the ladies in the shop to help out while the ceremony takes place?" He knows how restless Colby gets when he's not stimulated.

"They're not being paid to babysit. It's rude to put that on them."

"It's not like that. They love Colby. He's their honorary grandson."

I shake my head. "Not happening."

"Okay, if you need me to take him tomorrow, let me know. He can help me with tours, and I'll let him drive the tractor."

"I'll figure it out." I grab my ax, prepared to lose myself in my work once again.

"Do you have dinner plans?" Lucas asks.

"Just some leftovers from Friday," I mutter.

"Jake's serving chili around six, and he told me to invite you. He said he texted, but you didn't answer."

"I've been working," I say, my mind a jumbled mess.

The holidays are already challenging, and the added stress only heightens my feelings of loneliness.

Lucas steps forward, squeezing my shoulder. "It's gonna work out. Don't worry about it.

"Thanks."

"Remember what Mom used to tell us as kids?"

"It's only temporary," I reply. Despite being six years younger, Luke recalls what our mother always said. And it's true.

I lift the ax with every ounce of strength I have left, and this time, the thick wood splits effortlessly.

Lucas stands off to the side. "You're not supposed to be working today. It's a rest day for a reason."

"No rest for the wicked," I huff, continuing my task.

I don't know how to be still when Colby isn't here. This is my chance to catch up on things, and I need to keep my mind occupied.

He shakes his head. "When will you learn to relax?"

"Maybe never."

"You weren't always like this, you know," he says, moving toward the trail that leads to Jake's cabin. The trail makes a big circle with offshoots leading to each of our cabins.

"People change," I call out. The sound of the ax biting into the wood echoes through the trees. When he's out of sight, I lose myself in the physical labor.

During my next break, I check my texts.

JAKE
You coming tonight?

HUDSON
I don't think it's a good idea. School early in the morning.

Honestly, I shouldn't see Emma.

JAKE
It's dinner. Not a slumber party.

HUDSON
Maybe next time.

58

JAKE

If you change your mind, the invitation is open.

HUDSON

Okay, thanks.

Last night, I fought an internal battle every second Emma was near. Her intoxicating presence tempted me like the devil. Something stirs beneath the surface, and I don't want to think about it. I roll my shoulders, realizing how easy it would be to see her again.

Maybe the awful booze was what fueled the attraction?

There's only one way to find out.

I fight the urge to run toward her.

But—there's always a but when my heart races—my relationships end in heartbreak, and I would hate myself for hurting her.

I can't be her Mr. November. I won't. That's a goddamn fact.

CHAPTER 7

EMMA

As I approach the trail's end, I notice it opens to a gravel road. In front of me stands a two-story log cabin with a hunter-green metal roof, surrounded by trees—an oasis in the middle of nowhere Texas.

I feel at peace.

After a few steps forward, I freeze when my eyes land on Hudson. My lips part as I take him in like expensive champagne, savoring every moment. This man is trouble, and I hate how I magnetize toward him.

"What are you doing?" I hear.

"Shit," I breathe, nearly jumping out of my skin as Lucas emerges from behind a tree. He's the most annoying Jolly brother.

His dark, messy hair curls upward at the tips. "You should take a picture. It'll last longer," he says.

"Excuse me?" I give him an incredulous look, realizing I don't know how long he's been watching me.

"You were eyefucking my brother."

Busted.

"Pfft."

All six-foot-two of him stalks toward me, his head held

high. If Jake has the personality of a golden retriever, then Hudson and Lucas are the rottweilers of the family.

His voice drops. "Don't worry, your dirty little secret is safe with me."

"You can tell him if you'd like." I raise my brows, unbothered by him. Men like Lucas are a dime a dozen.

"Oh, I love it when you're feisty. Let's call your bluff," he playfully threatens, his cocky smirk never leaving his perfect lips. Lucas puts his fingers in his mouth and lets out a high-pitched whistle. Hudson immediately turns and glances our way, scowling.

Lucas gently wraps his large hand around my wrist, pulling me toward the clearing.

"Is this what it's like to have a younger, annoying sibling?"

Lucas waves and grins like the Cheshire cat, displaying his perfect teeth. I play along, pretending to be unbothered, but I struggle to keep the facade up as Hudson lifts his black T-shirt to wipe the sweat from his forehead. Muscles cascade down his stomach, and dark hair trails into his jeans. I gulp hard as naughty thoughts fill my mind. Kittens and bubbles, Emma.

Lucas cups his hands around his mouth. "Emma was eyefucking you!"

"You're an asshole," I whisper under my breath.

"Sure am." He chuckles, casting a sideways glance at me.

Hudson shakes his head and resumes his work, slamming the ax into the wood, clearly annoyed.

I lean into Lucas and whisper, "I heard Southern boys have the best manners. You wouldn't want to disappoint your mother, would you?"

"I like you, Emma." Lucas releases my wrist and turns to face me fully. "I think I can help you."

"Do I look like a damsel in distress? Because I'm not," I snap back.

Hudson continues chopping. Each swing rings out sharply through the woods, and I can't seem to tear my gaze away from him as he works. When he releases a deep grunt, my body instinctively responds. Fuck, I need to get a grip.

Lucas narrows his eyes, noticing. "I see the way you two look at each other. And everyone knows what happened on the porch last night."

"*Nothing* happened," I assert.

He licks his lips. "But you wanted it to."

I can't deny that. To do so would be a lie.

Everything faded away when we were close. No one else mattered. It was just us—before Jake ruined it all.

"I was by the fire. A handful of us watched the two of you. Why didn't you just do it? You're Emma fucking Manchester."

"That means nothing," I explain.

"I've researched you because I knew you'd be back eventually, so I wanted to be prepared. I know you date a different man every month and haven't settled down since you broke up with that jerk nearly two years ago. You're a hopeless romantic who would be perfect for my brother."

My heart races. "You don't know me, Lucas."

"I know enough, and I can see right through your facade. The two of you are meant for each other. Why play it safe?"

I stare at him. "He's unavailable."

"Bullshit," he snaps. "No one has tried. He pushes them away, and they give up every single time."

I hesitate to trust what he says. I have no reason not to trust him; I know he has his brother's best interest at heart. Claire told me how close they are.

"Hudson won't make this easy for you."

His words make me laugh. "No kidding. But I can't resist a good challenge."

"So you're in?" he asks.

"I never sign a contract without reading the fine print," I reply, aware there's more to this deal. "What do I have to do?"

Lucas shoves his hands into his pockets. "Oh, right. You just have to play along with my advances."

I laugh sarcastically. "He's smarter than that."

"He is, but it will work. Guaranteed." Lucas exudes confidence. "Before you agree, let me clarify—you're not my type. I don't want you to think I'm hitting on you. I'm not."

"I don't know whether to be flattered or offended," I tell him. "What do you get out of this?"

He smiles. "I get to see my brother happy again."

I glance back at Hudson, unsure if this is a foolish idea. "I'll think about it."

Lucas wraps his strong arms around me, pulling me into a hug that envelops me completely.

"Hug me back," he mutters.

I squeeze him, inhaling his cologne. There's nothing between us—no spark, no attraction.

We pull apart, and his green eyes travel down my face. Like his brothers, Lucas is tall and handsome.

"So, what's your story? Why are you single?" I ask.

"Because I have standards," he replies. "Looks like phase one has begun."

"I didn't agree to this."

"You don't have to. Your actions speak louder than words. I'll see you later." He walks toward Hudson. "I gotta brag about getting your number."

"I didn't give you my number." I shake my head.

"Oh right." He pulls out his phone and hands it to me. "Program it in, please."

I take his phone and text myself. "And what if this backfires?"

"It won't," he says, taking back his phone and sliding it into his pocket. "I know Hudson better than anyone, and he's never looked at anyone like he looks at you. That's a promise, Emma. If I hadn't seen it myself, I wouldn't believe it either." His sincerity makes my heart race.

"It's a deal then. Oh, and when this works, I might need one tiny favor from you."

I lift an eyebrow. "Ah, there it is. I knew there was more to this."

"I need you to be my date to a wedding."

I place my hands on my hips. "Who are you trying to make jealous?"

"I have a point to prove." He stares off into the distance, his expression turning serious.

I realize we have more in common than I thought. "I know what that's like. I'm sorry."

He shakes his head. "Don't be. Everything works out the way it should. Anyway, I hope you're ready to have fun," he says with a grin. "This is going to be an unforgettable holiday season."

Lucas crosses the street and approaches Hudson. They chat, but based on Hudson's body language, it's clear he couldn't care less. I wish I could hear their conversation.

On the way back to Jake's, I text my besties in our group chat, sharing every detail of my whirlwind arrival.

HARPER
This is how it starts.

EMMA
Am I making a mistake?

BILLIE
Time will tell.

HARPER
So Hudson's your Mr. November?

The thought makes me snicker.

EMMA

No way.

HARPER

Maybe he's your Mr. Forever.

Harper sends a GIF of Michael Jackson eating popcorn.

HARPER

I'm here for the entertainment.

BILLIE

Me too!

EMMA

I'll keep you updated.

When I walk into Jake's house, I find my sister on the couch with Tinsel sprawled across her belly. They're watching TV together.

"Hey! You just missed Lucas," Claire says. "He was looking for you. I told him you were on the trail."

So, he expected to find me. *Sneaky bastard.*

"Ah, yes. He found me. He's very..." I trail off, unsure of how I truly feel about him yet.

She laughs. "He's great."

"I have so many questions. It feels like a different world here." I sit at the end of the couch, resting my head against the cushion while staring at the high ceilings. Tinsel purrs contentedly.

"I spoke to Dad earlier and told him you'd be staying here for the holidays."

"I only agreed to stay through December first."

"Of course, but I know you'll change your mind. Anyway, he wants to spend Christmas with us," she says, scratching Tinsel's chin.

My relationship with our father has been rocky over the years. He's all business, and professionalism runs through his veins. Claire was the golden child who followed in his footsteps, while I never showed the same interest. I've come to terms with being the Manchester disappointment.

Since moving from New York to Texas, Claire has worked hard to improve her relationship with him. I haven't made an effort, nor has he.

I love my father, but he's strict and opinionated, particularly about my career choices.

I take a deep breath. "I'm really sorry, but I can't commit to that right now. I don't know if I'm ready."

"Can you at least think about it?"

I glance at her. "I promise I will.

CHAPTER 8

HUDSON

After showering, I wrap a towel around my waist. My body aches from the relentless manual labor of the day, and I might regret the hours I spent chopping wood.

The fireplace, the woodshed, and the garage are all fully stocked. This should last us through November, as long as we don't encounter any freak snowstorms, but caution is always wise.

The blade of a sharp ax cuts through my frustrations, even if only momentarily. As a stressed and upset teenager, I would chop wood relentlessly on weekends to keep my mind busy.

Chopping requires both physical and mental focus, leaving no space for thoughts about anything or anyone else. I'm sure Lucas noticed my behavior, but he didn't comment on it.

As I enter my bedroom, I glance out the panoramic windows facing the backyard. The sun hangs lazily in the evening sky, casting a golden-brown hue over everything—the grass, the trees, and the light filtering through the branches.

Night will fall soon. Colby will be home, and I still haven't decided what to do about tomorrow. Keeping him home is the only logical choice, but I know he will resent every moment of it. I'll sort it out.

Once dressed, my eyes fall on the silly T-Rex in tennis shoes on my dresser, a gift from Emma for Colby.

I met her briefly a few months ago, and that day remains etched in my memory. Her dark red hair swayed in the summer breeze as she met my gaze with a warm smile. Our eyes lingered a moment too long, and in that instant, my world shifted. She left after a few days as if running from something.

My trauma whispers it was *me*.

I realized then that she was a dangerous temptation. I had almost convinced myself she was just a figment of my imagination until yesterday.

I shake my head, desperate to rid my thoughts of her, but it feels nearly impossible.

Instead of wrestling with myself, I slide on my boots. Stepping onto the porch, I shove my hands into my pockets and inhale the fresh air. I gaze into the woods, where she was watching me.

Emma already can't resist me, and she hasn't even had a real taste of what I have to offer.

A part of me wants to know her, the real her, because the online persona is curated bullshit. That version of Emma Manchester doesn't intrigue me. No one can be that cheerful or enthusiastic about everything—not even Little Miss Sunshine. Yet, somehow, she manages it.

Damn it.

I'm battling myself, questioning if what I felt last night was just the result of too much tequila. Deep down, I know it wasn't. The third time's a charm, right?

I should walk back inside, eat leftovers, and forget about everything, but... I know she's at Jake's house waiting for me, secretly hoping to see me.

With determination, I step off the porch. Once in my truck, I back out of the driveway with more purpose than I've felt in a long time.

What the hell am I doing?

Jake lives five minutes away, but I slowly take the gravel road, gripping the steering wheel with white knuckles as I replay being with her last night. Watching her squirm after not getting her way was oddly satisfying.

Emma isn't accustomed to rejection, and I almost hated being the one to deny her. But she needs to learn a lesson— cheap shots won't work with me. She's smarter than that, and I'm too damn old for childish games. My motto is: say what you mean and mean what you say, which is why I don't say much.

I'm craving her like she's my new addiction.

Lucas is already here. His dirt bike is parked next to the porch.

After taking a deep breath, I enter the house.

Emma and Claire stand in the kitchen, laughing, while Lucas and Jake sit on bar stools across from them. They glance my way when the door snaps shut.

"Am I interrupting a double date?" I ask, unimpressed.

Emma looks at Lucas, but my gaze is fixed on her.

"You are," Lucas replies. *Cocky bastard.*

I can't tell if Emma's laughter is directed at him or if she's laughing with him. Our eye contact lingers, something common between us. But it quickly grows too intense.

"Glad you made it," Jake says, pulling my attention away from Emma. "We were just getting started."

A bell jingles behind me, and I turn to see Tinsel prancing toward me. She sits at my feet and paws at my jeans, digging her claws into the fabric. Bending down, I pick her up and hold her as everyone grabs bowls for chili.

"Hey, baby girl," I say, kissing Tinsel's furry forehead. She purrs and leans into me. "Want to finally come home with your real daddy?"

"For the last time, you're not catnapping Tinsel. I found her first," Jake warns over his shoulder. I've teased him about stealing her for thirteen years, and if he weren't so attached, I

69

probably would. There's a reason he only trusts me to watch her when he travels with Claire.

"You love me more than him, don't you?" I ask, and she paws at my jaw. "Sweet girl."

"Tinsel! Attack!" Jake calls out, retrieving an extra bowl from the cabinet for me.

"You're so cute," I say, holding her tightly against my chest.

After a few minutes of snuggling, I set her down and she promptly attacks my leg. Things need to be on her terms or she gets angry. "Hey! I have to eat. I'm starving."

The furry ball gives me a death glare as she flicks her tail and prances away. Jake chuckles and takes a seat on the stool next to Claire.

"Come on. Come eat while it's hot. We have cheese, sour cream, and cornbread. All we're missing is a dozen chewy chocolate chip pecan cookies," Jake says, grabbing spoons.

I narrow my eyes. "Then you should've made some."

"Hm. Maybe you should've?" he quips.

I know what he's hinting at. My brother is convinced that I bake when I'm in love. Maybe I do, but I haven't made those cookies since before Colby was born. "Don't think so."

"Actually, ooey gooey chocolate chip pecan cookies are my favorite," Emma sings.

"Maybe you can ask Santa for some," Claire replies. "Not sure if Hudson can deliver."

I tune them out as I ladle several scoops of hearty chili into my bowl. The aroma of onions and large chunks of garlic is heavenly. "Mawmaw's recipe?" I inquire.

"You know it."

Lucas sits next to Emma, and I hear her giggle. A pang of jealousy hits me—an emotion I haven't felt in years—and I tense up.

Jake clears his throat. "I brought Granny a big bowl about thirty minutes ago, and she said it was perfect."

"Suck-up," Lucas shoots back.

"I can't help being her absolute favorite grandson," Jake brags.

"She told me I was her favorite first." I add the fixings to my food before taking the stool in front of Emma. When I look up, she's staring at me.

"Grandma is super excited to meet Emma," Jake explains.

"She'll adore you," Claire adds. "And she'll probably try to hook you up with one of these goons."

Lucas winks at Emma, and I roll my eyes, focusing on my food. He's relentless and trying too hard. It reeks of desperation.

"Heard you needed help with Colby tomorrow," Jake notes, keeping the conversation flowing.

I glare at Lucas, wishing he hadn't opened his mouth. His brow raises as he gives me a cheeky grin.

"I'm glad to know I was the subject of your conversation," I say, setting down my spoon. It's hard to be angry when I know they mean well. "But I have it under control."

It's a lie, and my brothers see right through it. They tend to know when I'm putting on a front. It's hard for me to ask for help, and I prefer solving my problems alone. I never want to be a burden.

"What happened?" Emma asks, concern evident in her tone.

I lick my lips, focusing on the meat and melted cheese in my bowl.

"Donna's moving," Lucas answers.

"What?" Claire turns to me.

Emma glances back and forth between us, unaware of my life.

"Who's Donna?" she asks, a faint tremor in her voice.

I meet her gaze.

"She *was* Hudson's nanny," Lucas mumbles, chewing a large piece of cornbread. Crumbs fall from his mouth; he has forgotten his manners around a lady, and I give him a disapproving look.

"Aww, you needed a nanny? To make sure *you* were behaving?" Emma jokes with a playful smirk on her face.

"Smartass," I mumble.

"What does that mean for tomorrow?" Jake asks.

"Look." I finish chewing and wipe my mouth. "I appreciate your concern, but I've got this under control."

"What does 'under control' mean?" Lucas presses.

"It means to shut the fuck up and mind your own business," I snap, having had enough of him for the night.

"I'd be happy to help," Emma offers.

"No, thank you."

Her brows furrow. "Why not?"

"Have you ever seen a nearly five-year-old throw tantrums like they're getting paid a million dollars for each one?"

"No, but—"

"My answer stands. Now, can we please talk about something else? Like how I'm stealing Tinsel when I leave here tonight."

Jake bursts out laughing. "I'll kill you."

Emma clears her throat. "We're not changing the subject. You didn't let me finish. I'm great with kids, okay? I've taken care of a very spoiled two-and-a-half-year-old who has zero manners. Hanging out with Colby would be fun."

Claire smiles and nods in agreement. It's not that I don't trust Emma, but I feel protective. She's a total stranger.

"No means no," I say, focusing on my food.

Emma glances at Claire, who gives her a slight shrug.

A minute passes in silence, with only the sound of metal utensils clinking against glass bowls.

"So, you two are going on a date next Saturday?" Claire asks Lucas.

"Yep," he replies, playfully elbowing Emma. "I had to beg her, but she finally agreed. We're gonna have fun."

She licks her lips, her brow arching. "If you say so."

I see how she looks at him, and I can't shake the feeling that she's faking it. But I don't know.

"Great. I guess we're planning two weddings next year?" I take a big bite of my chili.

Lucas needs to step it up if he wants to convince me. I can see right through him—he's trying to make me jealous.

"Maybe before Jake and Claire," he quickly adds. "We'll see how next weekend goes. Apparently, I'm easy to fall in love with," he warns Emma.

"Can't wait," Emma replies. "I already told my besties about you."

"Hm," I grumble, not buying any of it.

Emma's brow furrows. "What was that hm for?"

"Wish you both the best."

Jake starts chatting about the weather while Claire shares the design of her latest snow globe for the shop. The prototype is incredible.

When Emma glances my way again, I choose to ignore her. I've confirmed that the alcohol wasn't responsible for last night's behavior. It's the two of us together. Emma Manchester is a rip current threatening to pull me under.

Something simmers between us, and the thin crust of the earth beneath me seems to crack. She'll drag me down to the depths if I let her, destroying every part of me that remains. I can't allow that to happen.

After scraping the last bite from my bowl, I wipe my mouth, knowing I need to leave. Emma stands as well.

"I'll take your bowl," I offer.

"No, thanks." She turns on her heels toward the sink.

I take Claire's and Lucas's dishes while Jake finishes eating. I go to the sink and move the spigot toward me.

"Excuse me?" she says, returning it to its original position. "I haven't finished rinsing."

"I'll take care of it."

"No means no," she mimics, using the same tone I used earlier.

I pause, wiping my hands on a dish towel, and turn my full attention to her. "Is this what you want?"

"I want you to stop," she whisper-hisses, giving me the dirtiest look. I've offended her. I've made her mad. Maybe that's for the best; perhaps pushing her away will actually work.

"Be specific." My gaze remains locked on her, and she doesn't seem to mind. Her hair is tied up in a high ponytail, exposing the softness of her neck, and I notice her pulse quickening.

As I take her in, my chest tightens. Maybe we could have worked out if circumstances had been different.

"Stop staring at me," she snaps.

"Make me," I reply quietly.

The hint of her sweet perfume is intoxicating.

Another silent conversation unfolds between us.

I can almost see the gears turning in her mind as she tries to figure me out. Unfortunately, she never will. I'm not like anyone she's ever encountered. That much is certain.

"You're..."

"Go on," I encourage.

"*Frustrating.*"

I grin. "Thank you."

After raising a toddler, my patience is unbreakable, and I have nothing but time. Emma dries her hands on a rag before tossing it on the counter.

She shoots me a death glare.

"You're playing games," she mutters under her breath, loud enough for only me to hear.

"You're projecting," I say, grabbing the scrubber and turning away from her. She walks off as Jake sets his bowl in the sink. I spray it out.

"Thanks," he says, squeezing my shoulder. "You good?"

"Never been better," I tell him. "Dinner was great. Thanks for the invite."

"I'm glad you actually came." Jake reaches into the fridge for a beer and offers me one, but I decline. "I didn't expect to see you, though. What changed?"

"Mom kept Colby for dinner, so I thought, why not? Plus, I love Mawmaw's chili recipe."

"Any other reason?"

"What reason would that be?" I raise an eyebrow as he fills containers with food. "Share what's on your mind."

"You know exactly what I'm talking about."

"I don't." It's easier to play dumb. I lower my voice and glance over my shoulder. "Can everyone stop?"

"Stop what?"

"Trying to play matchmaker."

He shakes his head. "I'm not."

I can't tell if he's being honest or not. "It feels like you're pushing. That's never going to happen."

"Why not?"

Claire and Emma share a laugh with Lucas.

"Not my type."

"Bullshit. Next."

"Too young," I reply.

He rolls his eyes.

"I'm not ready for a relationship. You know that's the truth."

"That sounds like an excuse. Give me the real reason."

I stare at him.

"I'm a curse to women, Jake. Every woman who's been with me has..."

He takes a long pull from his beer and moves closer. "Meredith leaving wasn't your fault."

My jaw clenches. "I don't want to talk about this, okay?"

"I'm not playing matchmaker, but I think the two of you

would be great together. You have a lot in common—unlike that fake shit between her and Lucas."

I laugh. "Glad you see through it as well."

"Painfully obvious."

I glance at the time and need to leave before Mom drops off Colby. "I should probably get going."

"Yeah, it's getting kinda late, and we have to be up early," he replies.

Nodding, I pat his back. "Thanks again for dinner."

"No problem. Want me to bring you some for lunch?"

"Absolutely." I dry my hands. "You spoil me."

As I walk past the breakfast bar, I announce my departure.

Claire hugs me goodbye. "Make sure to squeeze Colby for me."

"I will."

Lucas waves at me, but Emma doesn't look my way again. She's glued to her phone.

"Well, I hope you all have a good night. Come on, Tinsel," I say with a laugh. Jake shoots me the middle finger.

As I close the door behind me, I realize just how fucked I am.

Emma Manchester is intoxicating, and I have to get the thoughts of her out of my head. It's for the best, or at least that's what I'll tell myself until I believe it is true.

It's for her own good. *Right?*

CHAPTER 9

EMMA

The historic City Hall, once an old bank, was remodeled into a local government building in the 1980s, or so the historical marker claims. Next door stands the courthouse, and the lawn is adorned with glittery ornaments larger than I am.

At exactly eight o'clock, the door unlocks, and I step inside with determination.

"Good morning. I'd like to get the application for the Christmas Cookie Contest, please," I tell the man at the counter.

"Good mornin'. Sure, just give me a second," he replies politely as he flicks on the overhead lights. He looks around my age, maybe a year or two younger. He pulls a stapled stack of papers from a drawer and slides it across the counter to me.

"You'll need a sponsor," he adds, his southern twang thickening his words. "I can tell you're not from 'round here."

"A sponsor?" I echo, taken aback by this new information. Jake hadn't mentioned it yesterday.

"It's a new requirement. You have to be a resident of Merryville or have an immediate family member who is a resident and can sign on your behalf. However, if they do that, they can't enter the contest themselves."

"Is it that serious?" Concern creeps in as I wonder if Jake's hesitation about my entry was justified. But no matter what, I am still committed to entering.

The guy narrows his eyes, intrigued. "Are you one of those celebrity bakers or somethin'?"

I try to suppress a laugh, but I fail. "Nope. I'm just a girl who can follow a recipe. Since I'm in Merryville for the holidays, I thought it would be a fun challenge. Kinda hoping for some beginner's luck."

"You'll need it, considering how competitive it is. But miracles happen every day. So, who are you related to?"

"Claire Manchester. She's engaged to Jake Jolly. Oh, sorry, most people call him JJ."

"Ah, Claire. Should've guessed." He swallows hard. "She's very... intimidating."

"I'll have to tell her you said that," I chuckle, knowing well the effect she has on people. Being a CEO is more than just a title; it runs deep in her veins.

With just one glare, my sister can make anyone cower.

Growing up with Claire was both a curse and a blessing. She taught me how to rise after being knocked down.

Watching her navigate a man's world without fear made me realize that I wasn't cut out for the family business. It was too cutthroat for me. I'd rather drift through life like a butterfly than climb the corporate ladder. I have no regrets.

He clears his throat and subtly glances at my left hand. No ring—definitely not married.

"It's really nice to meet you," he says.

"Emma," I reply.

He smiles wide. "I'm Brent. Maybe I'll see you around town."

I laugh. "I'm sure you will, especially after I win that cookie trophy," I say confidently as I take the application.

"Good luck!"

"Thanks! I'm gonna need it, right?"

"You will," he assures me.

I push open the door, and the jingle bell above rattles lightly. With one hand in my pocket, I hold my Hall of Fame golden ticket in the other.

The more I think about it, the more I crave that cookie trophy. I just need to perfect my recipe in three and a half weeks—definitely doable, right?

Tourists pass me on the sidewalk, wearing Santa hats, ugly sweaters, and jeans. Carolers sing as I stroll toward the heart of the town square. It's the second of November, and Merryville is already in full holiday mode. I can't wait to see how it will transform as December approaches.

As I enter Glenda's Café, the enticing aromas of bacon and freshly brewed coffee fill the air. "Jingle Bell Rock" plays on an old radio at the counter, where a glass case displays an array of pies—pumpkin, chocolate, lemon meringue, and strawberry cream. My mouth waters at the sight, and I realize how hungry I am.

A stack of yesterday's newspapers spreads across the table next to the counter. While I wait to be seated, I catch the bold headline of one.

MERRYVILLE POST
Season's Greetings: Jolly Christmas Tree Farm Seasonal Celebration on Nov. 2nd

The front page features a large picture of Jake, Lucas, and Hudson smiling widely with their perfectly straight teeth and dimpled cheeks. Men like the Jolly brothers aren't part of my social circle.

Ashton Banks certainly wouldn't get his hands dirty, nor would his brother Dyson. The men who have tried to date me over the past two years lack adventure—they're just wealthy.

But I already have more money than I could ever spend, so that doesn't impress me. Money has never bought my happiness; my father learned that long ago.

I glance back at the photo of the Jolly brothers. With their solid muscles, they work and play hard.

I can almost picture myself as a regular here, greeting those I know by name. The thought makes me smile, but it also scares the shit out of me. Settling down isn't something I've considered much, but my sister loves it here. She would say it's the magic of Merryville.

"Hi, honey. Good mornin'. Just one?" A friendly older woman asks, jolting me from my thoughts. She has strands of silver-gray in her hair.

"Bring it with you. They're complimentary," she adds, picking up a menu along with napkin-rolled silverware.

"Thanks. And yes, it's just me." I grab one, tucking the pages under my arm as I follow her. The ruby-red slippers she's wearing scatter bits of light against the wall like a disco ball as she leads me through the busy diner.

This must be Glenda, the owner of the café.

She glides between tables and chairs, setting a menu at a booth surrounded by windows. The warm morning sunlight spills in, and I feel like I have the best seat in the house, overlooking the town square.

"Would you like coffee, orange juice, apple juice, chocolate milk, or regular milk?" she asks.

"Coffee with cream, please."

With a nod, she turns on her heels and strolls away.

The sounds of clinking plates and lively chatter fill the room. I overhear someone mention the Jolly Tree Farm.

As I eavesdrop on the conversation at the table behind me, I realize it's the morning's hot topic.

Glenda returns. "Sugar's on the table. Ready to order?"

I nod. "I've been told the pumpkin pancakes are a must. And I'll have some sausage, too."

"Excellent choice. Links or patties?"

"Surprise me," I reply. "Either is fine."

She smiles and glances down at the newspaper that has captivated me for the past few minutes. "Have you visited the farm yet?"

"Sort of." It's not a lie, but I haven't taken an official tour.

"You should go today. It's a lot of fun, but it'll be busy, so get there early. Bring a sweater—it's the first big event of the season and a really big deal for the locals. Also, two of the Jolly boys are single," she adds playfully.

I chuckle. "Thanks for the tip."

Everyone seems to know I'm from out of town. I promised Claire I would visit the farm today.

Another table catches Glenda's attention, and she excuses herself to refill their coffee. Steam rises from my mug as I add a spoonful of sugar and a splash of cream. I snap a photo of it next to the newspaper; a big, fluffy cloud casts a shadow across half the page.

As I zoom in on the picture, I make sure nothing in it reveals my location. Most people know my sister lives here now. However, I've only told my close friends that I'm in Texas and want to keep this visit private for as long as possible.

The last thing I need is for the paparazzi to follow me around Merryville. This town is too small to hide in. I want to blend in for one season and not be Emma Manchester. Is that too much to ask?

The upcoming week's weather forecast is at the bottom of the paper. Before I flip the page, a gigantic plate of orange, fluffy pancakes with white, gooey icing is set in front of me. I gasp—it's beautiful.

Glenda beams at my reaction. "If you need anything else, just let me know. Enjoy, honey."

"Thank you so much." I grab my fork and cut into the moist pancakes. Steam rises from the middle, and the icing oozes down the sides. The sweet bite nearly melts in my mouth, and I'm in heaven as a delighted moan escapes me. Jake was right; these are amazing.

My attention drifts back to the newspaper and then to Hudson. Though his eyes are kind, I can see the hurt behind them. I look forward to the day he shares what happened with his ex. Slowly, I've pieced together fragments of his story, but it remains unclear. His past looms like an elephant in every room and conversation, and I want to understand why.

Curiously, I type his name into Instagram, and one account appears.

This is unmistakably him:

> *The only person who matters calls me Dad.*
> *Manager of @jollychristmastreefarm.*
> *Heartbreaker is my middle name.*
> *Did you find what you were looking for?*

"He follows me," I whisper, wondering how long he's been watching my posts.

Does he read them? Does he comment? He must know I'm usually just posting and ghosting, ignoring most messages.

I scroll through his feed and notice he posts several times a week. Today, he shared a picture of himself smiling at the front gate.

There are countless photos of him shirtless while chopping wood, riding four-wheelers on the farm, and enjoying moments with his brothers. It's evident that he's a dad who shares private glimpses of scattered dinosaurs on the floor and crayon scribbles, but Colby is never shown directly. Only his tiny fingers, toes, or the back of his head appear.

I continue scrolling, fascinated by the curated glimpse into his life. He's maintained this account for years, accumulating over a thousand posts.

I rush to the beginning, eager to see the first picture he

shared—newborn baby feet, taken on December first, five years ago. That must be Colby's birthday.

The caption reads:
Today is the happiest day of my life: the day my son was born. I love you, Bee. Forever grateful for you. Thank you for changing my life for the better. Always your dad.

A bee emoji follows the heartfelt words, stirring unexpected emotions within me. I can feel the depth of his love and care for his son.

As I read, I feel like I'm intruding on his intimate thoughts, as if I'm rifling through his diary. Each post reveals his adoration for Colby, shining through every word.

I click on one of his shirtless wood-chopping photos, noticing it has a few thousand likes, with several comments calling him "lumberjack daddy." This man knows how to be a professional thirst trap online, playing into his emotional unavailability.

As I scroll further, my finger slips, and I accidentally like a video he posted two years ago.

"Shit," I whisper-hiss, annoyed with myself for being so clumsy. "Shit."

I set down my fork and chew the bite of food in my mouth, washing it down with coffee, wishing I hadn't been so careless. But it's too late; the notification was sent to his phone.

I could pretend it didn't happen, but he doesn't seem like the type of man who would let me live that down. I could blame Claire, but why would she have scrolled so far back?

I stare out the window, searching for another solution.

I could follow him back.

The superfans who stalk me would notice my follower

count increase. I could follow him from my secret, private account, but that would make me an even bigger stalker. I have to own this.

Hudson is popular with the ladies, so maybe he won't even notice.

My heart races as I read the caption of the photo I stupidly liked. Most comments focus on the muscular V leading to the impressive bulge in his khaki shorts. His tanned, sweaty skin and messy hair, combined with that smirk, are too much to handle.

Seeing him makes my heart palpitate; the attraction is almost overwhelming, even through the screen.

The caption reads: *What you see is what you get...*

Typical. But I see the real him—the king of playing hard to get, the man struggling with demons that I want to help him conquer.

I was tricked into believing that love exists, too. Now, I'm like Indiana Jones, searching for it as if it were the Holy Grail. I know I'm worthy of true love—even if I haven't found it yet —and I'll keep searching until my last breath. That's the difference between me and Hudson; he isn't even trying. Liking that image was reckless, and I'm annoyed with myself.

Before I stress too much, I text my best friends because they provide sound advice when my thoughts spiral. Plus, they're honest, even when I don't want them to be.

EMMA

Let's hypothetically say you were stalking someone and accidentally liked a photo from two years ago... What would you do?

BILLIE

As long as it wasn't Maddox, I'd pretend it didn't happen.

EMMA

It wasn't Maddox.

Maddox was the man the entire world thought I'd marry. Our relationship was private, which I didn't mind. I loved staying out of the spotlight with him. Rumors about rings and secret pregnancies circulated, but that's all they were. Maddox never proposed, even though we had discussed it several times.

One night, lying naked and alone in Paris, watching the glittering Eiffel Tower, it struck me that nothing would change between us. He was content with his extravagant but quiet life. I felt like nothing more than an ornament on his tree, and I craved more.

We were always on opposite sides of the same coin. It took me years to realize that it wouldn't have worked out. Discovering that I wasn't wife material for the man I loved nearly destroyed me. But I rose from the ashes and found myself again.

Now, I know my worth, and I won't settle. I want to be with a man who can match my obsession.

HARPER

Is it someone who would start drama? We can create a cover-up story. Blame me for anything. I'm so loved by the public right now that they'd devour a silly rumor like this. But you have to tell me who it was first.

My friends always have my back; I'd do the same for them.

EMMA

It was Hudson.

HARPER

Jake's brother?

BILLIE

😍😍😍😍

85

. . .

I laugh at Billie's heart-eyed emojis.

EMMA

YES! Ugh.

HARPER

What's the issue?

Billie's chat bubble appears and then disappears.

BILLIE

Why were you looking at photos from two years ago?

EMMA

I was curious.

BILLIE

Right! So believable. You're already crushing on this guy. Let me look him up.

I take a bite of my delicious pancakes.

BILLIE

Damn. He's... wow.

EMMA

Look, things are really awkward between us.

I share what happened last night and how he was standoffish.

HARPER

It does sound like you're crushing. HARD AF!

They won't let me escape it.

EMMA

I just want to get to know him better. That's all. He's so quiet.

BILLIE

You're trying to piece him together like a puzzle. You always loved those.

EMMA

UGH! I'M DOOMED.

HARPER

Just follow him back. Your sister is marrying his brother. That's a perfect reason.

My finger hovers over the follow button. Glenda walks by, and I stop her.

"Do you have a quarter?"

She digs into her apron pocket and loose change jingles. She hands me one.

"Heads or tails?" I ask.

Whatever she calls will decide my next move.

I flip the coin as "Run, Rudolf, Run" plays on the radio.

"Heads," she calls as it spins. Heads means I follow Hudson; tails means I block him. One extreme or the other.

I catch the coin and slam it down on the table. Glenda leans over my shoulder, eager to see the result. I take a quick breath and glance down.

Heads.

"Hope it was the right call," she says.

"I guess we'll see," I reply, returning the quarter.

I click the button, and it changes to FOLLOWING.

CHAPTER 10

HUDSON

"I want to go to school!" Colby yells, stomping his feet as I lead him off the sidewalk and away from the crowd of happy people.

I kneel to adjust the bright green Jolly Christmas Tree Farm baseball hat on his head. "Listen, I know. I'm really sorry, but sometimes when you work on the farm, you have to choose the farm. One day, this will be yours, and you'll understand why I made certain decisions. Now, Grandma and Pawpaw are here, and we should go say hi real quick. Uncle Jake and Uncle Lucas are here too."

"Aunt CeCe?" he asks.

"Yes."

He sniffles and pulls out the dinosaur Emma got him from his pocket. I gave it to him last night before bed, and he grabbed it this morning before we left, smiling the same way I had when I first saw it.

"Are you good now? We need to find Jake and Lucas, or we're going to run out of time. Let's get moving."

His brows furrow, and he wails again.

"Noooo!" His high-pitched scream grates on my nerves, drawing stares from passersby who might think I've whooped him. That's not how I parent, even though I got plenty of spankings as a kid.

It used to bother me when he'd break down in public, but now I don't care. I focus on him and try to bring him back to reality.

"You're tired." I blame the endless amounts of sugar my mother showered on him for two days. Last night, it took him over an hour to settle down. I made it to the end of Goodnight Moon before laying with him, thinking about Emma as he counted out loud. He reached twenty-two before finally falling asleep.

Today, I can't let him nap. I want him to fall asleep right after dinner.

"Bee, today is super special, so you have to be on your very best behavior. You promised me at breakfast you would."

This morning, I made his favorite—green eggs and ham with a side of sliced strawberries. We talked about today, and I made a deal with an almost five-year-old. Stupidly, I believed him.

"No!" Colby swings his arm but doesn't hit me. He doesn't even try. Tears stream down his face.

The teenage years will be hard; I can already tell. He's more stubborn than I am.

"Grandma used to tell me all the time that life isn't fair. But you know what?"

He stares at me, and I see a mini version of myself—the same hair, eyes, and smile.

"We're Jolly's, Bee. We persist no matter what. We keep going even when it's hard or when we don't want to. Rain or shine, we show up. Lots of people's livelihoods depend on us. Got it?"

He huffs and crosses his arms, scrunching his face.

"Oh, I almost forgot to mention—tonight, I'm making your favorite for dinner."

It's the only ammunition I have, but I change the subject, hoping to distract him.

"Sketti?" His green eyes light up.

"With big fat meatballs the size of your fist."

He smiles, glancing down at his balled hand.

"You good now?"

He looks past me, avoiding eye contact. His expression shifts just before he bolts away. I try to grab him, but I end up falling onto my backside as he darts into the oversized crowd. It's a mix of locals and tourists, and when I stand up, I lose sight of him.

Colby is fast. I whistle loudly, hoping he can find and return to me quickly.

"Bee," I yell, cupping my hands around my mouth.

Anxiety floods me.

I've been awake since sunrise, juggling customers and Colby all day. It feels like two full-time jobs. I know he sometimes bolts under pressure—a trait he inherited from his mother.

"Shit," I mutter.

"What's wrong?" Lucas asks, noticing my panic.

"Colby ran away."

"We'll find him. He's around," he reassures me, squeezing my shoulder.

"Colby!" I call out again. We've discussed this before; I've instructed him never to run away from me, especially in public.

Lucas quickly finds Jake, and my brothers join the search. They saw what he was wearing this morning before our office pre-meeting.

There are at least a thousand people on the farm, taking tours and enjoying various activities. We really don't need this right now.

My heart races, but I remind myself he's safe here.

"Bee!" I say, frustration mounting as I push through the crowd.

I scan for the bright green hat he's wearing and make my way to the center of the thoroughfare, where foot traffic swirls in every direction. Just as I turn, I spot Claire holding Colby's hand, while Emma kneels at his eye level.

"Colby," I call out. Emma pauses but remains where she is, at the edge of the sidewalk.

"See? I told you that once you stopped crying, we'd find him," Emma says, standing to give way.

I stride closer, realizing he's been playing them. He wasn't crying out of fear of being lost—he's clearly wrapped them around his little finger.

"I was worried about you, Bee," I say. "Please don't do that to Daddy again, okay? You can get lost."

"Aunt CeCe found me," he replies, glancing at Claire as if she were his savior.

I'm furious. A five-year-old is manipulating us all.

"And Emma helped," he says, smiling at her.

He treats them like they're heroes. "Great, let's go find Grandma."

"No!" He clings to Claire as if she's his lifeline.

"Hey, hey," Claire says, meeting his gaze. Her serious demeanor is reminiscent of a strict schoolteacher. "Did you run away from your dad?"

Emma watches me intently, nearly boring a hole through my skull, but I maintain my focus on my son. I'm grateful Claire recognizes what truly happened; nothing escapes her.

As Claire waits for Colby's response, I steal a glance at Emma.

She's wearing a black cashmere sweater, her hair half-pulled back. Her crimson lips curl into a smirk, and when the breeze blows her way, I catch a hint of her sweet perfume. She smells like a Georgia peach.

Our eyes meet briefly before I look away.

"Tell Aunt CeCe the truth," I say, shoving my hands into my pockets.

"Yes, but..." His lower lip quivers. "I was sad because I missed a birthday party for my friend Davidson at school today."

My expression shifts into a frown.

"Oh, Bee. I'm sorry. I can't know these things unless you tell me," I reply, trying to sympathize. "Maybe we can get Davidson a birthday present, and you can take it to school tomorrow?"

"Really?" His face brightens immediately.

"Yes, we'll stop by the gift shop before we leave. But please, no more running away from Daddy, okay? I was worried about you. You're my world." I adjust the collar of his shirt, which matches my own.

I think I hear Emma exclaim "aww," but I brush it off.

He looks up at me as if he understands. Someday, he will, and hopefully, he won't hold my protectiveness against me. "Okay. I'm sorry."

"Hudson, we need more wood bundles," my cousin Eli calls from behind me. He's a few years younger than Lucas, but everyone assumes he's my brother, too. "I'll let them know on the radio. Some helpers will meet you by the lowboy."

"Sounds good," he replies. As he walks away, I quickly make the call, then turn my attention back to Colby. "Time to get back to work, little man."

"Can I stay with Aunt CeCe and Emma?"

Claire shrugs.

"No, they're spending time together today, without any little boys around."

"It's honestly fine, Hudson," Claire whispers. "It would give us an excuse to play the kid games."

Emma snickers.

I shake my head. "I'm not going to do that to you. You should spend quality time with your sister."

93

"Oh, don't use me as an excuse. I'd love to have him around," Emma chimes in. "There's a merry-go-round where I could use a partner."

Colby's eyes light up, and he nods eagerly. "Please?"

"You both don't have to do this," I mutter.

Claire smiles. "If you allow it, I would be honored. Seriously."

"She doesn't lie," Emma adds. "If my sister doesn't want to do something, she'll tell you. Trust me. And she never does favors." She lowers her voice. "We're not doing it for you. Also, depending on your answer, one of us stands to win $500."

I glance between them, confused. "Wait, you bet?"

Claire laughs. "What's your answer?"

As I look back and forth, trying to decipher their bets, Colby tugs on my shirt. "Pleeeeease, Dad?"

In this moment, am I the problem? They stare at me like I am.

"Are you sure?" I ask Claire one last time.

"Is that a yes?" she replies.

"Yes," I hiss.

Claire points at Emma, who is laughing. "Told you. I won!" She does a little dance.

"You must have been a nightmare growing up," I remark.

"She was," Emma agrees.

I'm not annoyed by her gloating; I'm frustrated that Claire knows me too well—probably well enough to understand how her sister affects me. I clench my jaw, determined to keep my guard up.

"Can't wait for you to pay Jake that $3000," Claire says, her tone teasing.

My brows furrow. "What?"

Then I remember the bet I made with Jake on Halloween night about finding a girlfriend by New Year's. He knew

Emma was on her way to stay with them. My mouth falls open. The bastard set me up.

"I'm lost," Emma says. "And I'm ready for some hot cocoa."

I place my hand on Colby's shoulder. "Be very good for Aunt CeCe and Emma, okay? I'll see you at lunch. We're eating Jake's chili."

Colby ignores me.

"Agree, or I'm not taking you with me today," Claire says, shaking his hand.

I smile at her. "If I said no right now, you'd technically lose, right?"

Claire's smile fades, and Emma crosses her arms over her chest.

"You wouldn't," Claire mutters.

"No, I wouldn't," I reply, not wanting to upset Colby when we're finally in a good place again. "But I considered it. He's tired. If he gets bored, I have activity books, crayons, and his iPad in the shop office—plenty of snacks, too."

She grins. "We've got this. Emma and I were heading over to the petting zoo, and then we're getting corn dogs at the concession stand."

"Oh, I can't wait to see the miniature ponies," Emma exclaims, raising the energy. "They're my favorite."

"I love ponies, too," Colby chimes in, getting excited.

I shake my head but smile.

"If you need anything, please call me. Anything. Nothing is too small or too big."

Emma clears her throat and opens her palm to hand me her unlocked phone. "I actually don't have your number."

I glance at Emma. "Smooth."

She licks her luscious lips and smiles. "What if I need you for something?"

I glare at her. She won't make this easy for me.

"Hudson, for the love of your grandma's chocolate pie,

hurry up. We have places to be," Claire snaps, losing her patience.

Colby laughs.

I take Emma's phone, knowing her entire life is on it. Then I program my number into it but don't put it under my name.

There's no way she'll find it quickly with the length of her digital Rolodex. I hand it back, locking it with the side button.

Jake and Lucas find us, relief washing over their faces when they spot us.

"You had us scared to death," Lucas says to Colby.

Jake slides his mouth against Claire's, murmuring, "You're so pretty. I want to marry you tomorrow," as he wraps his arms around her waist and lifts her up.

"Be careful what you wish for. We could make that happen," I remind them. I haven't officiated anyone in over a decade, but I agreed to do their ceremony when they finalize their date.

Lucas waggles his brows at Emma, but she's looking at me with a sexy smirk. This is a game to her—one I won't play. Her reputation precedes her, and I know Emma Manchester never commits.

The alarm on Lucas's phone dings. "We've wasted enough time. We have an interview in ten minutes by the pavilion."

"Shit." I almost forgot.

Colby starts, "Umm. Bad word."

"Hush."

Before we go our separate ways, I stop Claire. "I'll meet you at the Gingerbread house at noon."

"We'll be there," she says just as Colby reaches for Emma. She takes his hand, and the three of them melt into the crowd.

I sigh, keeping my eyes on them until they disappear. "I feel guilty."

Jake laughs. "Are you kidding? Claire's been scheming to steal him away from you since yesterday."

I chuckle. "I knew it."

"We're trying for kids," he blurts out.

I stop walking, excitement bubbling up as I realize my brother is leaving the decision up to Claire. He would've been happy either way. "That's great! I'm going to spoil the ever-loving hell out of your little crotch goblin as payback! Excited Colby will have a cousin."

"Maybe eventually cousins. I just don't know how to be a dad," Jake admits, looking stressed. "But the thought of seeing her pregnant with my baby..."

I resume walking. "Okay, keep those private thoughts to yourself."

"What if she's already pregnant?" he whispers, and I can see his excitement. "You make being a dad look easy."

I burst out laughing. "I just make that up as I go, teaching with compassion—just like I did with you growing up."

Jake smiles and nods. "You'll help me not suck?"

"Yep. I promise. I've been through it all, so I've got your back."

Pride washes over me. I am a good dad, or at least I'm good enough.

"So you and Emma," he mumbles.

"Absolutely not. There is no me and Emma."

"Yet," he replies. "You two have a lot in common."

I roll my eyes. "You said you weren't matchmaking. You lied."

"What are you two chatting about?" Lucas asks.

"Hudson and Emma," Jake tells him.

"We're going on a date this weekend. Kinda claimed her," Lucas says.

"Yeah right. We all know it's fake, Lucas. You can drop the act," I say.

He doesn't smile. "It's not an act."

My grin fades; he seems serious.

"I'm interested in her, so back off," he says, his tone serious.

"Hey, you have nothing to worry about," I confirm.

I glance at Jake, who shrugs, and we share a silent conversation as Lucas leads the way. This only cements her name on my off-limits list.

Jake and I move toward the local news van when a woman in her early twenties approaches me, a permanent marker in one hand. When she gets close, I smile.

"I follow you online," she says. "You're my favorite lumberjack."

Jake watches me, amusement dancing on his face as I scribble my name across a log. "There are others?"

"You have no idea. By far, you're ranked at the top," she replies.

Jake chuckles.

"Oh, would you mind if we took a picture together?"

I don't get a chance to answer before she steps in closer, wrapping an arm around my waist. I keep my hands crossed in front of me; I know how rumors spread in a small town.

"I honestly thought being grumpy was an act," she says. "It's even hotter in person."

Jake offers to take the picture. As soon as he grabs her phone, I notice a small crowd of women lining up to see me like I'm the main attraction.

"We need to go," Jake whispers as he hands the device back to the woman.

"What should I do?" I ask.

He lets out a sigh and turns to face them. "Sorry, ladies. If you want to see Santa, he's just a quarter of a mile that way. We have some official business to attend to, but you'll be able to chat with Hudson later," Jake says, flashing them his boyish grin before pulling me away from the crowd. Lucas continues walking without stopping.

"I can't believe this is still happening," I mutter, feeling annoyed.

"It's great for business," Jake replies.

"I told you last year that I wouldn't be the farm's entertainment. That hasn't changed."

"You're the star at the top of the tree until you find a wife. Trust me, even an engagement won't stop them from trying."

"I don't like this," I grumble, keeping my eyes on the ground and avoiding eye contact with anyone.

This situation reminds me of last year when Emma shared the farm with her millions of followers. We became celebrities overnight.

"I'd hoped the attention would be temporary," I say.

Jake chuckles. "Oh, we've only just begun."

We find Lucas, and the attractive reporter greets us with a million-dollar smile, showcasing her perfectly straight, white teeth. Her big blue eyes meet mine. "And you must be Hudson Jolly."

Even she seems starstruck.

"Nice to meet you."

"I've heard a lot about you," she continues, her gaze lingering a bit too long.

Lucas clears his throat as the camera operator begins setting up the tripod.

"Hopefully, it was all good."

"My expectations have been met." She's flirting. "I'm Zella."

"Nice to meet you, Zella."

I glance at Lucas, trying to decipher his expression. We'll have to discuss his recent outburst later.

The light above the camera flicks on, shining brightly in my face.

"Five minutes," the guy says.

Zella smooths her blonde hair and applies a fresh swipe of lipstick.

"We'll be doing a live shot from the farm today. Everyone in the studio is really excited to be part of this."

"We can't wait," Jake tells her, stepping between me and Lucas. "Don't be nervous."

"Nervous?" Lucas mutters. "Just try not to be cheesy."

Impossible.

Even though Jake isn't a dad yet, he already has the corny jokes down.

I check the time on my phone and quickly skim through the notifications on the home screen.

Emma Manchester liked your photo.

Emma Manchester followed you

My mouth slightly drops open.

"What's up?" Jake notices my sudden shift in mood.

"Nothing." I lock my phone, shoving it into my pocket, though I can't ignore how my heart races.

Why would she do that? What photo did she like?

"One minute until we're live," Zella announces, holding her microphone. She stands beside me with a smile, waiting.

"Thank you, Janice. We're live today at the Jolly Christmas Tree Farm with the Jolly brothers—Hudson, Jake, and Lucas. Right now, there are close to a thousand people here at the farm, and as you can see, most are already in the holiday spirit."

She laughs. "Hudson, can you tell the folks watching at home and in the studio what they can expect when they arrive?"

"Joy. Family. Fun. The holiday spirit is alive and well on the farm today." I grin and step back to let Jake take the spotlight.

He slides in seamlessly like we planned the transition.

"Not to mention, Santa came all the way from the North Pole to celebrate this special occasion. Did you give him your list?" Jake asks Zella.

"I sure did. Had a few things on it." She glances at me

before focusing back on the camera using her television voice. "Absolutely, Janice. There are plenty of reasons everyone should put Jolly Christmas Tree Farm at the top of their holiday to-do list this season. This is the only place to be, and I genuinely wish those watching at home could feel the magic in the air right now." She turns to Jake. "Tell everyone where they can find you and how to get here."

"Sure thing." Jake's twang becomes more pronounced, a sign of his excitement.

As he promotes our social media accounts and lists our extended hours, I glance past Zella. My eyes land on Emma, sipping a cup of hot cocoa. Colby gives her a high-five, and they share a laugh.

"Isn't that right?" Jake nudges me.

"Absolutely," I reply, unsure of what he just said. Emma's gaze captured me.

"Thanks, Janice! We're going to have a blast. Yep, come on down and check this place out for yourself. Highly recommended."

We freeze for ten seconds before Zella relaxes. The camera light shuts off, and she expresses her gratitude. Before I can walk away, Zella stops me.

"Would you like to grab a drink sometime?"

"Well—"

"He would," Lucas interrupts.

I glare at him.

Zella steps forward and hands me her card. "My number is on there. Call me sometime. I'd love to hang out."

"Nice meeting you."

"The pleasure was mine," she replies, grabbing a bag of gear and heading toward the van with the Channel 6 logo on the side.

Lucas looks at me. "You should go out with her."

"I don't want to go out with anyone," I insist for the

hundredth time. Yet as soon as the words leave my mouth, my faithful excuse feels like a lie.

Shit.

Two hours pass quickly, and I haven't had a minute to myself since the interview until now. The sounds of the crowd chatting, children laughing, and the band playing drift through the chilly breeze.

A smile touches my lips as I think about Colby. I hope he's having fun and behaving, but then again, he's always loved Claire.

I'm so glad my brother is marrying her. They were made for one another, and their happiness is evident. They're lucky.

Sometimes, I wonder if I've ever truly experienced love. My heart now tells me I never will, and that's a hard reality to face.

I load several fifty-pound bags of popcorn kernels into the back of the side-by-side. It takes me a few trips, but this should keep my cousin BJ—Bella Jolly—supplied into the afternoon.

The girl is a spitfire who knows her worth. As her oldest cousin, it's my responsibility to teach her how to stand her ground, especially with men. I'm already praying for whoever she ends up with because BJ doesn't tolerate nonsense from anyone. Perhaps that's why she's determined to open another coffee shop after graduation. She's been sneaky, working there during her college breaks, on weekends, and over the holidays to learn everything about running a shop.

I told her it was shady and that she'd be the talk of the town once she does it. She laughed and said she loved free advertising. Heart of coal, that one.

I try to be as efficient as possible, knowing I'll have Colby with me the rest of the afternoon, and he tends to slow me down. I spent the summer planning for this event but never imagined I'd have my son here with me. Today is the culmination of every free minute I've focused on.

My grandmother is convinced that I work so hard to avoid dating. She's not wrong, but I'd never admit it out loud because that woman loves to say, "I told you so."

Before heading back to the concession stand, I queue my radio.

"Calling the snack shack," I say, waiting for a response.

"Concessions," BJ replies.

"I've grabbed the kernels; need anything else?"

I give her a moment to check back.

"Hot dog buns and pretzels, please. As many as you can carry."

"10-4." Thankfully, I have plenty of room to carry whatever they need. Once I load the oversized bag of buns, I grab a gigantic box of individually wrapped pretzels and buckle it into the backseat. Before leaving, I take a quick inventory, knowing I'll need to order more food for the morning to be ready for the weekend. We're expecting thousands of guests on Saturday and Sunday, with a goal of 2,000 trees sold. Jake thinks it will be more like 3,000, which would set a record for Jolly Farm.

I lock the door and head toward the stand. It's not far, but the constant flow of people has me creeping across the grass.

"Hi," I say, smiling at one of the ladies eyeing me like her next meal. I keep my gaze ahead. I never wanted this kind of attention in real life. Online is different; I can create boundaries there. Most of the time, I post and ghost.

That's when I remember that Emma followed me on Instagram. After parking behind the food stand, I pull my phone from my pocket and log into the app. Immediately, I'm overwhelmed with notifications, and my follower count has skyrocketed. I nearly panic-scroll, trying to find Emma's name.

I check my profile and see that my follower count has jumped from under 10,000 to over one million.

I nearly drop my phone. "What the fuck?"

Then I visit her profile: @therealemmamanchester

The gray button says FOLLOWING, just like I remember.

She's responsible for this attention.

I do the only thing I can: deactivate my account until the situation stabilizes.

In this moment, I exist to no one—not even her.

CHAPTER 11

EMMA

I kneel in front of Colby, holding several wet napkins. "You've got cotton candy on your face. May I help you clean it off?"

I wait for his response, but he remains silent.

"Or you can do it yourself if you'd prefer," I suggest gently. "Or maybe Claire could help?"

It's important to let him decide, especially since he's at that age when kids want to do things on their own.

"You can," he replies, stepping closer with a grin that highlights his dimples.

I smile back, removing his Jolly Christmas Tree Farm baseball hat. Colby blinks up at me with those long, curly eyelashes. I gently wipe his chubby little cheeks. "We're meeting your dad soon."

He shakes his head and scowls. "No! I want to stay with you!"

It takes all my strength not to laugh; Hudson has given me the same look several times already.

"You promised," Claire chimes in from behind me. Her voice is calm yet firm as always. "And if you don't argue, we'll have ice cream very soon."

"Two scoops?" Colby asks.

"As many as you want." My sister has a knack for negotiating with kids. I'm convinced she could strike a deal with the devil and come out on top.

"Chocolate?"

"Any flavor your heart desires. Strawberry, vanilla, cookies and cream, mint chocolate chip..."

As I clean his other cheek, Colby watches Claire with interest.

"Did you know mint chocolate chip is the fourth favorite ice cream flavor in the United States? It was invented in France for a princess's wedding."

"Really?" I reply, intrigued. "Huh. I learn something new every day."

Colby giggles.

Claire glances at the expensive watch on her wrist. You can take the girl out of the city, but you can't take the city out of the girl. She's still a stickler for time. "We have five minutes," she informs us, embodying little Miss Punctuality.

Colby looks at me and says, "Your hair is pretty."

"Thank you. You can touch it if you want." He reaches forward and twirls a few strands around his fingers. "Now you're clean with hardly any evidence left."

"We're so busted," Claire shakes her head as I stand. "His cheeks are tinted blue. Hudson will know."

I grin. "But it was yummy, wasn't it?"

Colby nods enthusiastically. "Yes! I want more! The pink one."

I glance at Claire. "You've created a monster."

"Rawr," Colby roars playfully.

"A T-Rex." Claire reaches for Colby's hand. He takes hers, then mine. "I'm sure Hudson is already waiting for us."

We've packed in as many activities as we could: visiting the petting zoo, taking pictures at the photo booth, riding the carousel, and even painting rocks shaped like Christmas trees at the craft booth. Each of us has one in our pocket, decorated with bright neon paints that resemble strings of holiday lights.

Three hours have passed in the blink of an eye, and I feel a pang of sadness. Having a kid around has been entertaining.

Colby swings my hand in his, and on the count of three, Claire and I lift him into the air. He kicks his legs out and laughs. My arm will be sore from the excitement today, but his giggles are well worth it.

"Today's been a good day," I tell my sister.

She nods in agreement. "Every day in Merryville is."

When I look up, my gaze locks onto Hudson, and I struggle to interpret his expression. Understanding him is still impossible, and I hope it doesn't always feel this way.

"There he is," Claire points out as Colby breaks away from us and runs toward his dad. Hudson scoops him up into his arms, adjusting the hat on his head.

"Did you have fun today?" he asks.

"Yes! We pet the animals and collected rocks and—"

"And ate too much blue cotton candy?" Hudson interjects.

Colby snickers, "Yes, Daddy. But shh! Aunt CeCe didn't want you to know."

He lifts a brow at Claire but acts as if I'm invisible.

"It's kind of hard to hide when it's all over you," Claire tells Colby, prompting a giggle from him.

"Are you hungry?" Hudson asks, setting Colby down. The little boy's shoes sink into the hay beneath him. "Uncle Jake is warming chili."

"Mm, with cheese?" Colby asks eagerly.

"If you want it that way," Hudson replies.

We head to the covered area with picnic tables, surrounded by chatter, but my focus remains on Hudson.

"I wasn't done hanging out with the little rascal," Claire admits. "We didn't get the chance to take the hayride."

Colby turns to Hudson, eyes wide with anticipation. "Can we go, Daddy?"

"I can't, Bee. Maybe tomorrow, okay? I'm super busy today."

Colby immediately pouts.

"I need to talk to Emma right now, okay? So go with Aunt Claire," Hudson says. Hearing my name spoken by him sends a shiver down my spine. My body shouldn't react this way, and my heart shouldn't stutter—but it does. I try to shake it off, but there's no denying it this time. No drinks to blame. It's all him.

Claire glances my way before narrowing her eyes at Hudson. "Come on, Bee. Let's find a picnic table."

Hudson's large frame turns toward me, and he gently takes hold of my wrist, leading me away from everyone. His touch singes my skin. Part of me wonders if I should run away, given how much I enjoy his strong, calloused hand around mine. It's too much.

Once we're alone on the other side of the building, he brushes his thumb lightly against my wrist, as if checking for a pulse. If he feels it, he'll know my heart is racing. As he releases me, I feel an immediate sense of loss.

With a smile on my face, I look up and meet his bright green eyes, but his mouth and brows are downturned. He's *pissed*.

"Why would you follow me on Instagram? I had to deactivate my account because you didn't consider what following me would do," he says, frustration evident in his tone.

His words hit me like a ton of bricks. "I—"

"I won't be your new trend, Emma," he replies, shaking his head.

"Hudson. I'm really sor—" I begin to explain.

"Don't. I'm too old to play games with you," he responds, stepping closer until my back hits the snack shack. His thigh parts my legs, and his mouth is so close to mine that my head swims.

"You're thirty-nine, Hudson. Do you want to be in the same situation you're in now when you're forty-nine? If you don't let people in, that will be your future."

He leans in, brushing his mouth against the shell of my ear. My eyes flutter shut, and I desperately want him to kiss me as he increases the pressure between my legs. I gasp, filled with need and desire, ready to beg for every inch of him. My body instantly reacts.

"You talk too much," he whispers, eliciting a breathless gasp from me. "Too. Fucking. Much," he mutters against my skin, making my breaths transform into ragged gasps.

"Are you going to punish me?"

"Oh, I already am." I feel his smirk against the softness of my neck, the scruff of his facial hair tickling my skin.

"Bastard," I whisper, craving his touch.

"Ahem," I hear someone clear their throat. Hudson pulls back, and I glance over to see Jake smirking with his arms crossed. He raises his brows between us as Hudson walks away.

"Do you always have to ruin a moment?" I begrudgingly ask.

Jake stares at me for a second before walking away, chuckling. "Little Sis, you're gonna make me very rich!"

"Ugh. I'm not your little sister yet," I groan, relieved to be alone. I take a moment to regroup, but my mind is spinning, and my body is on fire. Yet, I can't help but smile.

That grumpy man frustrates me, but I like it. When I glance down, I realize how hard my nipples are beneath this thin sweater and quickly cross my arms over my chest. He had me melting like a popsicle on a hot summer day.

My sister notices my demeanor as I approach her. "Are you okay?"

There's no way I can share the dirty thoughts swirling in my head right now.

"I followed Hudson on Instagram, and he's pissed about it."

"Em. You didn't," she whispers, wide-eyed.

"It was inconsiderate, and I didn't think it through," I admit.

"Have you forgotten who you are? Because don't. You can't escape it, not even here, even if it feels safe. The paparazzi still come and go, Em. Don't be fooled, okay? Hudson's very private. You have to respect that."

"I know," I reply. I won't slip up again.

Hudson laughs at something Colby says, and when he glances at me, it feels like he's already moved on.

"Something's going on between you two."

"I'm not sure what it is," I admit, thinking about the marks he left on my neck.

My phone buzzes, and I pull it from my pocket to see our girl group chat lighting up. Claire watches me as I unlock the screen.

BILLIE

Already broke the internet.

HARPER

I'm so jealous.

I furrow my brows and click on the link. At the top of the page, it reads:

Hudson Jolly is Mr. November. What we know about him...

Hudson Jolly, 39 Years Old. He manages a Christmas tree farm, is a dad, and is single, ready to mingle with a maneater for the holidays.

There's a photo of Hudson leading me away from everyone on the farm. I'm looking up at him with googly eyes while he smirks at me. His hand is firm around my wrist.

Shit.

I can see *it* in my expression.

EMMA

OMFG! The look...

BILLIE

😳 Uh-oh!

HARPER

I'd have the same expression if he were manhandling me like that. He's FINE.

Before I can process it, I shove my phone back into my pocket.

"Was it important?" Claire asks.

"No, just Billie and Harper being themselves."

She snickers. "Billie still denying she's in love with Asher Banks?"

"Yep," I reply.

The internet is going wild over one silly picture. I decide to show Claire.

"I told you they were watching. You are too high profile." She glances at the screen and grins. "You're wearing the in-love face."

"Shh!" I hush her. "What do I do?"

"Enjoy it," she responds. "Look at you. Look at him."

I tuck my lips into my mouth, trying to contain the wave

of realization. This push and pull began months ago, back in July, the day we met.

"I want to disappear," I confess.

"Then follow his lead and deactivate your accounts too. It redirects the focus back to you."

My notifications are overflowing on every social media platform. I get so many that I've muted them, but I still see the numbers.

"You don't need permission to take a break and let things die down," Claire assures me.

Her suggestion makes sense.

I unlock my phone and do something I've never done before—I deactivate every account. Let everyone speculate about that instead.

I expect a rush of existential dread, but I feel...nothing. I laugh and shove my phone into my pocket. Maybe I really am dead inside. But after Hudson pinned me against the snack shack...

I feel more alive than I have in a long time.

"Always stay two steps ahead," I tell Claire. "You're smart."

"I know," she replies, laughing. "Looks like your hiatus begins just as the magic of Merryville takes hold." She wraps her arm around me, guiding me to the table as Jake approaches, carrying a steaming pot with gloves.

I smile, feeling safe and at home, cherishing my sister's presence. I've missed her so much over the years.

"Come on, y'all. It's time to eat." Jake lifts the lid.

Steam rushes upward, and Colby climbs onto his knees. He tries to poke his finger inside, but Hudson quickly stops him.

"It's scorching hot," he warns, gesturing for him to sit. Jake and Claire shift around him, leaving one seat open. I slide in next to Hudson, carefully leaving enough space so our thighs don't touch. Just being able to smell him is torture enough.

The tension between us slices through the air. Goosebumps rise on my arm, and I try to ignore them, but he takes my breath away with a single glance. That should be impossible.

"How was the petting zoo?" Hudson asks Colby while I scoop chili into my bowl.

"Great! There were rabbits, goats, chickens, and ponies!"

I smile at the thought of the fun we had today. That kid has boundless energy, but surprisingly, he never acted out.

"What's on your mind?" Jake asks, eyeing me cautiously. I wonder when he'll mention to Claire that he saw us together. Or maybe he won't.

"Just thinking," I reply, taking a bite of my food.

Claire quickly grabs Hudson's attention. "You should let me keep Colby for the rest of the day."

"Yes!" Colby exclaims, nodding enthusiastically. His laughter is contagious, and he's absolutely adorable. He's genuinely happy, and it's clear how much love and attention Hudson gives him. "Aunt CeCe said she'd take me to the place with lots of ice cream, and I get to pick as many as I want. And I've been good!"

"Let's finish eating first, then we'll talk about it, okay?" Hudson replies to Colby, giving Claire a nod of agreement.

It's a silent endorsement—a yes.

I understand my sister's affection for Colby. He has a big heart that needs to be protected. I've listened to him share stories about kids at school, monster trucks, and T-Rexes. His imagination is wild, and I'm impressed at how well he can remember details.

Jake checks his watch. "We need to head out in about five minutes. We're supposed to take over tours from Lucas at 1:30."

We haven't been here long. I guess this is standard for every season—eat quickly, then say goodbye.

"Where are you meeting him?" Claire asks as everyone finishes their meals.

"At the drop-off zone on the west side of the property," Jake replies politely, leaning down to steal a kiss.

"Don't keep Lucas waiting." My sister playfully grabs a handful of his butt.

Jake laughs and pulls her close, "Don't start something you won't finish."

"Just go," she tells him.

"It's not my fault he didn't join us and made plans with *someone else*," Jake says, glancing at me. "But I guess you're right."

"Who?" Hudson asks, curious. "Is *she* back?"

"Actually, we're hanging out together," I say with a smile. "That's why Claire wanted to keep Colby—so they could have some quality aunt-and-nephew time."

My phone vibrates, and I pull it from my pocket. After swiping out of the group chat with my friends, I see a message from Lucas.

LUCAS
Well?

EMMA
I'm convinced you're the actual devil. Love how you got Jake involved.

LUCAS
I didn't get him involved. He's just in on it.

I chuckle lightly and put my phone away.

"Lucas said to hurry," I inform them. "He just texted me."

114

I sneak a glance at Hudson, whose jaw tightens.

Is he jealous? *No way.*

"What time should I meet you?" Claire asks Hudson as she rises from the table.

"I'll take him to the tree lighting ceremony at sunset. Unless you're leaving early—then just text me."

"I wouldn't miss that for the world," Claire says.

"Great! We'll meet up and do a trade-off: your kid for mine?" He pats Jake's shoulder, eliciting a laugh from him.

Claire leans into Jake and plants a kiss on his lips. "I love you," she whispers. "I'm going to miss you."

"Love you, miss you already," Jake replies, his gaze dreamy as he looks at my sister. They are clearly lovesick, and I'm a tad jealous.

"Are you riding with Jake?" she asks, reaching for Colby.

"Yep," I respond. "That's the plan!"

"I was just going that way too," Hudson interjects.

Jake glances over at him. "No, you weren't."

"I am now," Hudson replies, his tone straightforward.

They share a silent exchange, and as we approach the work truck, I realize it's a single cab with one long seat.

"I'll drive." Hudson takes the keys from Jake.

"Actually, why don't you go ahead and relieve him for thirty minutes since you're heading that way? If you need anything, call me on the radio," Jake says.

Hudson glares at him. "I call the shots. I'm in charge."

"Sure, you are, bud." Jake taps the side of the truck and winks at me before walking away.

Hudson opens the driver's side door for me, and I slide inside, scooting to the middle as he joins me. He backs out of the driveway, and we travel down the gravel road.

"I saw you with Colby today," he admits.

"He's a really good kid—has manners. You've done a great job."

A small smile spreads across his lips, filling me with

happiness. He's a fantastic dad; Colby is incredibly lucky to have him.

"Let me help you," I say. "I can be your temporary nanny."

"Are you sure you're not Lucas's?" He glances at me.

I lick my lips. "Is that jealousy I hear, Mr. Jolly?"

He smirks. "You're gonna be the end of me."

"I already am."

The truck stops at the end of the road, and Hudson opens his door. Before he can get out, I climb over his lap, straddling him, meeting his eyes for a brief moment.

"Thanks for the ride," I whisper, slightly grinding against him; he feels thick beneath me.

Fuck.

This man...

Just one kiss; that's all I need. It's all I can think about as my mouth inches closer to his. When his breath catches, I slide off him and hop out of the truck. Lucas walks toward us and I pick up my pace, meeting him.

Once we're close, he wraps his arms around me. "How sweet. He drove you."

"You know him well," I reply.

"Told you," Lucas says, grabbing my hand and interlocking his fingers with mine.

Hudson's gaze lands on our hands.

"Can I get those keys?" Lucas asks, and Hudson drops them in his palm. "The tractor's on the side."

As we walk away, Lucas leans down and whispers in my ear, "Laugh like I said something funny."

I do, and he pulls away with a smile. "You are a pro."

"We could've had fun if I'd met you in New York—tag-teamed them all."

"Ah, I'm sad I didn't have the opportunity. Especially since I look hot as hell in a suit." He releases my hand and opens the door for me.

"I'm sure you do." I climb inside.

Lucas adjusts the baseball cap on his head, identical to the one Colby wore earlier, then we leave. The road is bumpy but we're not very far from the farm, maybe five minutes.

I'm not sure what I expect when we finally arrive at his place, but a two-story cabin with large windows isn't it. "You live here alone?" I ask.

"Yeah. I've had roommates over the years, but I kicked them out for pissing me off. Now it's the bachelor pad."

We climb out of the truck, and I ascend the wide steps to his porch. As Lucas walks inside, I'm struck by the amount of natural light streaming in. Not to mention, his house is immaculate.

"Wow. Impressive. Bet you've hosted some wild parties here."

"I have," he admits as he moves into the kitchen.

He places a plate in the microwave and then turns to me. "So, tell me what happened today. Where are we with this plan?"

I fill him in on the Instagram situation, and he reacts just like Claire did.

"It was stupid, I know."

"He forgives easily until he doesn't," Lucas explains.

"Do you think he'll ever be able to love someone again?" I ask seriously.

"Yes," he replies. "*You.*"

"Stop," I tell him, a hint of excitement creeping in.

"You're the one for him, Em. I haven't seen him smile genuinely in a long time. It took a pink Power Ranger less than five minutes." Lucas removes his macaroni from the microwave. "Want some?"

"Nah, I just ate five pounds of chili. Do you mind if I look around?"

"Make yourself at home," he tells me as I wander toward the mantle.

Various photo frames are displayed. I'm so interested in the family photos because each one tells a story while capturing a moment in time. There's a few of the farm, some of Lucas with his friends, but my gaze settles on three young boys holding up Christmas gifts, wrapping paper strewn on the floor. "Oh my God, is this the three of you?"

"Probably, there are several up there," he says, glued to his phone.

In the back, I spot a photo of Lucas with a guy who has dark hair and a girl with the same eyes as him. They're early teenagers, the three of them.

"Who are they?"

He shrugs, so I grab the frame and hold it up. His eyes flicker over it, and a sad smile touches his lips. "My best friend Sammy and his twin sister."

He takes a big bite of food.

"What was that eye twitch for?" I ask. "Oooooh, is this the woman you're trying to impress? She's pretty. Oh my God, it is!"

He finishes chewing and swallows. "I didn't admit to anything."

"You don't have to."

CHAPTER 12

HUDSON

My mind drifts as I drive the tractor for the hayride around the field.

Is it possible that Lucas is serious about dating Emma? Is it possible Emma is into him?

Both scenarios seem plausible. They're close in age, and my brother carries no emotional baggage. No children from a previous relationship. He hardly dates and is still friends with every single ex-girlfriend of his.

Lucas would be a good match for her.

I grip the steering wheel tightly, recalling how close our mouths were when she straddled me. It was payback for almost crossing the line with her again. Like a siren of the sea, she beckons me into her murky depths, pulling me under with her.

I'm acutely aware of the emotional damage I could cause her. Claire would never forgive me if I hurt her baby sister.

The tour guide, Susie Lynn, speaks excitedly into a microphone as she shares facts about the farm. Her high-pitched voice jolts me out of my thoughts. But as I scan the distance, I realize Lucas is late.

When the farm truck finally pulls into the parking lot, he's alone. His hair is a mess, as if someone has been running their hands through it. I clench my teeth at the thought.

Once the tractor comes to a complete stop, I cut the engine. The next tour begins in ten minutes. As soon as Lucas approaches, he smirks.

"How was lunch?" I ask, extending my palm.

"She was great," he replies, his cockiness evident as he wipes the corner of his mouth. He places the keys in my hand, and I grip them tightly.

"Why are you doing this?" I ask, frustration creeping into my voice.

"Doing what?" He feigns innocence.

"You're faking it," I say. "It's obvious."

I wait for him to confirm or deny it, but Lucas is unpredictable. The truth is, I have no idea what's happening between them right now, but Jake also believed this was just an act.

"You can have her when I'm done," he says.

"Don't disrespect her," I warn.

"Just admit you're into Emma, and I'll back off," Lucas says, crossing his arms over his chest.

"Absolutely not," I retort.

"Fine." He flashes a cocky grin that I find infuriating. "Emma chooses who she wants, and until she does, she's fair game."

I laugh at him as if he's lost his mind. "I'm not competing with you."

"You will," he singsongs.

My phone buzzes, interrupting the conversation. I roll my eyes at him and focus on the text message, though he stands in front of me, clearly waiting for the discussion to continue.

MAMA

I can take Colby this week after pre-school, but only if I can keep him on Saturday night again.

HUDSON

You know I don't like him being gone every Saturday.

MAMA

Honey, you need to rest this weekend.

I feel guilty knowing how much my mom worries that Colby is growing up too fast. She said one day, she blinked, and we were men.

HUDSON

Let me think about it. I love and appreciate you.

I sigh with relief, knowing she can pick him up after pre-school. It eases some of the pressure and makes this manageable.

MAMA

Oh, and I just spoke with Claire and Emma. They looked like they were having fun with Colby. Maybe Emma can be your temporary nanny? And before you give me an excuse, she told me she already offered to help, but you won't let her. Is that true?

. . .

I scoff, disbelieving that she told on me.

HUDSON

I don't know her. Not happening.

MAMA

Claire wouldn't have her around if she weren't trustworthy. Emma can stay with him at your house instead of being stuck working beside you all season. Let him be a kid, especially while he still believes.

HUDSON

Can we talk about this later? I gotta get back to work.

MAMA

Sure, honey. Have a good day!

"What's with that face?" Lucas asks.

"Nothing," I reply, drawn back to earlier today when I saw Emma with Colby.

I wondered how differently my life could have turned out. I envisioned our future so vividly that it felt like déjà vu.

"You make everything so much harder than it needs to be. Live in the moment," Lucas tells me. "Take advantage of right now."

"You'll understand my decisions once you have kids, okay? Everything I choose affects him, and I have to prioritize his best interests."

I still can't tell if he's trying to win over Emma's heart or trying to convince me to do the same.

"Did she follow you on Instagram?" I ask as he walks away. It's almost time for the next tour to begin.

"She deactivated her account. She said she was going on a hiatus to think. See you at the tree lighting ceremony."

"I'll be there." I move toward the truck, wishing I understood Emma. When I think I have her pegged, she does the unexpected. Social media is her entire identity, so I never imagined she could switch it off.

As I climb into the truck's cab, the sweet scent of her perfume lingers in the air. It's utterly intoxicating. I back out of the driveway, kicking up rocks as I turn onto the main road. She's the only thing on my mind.

Three hours later, I meet up with my dad, who still has a long line of kids waiting to sit on his lap. Today, he's wearing a special Santa suit adorned with golden jingle bells. Whenever he's jolly, he jingles, and it's impossible not to smile.

He's the official Santa Claus of Merryville. It wouldn't be Christmas without him. Colby knows his grandfather is Santa, which is why he behaves his best around my parents. After all, Santa is always watching.

As the sun sets behind the horizon, I join Jake and Lucas. The crowd has gathered around the dark tree. They perk up when they see me making my way through the crowd. Before I take the stage, I search for my son.

I step up to make myself visible and whistle over the

chatter. Scanning the crowd, I spot Colby waving at me from on top of a picnic table.

"I'm over here!" he yells. Then I notice Emma beside him. Our eyes lock, and I see her chewing on her bottom lip. An electric current passes between us, and for a brief moment, everything else fades away.

I force myself to look away from her.

"Come on," Jake says to Colby, motioning for him to hurry.

My son jumps off the table and sprints through the crowd, parting it as he calls out, "Excuse me!" repeatedly.

When he's close, I scoop him in my arms and squeeze him. "There you are! Did you have a good day?"

"Yes! I had so much fun!" he replies, beaming with chocolate smudged on his cheek.

"Are we ready now?" Lucas asks, and we each nod in agreement.

This has become a cherished family tradition every year since we were kids. Being with my brothers and continuing this ritual means more to me than they will ever know.

"Is everyone ready?" Lucas yells out to the crowd.

"Yes!" they respond as a cymbal roll begins behind us. The band is queued and ready to play "All I Want for Christmas." We chose this song when we were kids, and it has stayed with us. When we're eighty, we'll probably still hire a cover band to play Mariah Carey's classic song.

"On the count of three!" Jake shouts into the microphone.

The crowd cheers, every face lit up with a smile.

"Three, two, one!"

Lucas flips the switch, and the sparkly lights flood the tree, illuminating it in red, green, and white. The lights glitter as they ripple up and down the tree, dancing to the music.

The lead singer begins, and the crowd erupts in cheers.

Happiness washes over me, filling me with joy. *I did it.*

I officially launched one of the most successful Season's Greetings in the farm's history.

"Make a wish," I say to Colby, who beams at me, his dimples deepening.

He looks up at the tree, his face aglow with bright white light. "Okay, I made my wish. Your turn, Daddy."

I glance back at the crowd, and my eyes settle on Emma.

"I just did."

"Hope it comes true," he tells me.

A smile crosses my lips. "Me too, Bee. Me too."

He hugs me tightly, and I hold him close. Despite my challenging circumstances, I feel incredibly lucky and grateful for this.

After a few more holiday songs, the event ends, and the crowd starts to disperse, heading to their vehicles. In the distance, I hear car doors slamming and engines revving. Colby falls asleep on my chest as I carry him home, and I smile, knowing the girls must have worn him out today. Admittedly, I'm exhausted, too.

Behind me, laughter echoes. I glance over my shoulder and see Claire and Emma giggling like teenagers tipsy on strawberry wine.

"Did you have fun?" Claire asks. "Tell the truth."

"More than I'd like to admit," Emma replies. "I'm just... happy. Excited."

I grin, unable to resist eavesdropping. Their voices carry through the forest, and they don't notice me ahead of them.

"Did you have fun with Lucas?" Claire asks quietly.

"Yeah, I did. Did you know he's in love with his best friend's sister?"

"No. What's her name?"

"Not sure," Emma admits.

Lucas would never utter her name aloud. He's superstitious about it because Holiday always shows up whenever he mentions her.

"And who are you in love with?" Claire asks.

"Life."

I chuckle, and they immediately quieten.

"Who's there?" Emma asks.

"Shh," I hiss.

"Hudson?" Claire whispers when she's right behind me, tiptoeing through the woods.

"If you wake him..." I mutter as Colby's arms and legs flop against me. He's sound asleep, breathing deeply and steadily.

When we reach the clearing by my house, I walk up the back steps of the porch. The two of them continue down the path toward Jake's.

"Good night," Emma whispers.

"Night," I reply, carefully unlocking the door and stepping inside. "Thanks for everything today."

"You're welcome," Claire says.

My heart feels lodged in my throat as I remove my boots and ascend the stairs to Bee's room. His pediatrician advised me to let him sleep during these times and to expect more rest when he's experiencing growth spurts.

I gently place him on his bed, carefully removing his hat, shoes, and pants. Then, I pull the fluffy blankets over him and tuck him in.

"Goodnight, Bee," I whisper, flicking on the lamp beside his bed. It has helped ease his fear of sleeping alone in his room, and now it has become a comforting routine.

I head downstairs and pour myself a glass of whiskey. The leftovers from Friday are waiting for me on the fridge's top shelf. As I pop them in the microwave, my phone buzzes.

UNKNOWN

Hudson Jolly, did you seriously program yourself into my phone as Lumberjack Daddy?

I burst into laughter, nearly spilling the whiskey across the bar top. I quickly save her number.

HUDSON

Guess you found me.

EMMA

Took over thirty minutes.

EMMA

I'm really sorry about what happened earlier.

HUDSON

Why?

EMMA

Can we have this conversation in person?

I glance down at her text, then down the double shot of whiskey. After some liquid courage, I type the first thing that comes to mind.

The microwave beeps, breaking my concentration.

My brother always tells me to live in the moment. Should I send it? I know the implications. I stare at the text for over a minute, the cursor blinking insistently. Finally, I hit send.

HUDSON

You know where I live.

Fuck it.

CHAPTER 13

EMMA

I reread his text.

It feels like an invitation, like he wants me to come over.

My heart flutters, and I place my hand against my chest, savoring the sensation. It may be a flicker in the dark, but it's there. And it scares me because he has made it very clear that he's emotionally unavailable.

I don't want to set myself up for heartbreak.

I've barely recovered from the last one.

Sitting at the edge of my bed, I revisit our brief conversation. Is he flirting? Do I want him to be? I could be at his house in ten minutes flat.

Before I can talk myself out of going, I change into warmer clothes and slip on my shoes. When I open the door to my room, the hinges squeak. I freeze, almost laughing at myself, then take a step forward.

The house is dark except for the warm glow of a lamp in the living room. As I move toward it, excitement courses

129

through me. The thrill of being with Hudson again is almost overwhelming.

"Howdy," Jake says, looking up from the couch, his black-framed glasses perched on his nose and a book in his hand.

I cover my mouth to stifle a scream, but the surge of adrenaline still races through my veins.

"You goin' somewhere?" he asks.

"Uh, yes," I stammer, aware of my bright red cheeks.

"Have fun," he replies, returning to his book. I head toward the back door. "Oh, Emma?"

"Yeah?" I ask, reaching for the doorknob.

"Tell Hudson I said hi."

A flutter spreads in my chest.

I could ignore Jake's words, but I don't. I turn back toward the couch. "Do you think I'm making a mistake?"

Claire says Hudson is a green flag, and I want to believe that. But Jake knows his brother.

His expression softens. "Sometimes mistakes turn into miracles. I don't think you have anything to worry about. Hudson's a Grinch with a huge heart."

"Do you think I can make it grow three sizes too big?"

His brows lift. "I think you already have."

A grin spreads across my lips. "Can you keep this between us, please?"

"Secret's safe with me. But tell me this..." Jake sits up and drops his voice to a whisper. "You and Lucas, that's fake as hell, right? Because—"

"It's fake," I admit. "And it wasn't my idea."

"Got it. Carry on, then. Looks like Lucas and I are on the same team." He chuckles. "Just making sure my brothers won't be fighting over the holidays."

"Lucas isn't my type. And apparently, I'm not his."

"And Hudson?" he presses.

A wide smile blooms on my face. "That's still to be determined. See you later?"

He nods and returns to his book as I leave.

Tonight is colder, and I'm looking forward to some cozy fireplace weather this weekend. The wind rustles the leaves along the dirt path as I shove my hands into my hoodie pockets, but my body is on fire.

Thoughts of what I'll say to Hudson swirl in my mind.

When I finally reach the clearing, his large house looms in the field like a fortress. Some lights shine, but the cabin remains mostly dark.

As I ascend the porch steps, anxiety creeps in, and I question my decision. A part of me considers turning back. But just then, the door swings open slowly.

Golden light spills from inside, revealing him looking at me like an archangel.

Our eyes meet, and I can't help but drink him in. As my gaze travels down his body, I memorize every rigid curve. Tree tattoos adorn his arms and chest, and I can't help wishing to trace them with the tip of my finger—or perhaps my tongue.

This man is stunning, an utter temptation. The fact that he's a father makes him even more alluring.

"You came," he says, almost as if he doubted I would.

"Not yet," I reply with a hint of sass.

He keeps a straight face.

"Okay, tough crowd. Anyone else would have enjoyed that joke."

"Hm. I'm not just *anybody*," he says.

He's absolutely right about that.

Hudson steps aside, allowing me to enter.

As I pause in the living room, I notice the fire roaring in the fireplace. The wood isn't fully charred, which means he just started it. On the coffee table lies a face-down book—the same one Jake was reading. It's cute that they're buddy-reading.

An oversized fluffy rug covers the floor, and I imagine how

it feels beneath my bare feet. The L-shaped couch faces the fireplace.

His home feels cozy, and I can sense the love within these walls. Colby is a lucky kid.

My eyes wander to the kitchen, and then I take in the hand-carved staircase leading to the second story.

"This is a big house for the two of you," I comment.

Hudson moves to the counter, ignoring my remark. Muscles ripple down his back, and his joggers hang low on his hips. That cocky Jolly attitude is on full display. It's my kryptonite that I both love and hate.

"Whiskey?" he asks.

"Sure." I want to relax, but my temperature rises each time I look at him.

"You need a shooter?" Hudson glances at me, and I swallow hard. Can he sense the heat beneath the surface?

"No, I can handle it straight." I move closer to him, running my fingers through my hair. Does he notice the effect he has on me? He has to.

Hudson pours double shots for both of us and pushes one across the counter toward me. Our fingers brush, and I swear the spot where he touches me feels like it's on fire.

"Thanks," I whisper, wishing I knew what he was thinking. A million unspoken words pass between us when our eyes meet. I down the whiskey, welcoming the burn as it slides down my throat.

"Well?" he finally asks.

"It tastes great," I say, setting the empty glass down.

He shakes his head in disbelief.

"What did you want to discuss?" Hudson cuts straight to the point, skipping any warm-up.

"I think we should start over," I say, sliding my glass back toward him.

He shakes his head. "You're not the first woman who's tried to fix me."

I smile. "But I'll be the last."

He narrows his eyes at me. "Are you always like this?"

"Yes. But for some reason, you're playing the part that I'm usually cast in relationships. It kind of sucks for you because I know the script already. *I'm a broken toy. Stay away from me. It's me and not you.*" I roll my eyes. "I'm not convinced you want me to stay away, given your contradictory actions."

He lifts the bottle and pours shots into our glasses. Hudson doesn't respond to what I've said, but he absorbs every word.

He remains silent, and I don't urge him to speak.

"I push people away because it's easier," he finally admits.

A tender expression meets my face. He didn't have to tell me that; I've witnessed it myself.

"You can try, but my sister is madly in love with your brother, and they're getting married. Eventually, they want to have kids. We're locked in as long as they are," I say, blinking up at him.

Hudson shakes his head. "Don't make this difficult."

I scoff. "Do you need a mirror to repeat that?"

This finally earns me a smile. I take a moment to gather my thoughts because the whiskey has made my brain foggy.

"You didn't have to deactivate your account," he mutters. I'm sure Lucas told him; he mentioned he would.

"I did it to protect you."

His expression twists in response.

"You're Mr. November," I say. "I don't have a choice in that. So, I disappeared with you, Hudson. I'm not afraid to risk it all."

I glance at the whiskey bottle, noticing its label—Devil's Tongue, one-hundred proof. Typical.

Hudson's gaze fixes on me, and I can tell something is on his mind.

"Just ask," I prompt. "You want to ask me something."

There are a million things he could ask, none of them I can predict.

"Tell me what happened with your ex," he says.

Every thought in my head is thrown off course.

"Why do you care?"

My heart pounds in my chest.

"You haven't really moved on since the breakup. Why?"

I take a deep breath. "Have you been keeping up with me?"

This revelation sends my mind spinning.

This time, he forgoes pouring the whiskey and drinks straight from the bottle. He slides it to me when he's finished.

"I'll share my deep, dark secrets if you share yours," I whisper. "Do you trust me?"

"No," he replies without hesitation. "Not yet."

His words give me hope that maybe one day he will. I drink more whiskey, watching the pulse at his neck throb rapidly.

Hudson moves to the couch where I imagine he was before I arrived. I grab the bottle and sit next to him, leaving enough space so we don't touch. I sink into the cushions and lay my head back, staring at the high vaulted ceilings.

He watches me. It's often the quiet ones who are the most observant. I can see the gears in his head turning as if he's deciding whether to trust me. If given a chance, I'd ensure he didn't regret it.

Hudson shifts his attention to the fire, and I glance at him.

"This is dangerous," he mutters, and his eyes almost darken.

"We meet in the middle."

"And you'll keep my secrets?" Hudson asks.

"Until the day I die. But you have to keep mine, too." I mean every word. My heart flutters for him, and I try to ignore it. "I usually have NDAs ready for occasions like this."

"That's protocol, then?"

"Everyone in my inner circle has signed one. It's for my

protection because people try to get close to me for personal gain."

His brows furrow. "I would never do that. You have my word. The time we've spent together won't be shared with anyone. It stays between us," Hudson promises.

I chew on my bottom lip. The only way out is through.

We both drink, and his original question resurfaces in my mind. "Why do you want to know about my ex?"

"Patterns tend to repeat themselves."

I look back on that relationship, wishing I had recognized the signs before I got in too deep.

"Maddox loved the idea of me and what I could do for his reputation, but he didn't truly love me. Sometimes, I felt like a checkmark on a to-do list or an afterthought. I was tired of being put last."

As I stare at the flames, I realize this is the first time I've voiced those feelings out loud. My best friends and sister know a summarized version but not the raw truth.

"In our final year together, he forgot my birthday. We were supposed to meet in Paris, but I spent the whole week alone. When I came back to New York, I ended it."

"Fuck. Him," Hudson growls, clenching his jaw.

"I'll drink to that." I bring the bottle to my lips. "A month later, he replaced me. We were together for years, and he moved on as if I meant nothing. And she's so pretty—blonde, tall—nothing like me. I'm convinced I wasn't even his type. It sucks, considering how much of myself I gave to him."

"I'm so fucking sorry," he says, his jaw tightly clenched.

"I am, too. But I ignored the red flags." I offer him a small smile. "I've healed, though. Now I know what I want and don't want in my next relationship."

We sit in comfortable silence as more whiskey disappears from the bottle, the wood crackling in the fire.

Hudson inhales deeply. "After my wife gave birth and came home from the hospital, she told me she'd made a mistake. She didn't want to be a mom or build a life with me anymore. Colby was just a week old when she left, eighteen days before our son's first Christmas. I tried to convince her we could figure it out together—go to therapy, rebuild our relationship. I told her I loved her and would do anything to keep our family together. I wanted to help her. But she calmly explained it wasn't postpartum or depression; she felt like she had been cosplaying a life with me. She wasn't in love with me anymore. She thought having a baby would change her mind. I realized I had been living a fucking lie." His voice trails off, and I watch as he mentally puts a wall between us.

"Hudson. I'm..." I swallow hard, wishing there was something I could do, realizing his trauma in his last relationship stems from being left. My heart breaks. "I'm so sorry."

"Yeah. So when I say you should stay away from me, I mean it. I've learned, and it's been reiterated several times, that I don't need anyone." He speaks bluntly without sugarcoating it.

"I wish I could help heal that pain," I reply, understanding that he's trying to push me away again. It's a protective mechanism, one I completely understand now. "Where is she now?"

He shrugs. "I don't know. She moves around a lot."

I hand him the bottle, and this time, he pulls so hard that bubbles trickle from the bottom.

"Are you still in love with her?" I don't know if I want the answer

"No." He meets my gaze. "And I'll never forgive her for what she did."

Hudson stands to add more wood to the fire. The tattoos on his biceps depict conifers, the very types that grow on the farm. He glances my way and my heart races. This time, when he returns, Hudson sits closer to me.

I crisscross my legs, turning toward him for a better look at the ink on his arms and shoulders. He smells like a fresh winter day in the mountains.

Hudson's jaw tightens. "Would you take him back?"

"I don't do second chances," I reply, avoiding his gaze. "It's one of my rules."

He raises an eyebrow, unimpressed. "Really? And I suppose there are other rules, too?"

"I won't lead anyone on if I know it won't work between us. I don't do flings."

This makes him scoff.

"There also needs to be a possibility of a future. And the final rule: every man I'm interested in is told the rules." I squeeze my eyes shut.

"Anything else I need to know, considering we're starting over?"

"Nope, that's pretty much it," I say, focusing on the fire. It flickers, casting our shadows on the wall, and I realize how tired I am. Part of me wants to stay up with him all night, asking every question I can now that the door is wide open. But my eyes grow heavy.

"One more question, then I'm going to head home," I say, thinking back to the first time we met in July. "And make it good."

Hudson takes a deep breath. "Did you want to kiss me on the porch?"

I nod, looking up into his captivating eyes and feeling the warmth of his breath against my cheek. Butterflies erupt in full force as the air around us thickens.

"Did you want to kiss me?" I ask, desperately hoping he feels the same way.

"Fuck yes. And now?" His gravelly tone sends goosebumps racing up my arms. He wears the same expression now as he did days ago.

"Please," I breathlessly beg.

This time, he doesn't hesitate.

His palm rests on my face, and his whiskey-scented lips slide gently against mine. We're a tangle of tongues and lips, enveloped in desperate passion. I feel like I'm falling into oblivion as his fingers move roughly through my hair. Nothing else matters in this moment— just us, just his mouth on mine.

A desperate moan escapes as our tongues intertwine. Hudson lays me back onto the couch, and I wrap my legs around his waist. I want and need more of him. His hard, thick cock presses between my thighs.

The mere pressure of him against me makes my eyes nearly roll back in my head. It's been too long since I've been with a man. He nibbles on my lip, and then his mouth trails around the shell of my ear. I gasp. The fire he ignited inside me threatens to consume me.

"I won't make you break your rules," he whispers in my ear, his teeth grazing my skin, his fingers tangled in my hair. My rules don't stand a chance with him. "But I could."

He briefly nuzzles into my neck, inhaling my hair before pulling away.

Dread follows my elation as we break apart, my vision blurring before the world comes back into focus.

Hudson has swollen lips and a noticeable bulge in his joggers. My hair is messy, and I quickly push it down as I sit up straight.

"I should go," I say finally, fully aware that I need to leave.

"Let me walk you home," he offers.

"No, it's okay. You should be here if Colby wakes up."

"Emma," he says my name like a prayer.

The alcohol swims in my system, and I feel intoxicated by him, but I know I need fresh air to clear my head.

As I walk away, he grabs my hand and pulls me back. He tucks loose strands of my wavy, damp hair behind my ear.

"We can't do this again," he states.

I force a smile.

"I can't get attached to you," he admits, desperation seeping into his voice.

"We both know it's too late for that," I reply, knowing I'm just as guilty.

Hudson inhales deeply.

"Hope to see you tomorrow," I say.

"Maybe," he echoes.

As I turn to leave, he calls out, "Emma."

"Yeah?"

He walks with me to the door. "You should spend the holidays with people who care about you."

I want to remember the softness in his expression and the kindness in his voice as my heart flutters involuntarily.

"Ask me to stay, and I will," I say.

Time stretches, and I wait for him to say something, but he remains silent. I understand why; every woman in his life has left. I close the door behind me, adrenaline coursing through my veins. I'm grateful for the chance to be alone to think and to replay every moment we've shared.

I gaze up at the night sky, the stars twinkling above. Excitement surges within me. This is just the beginning.

As I step off the porch, I realize that the magic of Merryville found me when Hudson Jolly kissed me.

CHAPTER 14

HUDSON

"Daddy!" Colby whispers loudly from the end of the bed. I jolt awake, my heart racing. Since becoming a dad, I've slept lightly—the sound of a pin drop could wake me.

"Hey, Bee," I grumble, half-panicked. "Are you good? Hurt? Sick?"

"No. I'm so hungry!" he whines, climbing onto the bed and plopping down on my chest, wrapping his arms around me. "Starving!"

I glance at the clock on the nightstand—it's just past five in the morning. Sometimes he wakes up earlier than usual when he goes to bed early. For once, I wish he wouldn't have. That extra thirty minutes of sleep would've been invaluable.

My head pounds from the fifth of whiskey I stupidly drank with Emma last night, but I don't regret it. I wanted her so badly that I'm still aching for her today. I swear she stole my soul because I haven't felt the same since I learned she was back in Merryville.

"My stomach is mad! It's growling!"

"Okay, okay. Eggs and bacon?" I ask, flicking on the lamp beside the bed.

"Green eggs and ham!"

"Alright, if that's what you want."

Since we started reading Dr. Seuss, he's requested it several times. He only enjoys eggs when they resemble slime. I know it sounds disgusting, and it took some getting used to, but now I think I could eat them in any color.

Colby hops down and runs out of the bedroom. The sound of his feet pattering across the hardwood floor in the hallway makes me smile.

"Foooooooood!" he yells as he bounces downstairs. The creaks in the stairs will come in handy when he's a teenager sneaking out.

This kid has an endless supply of energy in the mornings, and sometimes I wish I could borrow just a sliver of it—far better than coffee.

With my feet on the floor, I rub my face, already exhausted before the day starts. Drinking last night was foolish, but I appreciated the liquid courage it provided. It sparked a candid conversation with Emma, one I wouldn't have had sober.

When I go downstairs, I find Colby standing in front of the fridge, peering in. He's on his tiptoes, carefully removing the carton of eggs.

"You're cooking with me today?" I say, placing my hand in his messy hair.

He nods enthusiastically, and I fetch a stool from the pantry for him to stand on. One day, he'll be taller than me, and I'll cherish these moments. Mama always said kids grow up fast, and I should've believed her.

As I brew coffee, I grab the food dye he loves while he gets himself into position. "How many eggs would you like?"

"Two for me."

"Two for me, too," he echoes.

"So how many is that total?" I ask.

"Four." Colby carefully cracks the eggs into a bowl. I scan for shells before adding a couple of drops of green coloring.

He won't finish two eggs, but I usually take care of what's left on his plate.

"Great job whisking," I tell him.

He grips one side of the bowl tightly and stirs with the other hand.

"Rawr," he exclaims, putting more muscle into the task.

Some mornings, Colby loves helping with breakfast, while other times he prefers watching cartoons on his tablet. Regardless, our routine is to spend time together before I take him to school.

"Strawberries or pineapples?" I ask as I pour myself a cup of coffee and a glass of milk for Colby.

"Pineapples!" he exclaims, waving the whisk in the air. Unfortunately, some eggs drip onto the floor and counter, prompting me to quickly wipe it up.

Once we have pineapples on our plates and the ham sizzling in the skillet, we turn our attention to the eggs. "Remember to keep stirring once it's in the pan, okay? Make sure the handle is pointed outward and be careful because it's hot."

"Yes, sir," he replies with an exaggerated nod.

When I was his age, my grandma let me help in the kitchen. Some of my favorite childhood memories are baking with her during the holidays. I cherish those moments and love sharing what she taught me with Colby.

"Ready?" I ask.

"Mmhmm!" he replies eagerly.

I pour the mixture into the skillet, and Colby stirs, ensuring it doesn't stick. Over the past year, he's learned to scramble eggs to perfection; I think he could give Gordon Ramsay a run for his money.

"Good job, Bee. Those are going to be fluffy."

"Like fluffy clouds," he says, grinning widely.

When the eggs are done, I place the food onto our plates.

Colby climbs onto a bar stool, and I slide his meal in front of him. He picks up his fork and takes a bite.

"Yummy! These are the best in the world."

"You did great," I tell him. "Best egg chef I've ever met."

"Mmhm," he agrees. "I get to go to school today?"

"Yes, and I have a present for Davidson."

"Ooh! He's going to be happy. Can I get a puppy for my birthday?"

"Hm. I'm not so sure about that," I reply, taking a bite of the bright green eggs.

He pops a chunk of pineapple in his mouth and smacks his lips.

"Manners," I remind him, and he immediately stops. "So, when school ends today, Mimi will pick you up."

"Today?" he asks, surprised.

"Where's Donna?" he continues.

I explain what happened yesterday.

"Donna moved away, Bee."

"Like my mama?"

That question pierces my heart, leaving me momentarily speechless. It's not something I can easily answer.

"Donna had to help care for some babies, and since you're a big boy now, I thought you'd be okay with it." He has a big heart, especially for kids smaller than him.

"Oh, right! I'm going to be five, and then Santa will come and bring me lots and lots of presents," he says, grabbing the glass of milk I made for him.

He grins and raises his eyebrows playfully before taking a sip.

Colby loves Christmas, and I've gone out of my way to make it extra special. My parents do too, since he's their only grandchild. Hopefully, Claire and Jake will change that soon.

On Christmas Day, my parents always prepare a big dinner, and we watch football, play games, and indulge in too much pie. Spiked eggnog is typically involved as well.

"Presents stacked to the ceiling!" he exclaims, lifting his arm high. "Up there. And there. And there. Is Mr. Stinky going to deliver me a birthday card this year?"

Oh no. I almost forgot about that silly little elf. Colby named him after finding him squatting with a pile of chocolate-covered raisins. I thought it was funny, but now I'm stuck with Mr. Stinky for several more years.

"You never know what Mr. Stinky is up to. But after Mimi picks you up from school, you'll be hanging out with her until I get off work."

"Can I go with Emma and Claire?" His face lights up at the thought.

"Claire has to work today," I reply, leaving out Emma's name. "Also, Mimi has some fun activities planned. You'll see Claire again, I promise." I give him a confident nod, and it seems to satisfy him for now.

"Okay. Aunt CeCe is taking me for ice cream, too." Colby stabs his eggs with his fork. "Strawberry is my favorite, but you have to put water on them first, then use a knife to take the grass off the top."

I chuckle. "Thank you for mansplaining how to wash strawberries."

"And slice them like this. Psh Psh Psh," he says, tapping his fork on the plate.

His mind is racing this morning; he must have slept incredibly well. I'm almost jealous. I tossed and turned for hours with thoughts of Emma before finally drifting off. I can't escape her in my dreams either.

After a bite of ham, he sets his fork down. "I'm done, Daddy! Stuffed like French toast."

"Kid, where are you getting these jokes?"

"At school. Davidson has an older sister who tells us things. She's about to be seven and has pretty hair, too."

"And what's her name?"

"Evie," he replies, and I swear I see his eyes sparkle like

they're filled with heart emojis.

"Don't you think Evie is a little old for you?"

His face twists, clearly offended. "No. Evie is smart. She knows things—big kid things. Her favorite color is pink, and she has a bike with sparkly streamers."

"Oh wow. Maybe I can meet Evie's parents to see who I'll need to share my grandkids with."

"Evie is seven years old, Dad. She's going to drive soon," he says matter-of-factly.

"Okay, enough about Evie." I stack our plates and quickly clean the kitchen while he watches. "Go get dressed. Brush your teeth. Wash your face."

"Can I watch my tablet?"

"Do what I asked first, and then you can for a little while before school." I glance at the clock over my shoulder as he darts up the stairs. "Clothes. Teeth. Face."

He mockingly repeats my instructions in a deep voice. He can repeat them as much as he likes if it helps him remember.

I hear the faucet turn on, and I move toward the edge of the stairs.

"Brush your teeth and wash your face!" I remind him, knowing he didn't bathe last night because he fell asleep too early. He's not filthy, and I won't fight him to get into the tub in the morning; that always ruins both our days.

As I pass his room, I see him in bed, dressed and watching his tablet.

"We leave in thirty minutes, okay?"

"Yes, sir."

Once I'm dressed, I find Colby asleep in his bed. His iPad is blaring with sound effects, and I'm amazed he can sleep through it all.

"Come on, Bee. School time," I gently say, stopping the show. "Did you brush your teeth?"

"Yes," he responds, kicking out his foot.

"Shoes. Up. Let's go," I urge, hoping he comes to life once

he's fully awake. His sleep schedule is a bit off, so I'll have to work extra hard to reset it throughout the week. Moments later, he follows me downstairs. I grab his lunch kit from the counter and hand it to him.

He picks up the pace and starts humming a song about frogs, probably something from the cartoon he watches. I glance at him and smile. "I'm proud of you."

Colby laughs as we head to the truck. "Little frogs. And big frogs. Some are as big as hogs. Ribbet."

"That would be huge," I say, holding out my arms to illustrate the size.

His eyes widen. "Daaaamn."

"Don't say that," I respond, trying to stifle a smile because I'm proud he used it in the perfect context. "That's a bad word. I know I say it too. I shouldn't. If I do, tell me not to."

"Okay, Daddy."

As we near the truck, he reaches for the door. I buckle him into his booster seat, and then we're off.

Christmas music plays on the radio, a staple year-round in Merryville, but now the temperatures are finally cooperating. Magic is in the air.

It takes us forty-five minutes to get to the elementary school. I had forgotten that this week would be busy with tourists arriving, and the traffic is a nightmare.

When I pull in, I find a spot near the main office.

Every day, I make it a point to walk Colby to his classroom —no matter what. I'll cherish these moments while I can.

Ms. Barker, his teacher, greets him with a smile as he hangs up his backpack. I bend down, hug Colby, and hand him the gift for his friend. "Give this to Davidson, okay?"

"Thank you, Daddy."

"Love you, Bee. Have a good day."

As I walk down the elementary school hallway—the same one I attended as a kid—the classrooms feel smaller, yet they still smell the same as they did all those years ago.

Before returning to the farm, I stop by Main Street Coffee where my cousin works. As I walk in, she greets me with a shit-eating grin.

"There's Mr. November now."

I scowl at her. "Excuse me?"

"Hudson," she snaps back. "You don't need to get your Grinch panties in a twist, okay? I'm just teasing you. What do you want to drink?"

"Two hot cocoas."

Her brow raises. "Two? Oh, it's already like that?"

"Large with whipped cream and a side of shut the fuck up, please."

She snickers, clearly enjoying getting under my skin. "That'll be $13.98."

"For two hot chocolates? Geez." I roll my eyes playfully at her and swipe my card, even adding a five dollar tip.

A few minutes later, a different barista approaches the counter, holding my drinks. "Two hot chocolates for Mr. November?"

I glare at my cousin as I take them.

"Have a great day, Bella," I say, deliberately avoiding her nickname.

"I'll have the last laugh, I promise!" she replies confidently.

Once back at the farm, I hop into my golf cart with the cocoas and drive to Jake's. It's barely past seven-thirty when I tap on the window of Emma's room.

Moments later, she pulls back the curtain, standing there in a T-shirt and panties. Her auburn hair is a wavy mess, and I catch myself wishing I could thread my fingers through it.

She narrows her eyes at me, as if she can read my thoughts, thoughts I shouldn't be having.

"Open the window," I say, keeping my voice low.

She struggles a bit but finally slides it upward.

"What are you doing here?" she asks groggily.

"Hung over?" I reply.

"A little," she whispers back.

"I brought you a hot cocoa. Thought you'd enjoy it."

She smiles. "Is this an olive branch?"

"A fresh start," I say.

Emma lifts the cup to her mouth, and I notice something written in neat, cursive handwriting on the bottom. It's Bella's.

HUDSON JOLLY WANTS TO FUCK YOU!

My mouth falls slightly open, and Emma notices.

"What? Is my tit out?" she asks.

"No, no, your tit is—" I clear my throat, realizing Bella is going to pay for this.

"My mother will have Colby today and tomorrow, so I thought if you're bored, you could meet me at the pavilion at noon."

A pretty smile spreads across her kissable lips.

"I'll be there. Thanks for the hot cocoa." She glances at the name on the cup. "Mr. November."

Before I can explain, there's a knock on the other side of the door. I hear Claire's voice, though I can't make out what she says.

"Have a great day," I whisper. "See you soon."

"Bye," she replies, closing the window and shutting the curtain. I hop back onto the golf cart and drive away, unable to stop a cheesy grin from spreading across my face.

As I reach the end of the street, I lift my cup to check the message on the bottom.

HUDSON JOLLY WANTS TO EAT YOUR ASS!

HUDSON

> You're gonna wish you hadn't written those crude things on the bottom of the cups.

148

BELLA

Oh, did she see it?

HUDSON

I delivered them to Pastor John this morning for Mawmaw as a favor.

My cousin sends a wide-eyed emoji, fully aware that she'd be in trouble if this got around town.

BELLA

Please don't get me fired!

HUDSON

I guess we'll wait and see what happens.

It's a lie, but I'll let her stew in embarrassment until I can properly return the favor. Meanwhile, I hope Emma doesn't see it because that could get awkward.

CHAPTER 15

EMMA

"Emma?" Claire's voice calls from the hallway. "Are you awake?"

I walk across the room and crack open the door.

She leans in, eyes wide with curiosity. "Did Hudson just deliver a cup of coffee to your window, or did I imagine seeing him stalk across the yard?"

A wide smile spreads across my face as I hold up the red cup with a white lid. "It's hot cocoa."

Her mouth drops open in disbelief. "I don't know how you do it. I'm honestly convinced you're a man whisperer."

"If that were true, I wouldn't be single," I mutter, sipping the cocoa with a smirk. I would have any man I want.

Claire reaches for my cup.

"Hey!"

She lifts it high, and I notice something written on the bottom.

HUDSON JOLLY WANTS TO FUCK YOU!

The handwriting is surprisingly neat.

I burst into laughter, and Claire quickly joins in.

"So, he's your Mr. November?" Her eyes sparkle with mischief.

"You're not playing into this, too. You know the internet decides, not me."

"Maybe this time they got it right?" she shrugs.

"Who knows? Oh, can you please sign my cookie contest form? I need permission from a resident."

She tilts her head, surprised. "You're serious?"

"A citizen of Merryville has to approve my entry, but they forfeit their right to compete. It's a new rule this year."

"It's that serious?" she asks, signing at the bottom. "Just remember me when you're the Christmas cookie queen, okay?"

I snicker. "I will. Oh, and speaking of rules, Hudson knows mine."

...and he kissed me last night.

I keep that last part to myself, tucked away with the butterflies that flutter each time I think of him. I'm so afraid of falling for this grumpy man.

I set a sweater and a pair of jeans on the bed, then rummage through my suitcase for my boots. I didn't travel light because I wasn't sure how long I'd stay. "You only give those to men you're interested in."

"It's not like that," I explain, knowing I can never share the details of our conversation.

A teasing smile stretches across her face. "You're lying."

"I wish he'd give me the time of day," I confess.

"Then let him. Fuck around and find out."

"What have you done with my sister?" I ask, raising an eyebrow, recalling how strict she used to be during her CEO days.

"Jake and I started as a fling. Highly recommend it. It was hot and passionate, and knowing there was an end date to our situation only made it more intense."

I'm surprised. "What? I had no idea."

"It was the catalyst, a part of our origin story." She smiles sweetly as if reliving the memories.

I take a moment to get dressed, sliding on my tight jeans and appreciating how they fit. There are perks to having best friends who are fashion designers. After I wiggle into my sweater, I turn to her.

"So, what rules did you give Jake?" I wonder if they're similar to my own.

"I didn't."

My eyes widen in shock. Claire, who has always been anti-love, was determined to protect herself after discovering she was the other woman. "Jake put rules into place? I didn't realize he had it in him," I mutter. He's too *nice*.

"When he's in a mood, he quickly turns into Hudson."

My curiosity piques. "Oh my God, tell me these rules. I'm invested."

"There were only two: no strings attached and no falling in love," she says, shaking her head playfully. "I agreed to it like I could control my emotions."

Laughter escapes me. "Yeah, that's hilarious, considering how obsessed you two are with each other."

"I came to Merryville to show Dad how ruthless I could be. Most men are good for only one thing, so I was happy to have a fling with a hottie for the holidays. After that, the rules didn't matter."

I wrap my sister in a tight hug.

"What's this for?" she asks.

"I've missed you so much," I admit.

"One reason why you shouldn't leave until after New Year's." She squeezes me and laughs, and I meet her gaze. The older she gets, the more she resembles our mom. "Who were you with last night? Is it safe to assume it was Hudson, considering he delivered hot cocoa to your room?"

"How do you know I was with someone last night?" I

wonder if Jake spilled the beans. If he did, I won't trust him again.

She shrugs. "The hickeys on your neck."

My smile fades immediately. I move to a full-length mirror in the corner of the room and tilt my head to the side. Dark spots pepper my skin, and memories of Hudson's mouth and teeth flash in my mind. He smelled so good like he had just stepped out of the shower.

I swallow hard as I meet Claire's eyes in the mirror.

She smirks. "Must've been a good night."

"He's a bastard," I whisper. He knew exactly what he was doing—claiming me as his.

"Do you think he'll be your Mr. December, too?"

I bite my lip. At the rate my heart is racing, he might be my Mr. Forever.

Claire moves to the door. "Be careful, Em. The Jolly boys are addictive. One minute they're leaving hickeys on your neck, and the next they're sliding diamonds on your finger." She wiggles her ring, which shines brightly in the overhead light.

"I'm already screwed!" I cry playfully as she leaves. I return to the mirror and grab my makeup bag, knowing I can't go out in public like this—though I can't stop smiling. He wants people to know I'm taken. Here I am, already marked by a beautiful, mischievous man.

The fantasy of him pressed between my thighs is quickly ripped away when I remember his words: *this can never happen again.*

I take a picture of my battle wounds and text it to him.

EMMA

Please explain.

A moment later, he hearts the image. I expect a follow-up message, but none comes. I wish I could see his reaction.

I apply concealer and blend it with a brush. Once the bruises are mostly covered, I dust on some powder. Now, it's like it never happened—well, until I shower.

After Claire leaves for work, I jot down the ingredients I need for the cookies I'm baking this weekend. I have two recipes in mind: a chewy oatmeal raisin and a raspberry almond shortbread. While I'm most excited about the latter, I need to research previous winners.

I'm determined to become the Christmas cookie queen.

Tinsel prances toward me as I leave my room with my grocery list. Her bell jingles as she dances beside my feet. I bend down to pet her, and instead of running away, she nudges her head into my hand.

"Aww, did we become instant friends?" I ask, squatting to scratch her chin. She purrs and rubs against my fingers.

"Did you drool?" I giggle. "Claire told me you hated people. That's a lie, isn't it?"

Then she bites me.

"Ouch! Okay, maybe it's not."

I pull my hand away, but she begs for more pets. "You're a Jolly. You give too many mixed signals."

I scratch under her chin a little more, and I pull away before she bites me again.

On the drive to town, I try to recall the name of the guy who helped me. Was it Ethan? Brandon? Brent. Yes, it was Brent.

Once on Main Street, I notice more people stroll the sidewalks than had a few days ago. Heads turn as I drive by, making me self-conscious. I slide into an open parking spot in front of the building.

A guy stops me on the sidewalk.

"I don't think I've ever seen an M5 in person," he says.

My brows lift, and I nervously laugh. "Excuse me?"

He smiles. "Your car. Expensive."

"Oh, it's a rental. I didn't pick it." I glance at the car, realizing how extravagant it is. "Anyway, have a good day."

"You too," he replies, and I decide it's time to trade that vehicle in for something else. I don't want attention. Not here.

I enter city hall and spot a familiar face. "Hey, Brent. How have you been?"

Today, he's wearing a bright red polo with a Santa beard and hat logo. "Hey Emma, great. Did you get your form signed?"

I smile, realizing I'm already on a first-name basis with someone who remembers me. It makes me happy.

"Ah yes, the paperwork." I slide it across the desk to him, and he checks everything. "So, is there a place where all the past winners are listed?"

He chuckles. "You sure you're not a master cookie maker? That's what they usually want to see, too."

I tilt my head at him. "Look me up on the internet. You'll learn plenty about me, but baking cookies isn't one of my hobbies." It's a secret; only those close to me know. I never flaunted my sadness; I quietly baked my way through it.

"The application looks good." He tears it off the back and hands me the rules packet. "Don't forget to turn in a batch of cookies on the first Saturday in December."

"Okay. Got it. The Hall of Fame?"

"Right, if you walk down that hallway and take a right, you'll find a glass case. You can't miss it."

"Thanks."

"Good luck."

"You said I'd need it," I remind him.

"Oh, you will, especially when the purple hairs find out you've entered."

"They're going down," I say with a laugh. "You'll see."

As I move down the hallway, I'm struck by how this part of the building resembles a museum. The guided tour begins with the history of Merryville. My eyes scan the billboards until I find one detailing the town's story.

Merryville was founded by three families whose names are synonymous with the holiday spirit: the Merrys, the Jollys, and the Mistletoes. This unique community quickly emerged as a sanctuary for individuals with Christmas-themed surnames. Six months after its inception, two additional families, the Gingerbreads and the Sleighs, joined the growing settlement. Within the first decade, Merryville experienced a steady influx of new residents, most of whom shared a common heritage linked to the holiday—a phenomenon locals attribute to the enduring "Christmas spirit." This distinctive characteristic makes Merryville unmatched, with only a handful of imitators managing to survive.

The legacy of Merryville, rooted in its founding families and their festive vision, continues to thrive, captivating visitors and residents alike with its enchanting holiday magic. The magic of Merryville is much more than an old wives' tale; it lives in the hearts of its townsfolk.

I continue around the room until I spot what I've been searching for—the Christmas Cookie Hall of Fame. Each winner has a professional photo taken of them receiving their trophy, with their names etched in golden letters alongside the year won and the type of cookie.

"Mostly gingerbread," I whisper, scanning down the names until I stop at Betty Jolly, who won consecutively for nearly two decades.

I text my sister.

EMMA

Who's Betty?

CLAIRE
Jake's grandmother.

EMMA
I want to meet her.

CLAIRE
What a coincidence! She wants to meet you too!

EMMA
Oh, can you set something up?

CLAIRE
I'd love to.

I can't help but smile mischievously; this woman must know the secret to winning that contest. There has to be an advantage. Excitement courses through me, and I can't wait to meet her.

As I leave the building, I notice a corkboard covered with various papers tacked to it. A bright green garage sale sign catches my eye. Next to it are a couple of photos of lost pets and a few help-wanted advertisements—one for Main Street Coffee and another for the grocery store. Then, I spot a hastily pinned notice at the bottom.

Temporary Nanny Needed
(Just for the holidays!)
Must be local and have a valid driver's license.
Job ends on December 31st.
In-person interviews will be held this Saturday.
Call to schedule an in-person interview.

At the bottom, numbered tabs flap in the breeze. Many have already been taken. I confirm the number in my contacts. It's him.

I frown, genuinely disappointed that I won't be helping out with Colby. He loves LEGOs, just like I do. The kid overloads me with his cuteness, especially when he talks a mile a minute. With Claire and Jake at work, I'll be lonely.

Now that I've deactivated my social media accounts, I have nothing to fill my time except for baking and my thoughts of Hudson.

Lucky me!

Hudson meets me by the pavilion at noon, looking deliciously attractive. He's wearing dark-washed jeans tucked into boots, with his hands resting in his jacket pockets. The Jolly Christmas Tree Farm baseball hat obscures his face, but I can feel his gaze on me. As I approach, a hint of a smirk flits across his lips.

"Hi," he says, his eyes taking me in.

"Hi." I admire the scruff along his chiseled jaw.

"I almost thought you wouldn't show."

His gaze drifts to my neck, and I smirk. "I'm a pro at keeping secrets."

He chuckles, unable to suppress his amusement.

Ah, I broke through already. Always a good sign when he's laughing. "So, what are we doing today?"

"I'm on stable duty," he replies.

"There are horses here?"

"Of course," he says, glancing at his watch. "And we should hurry. We don't have much time."

Hudson unlatches the radio at his hip and speaks into it. "It's Hudson. Goin' to the barn."

"Heard," Jake calls back.

I follow him across the pasture to the four-wheeler. He hops on and then looks back at me. "Coming?"

"Yes," I reply, eager for the adventure. I swing my leg over the back and scoot closer to him.

"Hold on to me," he instructs.

Carefully, I wrap my arms around his body and hold on tight. He lifts my thighs effortlessly, pulling me closer. My breasts press against his back.

"That's better," he says, releasing me. I can't help but smile, relieved he can't see the giddiness on my face.

I squeal, tightening my grip as we take off. He smells like leather and earth, and I inhale deeply, wishing I could bottle it.

"Wow," I exclaim as the breeze tousles my hair.

He laughs as we continue down a trail wide enough for a truck. I bask in the warmth of his body while my heart races.

Conifers line both sides of the trail, stretching as far as I can see. I imagine what it would have been like to grow up here, playing freely on this property. I would have loved it, but instead, I was shuttled in and out of boarding schools. Often, I wonder how different my life would have been if I had experienced a normal childhood without all the glitz and glamor.

When we reach the big red barn, Hudson shuts off the engine. I reluctantly release my grip on him as he climbs off.

"I envy you," I say as he helps me to my feet, feeling steady on the ground. "I don't know if you realize how lucky you are."

He grins. "I do know, and these days, I don't take any of it for granted. After becoming a dad, I truly understood how wonderful life is on the farm. It's why I never want to leave. This is home."

I study him, appreciating that he trusts me enough to share something personal. Hudson could keep it simple with short sentences and straightforward answers, but he's making an effort.

"Well, the farm feels like home. I can almost imagine living here."

He's filled with gratitude. The fact that he can express that after everything he's been through shows he's not a Grinch. Hudson's just trying to protect his heart from being shattered; I can't fault him for that, but I won't be the next woman to hurt him.

"Would you move here?" he asks, leading me into the barn.

I glance at him as we walk down the center aisle. "When my sister has kids, I want to be involved."

"That was a non-answer," he replies. "It's a simple question."

"Is it?" I ask, looking around the barn. Ten stalls line each side, and hay bales are stored in the loft. I peek into the tack room and see a handful of saddles.

"Another non-answer."

I turn to face him. "There are a lot of hypotheticals that come with that. Is the love of my life here? If so, yes. Without question. If not, I don't know. I won't settle down until I find the person I'm supposed to be with. My original answer was easier."

Hudson steps closer, and my back presses against the doorframe. My heart races as I feel the heat rising within me. "This is why we shouldn't be alone."

"Why?"

He leans in slowly, my jaw tilting upward. "Because I want to kiss you."

"Why do you resist it so much? Am I not your type?"

His mouth hovers over mine, and my eyes flutter closed. "You're everything I want."

I gasp, warm breath escaping in quick bursts. I feel weak in the knees, his closeness makes me dizzy. "I'll take the risk if you do," I whisper.

"Fuck, Emma," he says, and our mouths collide. This time, we're dangerously falling, tumbling through space together as his fingers weave through my hair.

I reach for his belt, and he reaches for my jeans, easily unbuttoning and unzipping them. I grab his hand and shove it inside my soaked panties as he continues to kiss me. As soon as his finger brushes against my clit, I groan. "No one...no one has touched me since—"

"Shh," he whispers, sucking on my bottom lip. "Right now, you're mine. And only mine."

"Fuck." I cling to his neck for support, and even though he's barely touched me, I'm ready to come.

"Hudson," I pant, wanting the orgasm to consume me as he slides a finger inside me while still teasing my clit. "Yes, yes. That feels so good," I huff, every muscle tensing as I climb toward ecstasy.

"Hudson!" a deep voice suddenly yells.

"No," I hiss, my eyes going wide as I hurriedly pull up my panties and zip my pants.

"Fuck. I'm sorry." Hudson meets my gaze and kisses me fiercely before walking away, adjusting himself. I lean against the wall, breathless and squeezing my thighs together.

I was so close; my heart feels like it might explode. I shut my eyes, realizing my rules have completely unraveled. My sister is right...it's time to fuck around and find out. I run my fingers through my hair as I listen to their conversation.

"Wasn't Emma with you?" Jake asks, his voice unmistakable. He is, without a doubt, the biggest cockblock on the planet. I step into the open and glare at him, hands on my hips.

"You have the absolute worst timing."

He looks at me apologetically. "Sorry, Claire told me to tell you your dad is in town. You weren't answering your phone."

"Shit," I mutter, remembering I put it on silent earlier. Lost in the moment, I hadn't paid attention to my notifications.

I check my phone—five missed calls and several texts.

CLAIRE

Dad thinks he's staying in the room you're in until Christmas.

"Guess I'm sleeping on the couch until December 8th," I groan.

Hudson watches me intently. "Why?"

"Because my dad just wrecked my plans. Per usual."

Jake gives me a sympathetic look. "I'm sorry. We can get the cabin ready this weeke–"

"No. You can stay with me," Hudson interjects. "The house has four vacant bedrooms."

"You have six bedrooms total?" I ask, surprised. I knew the house was large, but not that big.

He locks eyes with me, and I can't shake the feeling of his stronghold over me.

"Great idea," Jake says, patting Hudson on the back. "Crisis averted, that's settled."

"It's just temporary until Emma leaves," Hudson clarifies.

I raise my eyebrows. "And what if I want to stay longer? Claire wants me here until New Year's."

"The invitation is open with no expiration date," Hudson offers, but I see something swirling in his eyes—pure obsession —that sends a thrill through me.

"And what if that's forever?" Jake asks with a laugh as he turns to leave.

Hudson and I both ignore him.

"See you two later," he singsongs walking to the truck.

When it rumbles down the road, kicking up dust, I know we're finally alone again.

The tension thickens.

Hudson slides the finger that had been buried deep inside me into his mouth.

"You have no idea what you've agreed to," he says with a sexy smirk.

"Mm. That's my line."

CHAPTER 16

HUDSON

We lost control...*again*. This seems to be our recurring theme whenever we're alone.

If these next three weeks unfold like this, neither of us will survive. The relentless push and pull, the thick tension, is almost overwhelming. My mind goes hazy when she's nearby. She disrupts my thoughts, dismantles my logic, and drives me to take risks with her.

Fuck me to tears.

Emma walks past me in the breezeway, her sweet perfume encapsulates me as she flips her wavy hair over her shoulder. The jeans she's wearing fit her so tightly that they almost look painted on. Damn, I want to peel them off her body with my teeth.

She glances back, catching me in the act of mentally undressing her. It feels like a hazy dream as her hair bounces.

I cross my arms over my chest and raise an eyebrow, completely unashamed.

"Claire saw the hot cocoa delivery this morning and noticed the hickeys on my neck. I didn't say anything."

So, Claire knows. Interesting.

"I'm not worried about Claire."

"You should be." Emma licks her lips and studies my mouth. "My sister is very protective. And don't get me started on my father."

That brings me back to reality. "Nothing is going on between us."

She throws her head back and laughs. "Oh, okay, then. I guess your finger buried deep inside me was nothing?"

My cock hardens at the thought. If Jake hadn't interrupted us again, she would be shaking under my touch, completely lost in pleasure.

"I don't remember," I shrug.

"You're so good at shutting it down, but I know better. I've almost got you figured out, Hudson Jolly." Her flirty tone amuses me.

"Unravel me," I reply, stepping into the tack room, knowing my time with her is slipping away. She leans against the stall gate and watches me disappear inside.

"If you're staying with me, we should probably set some rules," I say, loud enough for her to hear.

I think I hear her laugh. "Oh, like give me a curfew? Ground me if I'm a bad girl?"

I chew on the inside of my cheek. It's like she wants to be punished. "Mm. Don't tempt me," I say as I walk past her, two lead ropes thrown over my shoulder.

As I pass her, she calls out, "Give me your rules, then."

I'm not even sure where to start. I walk into the stall where Jingle is, clipping the rope onto his halter. I lead him out into the open and tie him to a hook.

"I don't want Colby to get the wrong impression," I tell her. That's my biggest concern. When I blurted out that she could stay with me, my son was the farthest thing from my mind. Guilt washes over me.

"I explained to him who I am and why I'm here. He knows I'm like an honorary auntie. And... I promise I won't seduce you in front of your kid."

"Sometimes, I don't know how to respond to you." I shake my head because she doesn't realize she doesn't have to try. A single smile, a smart-ass remark, the way her eyes soften when she looks at me—she tempts me without even trying.

"Anything else I need to know?"

"I'm hiring a nanny for Colby. I have interviews set up on Saturday. So, I need the house empty."

"Will do. I have plans anyway." Emma twirls her hair. "Good luck. Hope you find someone perfect for him."

I expected a different reaction, considering her conversation with my mother. "Thanks. I have a good feeling about it."

Emma watches me with curiosity. "So, are you going to introduce me?"

I nod and step aside. "This is Jingle, and that lovely lady in the stall at the end is Bells."

"He's huge!" she exclaims, her hand gently gliding down the side of his neck.

"They're Clydesdales. Jingle is a gentle giant."

"Kinda like you," she smirks as I pick up a brush.

"Can I?" she asks.

I hand it to her, and she runs her fingers along the bristles before brushing Jingle's neck, skillfully avoiding the sensitive areas. It's clear she has some experience.

"Do you know how to ride?"

She licks her lips and meets my gaze. "You're observant. You pay attention to the fine details."

I take a step back to watch her.

"Keep it up, and I'll put you to work," I tease, moving past her to grab Bells.

When I glance back, her eyes are on me, her smile bright and inviting. I clip Bells on the other side of the barn and grab another brush.

"So, are we riding today?" she asks, struggling to reach the top of Jingle's back. He's a large horse, and even I sometimes find it challenging, standing at 6 '2". Emma doesn't seem to be much more than 5 '8".

"We need to deliver a wagon to my father in an hour," I tell her, retrieving a stool.

I bend down to set it at her feet.

When I look up, her lips curl upward as she places her hand on my shoulder and steps up. Our gazes lock, and time seems to stand still as I admire her pretty face. A lifetime passes between us, and she takes my breath away.

Realizing how deep I'm in already, I clear my throat, rising to my feet.

We're eye to eye as I tuck a loose strand of hair behind her ear. "How long are you stayin'?"

"I'm letting you decide."

"And what if I never want you to leave?"

She inhales sharply, licking her plump red lips, and I feel a shift between us. "I'm letting you decide that, too," she whispers.

I smile, leaning in to kiss her before stepping away. She returns to brushing, and I move to Bells, needing to create some space. Emma doesn't respond.

"When I was a kid, I begged my dad for a pony. Growing up in New York, it was impossible, so he sent me to horse camp every summer until I graduated high school. That's when I became obsessed with cowboys. I've never shared that with anyone before." She nods and glances at me. "It's because you actually listen. Most people don't."

"I'm not most people," I reply. I'd listen to anything she wanted to share in her gentle tone. Her voice flows like a calm melody on a warm summer day.

"Riding is how I've spent my summers since I was old enough to remember."

"I can almost imagine it. A young you, riding around the farm, shirtless." She smiles.

"Basically, winters were for farming, and summers were

for planting. I love trail riding a few hours before sunset when everything shines like gold," I say, getting lost in the thought. "Maybe one day I'll introduce you to my boy, Dakota. He's a beautiful white Arabian I rescued after he retired from competing, and he loves to run. Colby's little wild thunder pony shares the same pasture. He's fire engine red, and his name is Thor."

Emma moves to the other side of Jingle, taking the stool with her.

"I'd like that. I haven't ridden in a long time," she replies, her back toward me. "Did you know Jake gave Claire rules last year?"

"I didn't know that." The first time I met Claire, I knew she was the one for my brother and that they would get married. Everyone in the family felt the same way. "I assume they were broken?"

"Oh, they completely decimated them," she laughs. "It made me think about my own rules."

"Mm. The famous five," I mutter.

"They're off the table. For you," she says, continuing to brush, not looking at me. I stare a hole through the back of her head.

"Absolutely not," I reply firmly.

She turns to face me. "My rules won't stop whatever this is. It will be your own that holds you back."

"That's usually the case," I admit, aware that I've halted every potential relationship I could've pursued. But no one has ever stopped me in my tracks...until Emma. "When do you plan on moving in with me?"

"I'm not moving in. I'm temporarily staying," she explains. "And don't ask me how long; I don't know."

I move toward her, grabbing her palm. Her breath hitches as I massage my thumb into the center of her hand. I pull a pen from my pocket and write the code to my front door. "Now you have the keys to my house..."

"Next up is your heart," she quips.

"Good luck, babe. You'll need it."

"And every person who's ever told me that, I've proven wrong with a smile on my face. Be careful; your luck might actually work."

I gently cup her cheeks and brush my nose against hers. "Is your heart fluttering right now?"

She grabs my shirt, fists tight. "You know it is."

Slowly, I lean in and kiss her passionately, my fingers threading through her hair. Warmth spreads across my cheeks as I smile against her plump lips, wanting her close. Everything else fades away, and emotions take over while our tongues dance together. The air is charged with electricity, and the spark between us nearly burns me the fuck down.

"Stay with me through Christmas," I whisper against her mouth.

"Consider it done."

We delivered the wagon to my father by the pavilion, and it was a nice ride. She sat close beside me as I showed her how to handle the reins. There were so many stolen glances and silent conversations that I couldn't stop smiling.

"Did you hear Emma's moving in with Hudson?" Jake asks Lucas as we load tree-cutting equipment onto a lowboy. His words pull me out of my thoughts about her.

"Temporarily," I reply, not reacting.

"She told me," Lucas says. "I think that's great. I hope you don't mind that she agreed to be my holiday hookup. We're not exclusive or anything, though."

I almost forgot Lucas was pretending to be into Emma. "You're still fucking lying."

"When I see her Saturday night, I'm going to ask her to move in with me instead. Let's see who she chooses." Cockiness drips from his tone.

"She's not going out with you," I shoot back. Emma mentioned that she would be busy on Saturday. Is that what she meant?

He shrugs. "Ask her. Guaranteed she'll be with me. I even asked her to wear a skirt for me. I can't wait."

I narrow my eyes and tense my fist. I'm five seconds from fucking him up.

"Hey, hey," Jake says. A single look from me is enough for him to know I'm about to explode.

"Emma is never exclusive with anyone, Hudson," Lucas says. "Not even you."

I step forward, but Jake pushes his hand against my chest. "Don't do this."

Lucas chimes in, "He doesn't want to claim her, but he doesn't want anyone else to have her either. That's chicken shit."

I walk away, taking off my gloves.

"Hey, we're not done," Lucas yells. I hop into the truck, exhausted from his attempts to provoke me. Jake climbs into the passenger seat, and we leave Lucas behind.

I pull my radio from my hip. "Hey, Mickey and Branson, can you meet Lucas at the equipment shed and help him finish loading saws?"

They respond and say they're heading that way. I'm not a complete jerk and won't make him do it alone, even if he deserves it; I need him to work on something else afterward.

"Were we as stupid as him at that age?" Jake asks.

I laugh. "Probably worse, but I don't have the patience for it. Once he pushes my buttons, I have to walk away."

We ride in silence for nearly ten minutes. The road smooths out but gets bumpy in spots. Before next season, we'll need to grade it because it's becoming washboarded. It's a road only farm workers use, and it slows us down. Time is money.

"Let me off at the front gate, please," Jake says. It's five minutes away. "Are you entering the cookie contest this year?"

I'm grateful for a topic other than Emma.

"You know I enter every year."

"And you lose." He turns to me. "I think you should make the chocolate chip pecan ones—the ones you bake when you're in love."

I groan.

"Emma's entering, and she's probably going to win it."

"Pfft. No way. I'm winning this year." I roll to a stop.

"Claire said Emma's a cookie shark. She got hooked on baking when she was dealing with her last breakup. Apparently, she got good at it. You'll need a miracle to beat her."

That breaks my heart. Baking is how she kept her mind busy when she was sad.

"Or maybe I'll recruit her to my team," I tell him.

He laughs. "Fuck, you're going to make me so rich. Remember, I want to be paid before Valentine's Day. Three big ones."

"Get the fuck out of my truck," I say, and he reaches for the door, still smiling.

"I'm happy for you," he says.

"Why?"

He grins, not needing to say it. The suggestion of falling in love lingers in the air.

Jake pats the truck and walks away. Claire awaits at the front gate, welcoming guests. As soon as he's close, he wraps his arms around her waist and kisses her neck. She turns, and their lips meet.

My thoughts immediately drift to Emma. I pull my phone from my pocket, seeking confirmation about something.

. . .

HUDSON

Do you have plans for Saturday night?

EMMA

I do.

HUDSON

Can I convince you to cancel?

My heart hammers in my chest. After everything that happened today, will my brother win her over, or will it be me?

Her text bubble appears and disappears several times.

I hold my breath, waiting for her reply.

EMMA

Sorry, I can't. I'm free next weekend, though. For now.

Maybe my baby brother isn't lying about his feelings for Emma. Perhaps she's exploring her options for the holidays.

I don't know if I can handle that I actually give a fuck. I thought I'd gotten rid of all those years ago.

CHAPTER 17

EMMA

After delivering the wagon to his dad, I drive home with a goofy smile, replaying every moment with Hudson. Christmas music blares on the radio, and I can't remember the last time I felt this way.

A tingle of anticipation washes over me, surrounded by a world of unspoken possibilities with this man. I'm on cloud nine just thinking about him.

As I pull up to the cabin, I spot a black SUV in the driveway. Its windows are thick like they're bulletproof.

I hesitate but then notice my father on the porch. When he sees me, he waves. Brody, one of his temporary bodyguards, stands beside him. He usually only comes around for special assignments, the kind where my dad wants to keep a low profile. I park, knowing I can't avoid my father while he's here. Sometimes, it's best to rip off the Band-Aid for quicker healing.

I glance around, checking for anyone else with him. It's just the two of them. As I approach, neither of them look like they belong here.

"Brody," I say, meeting his eyes. He's muscular, covered in

tattoos, and tends to be quiet. Over the years, I've heard him speak only a handful of times. He's also Billie's cousin.

"Father," I acknowledge. "Didn't expect to see you this year."

"Surprise! I thought I'd spread some cheer in Merryville with my beautiful daughters." He smiles broadly, too cheerful for my liking.

"What's with the act?" I question.

His brows rise. He's still dressed in a three-piece suit, slacks, and a tie, as if he flew straight from New York to Merryville. "What act?"

I glance at Brody, hoping for at least a supportive look, but he ignores me. My dad is never this nice.

"Claire's on her way," he informs me, glancing down at his phone.

They exchange glances, and I turn the doorknob, step inside. "They keep it unlocked."

"That seems unsafe," my father says, but I keep moving forward because I need to pack. I lift my suitcase from the floor and place it on the bed. Moments later, Tinsel dashes past my door, her bell jingling.

"Tinsel. Psst Psst Psst," I call out. The jingling stops, and I can picture her frozen in the hallway. The sound gets closer, and I wait as she slowly peeks around the corner. I pat my hand on the hardwood floor. "Come here, please. I'd love to give you a proper goodbye and a kiss."

She takes a step forward but then stops. I lean down, reaching for her chin, and she darts away.

"I thought we were besties!" I yell.

I lie back on the hardwood floor, staring at the ceiling, replaying my day in my mind—too many cute smirks and stolen glances.

"Emma," Claire says at my doorway, startling me.

I sit up. "Oh my God! Why does everyone around here always do that?"

"I'm so sorry. Please don't be upset with me. You don't have to stay with Hudson, if you'd prefer not to."

"It's not your fault. I should have planned better." I shake my head and lower my voice. "Or Dad should have. He mentioned wanting to spend Christmas here. Why is he here so early?"

"I don't know. Between you and me, I think he'll announce his retirement in January. I bet he's here to scout property to be closer to us."

"Us?" I shake my head. "Claire. I'm not moving here."

"Yes, you are." She laughs. "I had the same look on my face last year."

"Pfft. Stop. Peer pressure doesn't work on me. I'm immune, remember?" I grab the cocktail dresses from the closet. Harper made me pack them, convinced I might need them for dinner.

"*Penis* pressure will."

"Eww, shut up," I tell her, but she's not wrong. If Hudson is *The One* for me, I'd never leave.

"How long do you think it will be before you're sleeping in Hudson's bed?"

I toss a pair of socks at her. "If I'm lucky... *tonight*."

"Damn. I almost feel sorry for him." Claire readjusts her ponytail and glances toward the living room.

"You should," I admit. "I'm going to give him hell."

Each time he pushes me away, I'll stumble forward—at least until I know there's no chance for us in hell. With his past, heaven is already out of the question, isn't it?

She laughs. "Just don't get pregnant before me, got it?"

"Please. It would be an immaculate conception."

"Miracles happen every day," she snickers.

"Claire!" My father calls from the living room.

"If you need any help, let me know, okay?"

I tilt my head and smile. "I wish I could say the same. He's your problem this season."

175

"Ugh." My sister shuffles toward them.

"Your cat bit me," my father says in his deep, gruff voice.

Claire laughs. "Do you blame her?"

I take the steps to Hudson's house, wheeling my heavy suitcases behind me. On my palm is the code he gave me—0704. I type it in, and the handle clicks open.

He might be the only Jolly who locks anything, including his heart.

I pause in the foyer, taking in the space that belongs to him. Pictures of Colby hang above the fireplace—he's a proud dad, and a great dad.

My gaze drifts to the couch, and memories of last night flood my mind, filling me with a gentle swirl of excitement that makes me feel alive.

Leaving my suitcases at the door, I ascend the stairs. A few boards creak beneath my feet, and at the top, I'm greeted by a wide hallway lined with doors on each side. The first door reveals a playroom filled with toys, which connects to a Jack and Jill bathroom leading directly into Colby's room.

Dinosaurs are on his comforter, curtains, and wallpaper. On his nightstand sits a lamp and a tablet protected by a shatterproof case. A child-sized desk in the corner holds a notebook and crayons. In it, he was working on a drawing of two stick figures: the tall one labeled "Dad" and the smaller one with his name above it. He's smart, just like his dad.

In the background is a pony with a sausage-shaped body and stick legs. A smile forms on my lips; that must be Thor.

I exit his room and cross to the door facing Colby's. It opens to reveal an empty space. I walk back through the bathroom, which mirrors the one across the hall.

I expect to find another empty room, but instead, I'm met with a four-poster bed. Dust coats the photo albums stacked on the dresser, and the closet is filled with suits of various colors.

It's clear that no one has been in this room in a very long time.

Curiously, I return to the dresser and open the first album. A gigantic wedding cake dominates the center of the ivory pages, making my heart sink. Then I come across pictures of a twenty-something Hudson in a tuxedo, convinced it's the start of forever with the love of his life. My favorite images are of him with his brothers; Jake and Lucas look like kids, but there they are together. The bond they share shines through.

As I turn the page, *she* appears. This must be Meredith. She's short with a blonde bob and bright blue eyes, she looks nothing like me. I'm not sure what I expected.

I flip through the pages where they're together, and he looks so happy that it breaks my heart. Their story didn't culminate in a happily ever after.

I shut the book and pick up another. In this one, Hudson is horseback riding, shirtless in neon green shorts and flip-flops, exuding the cocky charm of a teenager. A Jolly Christmas Tree Farm baseball cap rests on his head as he gives a middle finger to the camera. I suspect Jake took the photo, especially since there are selfies of the two of them right after. It almost feels like I'm there with them.

The albums showcase his life from his perspective, and I'm captivated, eager to learn more through these snapshots. I want to flip through them all.

The next album is of him and his grandma baking throughout the years, with several pictures from the Christmas cookie contest. In one photo, he's proudly holding a sign that reads: "My recipe won!"

My mouth drops open. "No fucking way."

"What?" he asks, standing in the doorway and watching me from behind.

I gasp. "Shit! Does everyone sneak up on people around here? How long have you been there?"

"Long enough."

I close the album and turn to face him.

"You're not supposed to be here," I say.

"That's my line." He smirks. "Did you find what you were searching for?"

"Nah. Just an album of wedding photos where the faces weren't scratched out. I can help you with that if you change your mind; I've had plenty of practice over the years." I suppress a grin. "It was weird seeing you so happy. Seriously, I half-expected you to blink twice for help."

He laughs, and I make it my mission to hear that sound more often. This man may act like he has a hard exterior, but he's soft like a M&M.

"Yeah, I used to fake it a lot. I wanted to be liked and loved. Not anymore. Now, life gets what it gives. People can take me as I am, or they don't get me at all."

"You deserve to be accepted for who you are. You're not so bad."

His expression relaxes. "I have a hard-ass persona to maintain."

"Your secret's safe with me. Always. I'll keep it forever, right here." I pat my heart.

"Same." He breaks eye contact and glances around the room. "If you don't like this space, I can move the furniture elsewhere. There's a master bedroom downstairs with a full bathroom, but I don't use it."

I want to ask why, but now isn't the time. Eventually.

"This is perfect, Hudson." I run my hand over the dresser. "Is this hand-carved?"

He nods. "Yep. My great-grandfather built this entire set and hand-carved it from an old oak that fell."

"Great. So, not to state the obvious, but I guess it's seen a lot of use."

"Tons. Generational lovemaking. Oh, and good luck sleeping on that goat fur mattress," he replies.

My eyes widen. "Guess I'll be taking your bed until I can get a new mattress delivered."

He laughs again. "Yeah, and where would I sleep?"

I adore his charming Southern accent.

"Next to me."

I swear I see his green eyes darken as that gorgeous smirk spreads across his perfect lips.

We're standing on the precipice of something bigger than us, and I've almost convinced him to take the leap with me. We'll face our fear of falling in love together.

I just need a chance... a real one.

CHAPTER 18

HUDSON

"Next to me," Emma says it like she means it, and it's music to my fucking ears.

No woman has been in my bed in five years because I didn't allow it. But her?

"Not sure you can handle it, sweetheart." Doubt doesn't exist in my words, just confidence, a challenge lingering in the air between us.

"We'll see," she says, moving gracefully to the closet. "I'd love to see you in some of these suits."

She holds up a sleek tuxedo, the fabric gleaming under the soft light of the room. She tilts her head, a playful spark in her eyes, as if she's imagining how it would enhance the lines of my body.

I lean against the door jamb, unable to take my eyes off her. "You weren't kidding when you said you were trying to figure me out."

"Good luck, babe. You'll need it. Isn't that what you told me?" She digs into the coat pocket of the tuxedo, her fingers brushing against the fabric as if searching for hidden treasures. In her hand, she pulls out an ivory piece of folded paper.

I take a step forward and snatch it from her before she can peel it open. "I doubt you want to read the vows I wrote to another woman."

"It doesn't bother me. You belong to no one, Hudson." Her voice is unwavering, laced with a strength that both intrigues and unnerves me. "You may have meant those words when you wrote them, but they're kinda meaningless now, aren't they? Words are cheap. Action is everything. It's the only thing that really matters. It's a hard lesson I've learned."

My heart lurches, aching at the thought of her pain, wishing she didn't have to experience such heartbreak. Emma walks past me, wrenching the paper from my hand. I follow, caught in her wake as she skips down the stairs, a whirlwind of energy. At the bottom, her two enormous suitcases and a pink duffle bag sit like sentinels, patiently waiting.

She grabs a pair of tongs, her movements fluid and confident, and lights the stovetop. We both stare at the flames, mesmerized. "I can make it disappear."

"Do it," I whisper, my voice barely breaking the silence. The fire consumes the edge of the page until it shudders and morphs into a ball of flames. Emma screams when it breaks off and tumbles to the floor. I grab the tongs from her hand, adrenaline surging through me, and fling the burning remnants into the sink. The faucet is flicked on, water cascades down and washes away the ashes of a past I'm desperate to forget.

"It's like it never happened." She laughs, a light, airy sound that dances in the air and pulls my gaze to her mouth.

My smile grows, want bubbling within me. "What were Jake's rules?"

Her brow quirks upward, a teasing glimmer in her eyes. "I knew you'd ask, eventually. Edging questions. I love that game. No strings attached and no falling in love."

"Because he knew what he was getting himself into and was trying to avoid it." But I can feel it—I'm falling faster and harder than he did. It took him and Claire a month. A playful smirk spreads across her lips; as if she can read my mind.

This is happening too fast.

Emma leads me deeper into the intricate web she's slowly weaving. Eventually, I'll be ensnared, captured in a way that I can't escape, even when she leaves at the beginning of the year. The very thought of her leaving town constricts around my chest, panic rising like bile.

Her lips transform into a straight line, her expression shifting as she senses my unease. "What is it?"

"I just realized how fucked I am." I force myself to walk away, needing space, air, and time to think.

"Hudson," she says, following behind me. Emma grips my shirt, spinning me around and standing in front of me. I grow stiff as she leans in, her ear against my chest, listening to my rapidly beating heart. Part of me yearns to run my fingers through her silky hair, to lose myself in the comforting familiarity of her presence.

"I've got you." She clasps my hands, peeling my clenched fists open, and then gently hugs me. My breath is shallow, and I remind myself that the unease is temporary. The wave of panic sometimes throws me off balance, but it's usually random, an invisible tempest that I can't quite predict.

This time, though, it was triggered.

I rest my chin on her head, closing my eyes as I wrap my arms around her, wanting to hold on to this moment forever, never willing to let her go. How is this possible? How could I already be so attached? It's not fucking possible.

"What color is a chicken?" she asks, breaking the silence.

Stillness hangs thick in the air, and I'm utterly confused by her random question.

"I'm sorry. What?"

"Imagine it: a chicken standing in a field. What color is it?"

"Red." I chuckle, the sound bubbling up like a pop of

carbonation. The smile forces my face to relax. "What about you?"

"Mine is red, too." Calmness dances in her eyes. "Sometimes when life feels overwhelming, I think about my anxiety chicken. By the time it cock-a-doodle-doos in my head, the panic usually passes."

I snort, shaking my head in disbelief. "Chickens don't cock-a-doodle do *that*."

"My imaginary chickens do, and they also lay shiny golden eggs. Sometimes polka dot ones."

"Ah, they're *hen*dependent." The playful banter feels like a breath of fresh air amidst my swirling thoughts.

"Okay, that was a good one." She laughs.

I break away from her, creating space, even though I know the damage to my heart is already done. "Thank you."

"You've given me too many glimpses of the parts of you that you won't share with everyone. I've seen beyond the mask and the walls you put up," Emma whispers, her voice a tender melody that resonates within me.

I gently lift her chin to better meet her gaze. "Why didn't I meet you sooner? Before I was..."

"Don't you dare say broken. Unless your junk doesn't function properly..."

She raises an eyebrow, teasing, and I can't help but laugh at the absurdity of it.

"Rest assured, it works perfectly fine."

"Good." She crosses her arms over her chest, a satisfied look on her face. "This was a great talk. But I have to unpack and get settled."

As she moves toward her suitcases, I can't shake the gravity of our conversation. "Do you have plans for dinner? Will you be hungry around seven?"

"No plans." Her smirk deepens, her eyes flicking from my mouth down to my cock. "And I'm starved."

"Great. Should I add *thirsty* to the list, too?" I ask, enjoying the playful energy between us.

She claps her hands together, her laughter brightening the room. "Hilarious. And the answer's yes."

"Knew it," I reply, shaking my head as I begin to move toward the front door. "I'll have dinner ready around seven."

"Can't wait," she tells me.

I turn and catch a glimpse of her watching me, her expression a mix of anticipation and something deeper I can't quite place. She chews on the corner of her lip, an unconscious gesture that makes my heart race just a little faster.

"I'm so fucked," I mutter as I shut the door behind me, the sudden sound echoing back at me. I don't even remember why I came home.

I lead Colby into the kitchen with his backpack in tow. He's just returned from spending time with my mother, and excitement radiates off him. "Come on. I've got a surprise for you."

As soon as he sees Emma, he runs to hug her, his face lighting up with pure joy. "Oh my gosh! I've missed you!"

"Aww, I've missed you, too," she replies, warm and genuine, a broad smile stretching across her pretty face.

"Can I sit beside Emma, please?" Colby interlocks his fingers together and pleads, his big, round eyes wide with hope. "Please, please, please."

"If she says it's okay," I state, watching the two of them with a smile.

"It's fine," Emma responds, giving him a playful high-five as I move his plate across the table to make room for him.

He plops down in the chair, his anticipation palpable as he gazes at the giant plate of spaghetti piled high with gigantic meatballs.

"Yay! My favorite!" Colby exclaims, picking up his fork with glee and stabbing into the meat. "Thanks, Dad!"

"You're welcome. Now, I want to talk to you about something," I say, trying to maintain a serious tone amidst the cheerful chaos.

Emma, meanwhile, grabs a breadstick and takes a bite, savoring the warm, buttery texture.

Colby nods, curious. "Okay."

"I invited Emma to stay with us for a few weeks. Her dad is in town, and she had to give her bed to him," I explain, watching the realization dawn on Colby's face.

His eyes widen, and he gasps audibly. "Really? You can sleep in my room. You can have my bed!" he offers eagerly, his youthful generosity shining through.

Emma laughs at his outburst. "That sounds super cool, but you have an extra bed upstairs, so I don't have to use yours. That was really sweet of you, though. I'm sure your bed is comfy."

"It is! The best bed and pillow you'll ever find," he declares proudly, puffing out his chest as if he were personally responsible for its comfort.

"Mmhm." Emma twirls the noodles on her fork and takes a bite, covering her mouth delicately as she speaks. "Wow. I completely understand why this is your favorite."

"Can you be my real aunt? Like CeCe?" Colby asks, his eyes full of hope.

Emma smiles, the corners of her mouth tugging joyfully. "Actually, I got all the details about that. So, it turns out, the only way to make that happen is to marry your Uncle Lucas."

I grip my fork a little tighter when Emma glances at me, a sudden rush of protectiveness flooding my veins. "But that would never happen," I interject hastily, my heart racing slightly.

"Who knows what could happen?" Emma shrugs, a playful glint in her. She's enjoying this.

"You should marry Uncle Lucas and be my aunt," Colby insists, as though it were the most logical suggestion in the world. His enthusiasm is infectiously naive.

"After dinner, it's bath time," I assert, trying to steer the conversation away from Emma marrying my brother.

He shakes his head vehemently. "No!" he barks, his voice rising in protest.

I know better than to argue with him at the dinner table.

"Okay. What's one thing you're grateful for today?" I prompt, a staple of our nightly tradition.

His eyelids droop; I can see the exhaustion creeping in.

"Today, Evie gave me a sticker and I put it on my folder. It was a heart," he recounts, the memory causing a smile.

"Who's Evie?" Emma asks.

"My future daughter-in-law, apparently," I say with a chuckle, reaching for extra napkins to mop up some sauce that splattered across the table.

"She's seven," he explains earnestly to Emma. "It's Davidson's older sister. She's nice and has pretty pink nails."

Emma's brows lift in surprise. "Seven? Whoa. Into older women?"

"Maybe," he mumbles, not quite meeting her eyes, a hint of shyness washing over him.

"*Emma* is too old for you," I chime in, trying to defuse the sudden tension.

"One day, I'll be a grown-up," he declares, as if it were an undeniable truth.

"Find me when you're thirty," she jokes, and I swear I see a hint of rosy color spring to his cheeks.

It's moments like these that show how she has us both wrapped around her finger.

Eventually, our plates are cleaned, and we're all stuffed, leaning back in our chairs with satisfied sighs.

"I'll take care of the dishes," Emma says, rising from her seat with purpose.

"I've got it," I tell her, sliding the plates on top of one another, balancing them carefully. "Bath time, Colby."

"No!" he screams, his voice rising again, and Emma turns to him, her brows lifted in both surprise and concern.

"Would you take a bath for me, please?" she asks sweetly, trying to coax him with her charm.

He crosses his arms tightly over his small chest, a tiny grimace forming on his face. "I don't want to!" he declares, his defiance firm.

She drops down to one knee, her big brown eyes gleam. "But I even said please. What if I told you I have some bubble bath in my suitcase that smells like blue gum?"

"No."

"Hm. Oh, did I mention it makes the water blue, too? It's soooo cool."

He tucks his lips inside his mouth and hooks his fingers together, a subtle sign that he's intrigued despite his initial resistance.

"Come on. Let's go try it out. I'm happy to share."

Colby grabs her hand, and they walk up the stairs together, the sound of their playful chatter fading as they ascend.

"I'll be right up," I tell her, rinsing the dishes in the sink. The warm water cascades over my hands, and I focus on the rhythm of cleaning. I'll load the dishwasher once Colby is in bed, ensuring everything is in order for the night ahead.

When I make it to the bathroom, Emma is perched on the toilet, chatting animatedly with Colby. The tub is half full of water and frothy blue bubbles, just as she promised. It creates a vibrant contrast against the stark white porcelain, making the whole scene feel almost magical.

"Thanks for this," I say, and she rises gracefully from her spot. "Happy not to argue about it."

"You're welcome." Emma stands and switches places with me, her playful demeanor lighting up the room. "You owe me," she whispers.

I grab her elbow. "Add it to my tab."

As she leaves us, Colby blows the bubbles onto the shower wall, giggling as they pop and disperse. "Emma lives with us now?"

"Just until January, and then she's going back to New York," I say, keeping my tone calm, willing to ease his curiosity.

"New York? Why?"

I answer his questions the best I can.

Once he's out of the tub, he dresses in pajamas, and I let him choose the book tonight. I read until his eyelids grow heavy, and he finally succumbs to sleep.

I make my way downstairs, cherishing the quiet house as I approach the living room. Emma is sprawled on the floor, her backside up in the air, focused on her workout. Carefully, she lowers herself downward in a plank, her determination evident. After a brief moment of watching her, I step into the kitchen, making noise so she knows I'm here.

When I open the fridge, I'm greeted by the sight of a spotless interior and everything neatly portioned into containers. Even the counters are wiped clean and organized. There's nothing for me to do.

I head to the living room where Emma continues her plank, muscles flexing with concentrated effort.

"You didn't have to do that," I explain, feeling a bit uncertain now that my nightly chores are complete. A shower and some reading sound like a nice way to unwind.

"It's the least I could do after you prepared that meal," she replies, maintaining her focus. Her breath becomes steady, and I can see the strength it takes to hold herself up. "And, in the future, when I do something right, the only response I'll accept is 'thank you' or 'good girl.'"

She steadies herself, taking in calm breaths as sweat glistens on her forehead.

"I might be MIA over the next few days. I promised my sister I'd help her unload a Black Friday shipment and prep the shop. She's short-staffed because of the storm."

"Emma. You don't have to check in with me," I say, my voice gentle.

She shifts down to her elbows. "'Thank you' or 'good girl'. Eventually, you'll learn."

Her hair is a mess on top of her head. When I scan down her body, I realize she's wearing tiny shorts and a fitted sports bra. The combination leaves little to the imagination, and my breath hitches.

Temptress.

"Thank you," I mutter, my resolve wavering as I move toward the stairs. If I don't put some distance between us, I fear my lips will find hers again and we'll lose control. And I can't continue doing that.

"Mm. See. You're a *very* good boy," she says, sultry and teasing.

It's so fucking sexy; I think I might just adopt a praise kink.

CHAPTER 19

HUDSON

TWO DAYS LATER

"Colby, what do you say?" I tilt my head, curious about his thoughts.

"Nice meetin' ya, ma'am," he tells Heather, slamming his face into the couch.

He's tapped out for the day, and I'm thankful that this is the final interview. We started at ten this morning and have talked to at least nine ladies, each one bringing a different personality into our home, filling the air with their laughter and hopes.

I walk her to the door, my mind already racing with considerations. "I'll make a decision tomorrow before noon. I'll only call you if you're hired, okay?"

"I hope to hear from you." She blinks up at me, her big, blue eyes glimmering with anticipation.

"Thanks," I awkwardly say, and as she bends down to wave at Colby, who's dramatically playing dead. I can't help but smile at their interaction.

"Bye, Colby," she says, sweetly.

He lifts his arm in a half-hearted wave but doesn't even

bother to look at her. When I shut the door behind her, I cross my arms over my chest and settle beside him on the couch.

"Sit up. That was rude."

With a huff that rumbles through his small frame, he does as I say, but he's clinging to his stubbornness.

"Thank you. Now, who did you like the best?" I ask, trying to pull him out of his funk.

He squishes his face dramatically and holds his fingers together to form a zero.

"Oh, come on. They all seemed really nice. Heather was great."

"She talked to me like a baby." His face scrunches like he's offended.

"Son, I think that's just her voice," I explain patiently. "People can't help how they sound."

He shakes his head adamantly, brown curls bouncing. "Dad, they were all so weird. Every one of them!"

I try to hold back a laugh, his honesty is refreshing, but he's right. It felt less like an interview and more like... well, an interview before a first date. Each lady had dressed up, trying to impress, but it was hard to imagine any of them getting down and dirty with Colby in the yard, building castles out of leaves and mud.

"We'll pick the perfect nanny. Okay?" I reassure him, giving his shoulder a gentle squeeze.

"Do better, Dad." His little face, serious and determined, is enough to make me scoff in mock offense.

"Can we call Donna?" he adds, his hope for a familiar face evident.

Before we can continue our conversation, the door swings open with a sudden swoosh. When I turn my head, expecting to see my mother, I'm surprised to find Emma standing there.

She lifts her huge sunglasses from her eyes with one hand while balancing a shopping bag in the other. We haven't seen her since the night she moved in; she's been busy helping Claire in the shop.

"Emma!" Colby yells, his face lighting up with pure excitement. "I missed you!" Without hesitation, he pops up off the couch and dashes toward her, arms wide, squeezing her tight.

"Aww, I've missed you, too! So, so much!" she coos, patting his back as he burrows into her side. She glances down at him, then back at me. "I got you the coolest thing today after helping Aunt CeCe."

"Ohh," he whispers, bouncing from foot to foot as they waddle over to the couch. She hands him the bag, and I watch as confusion washes over his face.

"What is it? I don't get it?" He shifts his weight, eyes darting between her and the bag.

Emma settles onto the couch, their eyes locking in an eager connection.

"It's magic!" she announces with a dramatic flair, tapping her finger on the packaging. "These tiny little capsules will grow into dinosaurs this big." She holds her fingers out, spacing them apart about three inches.

"Woooow." His eyes widen, fully captivated by her. Hell, I am, too; the way she lights up while describing it is infectious.

"I was thinking we could use them at bath time!" Emma adds, excitement lacing her voice, and Colby's face instantly breaks into a grin, his earlier disinterest forgotten in this new adventure.

There it is. I narrow my eyes at her, realizing she has found the perfect solution to a temporary phase. "Smart," I mutter, a touch of admiration in my voice.

Colby pulls several shiny capsules out of the bag, his excitement radiating through the room.

"All of these are for me?" he squeaks, his eyes sparkling as he circles the living room like she handed him a million dollars. "Can I take a bath right now?"

Emma shakes her head, her grin never wavering. "Not yet. Only when your dad says you can." She moves in close to him, her presence inviting, and his eyes widen as he looks up at her as if she's an angel. *She is.* "You have to promise to show me which dinosaurs hatched, okay?"

"I will! I promise!" His voice is filled with uncontainable glee.

I clear my throat. "Okay, Bee. I think I hear Mimi pulling up right now."

"When I get home, I get to take a bath?" Colby's eagerness is palpable.

I chuckle, feeling a warmth spread through me. "You're staying with Mimi tonight, remember? Pizza slumber party?"

"Oh yeah!" His face lights up in realization. He turns to walk away, but then rushes back to Emma, thrusting his arms around her in an impulsive hug. "Thank you very much!"

She squeezes him back tightly, her affection evident. "You're very welcome."

When he's out of sight, I lean back in the oversized chair, watching Emma as she collects herself. "A problem solver. I like that."

"All stinky little boys at that age hate bath time. Hope you found someone who's perfect for you," she replies, casting me a playful glance.

"Yes, actually, I did," I say, my heartbeat quickening at the thought of her.

You, I want to say. It's more than obvious. Crystal fucking clear.

Emma stands, her energy shifting as she prepares to leave. "Welp, I gotta get ready for my date tonight. Can't be late." She turns gracefully on her heels and starts up the stairs, her confidence a sight to behold.

"You're adorable," she comments lightly, passing Colby as he heads toward me with his overnight bag, packed full for a night at my mother's. A few kids from church that she used to help watch are coming over too, all around Colby's age. Mom enjoys chatting with their grandmothers while the kids play. At first, I told her no, concerned about the chaos, and she got upset, launching into another lecture about how he wouldn't be this age forever.

A car door slams, and Colby darts to greet my mother. As soon as she enters, he climbs into her arms, laughing like he hasn't seen her in ages.

"Did you gain ten pounds since last week?" she teases, her voice filled with affection.

I stand, my arms folded across my chest. "Probably from all the Halloween candy you fed him."

The water turns on upstairs, its steady flow a reminder that Emma is getting ready for a date. My mother glances upward.

"You still want a large pepperoni to go?" she asks, shifting her attention back to me.

"Yes," I reply, handing my card over to her.

She doesn't take it. "No."

"Please let me pay," I offer.

"Absolutely not. I'm treating my grandson and his hardworking dad. I'll see you in the morning." She casts a glance at the colorful dinosaur capsules on the coffee table, approval in her eyes.

"You should hire whoever brought those. That was genius. Sad I didn't think of it," she remarks as Colby nearly drags her down the porch, his little legs working overtime.

"The weather is supposed to be bad in the morning," I say as I move to the door, a hint of concern creeping into my voice.

"We'll play it by ear," she reassures. "The worst thing that could happen is I get to keep this little booger until Monday."

"Sure. Hope you get all the juicy gossip tonight," I say, sharing a smile before watching her disappear down the steps.

I return inside, flipping through my notes for everyone I

interviewed today, the pages filled with ambitious dreams. Some resumes even have headshots attached.

Twenty minutes later, Emma walks down the stairs with her hair freshly dried and shimmering like copper. She's wearing a short-as-fuck shiny red skirt that hugs her curves perfectly, paired with a white fuzzy sweater that contrasts against her tanned skin. In that moment, she seems like she just stepped out of a dream—a vivid, surreal fantasy that dances tantalizingly at the edges of my imagination.

My mind races, each thought a jumbled mess of admiration and bewilderment. "Wow. You're..."

Words scatter like leaves in the wind. I'm left speechless.

"Going to be late if I don't leave right now," she says, glancing down at her phone, the glow reflecting in her eyes. When she passes me, I can't resist the urge to reach out. I grab her hand, pulling her back to me with a gentle tug.

"You act like you missed me," she remarks, teasingly.

"And what if I did?" My heart races as we draw close; my mouth hovers above hers, but I hesitate, caught in the dizzying whirlwind of my feelings.

She groans. "You're so frustrating!"

"I'm the frustrating one? Look at you! Dressed like this and smelling so fucking pretty." The scent of her perfume wraps around me, intoxicating, but the knowledge that she's going out with my brother stings deeper than I'd like to admit.

She moves across the living room, stepping outside, her silhouette illuminated by the yellow glow of the porchlight. Smoke billows from her mouth as she exhales, cutting through the chilly night air while she gazes at her vehicle. With a press of a button, the engine roars to life, and the headlights flick on.

"What's wrong with you?" she asks, shaking her head, a half-smile forming at the corners of her mouth.

I grab her elbow, pulling her close, the warmth between us

palpable. "I'm fucking jealous, okay? Is that what you want me to say? The thought of you being with anyone else..."

Her doe-like eyes meet mine. Laughter blooms and fills the space between us. I don't find anything about this situation funny.

Emma's expression softens, and her hand lifts to rest on my cheek, a gentle touch that sends a shiver down my spine. "Do you trust me?"

The edge of my anger fades as I close my eyes, focusing on her touch against my skin. "I don't know."

"This is your chance," she says, taking a step forward, her confidence radiating like a beacon.

I stand transparent before her; Emma sees straight through my defenses. Closing the distance, I lift her chin, forcing her to meet my gaze. Slowly, I lean in and capture her lips with mine. Her hands clutch my shirt, fingers twisting in the fabric as she pulls me closer. An unexpected moan escapes her.

"What was that for?" she asks breathlessly, her eyes wide with surprise.

"You never miss the opportunity to kiss a pretty lady under the mistletoe. It's bad luck," I reply, feeling the warmth of her breath mingling with mine.

She smirks, and I can see the wheels turning in her head, ready to fire back with a clever retort.

"You have the job if you want it," I tell her, my heart pounding with both eagerness and dread. She could say no.

Instead, a smile lights her face, revealing her perfect teeth. "Seriously?"

"You make Colby happy," I mutter, the words tumbling out before I can second-guess them. "Like T-Rex's and water parks. LEGO and chocolate birthday cake with sprinkles. I can't deny him that."

"But you can so easily deny yourself that," she counters, her voice tinged with a hint of disappointment. Her words cut through me like a knife, and I realize how painfully accurate she is. I suck in a ragged breath, moving beside her, my lower back resting against the railing as I watch her.

She doesn't meet my eyes. The fun, playful person she was just moments ago has vanished, replaced by seriousness. The mood grows heavy.

"The biggest difference between you and me is you're determined to run away from love. I will *always* run toward it."

My large hand threads through her hair and gives a slight tug. Our mouths crash together, and I taste her spearmint toothpaste. Another whimper escapes her lips, and I know we're spiraling out of control, like a kamikaze pilot with only one fate. The air thickens. It's electric and consuming, forcing me to confront the chaos brewing between us.

"Neither of us will survive this," I whisper against her mouth, my thumb brushing softly against her flushed cheek. Her eyes—full of want and need—widen at my words, and I can sense her heart racing beneath the surface.

"I don't care." With those bold words, she tugs on my lip, a playful yet intoxicating gesture that sends shivers down my spine. My eyes roll back in pleasure, overwhelmed by the pull of desire and the gravity of our situation.

"Cancel your plans tonight," I insist, the urgency in my voice laced with desperation.

"I can't." She takes a step away from me, and in that instant, I feel the loss of her warmth like the abrupt chill of an autumn breeze. Her cheeks are flushed a deep pink, and her lips are slightly swollen from our closeness. I'm convinced that NASA must have invented her lipstick because somehow, amidst all this, it remains untouched and perfectly in place.

Emma doesn't glance back as she descends the steps of the porch, her silhouette framed by the headlights of her car.

I cross my arms over my chest, frustration bubbling within me at my inability to convince her to stay. "Tell Lucas I said he can go fuck himself," I call out, the bitterness of my words echoing in the still evening air.

"I will," she responds, her voice steady yet tinged with uncertainty. "Wait up for me, okay? We'll talk when I return."

With that, Emma climbs inside her car, the sound of the slamming door echoes in the silence. She backs out of the driveway, and once the taillights vanish into the gathering darkness, I turn away, the weight in my chest growing heavier.

I change clothes, each movement feeling oddly robotic, as if I'm preparing for battle.

Right now, there's only one person on this planet who can help me.

And I need to speak to her before I do something I will undoubtedly regret.

CHAPTER 20

EMMA

Leaving Hudson with that expression on his face was difficult, but he needs to learn to trust me, even if it means taking the hard road.

When I return tonight, we have a lot to discuss. I've spent the last two days reflecting on what we're going through. The higher I climb with him, the harder we'll fall together. My mended heart can't withstand another break, but I'd risk it for him if he's willing to take the same chance, even if it's just until January when I leave.

Having him for the holidays is better than not having him at all—I truly believe that. Hudson Jolly, Mr. Grumpy, makes me smile. Butterflies swarm in my stomach again, and after I park, my nerves start to get the best of me.

Taking a deep breath, I get out of the car and knock on the door.

I hear footsteps lightly thump across the floor, followed by gentle laughter. The door swings open, revealing an older woman with bright green eyes. She draws me in instantly.

"You must be Mawmaw."

Her smile radiates like golden sunshine.

"And you must be the woman who's marrying my

grandson." She pulls me into her arms, and her scent is reminiscent of brown sugar.

I hug her back as if I've known her my entire life. "You flatter me. But... which grandson?"

"I already love you," she exclaims. "But you *know* which one."

Claire warned me that she's the town gossip. I wouldn't be surprised if she had a file on me hidden somewhere among the Texas Monthly magazines scattered across her coffee table. A crocheted blanket hangs on the back of her couch, and behind it sits a stand filled with dozens more; I suspect she made them all herself.

I follow her down a narrow hallway adorned with pictures of children. The delicious aromas of food waft through the air. My stomach growls, but I slow down to examine each photo.

It's clear she's a proud grandmother and great-grandmother.

"Whoa," I say, halting at a picture of Hudson in a cap and gown. His green eyes seem to look right through me, as if he knows something I don't.

"Cookie graduated with his master's degree in agriculture," she shares. "He was the first grandbaby to do it —top of his class, too."

"So he's a smart cookie?" I quip, and she laughs. The fact that she calls him Cookie is so endearing I can hardly contain it. I have so much more to learn about Hudson, and I hope one day I'll know him like the back of my hand.

The thought makes my smile linger.

She steps into the dining room, and that's when I spot Claire. Of course, she's early; being late is a cardinal sin for her. She must have parked on the opposite side of the house.

On the table, there's a feast of golden-brown fried chicken, cheesy macaroni, and green beans laden with large chunks of bacon.

"Mawmaw," I say, astonished. "You didn't have to do all of this for me."

We sit down, and she pours me a glass of thick eggnog.

"Sweetie, it was no trouble at all. First impressions matter."

I take a big gulp of my drink and catch a hint of alcohol—it's spiked.

"Be careful with that. I added a little giggle juice," she says, taking a sip herself. "By the way, I love that skirt. It makes you shine like the diamond you are."

"Thank you! I do love shiny things," I reply, feeling the conversation flow effortlessly. I nearly laugh at how nervous I was earlier.

Claire flashes a cheeky grin. "I was worried you'd be late."

"No way." If only she knew how close I came to ditching. Hudson almost convinced me to drop his grandma.

"Oh, by the way, Hudson thinks I'm on a date with Lucas right now."

"You canceled that days ago. Didn't you clarify that with him?" Claire asks.

Mawmaw watches me intently, noting the small details.

"I asked him to trust me." I take another drink of nog; I think it might be my new favorite holiday drink. The recipe is a must-have for sure.

"Honey, when it comes to men, sometimes it's good to let them squirm a little."

I burst into laughter.

She continues, reminiscing, "I remember when men would do anything to win my attention. If only I could be young and flirty again. But anyway, tell me ab—"

A knock sounds at the front door, interrupting her. We both stop talking and listen.

Knock. Knock. Knock.

"Were we expecting anyone else?" Mawmaw asks Claire.

My sister shakes her head. "It was a girls' night only. I told Jake and Lucas no boys allowed."

The door creaks open, and heavy footsteps echo across the wooden floor.

"Mawmaw! Where are you?"

I freeze—I recognize *that* voice.

Claire smirks and lifts her glass, raising an eyebrow but she doesn't take a sip.

"In the dining room, Cookie."

My blood races, and my heart begins to pound.

He's here.

"I'm sorry to interrupt. I need to talk to you. I think I'm fall—" Hudson pauses at the entryway. His scowl vanishes as he spots me, and the realization of my presence in his grandmother's dining room washes over him. He gradually relaxes.

"Ah, this is why you reacted that way."

A playful smile spreads across my lips. "I asked you to trust me."

Hudson glances from Claire to Mawmaw and then to the food laid out on the table.

"What were you saying, honey?" Mawmaw asks as she grabs tongs to serve a crispy chicken thigh. "Girls, go ahead and fix yourselves a plate. We're eating family-style here."

The electricity between Hudson and me is palpable.

"Have you eaten dinner already? Join us." Mawmaw gestures for him to hurry. "Come on now, no time for shyness, honey. What's on your mind?"

Hudson clears his throat. "Mom's picking up a pizza from town."

He steps fully into the dining room, wrapping his arms around Mawmaw from behind as she stays seated. "Love you, Mawmaw." He plants a kiss on her cheek. "I'll come over and visit again soon. I promise."

"You better bring your Cookie Cutter," she playfully pats his arm before turning to him. "Let me walk you out."

"No, no, apologies for interrupting. Y'all have fun." As he excuses himself, I catch a glimpse of a smirk on his face. The cocky bastard is pleased I wasn't with Lucas. Truthfully, I am, too.

His grandmother doesn't take the hint and follows.

Once they're out of sight, Claire's mouth drops open. "Holy shit. He's totally obsessed with you."

I roll my eyes playfully.

"I'm serious. I've never seen him act like that, Em," she insists. "You need to tell him that you and Lucas are a prank before it goes on any longer. Imagine if the roles were reversed."

Just the thought of Hudson with someone else makes my head spin. "I'm going to talk to him after dinner tonight."

"Oh my God. You're falling in love with him," she whispers.

My cheeks flush, and I wonder if it's the eggnog or just my thoughts of Hudson.

"I—I don't know," I admit. "But he makes my heart flutter."

"You felt butterflies?" she asks in a whisper.

"Yes," I reply.

She stares at me until Mawmaw returns to her seat. "Well, go on, finish your conversation and eat up."

We each reach for a different dish. I go straight for the green beans and swap them for the macaroni with Claire.

"That was interesting, wasn't it?" Mawmaw glances at me, her lips curving into a smile. "Witnessing how Cookie looks at you... well, I've never seen him like that with anyone. Destined hearts and Christmas miracles," she says.

"Are you sure?" I desperately want to believe her.

"Does the sun rise every day?"

We pass around oversized food bowls, serving ourselves

generous portions. The savory aroma of fried chicken makes my mouth water.

"Yes." I hiccup as the spiked eggnog finally kicks in. "Excuse me, sorry."

"Help yourself," Mawmaw offers.

"You're a very bad influence." My cheeks tingle.

She chuckles. "Oh, honey, I've been told that many times in my life. Now, tell me about you and Cookie."

"I, uh..."

She winks at me. "And don't forget to grab yourself a biscuit. And make sure to add more to your plate. There's more than enough to go around."

I obey, not wanting to offend her, though I'm unsure how I'll eat all this food. I'll figure it out. I pick up a chicken leg and take a crunchy bite. The outside is crispy, while the inside is juicy and tender. "Oh my God."

Claire chuckles. "Right?"

I glance at it. "How is this so good?"

"Now who's flattering whom?" Mawmaw asks, taking a bite of her own.

"Mawmaw's being modest," Claire chimes in. "But she makes the best food in the South."

"It's pretty good. So, you're living with Hudson and Colby?" Mawmaw redirects the conversation.

"I'm only temporarily staying there while my father is in town. At least until December 30th, then I'll return to New York."

Claire's jaw nearly drops. "Wait. You'll be here for Christmas?"

Tears fill her eyes, and I feel a swell of emotion. I want to stand up and hug her. I hate seeing my sister cry, even if they're happy tears. "I'm sorry. I'm just overwhelmed. I've been hoping for this."

"Aww, don't do that." When she cries, I cry too, just like we did as kids. "Hudson interviewed nannies today, and I think they all sucked. Tonight he told me that if I wanted to help with Colby, I could. The kid and I are going to have so much fun. I seriously can't wait." The thought of not being alone while everyone else works fills me with excitement.

Mawmaw notices my mood. "He's a sweetheart, just like his daddy. Colby reminds me so much of Cookie when he was little."

I take a forkful of velvety macaroni that's creamy and smoky. It's the most delightful taste I've ever experienced. "This is my new favorite food."

Claire chuckles. "I love it too. But this woman is super secretive with her recipe. Every time I make it, it never tastes like this."

"Honey, you know I don't measure anything. It's tricky to get it right when I go by taste alone."

"Did Jake tell you my sister's entering the Christmas Cookie contest?" Claire shifts the subject.

"Oh, fantastic! I love hearing that. Any idea what you're baking?" She looks at me with curiosity.

"Not yet. I wanted to get your opinion. Gingerbread is the most popular cookie, followed by chocolate chip."

She smirks. "You did your research. What do you want to know?"

"What would you bake if you were me?"

"Hmm." She drinks her eggnog and refills our glasses. "My favorite cookies are gingerbread. It's a secret family recipe that no one's cracked yet."

"That sounds like a challenge." I laugh. "I'd love to taste them."

"I have," Claire replies, taking a bite of green beans. "The night Jake and I made gingerbread houses together was magical. I'm pretty sure that's when we fell in love."

"But you don't know the recipe?" I ask.

"No, Jake takes that secret seriously. He won't even prep it in front of me."

My mouth drops open. "Okay, so I guess the only way to get it is to marry a Jolly, right?"

She rests her chin on her hands. "So, when are the weddings?"

I burst into laughter and lift my left hand. "Ringless, Mawmaw."

"Just wait," she says and then turns to Claire. "I had a dream about you, honey. You were pregnant."

"That's so random." Claire laughs nervously, and I notice she hasn't taken a sip of her eggnog. Our eyes meet briefly as she catches me staring.

"I made chocolate pie," Mawmaw says, redirecting the attention in the room. I watch Claire let out a breath of relief. This conversation may be over for now, but I won't forget.

We chat about the weather, the farm, and the snow globe shop. Mawmaw shares tidbits about contestants in the cookie contest, so I make mental notes of what to expect.

Mawmaw makes a pot of coffee and pulls out the Baileys from the fridge. "Do you want a pour?" she asks.

"Sure," I reply, and we enjoy our chocolate pie with homemade whipped cream, smiling so hard my face starts to hurt.

Once we finish eating, Claire answers a call from Jake while I help clear the table. "Mealtime is special. It's not just about nourishment; it's about bringing joy to the table and sharing an experience with loved ones. I know you're looking for the secret to winning the cookie contest."

I nod and gather the silverware. "I went through a tough breakup a few years ago, and whenever I felt myself slipping into depression, I would bake. I baked a lot. For months, I perfected my recipes because baking was all I had. Winning this isn't just a contest for me; it's proof that I can bake for fun, not just as an escape from a difficult time in my life," I explain.

It's just the two of us now. She puts the leftover chicken in a plastic storage bag.

"You want to know how to win, and it's simple: Bake with love. It always shines through and makes everything better." Mawmaw pulls me into a tight hug. "Plus, you have my Cookie to help you. He was always my good luck charm."

Claire returns to the kitchen, moving directly to Mawmaw who releases me from her embrace.

"Well, I'm going to head out. Thank you for everything. It was incredible, as always," Claire says, kissing Mawmaw on the cheek as if they were at an art gallery.

"I should go, too," I tell her, and she pulls me into another hug.

"Take care of him," she advises. "You're what he's been waiting for all his life."

"Thank you," I whisper as I step away.

I follow Claire to the porch.

"Are you pregnant?" I suddenly ask.

If I were guessing, I'd say she doesn't blink for at least twenty seconds.

"Oh my God, you are," I whisper, realizing the truth.

"Shh," she replies in a whisper. "I'm not. Not yet. We're trying, though. It's my Christmas wish."

I wrap my arms around her and squeeze tight, and she screams with joy. "No one can know, okay?"

"Okay. Oh my God. It's going to happen," I say. "Even if it doesn't happen by Christmas, okay?"

"I'm excited. I think everything went great tonight. She likes you," Claire ensures.

"It did. I already love her," I say, giggling, realizing how tipsy I am.

"Do I need to drive you home?" she asks.

I shake my head. "I'm going to text Hudson."

Claire wraps me in a hug. "Okay. Goodnight. I love you. Oh, I parked over there."

"Goodnight," I say, and we exchange a smile. Seconds later, the engine cranks, and she slowly drives down the driveway onto the main road. I look up at the night sky and find myself wishing upon the stars.

As I approach my car, I pull out my phone to text Hudson. When I look up, I see his truck parked beside my car.

He leans against it with his arms crossed, staring at me as if I'm the only star in the sky. He's a wet dream.

I take a deep breath, a smile spreading across my lips.

He shakes his head, and the silent conversation moves me forward. "I'm not letting you drive after drinking Mawmaw's giggle juice. It's tons of spiced rum, and you're a lightweight."

He opens the door for me, and I climb inside. "I was going to text you."

"I know," he says, gently shutting the door.

The scent of his clean skin and aftershave fills the cab as soon as he joins me. When he backs out of the driveway, gravel crunches under the tires, and a country song plays on the radio.

"Oh, by the way, I gave Lucas your message. He said you can go fuck yourself back," I say.

Hudson shakes his head but can't hide his smirk. "I was going fucking crazy. I almost drove to Moonshiners and threw you over my shoulder like a caveman."

"Please," I reply. "Men don't actually do that."

As we park outside his house, he opens my door. Moments later, to my surprise, he lifts me over his shoulder and carries me across the yard. I squeal and burst into laughter.

"Real men aren't afraid to carry their women," he teases, giving my ass a playful smack before he strides through the living room and places me down on the couch.

He leans over me, his intense gaze locking onto mine.

"I'm your woman?" I ask, half amused.

"Do you want to be?" he responds.

Our lips collide, our tongues dancing in perfect harmony.

He grinds against me, and I can feel him through my soaking wet panties.

"Be mine," I whisper. "At least until Christmas."

"Fuck, Emma," he breathes, his teeth grazing the delicate skin of my neck.

"No strings attached, and no falling in love?" I question, my hands reaching for his jeans button.

"I can settle for no strings attached. The other part? It might be too late for that," he admits.

I place my hands on his face, leaning in to ghost my lips over his. Even though it's early winter, it feels like the height of summer in here. "Hudson."

Just then, the front door swings open. "Sorry, I forgot—"

Hudson jumps up, and I turn my gaze toward the door.

"Shit. Mom!" he exclaims.

I close my eyes tightly, wishing I could vanish.

The front door shuts, and I hear her instruct Colby to return to the SUV.

Hudson chuckles lightly into my ear.

"Did she see us?" I ask, a hint of panic in my voice.

"Yes," he replies, sitting up and brushing my hair away from my face. "I don't care who knows. If you're mine for the holidays, then you're mine, Emma. Just make sure that's what you want."

The doorbell rings, and he takes a deep breath. "Surprised that thing works. No one ever uses it."

He adjusts himself and buckles his belt as he stands, and I sit up as he makes his way to the door.

"Oh, hey, Mom. Didn't expect to see you here," he says like she didn't just witness our tongues in each other's mouth and him grinding against me.

"Forgot to grab Colby's overnight bag," she tells me. I glance back and spot it beside the couch where he had placed it earlier.

I hand it to her, and she studies me for a few seconds. "Have a good night."

"Good night, Ma," Hudson replies, and the door closes behind her.

Before he walks away, the deadbolt clicks into place.

Hudson turns to me, a grin on his face. "Want some more eggnog? I've got Grandma's giggle juice in the cabinet."

"Fuck yes," I whisper, eager to relax after being caught by his mother.

CHAPTER 21

HUDSON

I move into the kitchen. My footsteps echo against the wooden floor, each stride resonates like a whisper in the quiet night. I reach into the fridge, grab the eggnog, and then turn my attention toward the cabinet where a bottle of spiced rum awaits. The amber liquid swirls slightly, catching the dim light as I set it on the counter.

Emma's presence hums at my back, and I feel her gaze tracking every move I make.

A thrill stirs in my chest, igniting a flicker of excitement I haven't felt in ages. It's a match struck in the dark, illuminating possibilities I had buried five years ago when my wife left me. I never thought I'd experience *this* again.

When I glance over my shoulder, our eyes lock. Her gaze is unwavering. Emma Manchester is looking at *me* like *that*.

A quiet curiosity lingers in her expression, and it holds me captive. My pulse quickens, each beat echoing in the room's stillness. I want to memorize how this woman is looking at me —as if I'm the only thing in the world worth watching, the center of *her* universe.

I savor this moment, indulging in the electricity that

courses between us. Her eyes radiate an intriguing intensity, drawing me deeper with each passing second.

She licks her swollen lips, the ones I was devouring like my life depended on it, and a heat surges through me. "Do you want it how Mawmaw makes it?"

She smirks, a playful glint in her eye that poisons my mind with vivid thoughts of her body pressed against mine. "Sure. I'd love to know her ratios."

Emma is buzzed; I can tell by how her cheeks flush, glowing pink. This drink will lead her straight to Wastedville. While reckless anticipation ignites, I can't cross the line with her. Not like this. I fill a glass a quarter-full with rum, the liquid dark and inviting, then top it off with eggnog before stirring it with a spoon. Unspoken words linger in the air.

"Ah, so what's the secret ingredient?" Her brows raise playful, curiosity etched across her face.

"Me." I dip my finger into the glass, then place it into my mouth, savoring the taste with a wicked grin. I wish it were *her*.

Her cheeks flush like she's remembering the other day. Fuck, how I wish I could read every dirty thought in her beautiful mind. I want to unravel the mysteries behind her every glance, knowing she's not the woman I assumed her to be.

I pour more rum into my glass before turning to face her. Excitement swirls within me, thickening the air.

Silence stretches between us, heavy with meaning and unspoken words.

"What is *this*? What are we doing, Em?" I ask, confusion weighing heavily on me.

Fear creeps up inside me. I'm falling too hard and fast.

"I don't know. I've never felt *this* before," she admits, her voice vulnerable.

My brows furrow in concern. "I'm so fucking sorry."

She shakes her head vehemently. "Why are you apologizing?"

I take a step closer, closing the distance between us. I brush my fingers down the side of her face, the warmth of her skin sending my heart racing. She smiles up at me, and in that moment, the world fades away. "I'm truly sorry that no one has ever made your heart skip a beat, and that it was me who did."

"What are you afraid of?" she asks, her warm gaze pulling me deeper in.

"Falling in love with someone who leaves when things get too real," I confess, the words spilling out like a secret. "Kind of like how you did after our night together in July."

She gasps, her eyes widening in shock. "You swore we'd *never* speak about that. We were starting over."

"Yeah? But you've told me several times you don't do second chances, and yet here you are. Explain that, Emma."

"Guess we're both liars," she responds, that same destructive spark igniting between us.

Neither of us stands a chance at winning this. The tension has been building for four months.

"I won't pretend we never existed," I admit. "I can't do that anymore."

She takes a ragged breath as my fingers weave through her hair, the silky strands slipping between my fingers. I tilt her head back when my mouth hovers just inches from hers, teasingly close. My girl likes it a little rough. "You've been thinking about me every damn day since you left, haven't you?"

"Yes," she confesses, her voice barely above a whisper. A fierce intensity swirls in the air. "You ruined me, Hudson. *So fucking bad.* I should've stayed away, but I can't. I'm drawn to you."

Hearing those words sends a wave of satisfaction through me. Spiced rum courses through my veins, encouraging me forward. I crash my lips against hers, knowing I'll never satisfy my hunger for her.

She's so desperate for me that she reaches for the top button of my jeans, her fingers trembling slightly with need. I want her, I want her so badly I can barely think straight.

"You've had too much to drink," I whisper, my voice low as I place tender kisses along her jawline.

"Hudson," she breathes, her eyes flickering with that familiar flame.

"I want to, but I *can't*. You need to decide if you're going to be mine for the holidays when you're completely sober. We both know tipsy Emma is a reckless girl who only cares about one thing." My cock, I want to say, but don't have to.

"You're still playing hard to get," she scoffs, trying to hide her desire, but I can hear the slurring creeping into her words.

"Trust me, I'm not, but I can if you'd rather do this the hard way."

"Speaking of hard." She runs her palm down the front of my jeans, her touch sending waves of pleasure through me. I nearly shudder; it feels incredible. "Why do you have to be so fucking respectful? I want you, Hudson. Sober or drunk."

"Emma," I growl. "If you keep it up, I won't touch you until Christmas."

Her mouth drops open in shock as she steps back. "You wouldn't dare."

My eyes narrow and I smirk. It's a challenge. "*Try me.*"

Emma tilts her head, feigning innocence as a sultry smile plays on her lips.

"It's so hot in here," she says before peeling off her sweater, revealing her soft curves. Her breasts are on full display, enough to make my breath catch.

"That's not going to work," I say as she slowly slips out of her shiny red skirt, the fabric glides down her legs. She's wearing a red thong and a garter belt, the lacy straps hugging her hips and accentuating her curves.

"Fuck, you're gorgeous," I tell her, my voice strained as

her hands explore every inch of her skin. "Emma," I warn, my cock throbbing with anticipation of having her again.

Together, we're electric and consuming.

Her fingers slide between her legs, and she whispers a moan that sends a jolt straight to my core. "This could be you."

I lean against the counter, downing the rest of my drink desperately trying to cool the fire blazing inside of me. She slips her fingers inside her pussy before placing them in her mouth. "Mm. Don't you want a taste? I'm so fucking wet for you, Hudson."

The alcohol burns my throat as I move past Emma, her intoxicating scent lingering in the air. "Well, good night."

She groans, and for a moment, I think she might throw a fit like a child denied a toy. "That didn't even break you?"

"I warned you I was a player in a past life," I say, taking the stairs two at a time. "I know the game, babe. Sexy as hell, but no means *no*."

"You're frustrating!" she calls after me, her voice a mix of annoyance and longing.

"I warned you about that too. And yet, you're still here. You're obsessed with the chase, Em. Like a goddamn addict."

She groans as I ascend the stairs, and I know I need to keep my distance before she breaks down my defenses. Emma is drunk and needy, a dangerous combination that threatens to consume us both. When we're together again, it won't be lost in a haze of alcohol and unspoken desires. We both deserve to fully experience the weight of our connection and feel its strength without the blur of impaired inhibitions. Last time was...*earth-shattering*.

I step into my room, shedding my clothes as I head to the bathroom. My cock throbs as I step under the hot stream; the hot water cascades over my skin. With a firm grip, I lose myself in thoughts of Emma.

Her name escapes my lips, and the image of her pretty lips

dances in my mind. The taste of our slow, passionate kisses has me nearly losing myself. I still remember the sound she made the first time I made her come. Her moans still echo in my ears. I recall how she tasted on my tongue—sweet and intoxicating.

We agreed to keep what we shared a secret—a careless deal made in the heat of the moment. But that night, our hearts truly bonded; together, we became something *more*. Yet she left unexpectedly the next day, departing without explanation and leaving my world incomplete.

I think about her grinding against me, her body slick with heat, my name escaping her lips like an incantation. It stirs something primal within me—a hunger that will never fade. The fact that she returned only adds fuel to the fire wreaking havoc on my thoughts.

My breathing quickens, and the orgasm rips through me, tearing through my body with an unspeakable force. Words don't exist, and I groan loudly, hoping she doesn't hear me. I stroke hard and long, every movement electric, the sensation nearly taking me to my knees. I brace myself against the bathroom wall, fighting pleasure. I've never come so fucking hard in my life.

"I'm in love," I whisper to myself, the realization crashes into me. "Fuck. Fuck. Fuck."

Elated yet terrified, I dry off and pull on some joggers, my mind still fogged with thoughts of her. I realize I left my phone on the kitchen counter, so I head that way.

The sound of running water fills the silence around me. When I pass Emma's door, I hear her cry out—a moan that sends a jolt of panic through my veins. I push the bedroom door open wider, my heart racing. When I catch a glimpse of her in the bathtub, I freeze. My breath catches in my throat as I realize her hand is between her legs.

"Yes, yes," she gasps, lifting her long leg onto the lip of the tub and rocking her hips. Water sloshes slightly as she works herself, urgency evident in her movements. Her back arches and the sight quickens my pulse.

"Fuck. *Hudson*," she whispers my name, breathy and pleading. "*Hudson*."

Against my better judgment, I move closer. I should turn away, allow her the moment.

"Emma," I manage to say, my voice steady despite the turmoil inside me.

Suddenly, she screams, water splashing onto the floor, surprise evident in her wide eyes. A rubber ducky is clutched in her hand. Its bright yellow color stark against the white tub.

"Oh my fucking God!" she exclaims, grabbing one of her shampoo bottles and hurling it in my direction.

"You summoned me," I reply, crossing my arms over my chest.

I glance down at the duck, its mouth moving as if it holds the secrets of our twisted encounter. "Is that a sex toy?"

Her cheeks heat with embarrassment.

"Fuck, babe. Don't you dare stop on my behalf."

Her eyes darken, an invitation wrapped in desire, as she slowly licks her lips. I lean against the vanity, my breath caught as she slides the ducky back down to her clit.

"What were you thinking about?" I ask, leaning into the moment and savoring every second.

She gasps, fucking that little duck's mouth. In the back of my mind, I know I'll be jacking off again before bed—there's no doubt about that.

"Your mouth on me," she confesses, desire spills from her lips with each ragged breath. "The first time we were together."

"I wanted you the moment I saw you," she admits. The tension between us is palpable as we walk through the door of Claire's house. Our mouths are desperate, our hands greedy, and the air is thick with desire.

217

"I felt that, too," I admit. It was as if the entire world tilted when our gazes locked, a sudden shift, one I couldn't deny. Knowing she's Claire's little sister...

Emma rips open my shirt, buttons flying across the floor like confetti at a chaotic celebration. "I don't do flings," she says with fierce determination as my fingers thread through those wild strands. "You're the exception."

"Keep it that way," I demand, kissing the inside of her neck. She gasps as I savor the taste of her sweet skin. Emma removes her shirt and carelessly tosses it aside, leaving it in a heap on the floor.

Claire moved out months ago, leaving this place echoing with memories, but it has been vacant since December. The Christmas decorations still loom in the space. Decorations hang like ghosts of holidays past.

Emma reaches for my jeans. "I want to lick every fucking ridge of you," she breathes out.

I pull away from her, abruptly aware of the uncharted territory we're entering. "You told me your dumb as fuck rules. Are you sure you can handle this? The next time I see you, are you certain you want me to pretend like this never happened?"

"Yes, it's for the best," she asserts, a determined glint in her eye as she slips out of her tiny shorts. The fabric falls away, revealing her smooth skin.

I kiss her passionately, pouring all my pent-up desire into every breath, wanting to savor every inch of her. It may be our first time together, but I'm convinced she's my soul mate.

"Fuck, Hudson," Emma groans, pulling me from my memory.

"Come for me," I whisper, my voice low and coaxing as she teeters on the edge of ecstasy.

She hisses through clenched teeth. "I'm...so close."

"You're so sexy," I growl.

Her body seizes and convulses as she rides the waves of pleasure.

"Hudson," she whispers, her eyes traveling up my body, filled with vulnerability and intensity. "I'm already addicted to you."

I inhale deeply. "All you have to do is stay."

"Then ask me to."

I move toward the tub and bend over, kissing her sweetly, leaving a lingering taste of hope and desire. I needed it as much as she did. "I'll never ask you to stay if you want to go. That's a decision you have to make on your own."

I pull away from her, seeking clarity in chaos. "I'm gonna grab my phone and another glass of eggnog. Want one?"

Her breasts rise and fall with each breath. "Yes, please. Just how Mawmaw makes it."

CHAPTER 22

EMMA

I lie back in the tub, allowing the blue bubbles and water to surround me. The warmth of the bath embraces me, and the alcohol still swims through my blood. My mind's delightfully calm as I sink deeper into its welcoming depths. Steam rises around me, curling and twisting in the air like delicate, ethereal fingers, creating a hazy veil that softens the stark edges of reality.

I close my eyes, letting the world around me fade into nothingness, as I think of the man who's haunted my thoughts since July. An effortless smile creeps across my lips as I imagine him—*us*.

Every memory of him sends a rush of heat through my veins, igniting a fire deep within. I want him so fucking bad it hurts—a longing that feels raw and insatiable. I can no longer pretend he isn't the man I've been searching for my entire life. Need and want grip my heart with fierce urgency, an unfamiliar sensation that both scares and exhilarates me. No man has ever affected me as profoundly as Hudson does. I crave him mentally, emotionally, and physically, a desperation that leaves me breathless.

Once I'm relaxed, I climb out of the tub, water trickling

down my skin in a gentle cascade. I reach for the plush blue towel on the counter, its softness beckoning me. After drying off, I slip into pajama shorts and a tank top. I remove my contacts, blinking hard to regain clarity before sliding on my glasses. The world blurs for a moment, then sharpens into focus, revealing the familiar surroundings of my room.

Over my shoulder, in the mirror's reflection, I catch sight of Hudson standing in the doorway. The light from the hallway frames his silhouette perfectly. A sly smile spreads across his lips, hinting at unspoken thoughts that make my heart race. If only I had the power to read his mind.

"I didn't know you wore glasses," he says, his voice smooth and casual yet laced with intrigue. In each hand, he holds a glass of eggnog.

"There's a lot you don't know about me." Our gazes lock in the mirror as I finish towel-drying my hair. Damp strands fall into place around my shoulders, framing my face. His intense gaze makes it hard to concentrate on anything else.

The thrill of his eyes on me nearly pulls me under. He's a current, drawing me deeper into a sea of unspoken words and shared secrets, an anchor holding me close, yet just beyond reach.

"What are you thinking about?" he asks, his voice low and inviting, as if drawing me into a world meant only for us. That tantalizing world can exist, can't it?

I chew on my lip, contemplating his question, my heart racing as I turn to face him. His presence wraps around me like a blanket, and I can almost taste the longing hanging in the air, sweet and intoxicating.

"You. Us. That night and how the stars aligned," I reply, my voice barely above a whisper.

I step into the dingy bar tucked on the edge of Main Street and Hot Cocoa Lane. The low lights cast a yellow glow, enveloping the room in an inviting hue that beckons weary souls. A faint trace of stale tobacco lingers in the air—a nostalgic remnant from the days when patrons could smoke freely indoors. Nostalgia wafts through the dimly lit space, transporting me to a time when laughter and clinking glasses filled the air, painting memories I can almost touch.

Tonight, I plan to drink until I'm tipsy and then stumble the three short blocks back to Claire's place, where I'm staying while I'm in Texas. Navigating the busy streets of New York after a few too many drinks is a challenge that I've mastered over the years. Merryville, with its quaint charm and slower pace, feels like a mere blip on my radar—an easy stroll compared to the chaos I usually navigate.

I've only been in town for two days, and my emotions are still in a whirlwind. Watching Claire get engaged, the golden glow of happiness surrounding her, was overwhelming enough. Meeting her fiancé—seeing the way they looked at each other, eyes bright with love—jolted my cold heart alive. And then, there was Hudson.

He's the first man in years who's made me take a second glance, stirring feelings inside me that I thought had died. The attraction was immediate and intense. Everything about him felt illicit, tempting me to consider reckless choices I would likely regret in the light of day. Or would I?

Suddenly, the bell above the door jingles, a cheerful sound that catches my attention. As I turn my head, I see Hudson Jolly—a vision as if he had been conjured from my very thoughts. His presence is magnetic.

"Fuck," I whisper as the air crackles with electricity.

His eyes lock onto mine, a moment heavy with unspoken words and potential. But just as quickly, he turns away, pretending he didn't see me. Deep down, I know he definitely did, but I don't take it personally; it's probably for the best, a protective wall against whatever this is.

I unlock my phone, the bright screen nearly blinding me in the low-lit bar, and text my best friends in our group chat, my heart racing.

EMMA

So, hypothetically speaking...

BILLIE

Oh God, here we go.

HARPER

Let her finish.

EMMA

If you met a really hot man who made you want to throw your rules out the window for one night, would you?

HARPER

How hot is he?

I pick up my Cosmo, the vibrant pink liquid swirling enticingly in the glass. I take a big gulp, enjoying the sweetness, then reply.

EMMA

Scorching.

HARPER

And he's single?

EMMA

Confirmed.

BILLIE

Who is he?

Just then, the stool beside me slides out, and Hudson settles into it, a relaxed confidence radiating from him. My nerves flutter like a thousand moths trapped in a jar as I lock my phone. His mere presence is overwhelming. The scent of his cologne grabs me—an intoxicating rich blend of cedar and something sweet, perhaps peppermint?

"You can't sit next to me and not speak," I say, surprising myself as

I find my confidence. His drink is placed in front of him, and I can't help but think it must be easy to remember what the locals order in a cozy small town like this. "We'll practically be related soon," I add, a teasing lilt to my voice.

He lets out a low, playful hum and brings his perfect lips to the rim of his glass. His relaxed demeanor makes my heart race because he's unaffected by me. I can't tear my gaze away from him; an invisible thread connects us.

"If you don't stop looking at me like that," he warns, his gravelly voice sending shivers down my spine and causing my heart to stutter.

"Then what?" I challenge, raising an eyebrow. "What will you do?"

He smirks, a playful glint igniting in his eyes, and the sexual tension nearly smothers me.

"Well?" I ask innocently, forcing myself to maintain a brave front.

"Be careful, Emma. You're gonna fuck around and find out."

"I want to learn everything about you," Hudson admits, his sexy voice pulling me back into the moment.

"I have nothing to hide from you," I reply sincerely, my heartbeat steadying as I lock my gaze on his. "Ask me anything. Anytime. I'll tell you the truth. Always."

His eyes sparkle with curiosity and charm, making him nearly impossible to resist. "Would you like to watch a movie with me?"

I laugh, not expecting that. "Sure."

I enjoy seeing him like this—carefree as if all the weight of the world has been lifted off his shoulders. This side of him suits him perfectly.

"Every season, I have a list of Christmas movies I watch. I wanna start at the top tonight." He pauses as he studies my expression. "Why are you looking at me like that?" A playful grin spreads across his chiseled face.

"You seem..." I shake my head, searching for the right word, "Happy."

The mood shifts and the air thickens. "Right now, I am."

I move closer to him, allowing our arms to brush together. I take a sip, savoring the rich flavors swirling in the eggnog. "Mm. I might be addicted..."

"The nog is good," he replies, a hint of pride in his voice. "Can only get this brand in Texas."

"To you," I add.

A cute-as-fuck smirk pulls at his lips, and it's exhilarating. He gently tucks damp hair behind my ear, his touch sending a shiver down my spine. "Are you happy?"

"Right now, I am," I repeat his words back to him, a smile playing on my lips. "What's your favorite holiday movie?" My curiosity piques, and I'm eager to hear his choice.

"Die Hard," he declares, taking a gulp of his nog as if it's the most natural answer in the world.

I scoff, a smile tugging at the corners of my lips as I shake my head. "That's not a Christmas movie."

"You gonna die on that hill?"

"Uh, yes," I say firmly. "Not a Christmas movie and never will be."

"Good. Was making sure you're not one of those weirdos who think it is." He winks at me, adding a layer of playfulness to the moment. "Tonight we're watching *Home Alone 2*."

"I love that one. The pigeon lady gets me every time," I admit.

Hudson grabs my hand, interlocking his fingers with mine in a simple yet electrifying gesture. I don't know if the eggnog is to blame or Hudson. Maybe both, but mostly him.

No one has ever chosen me like this when we're alone, and the feeling is both exhilarating and terrifying.

I'm falling in love with this man.

He leads me down the low-lit hallway, and the faint scent of his soap lingers in the air like an invisible trace, making the atmosphere even more intimate. When we reach the door to his room, he pauses.

A mix of excitement and hesitation swirls within me. This is his bedroom, and it's not lost on me how damn sacred it is. Has he allowed another woman in here with him?

"Wait, you want some popcorn?" he asks, his voice filled with genuine consideration.

"Oh my God, yes," I reply, unable to suppress the smile that spreads across my face. "With butter?"

"Of fucking course. Is there any other way to eat it?" he asks, opening the door and leading me inside. As I step over the threshold, the scent of cedar and something faintly floral floats through the air as I cross the threshold.

Windows overlook the backyard where the moon's glow casts long, silvery shadows across the grass. A fireplace anchors the room, its mantle adorned with pictures of happiness—Colby's smile captured in joyful moments. Above it hangs an oversized TV displaying a fireplace screensaver, the flickering flames adding to the cozy ambiance.

"I'll be right back. Get comfy," Hudson says, his voice playful yet soothing.

"Okay," I reply, feeling a mix of anticipation and nervousness wash over me. He releases my hand, leaving a lingering sense of loss in its wake. My eyes remain locked on him as he turns away, and before he disappears from view, he glances back, his expression softening. I smile, and it's immediately returned, that shared moment amplifying the unspoken connection between us.

I drink my eggnog, realizing it's already halfway gone. With a swift gulp, I down the rest and place the glass on his nightstand with a gentle clink that reverberates. I fall back onto his big bed, giddy like a teenager with a crush. The blankets are fluffy, inviting, and the pillows—a festive assortment in shades of cream, red, and green—seem to beckon me into their embrace.

The comforter faintly smells like him, a blend of his cologne and the faintest hint of laundry detergent, and it brings an overwhelming sense of comfort. I close my eyes, letting the plushness hug me.

I'm falling for him way too fast, and if I don't take control, I'll spiral out of control. But would that really be so bad?

"Em, are you asleep?" he gently whispers, his strong hand resting reassuringly on my thigh.

My eyes flutter open, slightly disoriented, as I shake off the remnants of sleep.

"Was I snoring?" I ask, half-laughing, the sound almost musical in the quiet space.

His brows raise in mock disbelief, that playful glint in his eyes making my heart skip a beat. "You snore?"

"Only when I'm drunk or exhausted," I explain, finally sitting upright. My head is woozy, a swirling fog that makes the room tilt slightly. When I stand, I stumble into him, giggles spilling out of me like effervescent bubbles.

"Yep, drunk," he says, his firm hand steadying me on my waist. Hudson glances at the empty glass on his nightstand, a knowing smile creeping onto his lips. "You're supposed to drink it slowly. Savor it."

"Not sure if you noticed." I hiccup, feeling a wave of embarrassment mixed with amusement. "I don't do anything slow. Not my style."

The delicious aroma of buttery popcorn wafts from a gigantic bowl. The scents are so inviting that I can almost taste the salt and butter on my tongue. Steam rises from the top, curling into the air, reaching forward like it's beckoning for me to grab a few kernels. So I do.

"Would you prefer to go to sleep?" He studies me, his gaze penetrating yet gentle, searching for an answer in my eyes.

"Hell no. I can hang, promise," I say with a nod, my confidence unwavering despite the slight wobble in my stance.

"On the bed then." His Southern drawl is sexy as sin.

"Mm. Kinda like when you say it like that," I reply playfully, a smile tugging at my lips.

I scoot to the middle of the bed, and Hudson laughs, the sound rich. He hands me the popcorn and adjusts the pillows behind me, creating a cozy nook where we can comfortably sit upright. I'm grateful for the carbs to soak up some of this alcohol because my head is swimming. He effortlessly slides in next to me until our bodies fully touch.

"Comfortable?" he asks, and our arms brush together, sending a flutter of butterflies in my stomach.

"Yes," I breathlessly reply, the word slipping out like a secret.

With a click of a button, the recessed lights lower, casting an intimate glow around us. He leans closer, his shoulder pressing against mine, making my heart race. The TV illuminates the dark room, its flickering light painting our faces in shadows as he starts the movie.

I hold the popcorn and the large bowl on my lap. Anytime he's near, his presence draws me in, making it hard to focus on anything else.

"The movie is that way," he says, pointing forward as he throws popcorn upward. He catches it with his mouth.

His perfect smile captures me, and his green eyes sparkle with mischief.

"You're captivating," I whisper, the words tumbling out before I can stop them.

He studies me, his eyes sliding down to my lips over to my neck. "Shit, those marks are dark," he comments, a smirk dancing at the corners of his lips.

My hand slams over the hickeys, my cheeks heating with embarrassment. "I forgot that I'm supposed to kick your ass for that."

A hearty laugh escapes his throat. "You can owe me one."

"I owe you two! Look at them!" I insist, pointing exactly where they are, a mixture of indignation and laughter coloring my words.

228

He leans over and peppers kisses on top of the marks, his lips teasing my skin. "I'd apologize, but you fucking loved it."

"I did." I rest my head on his shoulder, welcoming his touch as he wraps his arm around me. We fall into a comfortable silence; the screen illuminates our faces as Kevin McCallister's mother realizes her son is missing. This scene parallels my past, and I can't help the ache in my chest.

"As a parent, this is my worst fear," Hudson murmurs, his voice low and rich with empathy.

"It's because you're an incredible dad." My throat tightens slightly. "It happened to me when I was thirteen. Claire had moved out to go to university. It was just me and Dad after Mom passed away. He would book vacations for the holidays, but he was rarely present. I boarded the wrong private jet, full of my father's business executives, and ended up in Tokyo."

Hudson turns to me, his jaw clenched, and I can see the concern etched on his face. "How did your father not notice?"

"I was forgotten about many times, and I still carry a world of resentment for it. No one has *ever* made me feel important or prioritized me—not even my dad," I admit, forcing a smile. The words feel heavy on my tongue, a weight that threatens to spill over. Sometimes the truth is ugly, but I've stopped making excuses for him, allowing myself to face the painful reality.

"That changes now," he states, matter-of-factly.

"I want to believe you," I say, holding on to every word he says. I clear my throat, the memories swirl uncomfortably in my mind. "It's why I do things alone now. I can always depend on myself. I won't ever let myself down."

"I'm sorry you experienced that. You deserved and currently deserve better," he says, holding me a little tighter. His touch is a soft barrier against the waves of old memories crashing down around us, reminding me of how drastically my life changed after my mother's death.

"Thank you. I have a confession to make," I add, wanting to change the subject. "The Lucas thing was a prank."

"I know," he says, his fingertips trailing down my arms, sending shivers up my spine. Goosebumps form along my skin, a tangible sign of the emotions stirring within me.

"But you were still jealous?" I ask, my voice barely above a whisper.

"Yes, because Lucas would be good for you. I know that. And my brother is an incredible person—caring, responsible. No emotional baggage. Or kids. He loves hard. Whoever he ends up with will be very lucky. He'll put her on a pedestal and worship the ground she walks on. Even if it was a joke, I could see him making you really fucking happy. And... I want that for you, Emma. But I want to try to be the one to make you happy. I was jealous that I might not get that opportunity."

I can't help but smile, warmth spreading through me like sunlight breaking through clouds. "Hudson," I mutter. "You might be the only man who can."

A spark of hope reflects in his eyes and I want to kiss him so damn bad, but I'm trying hard to respect his boundaries. No means no.

"I honestly thought it was obvious that grumpy single dad lumberjack with a chip on his shoulder is my type."

"Oh really?" This earns me a genuine laugh from him, the sound infectious.

"I'm sorry if I hurt you," I admit, biting my lip in remorse.

"You didn't and don't apologize, please. This is how my brothers and I are with each other. We push hard. And eventually, I'll get him back tenfold. He fucked around and will absolutely find out when he's interested in someone."

My mouth falls open in disbelief. "Oh my God. You're evil."

"No, I'm not. But he started something that I will finish. I have older sibling duties to uphold."

We continue munching on popcorn, and I can't help but laugh when Tim Curry makes his grand entrance. "I love him," I say, my heart lifting with the familiar joy he brings.

"Me too," Hudson agrees, sharing the moment with me.

I don't remember the last time I sat down and watched anything. Life has been a whirlwind of travel, social media, and avoiding my emotions—the endless list weighing heavy on my shoulders.

"What?" he asks, glancing at me. "You tensed."

Of course, he noticed. He always does.

"It was nothing."

"Lie."

I exhale slowly, the weight of the moment pressing down on my chest. "This is the first time I've relaxed and laughed in years. When I'm with you, I have no worries."

Hudson leans over and kisses my forehead, his lips brushing against my skin in a gesture that feels both tender and grounding. "You're already the calm in my storm, Em. Let me be the calm in yours."

CHAPTER 23

HUDSON

The credits roll, and Emma's sound asleep. Her lips are slightly parted, and she looks like she doesn't have a care in the world. Her chest rises and falls in a calming rhythm. A glow from the screen highlights the gentle curve of her cheek, and I can't help but notice how peaceful she looks. What's she dreaming about? Me?

A smile touches my lips as I watch her, and the moment grabs me in a chokehold. I wonder if I can be the man who makes her happy. She deserves someone who appreciates her and chooses her every fucking time.

Emma could have anyone in the world—not an exaggeration—yet she still chose me. Call me cocky, but I don't ask why—I *know* what I bring to the table. And so does she.

Waking her when she's sleeping so peacefully almost seems cruel. I linger for a moment, admiring her as I watch her breathe. This is a memory I want to remember, one I'll visit on dark, lonely nights.

I reach forward, gently removing the glasses from her pretty face, and place them on the nightstand.

"Mm," she murmurs. Carefully, I slide the decorative

pillows from under her, the fabric whispering against the sheets as I lightly toss them onto the floor. Then, I lift the comforter over her. I've had plenty of practice doing this with Colby. If I've learned anything, you should never wake a sleeping baby.

Emma rolls onto her side, getting comfortable. Her wavy hair splays against the pillow.

I turn off the TV, and the sudden silence is almost palpable. Moonlight filters through the room, and I gather the empty popcorn bowl and our glasses. Once downstairs, the spiced rum calls me from the counter where I left it. Its amber hue glistens in the overhead light, and I take two long pulls. The liquid burns as it slides down my throat. It may be harsh, but it does the job of relaxing my mind. Or so I thought.

I lean against the counter, recalling my past while trying to predict my future. The night Emma and I spent together during the summer was so fucking magical that it continues to swirl in my mind. Being with Emma changed me, and I'm a different man, a better man because of her.

I freeze, staring at the harsh glow of the overhead lights that flicker off and on. The sound of the strong wind howling outside pulls me from my thoughts. I turn toward the windows overlooking the backyard. Tree branches whip violently in the gusts, their silhouettes casting eerie shadows on the ground. Almost on cue, heavy rain begins to pour. The rhythmic drumming against the roof creates a symphony that soothes and unnerves me.

The town folk were made aware of the cold front moving through with freezing conditions. Yesterday, I stocked up on food to last us for two weeks, but our outages never last that long. The temperatures are near freezing, but the rain stalled yesterday. It arrived with gusto.

"Shit," I mutter as the potted plants tumble off my back porch, their ceramic bodies crashing to the ground. The wind chimes, usually a source of gentle music, now clash violently together, creating a discordant symphony in the howling wind. Just then, the power cuts out, plunging everything into darkness. I find my way back to my room, each step uncertain, but that could be the spiced rum taking hold.

The backup generator hums to life almost immediately. I relax, knowing our food won't spoil.

Quietly, I enter my room. Moonlight spills through the oversized windows, splashing across the floor in silvery hues as I move toward the bed where Emma still sleeps. I slide beneath the blankets beside her, feeling warmth radiate from her body. She instinctively scoots closer, placing her arm over my stomach. Her breath tickles my skin as she nuzzles into me, seeking comfort.

"Good night," I whisper, brushing my fingers through her hair. She doesn't respond, already too lost in her dreams.

I hold her like she might disappear in the middle of the night. With her in my arms, the weight of the day finally crashes over me. And despite the storm raging outside, the world quickly fades away. I instantly fall asleep.

When I wake, for once, I feel rested. I reach over, my palm rubbing across the sheets where Emma was, and it's cold. The sheets are slightly rumpled, and the faint scent of her bubble gum bubble bath lingers in the air.

When did she wake? The question hangs in my mind.

I reach over to click on the bedside lamp, but it does nothing. The room remains shrouded in shadow, the morning light struggles to penetrate through the clouds.

"Great," I mutter, the cool air brushing against my skin when I sit up. I grab my phone from the bedside table, the screen illuminating my face with a harsh glow. It's just past six, and I have already missed notifications.

I check my texts.

MAMA

> Power is out, thanks to high winds. Ice is on the way. The farm's closed until it's safe for people to travel on the roads. Announcement has already been posted. I'd bring Colby home, but some down trees are blocking the driveway.

HUDSON

> He's safe with you for now. Need me to come over and help with the trees?

My parents are early birds, so I'm not surprised when her text bubble pops up.

MAMA

> No. Lucas is taking care of it as soon as he can since he's closer.

HUDSON

> Let me know when it's clear, and I'll come get Colby so you don't have to leave.

MAMA

> I will. How are things there?

HUDSON

> Not sure. Haven't been outside yet.

I slide out of bed, and the morning air's chill wraps around me. It's fucking cold in here. I move to the window and see tiny ice pellets cascading down like a curtain of shimmering crystals. The brunt of the storm hasn't arrived yet. This sleet is a prelude to the chaos that's sure to come.

I hear the water shut off in my bathroom, and the door creaks open moments later.

"Hi," Emma says.

I turn to face her, my gaze flickering down from her bright eyes to her perky little nipples, barely concealed by the thin fabric of her tank top, before returning to her mouth. She leans against the door jamb, her silhouette framed by the muted light of the overcast morning. I drink in every single curve, how her hair falls around her shoulders, the rosy hue of her cheeks.

She's *breathtaking*.

"Hi," I reply, my voice rough from sleep.

When she shivers slightly, I pull a quilt from the wooden storage chest at the end of my bed, feeling its weight in my hands. I move to her, wrapping it gently over her shoulders. "I'm sorry. The electricity is out. Could be like this for a few days."

"Days?" she looks up at me, her expression a mix of surprise and concern, then glances down at the blanket. "Did Mawmaw make this?"

"Yes," I say, chuckling at the memory of my grandmother's hands stitching the quilt together with love and care. "It was a gift."

"For what?" she asks.

I swallow down the lump in my throat. "It was a wedding gift, to be specific, but Meredith hated it despite it holding sentimental value. It was special to me."

"It's beautiful. These specific flowers are her style." A warm smile spreads across her face as she runs her fingers along the intricate patterns of the fabric. "Why do you keep it locked away?"

I don't know how to answer that, so I say nothing.

"Well, you shouldn't hide it. That's all I'm saying," she

says. The quilt is a piece of home, and it holds a reminder of comforting memories woven into every stitch.

"You're absolutely right about that," I admit, the tension easing slightly as I contemplate her words.

Emma reaches for her head, a playful frown creasing her brow. "Ugh. I think I drank too much last night."

"I was worried that would happen. Let's get you some coffee, water, and food."

"Yes, please." Her hand reaches upward and runs her gentle fingertips down my chest. Goosebumps trail over my skin, which always happens when she touches me.

"Are you cold? You've got chill bumps. I'll share my quilt with you," she says. The considerate offer makes my heart thump a little harder. She's always so considerate.

"It's not the temperature, Em," I say, meeting her eyes, hoping she understands the unspoken meaning behind my words.

A grin meets her lips, and she pulls her arm from the quilt. "You do the same to me."

"We're fucked," I tell her, the gravity of our situation settling in.

"I know," she replies, chuckling as if the absurdity of it all is both terrifying and exhilarating. Emma moves beside the bed, snagging her glasses and slipping them onto her face. "Wow, it's like viewing the world in 8K. Now your face isn't blurry."

I smile at her. "Breakfast time, babe."

"Am I on the menu?" she asks playfully, a teasing glint in her eye. "Because I'd love to be."

I glance at her, curiosity piqued. "Is that your answer?"

"I told you last night, I want you sober or drunk. Doesn't matter, Hudson. I know what I want for Christmas."

My brows quirk up, amusement dancing in my gaze.

"You," she states, her voice sultry and direct. "I want you for the holidays. Do I need to sit on Santa's lap and ask? I know I've been a bad fucking girl, but I promise to be *very* good the rest of the year."

I narrow my eyes at her, my heart racing as I move closer. She takes a step back, her body pressing against the cool wall behind her. A delicious but dangerous temptation lingers between us. I breathe her in, reveling in how sweet she smells. I kiss along her neck, feeling her shiver beneath my touch.

"Are you sure I'm what you want?" I ask.

"Not a single doubt," she confirms, a gasp escaping her as she drops the quilt onto the floor. The fabric pools around our feet. "Kiss me, please."

"I fucking love it when you use your manners."

Her fingers thrust through my hair, and our lips crash together in a fiery, desperate union. Greedy little pants escape from her throat, and I think I might stop breathing as we spiral into the abyss together. Her moan is a confession, audible proof that she's mine.

"I need you, Hudson. Begging isn't below me."

"Mm." My voice is low and teasing, but she surprises me as she falls to her knees. Emma looks up at me with those bright brown eyes behind black-framed glasses. Her expression is full of desire. She licks her plump lips, and my breath catches. The charged air swirls around us, and every cell in my body awakens.

"I want to be yours for the holidays, *pretty please?*" Her hands slide up my thighs, sending jolts of electricity through me.

"Emma," I growl, the sound pulling from deep within me as she peels my joggers down, releasing my cock. Her back straightens, and she looks up at me, silently asking for permission.

"I need *you* so fucking bad," she whispers. Her tongue flicks across my tip, and my eyes slam shut. "May I have you?"

I study her, brushing my thumb against her cheeks. A world of emotions mixes with the silent conversation we share.

This woman is my everything, and I knew that the first night we were together. Denying her means denying us the possibility of true happiness, but more importantly, love.

"I've been yours since July," I admit, hardly able to contain the rush of sensations that flood me.

"I've been yours, too," she says.

The confession is music to my fucking ears.

Emma stands, capturing my mouth again. We stumble backward to the bed until my ass presses against the mattress. We climb onto the bed and Emma takes me into her greedy mouth. She licks up and down my shaft with her tongue, moving slowly like she's memorizing every vein.

"Fuck," I hiss out, the word escapes like a prayer.

The early morning sunlight makes the room hazy, and I almost pinch myself to make sure I'm not dreaming. Her hands trail up my stomach and under my hoodie as she tweaks one of my nipples.

"Mm." She strokes me long and slow with her hand. "So much pre-cum."

She licks the cum that pooled on my dick. "I love the way you taste."

I run my fingers through her hair, gripping it tightly as she returns her mouth to me. She bobs up and down, nearly choking, trying to take me all in.

"Come here," I whisper, and Emma defiantly takes me to the back of her throat before doing as I ask. She lays on the pillow beside me, and I roll onto my side, fully facing her.

My hand trails down her body, fingers grazing her smooth skin as I slide into her panties. Her breathing grows ragged as her beautiful brown eyes lock onto mine. A silent agreement passes between us—a commitment.

For how long? I don't know. It's something I'll think about later.

"So fucking wet for me," I murmur, feeling the heat

radiate from her. We both know she wants and desperately needs it.

"Always," she mutters, her breath quickening as I gently tap my fingers against her clit. She pants, arching her back and pressing her pussy upward, seeking more of the pleasure she craves.

"There are rules, Emma. If you're mine, you're *mine.* I don't know how to share," I say, my voice low and intense.

"Agreed," she whispers, her voice barely above a breath as she removes her glasses.

I swirl my fingers in tight circles around her sensitive nub, a rhythm that matches her eagerness.

"We should keep this to ourselves. It will be easier when you leave," I say, hoping she understands the weight of my words. If she wants and needs an out, I will give her one.

"I don't know what the future holds," she says.

"I know. Also, we have to be careful in front of Colby."

"Of course," she replies, her tone shifting slightly, a hint of seriousness threading through her words. "Being with me also comes with consequences, Hudson. I don't want that to scare you, but we'll be watched, and privacy doesn't ex—"

"I know what I'm getting myself into. It's us against the world, Emma. Me and you. We can handle anything together." The declaration hangs in the air; a magnetic force intertwines us.

"Do you promise?" Her voice is barely above a whisper, tinged with vulnerability.

"Until my last fucking breath," I tell her.

She pulls me back to her mouth, but my lips hover above hers. We're frozen in time, and the world around us fades into a distant memory.

"I'm falling in love with you, Hudson," she whispers, her breath warm against my skin.

"Oh, Emma," I barely say, pulling back so I can meet her eyes. She smiles as if she already knows the secret I've kept.

My heart beats harder in my chest, resonating with the truth of the situation.

We're falling in love.

"Me too," I admit, a secret only we share. Our lips dance together slowly, a gentle exploration that feels electrifying and tender. I'm convinced she has me under her spell. Each brush of her tongue against mine nearly takes me under.

I kiss along her jaw and neck, peeling up her tank top with a gentle tug. My lips travel down her flat stomach, leaving a trail of warmth in their wake as I remove the tiny shorts from her body.

"No panties," I murmur, not surprised by the revelation.

"I hardly ever wear them," she admits, a playful glint in her eyes. It's a fact I file away for later as a smirk slides over my lips. I move between her legs and continue my trail of kisses to her pretty little pussy. With my tongue, I slowly part her, savoring the taste of her and the intoxicating scent of her arousal.

She sighs as I apply more pressure, flicking my tongue over her sensitive clit. Her fingers tangle in my hair, urging me closer. She pushes me against her, lost in the sensation as she rides against the scruff on my chin. And while I want her to fuck my face, not yet.

For once, Emma isn't in control. *I am.*

I shake my head, pulling back just a bit and sucking her hard, reveling in the sounds of her pleasure. "Patience, or I'll edge you all fucking day," I warn, my voice low and teasing, as I slowly slide a finger inside her tight cunt.

Long moans escape her lips, a melody of desire that only encourages me to continue.

Emma writhes under me, responding to my touch, and I curl my finger, teasingly tickling her G-spot. I fucking love watching her body arch in response to the growing waves of pleasure building within her.

"Every time I touch myself, I think of you," she admits,

her voice trembling with vulnerability. "Of being with you again. Just like this."

I kiss the softness of her inner thighs, savoring the silky warmth of her skin against my lips. "So, I'm your fantasy?" I ask teasingly, my breath hot against her sensitive flesh.

"Yes." She sucks in a sharp breath as I slide two fingers inside her. She clenches around me like a vice, eager and responsive. Not to mention greedy.

"You're just in luck, sweetheart. Because you're mine, too." A surge of possessiveness takes over.

She smiles at me, her eyes shining with longing. "I need you inside me."

I can't wait—I won't wait. The urgency coursing through me is primal.

I slide off the bed, quickly remove my hoodie, and move closer to her. My cock waits, poised at her wet entrance, and I press my lips against hers for a brief, searing kiss before continuing.

"It's only been *you* since you," she whispers, her breath hitching in anticipation. Before me, it was her ex, no one else.

Knowing she waited for me, has me slamming deep inside her. She adjusts her body, widening her hips, wanting to take more of me in. Our ends meet and the world around me blurs. Stars explode behind my eyelids, and my head swims as we become one again. I groan, overwhelmed by the feeling that Emma is my home, the only woman I've ever truly belonged to.

"My other half," she says as if she can read my mind. Her voice is heavy with emotion as she rocks in rhythm with me. I go slow and hard, savoring every moment, sucking and nibbling on her neck, tasting the salt of her skin. Her moans grow louder, guttural, echoing in the space between us.

Being with her is an out-of-body experience that transcends time and space. It's an electric and eternal connection that pulses with every heartbeat, weaving our souls together in a mosaic of desire. I grunt, maintaining my rhythm, wanting her to feel how deep I'm inside her. I want her to know who she belongs to in every step she takes tomorrow.

"I'm so..." Her voice is barely audible, a breathy whisper lost in the haze of our movements. The air around us is thick with want, charged with desperate energy as we become something more than ourselves—animalistic, driven by an unquenchable thirst for pleasure as we chase our high. I will never, ever be able to get enough of her.

I tug on her earlobe with my teeth, then suck on it before I whisper, "Come for me, pretty girl. Come around my cock that's filling you so goddamn full right now."

As if I snapped my fingers, she surrenders to the wave of her orgasm, her body quaking with intensity.

Emma does exactly what I demanded, so I give her what she craves.

"Good girl," I growl as I gently squeeze her throat. I don't recognize the sounds that escape from her, but they're raw and primal. Her nails dig into my back, leaving trails of fire and satisfaction along my skin.

"Keep fucking me," she cries out, her voice a desperate plea filled with urgency. "Claim me, Hudson. Prove I'm really yours."

So, I do.

CHAPTER 24

EMMA

"I've missed you so fucking much," Hudson says, his mouth hovering at my ear, his breath warm against my skin as he slams into me like tomorrow will never come. If the world ends today, I'll die a happy woman knowing I had this moment with him *again*. The last time we were together is etched in my memory, a euphoric experience I'll never forget.

I saw what could've been between us, and it scared the shit out of me.

"I missed you, too," I admit. Goosebumps trail over my skin, a delightful shiver that reminds me this is exactly how it's supposed to be. Every sensation is heightened as we lose ourselves in this moment of passion.

My mouth falls open, and my back arches as the second orgasm rips through me like a wave crashing against the shore. Our pants and moans create a symphony of sounds, each note resonating with the intensity of our connection. He feels so good buried deep inside me, as if it's where he belongs—we're two puzzle pieces who fit perfectly, even with our jagged edges.

"I'm so fuckin' close," he mutters, his warm breath brushing against my skin. His movements slow down, as he

244

climbs to the edge. I savor every second as time seems to stand still.

"I'm still on birth control," I whisper, meeting his gaze, hoping he understands what I want. The fire behind his eyes ignites something deep within me, and I capture his lips. I pour every part of myself into him as the heady rush of desire fills the air around us.

"Em," he whispers, his voice low and filled with urgency.

"Please," I beg, my heart racing. "I want *all* of you, Hudson."

His breathing grows erratic. Each inhale is a reflection of the pleasure mounting within him. I can see the flush spreading across his cheeks and notice how his muscles tense in anticipation. And then, with a shudder that sends a thrill through me, he loses himself inside me. Waves of pleasure that crash over him and he moans out my name.

We remain connected, our bodies entwined as we lock eyes, the world around us fading into a blur. Everything else ceases to exist, leaving just the two of us suspended. I felt the major shift between us, and I think he did, too. That wasn't just two people having sex. It was too raw, too emotional, too *vulnerable*.

I'm convinced I'm having an out-of-body experience. Our breaths are ragged, and my heart thumps like a drum. Hudson watches me, his cock still buried deep inside me, as if he's tethering me to him forever.

Sex has never felt this good before; it's as if we were made for each other as if he were sculpted to satisfy me in ways I never thought possible. The incredible sex has left me stunned and silent, my body still tingling from every tantalizing touch.

"Did you feel it?" I ask, my voice still breathless. Lingering emotions wash over me like gentle waves on a warm shore. My body is buzzing.

"Yes," he admits, his gaze piercing into mine as he rubs his nose against mine, giving me sweet Eskimo kisses. His lips finally capture my own, sending another jolt of electricity through me. "Join me in the shower. It will be good for your trembling muscles."

"Okay," I reply, my heart fluttering. Hudson moves off me, but not before effortlessly lifting me into his arms and cradling me against his chest. I'm a ragdoll after that.

He carries me to the bathroom and gently sets me down. Seconds later, he turns on the shower, and the sound of cascading water surrounds us, filling the cool air with steam. We step inside, and I welcome the warmth.

He studies me with severe intensity as if trying to memorize every freckle on my face.

"Jake told me you were entering the Christmas cookie contest," he says in a low voice. He grabs the soap and begins washing over my shoulders, his strong hands kneading into my muscles.

I squeeze my thighs together, still feeling the remnants of pleasure pulsing within me, each movement a reminder of how much he stretched me to fit him.

"I am," I confirm, allowing my neck to roll lazily on my shoulders, savoring his touch.

"You're going down, Emma," he declares playfully, a smirk breaking across his lips.

I burst into laughter, the sound echoing off the tiled walls.

"No way! You're joining *my* team," I counter, grabbing a loofah and washing him. "Your grandma said that's what should happen. Don't want to disappoint her, do you?"

His large, calloused hand slides down to grip my ass, his palm warm and possessive. "That trophy is mine this year. You need to join *my* team."

"Oh my God. You're super competitive, too." I narrow my eyes playfully, then smirk mischievously, like the Grinch who's about to steal Christmas. "You're either with me or against me."

"I'm gonna tell Claire to take back her permission," he singsongs, his tone laced with teasing mischief.

I gasp. "You wouldn't!"

Hudson's lips trail across mine, leaving warmth in their wake. "Good luck, babe. You're gonna need it."

"The last time you said that to me, I—" Before I can finish, the power unexpectedly comes on.

"Weird," Hudson comments, glancing toward the bedroom. His eyes fixed on the recessed lighting, which had dimmed low while we were absorbed in our movie. I half-expect it to flicker off again, but it remains steady. He clears his throat, bringing my attention back to him. "Welp, I guess the power is back on. Amazing! It's a sign that you're going down!"

I smirk, my gaze sliding playfully to his cock, still rigid and inviting. "I'll go down on you anytime you want."

The air thickens between us as I lock eyes with his sexy grin.

"Anytime? Maybe we can try that soon." He pauses, a thoughtful look crossing his face. He grabs the shampoo, massaging my scalp with his strong fingers, sending tingles racing down my spine. My eyes roll back in pleasure, lost in the bliss of his touch.

"Do you want to keep us a secret until we figure out if this is forever?" he asks, his voice softened by vulnerability.

I give him a smile, feelings swirling inside me. "Do you think that's the best decision?"

There are benefits to not telling anyone. I've gone back and forth between the options and still don't know the correct answer.

"I don't want to, but I also think that everyone knowing will put unnecessary pressure on us," he explains, his voice steady but tinged with concern. "I want us to both be certain this is what we want. I want to enjoy you, Emma, without the weight of the world, at least while we can."

I brush my thumb gently against his cheek. My heart swells with a mixture of emotions. "Let's decide on New Year's Eve," I propose, my voice barely above a whisper. "I'm attending a friend's party. If you want me forever, be there and kiss me at midnight. And if not, then I'll know, and we won't have to endure the awkward goodbye. We can pretend nothing happened when and if we see each other again." The finality of my words hangs in the air. I might stop breathing.

Hudson's eyes, typically vibrant, reflect a depth of sadness. "Why are you leaving this up to me?"

"Because I've already made up my mind," I reply, my hands instinctively finding their way to his chest, feeling the rhythm of his heartbeat beneath my palms as the water streams over us. "And...don't say you have as well. I want you to contemplate being with me, Hudson. My life is chaotic, and yours will change forever once you're linked to me. You may decide it's best to stay single until Colby is older, or you may realize I'm not the person for you after this newness has worn off. You have to think about more than just yourself," I whisper, feeling the weight of my words settle between us.

He gently helps rinse the suds from my hair, his fingers tenderly gliding through the strands. "You're sure that's what you want?" he asks, his voice reverberating with concern.

"Yes," I respond firmly. "I can leave Texas with a grateful heart, cherishing what we had without the 'this was only temporary' talk. I want to avoid that conversation. My heart might not be able to handle it," I explain, my words painted with the colors of my apprehension.

"Okay," he agrees, the acceptance of my proposition is wrapped in a heavy silence. "And if I don't show up?"

"I'll start the new year with you as a beautiful memory, but in my past," I say, trying to mask the tremor in my voice. The thought of it nearly breaks my heart, twisting it like a taut string. It's a precarious leap into the unknown, and deep down, I wonder if I'm cut out for this. Regardless, I must prepare my heart, so it doesn't destroy me.

"Now, can we return to living in the moment where there's little to no pressure? Just us," I plead, craving simplicity.

"Just me and you," he murmurs against my lips.

He presses his palm against my cheek and kisses me sweetly, shielding us from everything outside. In this moment, the world fades away, leaving only the promise of the present hanging in the air.

CHAPTER 25

EMMA

ONE WEEK LATER

"Nice minivan," Hudson says after I park in the driveway, his voice breaking the comfortable silence surrounding his house. He sets the ax down with a thud that resonates in the crisp air, then removes his leather gloves. A pile of freshly chopped wood is stacked neatly next to the storage shed like a monument. I glance at the logs, then back at him, noticing how his broad shoulders relax as he approaches me.

"Aren't you supposed to be at lunch?" I ask, almost shocked to see him here. The midday sunlight casts a warm glow on his gorgeous face.

"This is how I'm spending it today," he explains.

"Everything okay?" I ask, my gaze narrowing, searching for signs beneath the confident exterior. He's so good at pretending everything is fine when it's not.

He tilts his head, a smile tugging at the corner of his lips. "Why would you ask that?"

"Lucas told me when you get stressed, you chop a lot of wood. Actually, he said you 'chop a *fuckton*.'"

Laughter erupts from his throat, rich and deep, as he

snakes his arm around my waist, pulling me closer. "It's cute you think that's a *fuckton*."

That cocky little smirk nearly brings me to my knees, erupting something playful and rebellious within me. I hold him close, hooking my fingers in the sturdy loops of his jeans as I look up at him. His eyes glimmer, and I don't want this moment to end.

I love how his cologne—a mix of cedar and something distinctly him—mingles with the faint scent of sweat, creating an intoxicating blend. He gazes down into my eyes, his expression earnest. "It's winter prep for when the real storm comes. I promise."

"If you were stressed, you'd tell me?" I ask, wanting to believe him but needing reassurance.

"Maybe," he says, his voice low as he slides his lips across mine, leaving me breathless, the world around us fading into a blur.

I scoff, regaining a sliver of composure. "Why maybe?"

"Because I could be stressed about you and me."

"Are you?" I press, a weight settling in my chest.

"I'm living in the moment, Emma. I'm trying not to think about that. I'll worry about it when the time comes," he replies, his eyes searching mine as if looking for something that might anchor him.

My smile fades the truth of my own uncertainty hitting hard. "You're right; because I'm here now. If I thought there was nothing worth staying for, I'd be out in the world searching for love like I was Indiana Jones."

Laughter erupts from him, bright and infectious. "So, you think I'm the Holy Grail?"

"Babe, I *know* you are," I say, my tone a mix of flirtation and sincerity, but the gravity of my words lingers. "Just waiting to find out if I'm yours."

He playfully lifts my chin, his thumb brushing against my

skin, and slides his perfect lips against mine, igniting every nerve in my body. "I'm counting down the days."

I reach forward, grabbing his side, and he squirms away, laughter spilling from him like music. "I *knew* you were ticklish."

When I take off running after him, a burst of adrenaline propels me forward. He's fast, and I love hearing his laughter trailing behind him like a melody. "You'll *never* catch me, Emma."

"I hate it when people doubt me," I growl playfully, putting more oomph into my stride. When he turns around this time, I'm right behind him reaching for the back of his shirt. I grab on, but I stumble and the two of us fall forward. Hudson takes the brunt, his body under me as I land on his chest. Laughter bubbles uncontrollably between us.

Time feels like it freezes when I meet his eyes, and everything around us fades away. I'm lost in his gaze, captured in the love haze surrounding us.

Nothing else matters. Has it ever?

"You're my Holy Grail, Em," he murmurs, tucking a loose strand of hair behind my ear, his touch a gentle promise. His smile is sincere, illuminating the space between us. My breath hitches, and Hudson rolls me over onto my back. His fingertips trace the outside of my cheek before gliding down my side. Then he tickles the shit out of me, forcing laughter from me. With a quick movement, I try to squirm away rolling away from him, but he has a firm hold on me. There is no escaping this man. I don't want to.

"Don't you ever tell anyone I'm ticklish because you are too!" he exclaims between my fits of laughter as I try to tickle him back.

"*Please!*" I yell between giggles, holding my thighs together. "I'm going to *piss* myself!"

"Hudson!" I hear a voice call from behind him, cutting through our playful moment.

We abruptly stop and turn to see a dark-haired woman striding toward us with purpose. As she approaches, I can't help but note the familial resemblance; she has the same striking green eyes as the rest of the Jolly family. I instinctively try to push my hair down, hoping to regain some semblance of composure, as Hudson stands, extending his hand to help me up.

"You're rude!" she scolds him, her tone playful yet stern, before her gaze softens as she turns to me. "Hi! I'm BJ. Nice to finally meet you, Emma. I've been hoping my asshole cousin would introduce us."

"Oh, BJ, yes. Great to meet you," I say, pulling her into a warm hug that feels welcoming and genuine. "Claire mentioned you worked at the coffee shop. You wrote 'Hudson Jolly Wants to Fuck You' on the bottom of my cocoa. Hilarious, by the way!"

Hudson's eyes widen in shock as he looks at me, disbelief painted on his face. "Wait, you saw it?"

"You didn't give it to Pastor John?" she accuses him. "You *lied*! Bastard!" Her brows furrow in mock disappointment. "I apologized for writing awful things on the bottom of his cocoa!"

Hudson howls with laughter, his hands patting his thighs as he points at her. "Now that." He gestures with mock seriousness. "Is fucking hilarious. Stop pranking me!"

"No," she replies stubbornly, an impish smile on her face. "What were you two doing over there? Ready to admit you're dating yet?"

Hudson and I share a fleeting glance filled with unspoken thoughts and nervous laughter.

"What do you want?" he asks her, a hint of annoyance creeping into his tone.

She turns her attention back to me, her expression shifting to one of earnestness. "Promise this conversation goes nowhere? Do you verbally agree? It's confidential."

"Yes, of course," I reply, my curiosity piqued by her sudden seriousness. She seems to be floating on cloud nine, radiating excitement but is also all business.

"In Texas, a verbal agreement is legally binding, and I have a witness." She points to Hudson, who looks torn between being supportive and slightly embarrassed.

"You're feisty! I can keep secrets," I say, extending my hand. We shake on it, sealing our newfound bond of secrecy with a smile.

"Okay." She squeals in delight. "You know the building on Main Street that's been vacant for a bazillion years?"

"The old bike shop?" Hudson asks, recognition dawning in his eyes.

I have no idea what they're talking about, but my interest is piqued.

"I put a down payment on it," she announces proudly. "I'm buying it."

Hudson's eyes widen in shock. "How did you afford that?"

"I've saved nearly every penny I've made since I turned sixteen. I finally saved enough to put down twenty percent, so I bought it."

I glance between them, trying to process the enormity of the news. "How much was the building?"

"Close to two million dollars," he replies, glaring at her with a protective undertone. "How will you pay the monthly payments?"

"I've been selling my drawings online," she explains with a hint of defiance.

Silence lingers for a moment.

"Bella, I'm so fucking proud of you!" Hudson exclaims, pulling her into a tight hug. I can feel the excitement radiating between them, a palpable energy that lights up the air around us. They pull away, and he looks at her with earnestness in his eyes. "What do you need? How can I help?"

She laughs. "Thank you! You're the only person who has

been happy for me. The problem with everyone is that most aren't betting on my success. We're the only ones who know what I'm capable of, and I can't wait to give them all a big fat stinky 'I told you so.' I can't wait!"

"Congratulations," I say sweetly. "I'll invest."

Her mouth falls open in disbelief. "What?"

"Pitch your idea to me."

Hudson holds back a smile as he glances at me, his eyes sparkling with amusement.

"Half bookstore, half coffee shop. Right now, we have a coffee shop in town, and it's not hip. The bookstore sucks, too. Neither are fun. It's boring and as bland as the gray paint on the walls. I want to create a cool hangout where friends can gather to play board games or hold book club meetings. I envision bright colors—pinks, teals—with an abundance of flowers inside. I'll have a detailed menu that's completely book-related. And the name? Sugar & Spine. And yes, we *will* feature all the dirty romance novels that make the Purple Hairs blush because we believe in love around here. And raunchy sex." She looks between me and Hudson, her grin widening as excitement dances in her eyes.

I gasp, my excitement taking over because I can picture what she's described. "Oh my God! That sounds like an actual dream. For you to launch something like this in Merryville is genius considering the tourist traffic. Wow. It's a billion-dollar idea."

"Right? I thought so, too."

"That's what I'll invest in. You could open locations in every tourist town and major city, and they'd do incredibly well. It's going to be *worldwide*. Who wouldn't want to hang out at Sugar & Spine?"

Her legs tremble and she loses her balance, nearly falling. Thankfully Hudson catches her. I move closer, concerned. "Are you okay?"

"Is this a dream?" BJ asks, glancing between us.

"Feels like it, doesn't it?" Hudson studies me, a thoughtful expression on his face.

"I have a lot of money." I shrug casually. "And it's a great concept. You have the fire to make it succeed, and most people are missing that. You're going to be huge," I say. "Also, you should talk to Claire. She navigates the business world like a shark. She could probably help you bust some balls."

BJ wraps her arm around me, wiping away her tears of joy. "Thank you."

"You're welcome. I'll contact my lawyers this week," I say confidently.

Suddenly, her phone rings, and she answers it on speaker.

"Where are you? You're late," a woman's voice chastises. "If you get another write-up, that's it."

"I'm on my way," she replies, her voice a mix of urgency and embarrassment, as the woman continues her lecture. With a quick wave, she says goodbye and hurries to her vehicle.

Hudson remains silent, his gaze fixated on me.

"Cat got your tongue? Is that how the saying goes?" I quip, walking toward him with a playful smile. "What's up?"

"You just gave away a billion dollars," he mutters, astonished.

I shrug nonchalantly. "Money doesn't make me happy. Besides, I can't take it with me, so I invest in people and businesses. And I thought you did your research," I tell him, winking mischievously.

Last year, Claire saved the Christmas tree farm from foreclosure. Every penny came from her own pocket—a true testament to her determination and kind heart. It runs in the family.

"I'm still paying you to be my nanny," he confirms, his voice steady.

"Can you pay me in orgasms instead? Life experiences are worth more to me," I tease, arching an eyebrow.

His brow quirks up, intrigued. "How does this currency work?"

"Hm," I say, my brow furrowing in thought. "I think every three hours of helping with Colby should equal one orgasm. These are big O's that I can cash in *whenever* I want—at any hour, even if it's three in the morning and I'm feeling particularly horny or a bit tipsy. No exceptions."

Hudson licks his lips, a playful glint in his eye. "But I already paid you for last week, though."

I laugh against his lips, the warmth of his breath mingling with mine. "No, you bought your kid an insane LEGO shopping spree." I can't help but smirk because we did a lot of online shopping yesterday.

Hudson is still quiet.

"Does it bother you that I have a lot of money?" I ask, a hint of worry creeping into my tone.

"No, honestly, I forgot about it," he replies, his gaze steady and reassuring. "You're down to earth, Emma. Your authenticity is what I love about you the most. You're not afraid to be *you* regardless of the company you keep," he whispers, pulling me closer as he devours my mouth with his.

I smile inwardly at his words. "You're the only person who's ever appreciated me for me," I say, feeling validated in a way that's as rare as profound.

Before we get too lost in the moment, the alarm on my phone blares, cutting through the moment.

"Shit. I have to pick up Colby," I say, reluctant to break the spell.

"I can go and be a little late returning to work," Hudson offers, his eyes sparkling with desire.

"No. I promised him this morning we were going on a date to the diner after school. Sorry, I've got plans with mini you," I say with a casual shrug, though my heart twinges at the thought of leaving him.

He pulls me back into his embrace, kissing me deeply, and

in that moment, I feel the weight of those three words I'm terrified to ever say again.

"I'll see you at dinner. Be careful," he says, his large hand grabbing my ass, sending a delightful rush of excitement through me.

"Sexy," I mutter playfully, moving away with flushed cheeks. My entire body is on fire.

I spend the drive to Colby's elementary school daydreaming about Hudson, focusing on the warmth that man leaves in my chest. I park the van curbside and walk through the double doors, where I have seen countless little feet trotting in and out. The ceilings are low, but the bright overhead lights keep the space cheerful.

Standing outside the classroom with a few other parents, I note the tight-knit community around me. Many of the moms smile in my direction, but no one approaches to start a conversation—perhaps they're intimidated by me or maybe they're shy. Everyone in Merryville seems to know who I am now.

The decorated door swings open suddenly, and out runs Colby, his face lighting up like a Christmas tree when he sees me. I bend down, pulling him into a hug. "Ready for lunch?"

"Yes! Are we going to the diner?" His excitement bubbles over, making my heart swell.

"Yep," I tell him as we walk to the van. I press a button on the remote, and the side door slides open automatically with a whoosh, showcasing the interior.

"Wow!" he exclaims, his eyes wide. "This is just like Davidson's mom's van! Ooh, it has a TV too!" He points up, marveling at the shiny black box fixed to the ceiling.

I climb in, making sure he's buckled correctly, then look up at the TV. I press a button, and the screen flips down.

"I don't know how to use this," I admit sheepishly.

"Daaaammmmnnn," he exclaims, awe dripping from his voice.

"Sir, that's a bad word," I remind him gently, suppressing a laugh. "We'll figure it out when we get home, okay?"

He nods vigorously and gives me a thumbs up, his enthusiasm infectious. I close the door, and as we drive to the diner, we chat excitedly about school, his stories spilling out in a rush.

As soon as we enter the diner, Colby races toward Glenda, who stands behind the counter. He throws his arms around her in a tight hug. "Glenda!"

"Colby!" she exclaims, her eyes sparkling with delight as she clicks her ruby-red slippers together in amusement. She pulls a colorful sucker from her pocket, and he beams at her, his gratitude overflowing.

"Thank you, ma'am!" he offers. His manners are top-notch.

We settle into the same booth I sat in the first time I came here, the familiar surroundings wrapping me in a cozy embrace. Colby immediately dives into the kids' activity sheet placed on the table, a green crayon firmly in hand. He tucks his bottom lip into his mouth, his concentration palpable.

"Do you know what you'd like to eat?" I ask him, my eyes sliding over the menu spread before us. The vibrancy of the diner, with its vintage wallpaper and the enticing aroma of coffee wafting through the air, makes it hard to concentrate. There are so many options—fluffy omelets, sizzling bacon, and golden-brown waffles, all capture my attention.

"Can I get pancakes? With *lots* of butter. When I say lots, I mean *lots*," he confirms, excitedly.

I try not to laugh at his earnestness, but it's hard to resist the charm of his enthusiasm. "Sure. Want strawberries with it?" I suggest, and his eyes widen like he's picturing the sweet, juicy fruit piled high next to his breakfast.

A server walks up wearing a kind smile on his face. "Drinks?"

"Coffee with cream, please," I say, glancing over at Colby, who is bouncing in his seat, full of anticipation.

"Chocolate milk, please," he pipes up, his small voice filled with delight.

"Am I going to regret all this sugar?" I ask, half-teasing.

"Nope!" he replies confidently, making me chuckle.

"That's fine," I tell him, and the server walks away.

A minute later, a hot coffee is slid in front of me with steam curling from the top. I add cream and sugar and savor the rich aroma. After we order food, the two of us are left to ourselves.

Colby grins wide as he picks up a crayon and colors intensely, the bright hues reflect his excitement. He stops and looks up at me with curiosity. "Do you like my daddy?"

"Yeah. I like you, too. And Jake. And Lucas. Your grandma and grandpa. And great grandma. BJ," I list, appreciating the bonds I've created with so many since I've arrived. Part of me wishes I hadn't left back in July, but...I wasn't *ready*.

"No. *Like* him," he clarifies, his little brows furrowing in concentration.

"What do you know about *liking* someone?" I ask, grinning at the innocent wisdom in his question.

He raises his brows, striking a pose that is all too reminiscent of his dad. This kid is going to be a heartbreaker. "Evie told me about it," he explains matter-of-factly.

I watch him, aware of how easy it is to navigate away from these conversations with him. If he were a little older, I think he might play matchmaker. "Aw yeah? So, how old is Evie again?"

"She's seven. Two years older than me," he explains, puffing out his chest with pride.

"Right," I say, adding a few cubes of ice to my coffee because it's still too hot.

"Emma. Will you tell me what this word is?" he asks,

pointing excitedly to the dessert menu, which is brimming with creamy cakes, flaky pies, and shake flavors that are every color of the rainbow.

I move beside him in the booth, bringing the menu closer so we can peer at it together. "We'll sound it out. What does that say?" I encourage.

"In," he says confidently, pointing with a small finger.

I cover the next small section of the word and prompt him, "This one?"

"Gee-ree," he attempts.

"Gree, like Gruh and eee really fast. Gree," I suggest, smiling at his effort.

"Gree," he parrots back, his face lighting up with determination.

I slide my finger further along the word.

"Dee," he states.

"Very good! You're *so* smart," I encourage, feeling a swell of pride. "And this little last part..."

"e-nuts."

"Hmm. Try again," I coax gently.

"E-e," he tries.

"Ents. Like hints without the H," I clarify, watching as comprehension shines in his bright green eyes.

He nods, slowly formulating his understanding. "Ints. Ints."

"Now we'll say the whole thing together," I announce, my voice filled with anticipation.

"In-gree-dee-ints."

I immediately smile when he articulates it. "Exactly. Ingredients. It's all the different items that go into recipes. Ingredients are important," I emphasize, recalling the mess of flour and sugar from my past baking disasters.

"Like for cookies!" he exclaims, jumping in his seat with excitement.

"Yes, exactly!" I reply, matching his enthusiasm.

"Like the gingerbread cookies me and daddy make," he says, and my eyes light up at the thought.

"You know how to make the Jolly gingerbread cookies?" I ask, savoring this delightful tidbit of information.

He nods vigorously, his curls bouncing.

"Oh, can we make some this week?" I inquire eagerly, picturing us covered in flour with laughter bubbling around us.

"Yes! I even know where Daddy keeps the recipe!" he beams. "But you have to swear you won't tell him."

"Cross my heart," I promise, my mind racing. No way I'd look at it knowing it's top secret. When I glance outside, I spot a man across the street with a camera and a long lens focusing on us.

My mouth falls open.

"Everything okay, Emma?" Colby asks.

"Oh yeah," I say. Before our food is ready, I stop the server as he approaches with our order. "Can we get our food to-go, please? We'll be standing by the pie counter."

"Sure," he replies, nodding. "Want your drinks to-go?"

"That would be perfect," I agree, turning to Colby to explain that we need to head home, the thrill of the day mixed with a hint of caution swirling in the atmosphere.

"Why?" he asks, his brow furrowed in confusion.

I slide out of the booth then bend down to meet his eyes, closing the distance between us. Leaning in, I whisper in his ear, "I'm going to *poop* my pants."

Suddenly, he bursts into laughter, his joyful sound echoing around us.

I smile, placing my finger over my lips in a playful gesture. "Shh. You might make me do it right here."

Straightening up, I take a moment to collect myself before we move toward the pie counter, which is bustling with activity.

"They need to hurry up! I don't want you to *shit* yourself," he exclaims, glancing toward the servers delivering food to different tables in the diner.

I can't help but laugh. "Shh. And don't say that word."

"Well!" he groans. "It's true!"

With a smile, I gently rest my hand on his shoulder, comforting him even though we do need to leave right now. "I know. You're right. Thanks for having my back, Bee. You're the best."

CHAPTER 26

HUDSON

Exhaustion covers me like a heavy blanket. Work on the farm was relentless today, each task piling onto the last. I barely had a moment to breathe.

I can't recall how many trees I loaded and unloaded, but my biceps ache, a reminder of the labor demanded by the season.

Two large diesel trucks arrived to pick up an order for a big-box store, and once again, we found ourselves short-handed. At the beginning of the year, I planned to hire more employees because this situation has become a problem. I've been running around like a chicken with its head cut off, and so have my brothers, each of us caught in the whirlwind of our responsibilities. This chaotic pace won't end until two days before Christmas.

Part of me wants to skip ahead a few weeks, but that would mean sacrificing precious time with Emma, especially since she's mine this season.

The New Year's Eve deadline looms ahead, casting a shadow of pressure, but I'm doing what she asked and considering the possibility of being with her. I already know my answer; I've known it for months, but I'm honoring her request to give it some thought.

The pros certainly outweigh the cons, yet those cons threaten me and Colby's privacy. It's a life-altering decision, and I'm prioritizing Colby's well-being over my desires. I have to. However, Jake hasn't had any issues being with Claire, other than the rumors and speculation online. But it's easy to turn that off.

As I drive home, a grin slides across my lips knowing Emma is partly responsible for keeping me up later than usual. I'm not complaining. I cherish every fleeting second I'm lucky enough to spend with her.

When I finally step into the house, music blares from the TV. Emma and Colby are dancing around the kitchen, wearing whimsical aprons and chef hats. Their lively voices sing along to Kidz Bop.

A smile that feels almost permanent stretches across my face as I watch them shout the lyrics at the top of their lungs, lost in their own world.

Emma turns, catching a glimpse of me, and her grin widens even further, lighting up her face. She waves me over, her foot tapping along to the beat, her energy infectious and she doesn't miss a single word of the song.

"Daddy!" Colby exclaims, extending his arms toward me, a beacon of innocence. I lift him up, feeling the warmth radiate from his small body, as he and Emma continue to sing at each other. They make goofy faces that send me into a fit of laughter. I'm only sad that I don't know the lyrics well enough to join in on their sing-along.

When the song finally ends, Emma gracefully moves to the TV to turn the volume down before the next track begins.

"How was your day?" I ask Colby as I set him down, his little chef hat perched precariously on his head.

"Emma almost shit herself at the diner!" he exclaims, shaking his head as if reliving the chaos. "It was wild."

"Hey, we don't say that word," I reply, glancing at Emma with my brows arched in mild concern.

"Yeah, I'll tell you all about it later," she says, her hand grazing across my back in a brief yet electric touch.

"What are you cookin'?" I ask them, taking in the sight of flour scattered across the counter, a testament to their culinary chaos. The kitchen is an absolute disaster, but it's one filled with warmth and happiness. Plus, the food smells incredible.

"Chicken fried steak and gravy," Colby proudly announces. "I asked for it."

My brows furrow as I glance at Emma. "You did not have to make him that. I planned burgers tonight."

"Not a big deal. It's been fun," she says, flipping one of the steaks with the tongs in her hand. The sizzle of the meat against the hot skillet fills the air, mingling with the hearty aroma wafting from the kitchen.

"You knew how to cook this?" I ask, moving closer to the skillet, the heat radiating against my skin.

"Nope," she says with a nod, a playful sparkle in her eyes.

"That's right, Daddy. You can make anything with the right ingredients." My heart swells as I hear my son's confidence.

"In-gree-di-ints," Emma says, pronouncing every syllable with exaggerated clarity. They give each other a high five, their laughter ringing through the kitchen. Happiness radiates from my son, his face lighting up with each smile, and I love seeing him like this. It's the most carefree he's been in a long time. Hell, me too.

"It was as easy as following a recipe," Emma says. "Anyone can do that."

Her lips tease and tempt me, and if Colby weren't watching us as if he were getting paid to spy, I'd lean in and kiss her. "What's in the oven?"

Emma takes a step back and swings open the door. "Garlic roasted potatoes," she announces, the steam billowing out.

"We even chopped the garlic like real chefs!" Colby says proudly.

"We did." Emma shuts the door and steals a glance at me, a flirtatious grin dancing across her face. Fuck, I need her like I need air.

I clear my throat, forcing myself to focus back on Colby. "How was school?"

"Great! Tomorrow is show-and-tell, and I have the perfect thing to bring," he exclaims, his face brimming with enthusiasm.

"Really?" Emma turns and asks. "I didn't know that."

"Yeah!" he says, bouncing on his toes. "Let me go get it!"

Colby removes his chef hat and apron, then races up the stairs. Our laughter trails behind him, and as soon as he's out of sight, my mouth finds Emma's. I push her against the counter, my hand sliding possessively over her curves.

"I've been thinking about this all day," she says, her voice desperate and breathless as she runs her fingers through my hair. We're too greedy, too ravenous, nearly losing control. I moan against her, losing my grasp on reality anytime she's nearby.

When I hear the top of the stairs creak, we break apart.

Emma's lips are swollen from our kisses, and she tucks loose strands of hair behind her ear, trying to regain her composure. Not sure how that silly chef hat stayed in place.

"Ready to see it?" Colby asks, a grin spreading across his face as he hides something behind his back.

Emma and I stand side by side as he pulls a bright yellow rubber ducky from behind him.

Emma's eyes widen in surprise as he skips toward us, his glee infectious.

"Look how cool it is!" Colby says, his excitement palpable.

I hold back laughter, biting my lip as I hold out my palm. "Give it to me."

"Dad, it has a motor on its mouth, and it's butt does this." He wiggles the ducky as he demonstrates its functions.

I glance at Emma, and her face turns as red as her hair.

"Please, put it in my hand, now," I keep my tone light but firm.

Colby's smile fades as he looks up at me, a hint of uncertainty in his eyes. He gives it to me.

"Where did you find this?" I ask, knowing it was in Emma's bathroom.

He turns his head away, avoiding my gaze.

"This is Emma's *toy*," I tell him gently, meeting her eyes, then focus back on him. "You don't take things that aren't yours, okay? You have to ask for permission."

His bottom lip quivers, and I can tell he's just as exhausted as I am.

Colby turns to her. "Emma, can I bring your toy to school tomorrow and show my friends?"

I turn to her, smirking as embarrassment sweeps over her like a tide.

She quickly flips the chicken fried steaks in the pan, as if that can distract from the moment. "Oh, honey. I'm sorry, you can't. I was going to use it tomorrow for my bath time."

Her eyes darken when she glances in my direction. I grow hard thinking about her in the tub, losing herself to thoughts of me.

"But can't you use it some other time? I just need it for a few hours." His eyes glisten with tears, desperation creeping into his voice.

"How about I get you an even better one? A *bigger* one. That one is actually broken; it barely floats. Oh! You should take the rock you painted at the Season's Greeting celebration! I'll even let you take mine, too. It's *way* cooler, and we made them together. Remember? Do you know where it is?"

"Yes," he says, a bright smile returning to his face as he

runs back upstairs, his little feet thumping excitedly on the floorboards.

I move forward and hand it over to her. "I would've loved explaining your rubber *fucky* to his teacher."

"I'd have been deceased!" She snatches it from my hand, tucking it securely into her apron pocket before returning to the oven. "I can't believe I left that out. Careless."

I lean in, kissing the back of her neck, the warmth of her skin beneath my lips sending a thrill through me. She leans into me, a sigh escaping her lips. "I want to watch you use it again."

"We can make that happen," she mutters. "I love your eyes on me."

The timer on the stove sounds off with its cheerful ding as Emma expertly removes the golden-brown chicken-fried steaks from the bubbling grease. My mouth waters as she carefully places them on a plate lined with paper towels to absorb the excess oil. I'm genuinely impressed by how effortless she makes it look.

"Let me get it," I say, grabbing the oven mitts and taking over the task. I place the potatoes on the cork potholder waiting in the center of the table, the subtle scent of garlic wafts through the air.

"Is dinner ready?" Colby asks, skipping into the kitchen with his beloved pet rock cradled in his small hands. He's already forgotten about the rubber ducky—at least for now.

Emma pulls plates from the cabinet, and I grab silverware. We move around each other in the kitchen with a seamless rhythm, instinctively anticipating one another's actions as if we've choreographed this dance many times before.

"Join my team," I say over my shoulder, flashing her a grin.

"Join mine!" she replies with a laugh, undressing me with her eyes.

"Daddy, for what?" Colby chimes in, his curiosity piqued. "Can I be on your team?"

I grin widely, my heart swelling with affection for both of them. "Of course. I've asked Emma a million times to join our cookie-baking team for the contest the weekend after your birthday, and she keeps saying no."

His brows crease in confusion. "Why, Emma?"

I can't help but smirk mischievously and enjoy this too much. I'm aware that Colby is one of her weaknesses, she'd do anything for him that he asks within reason.

She narrows her eyes at me, twitching her lips in mock scowl. "You're evil."

"Please join our team!" Colby pleads, his green eyes wide with hope.

"I'll think about it," she tells him, playfully removing her apron. The duck's head pokes out.

"Come on, time to eat dinner," she says.

We move to the table, the wooden surface polished and inviting, and I pull Emma's chair out for her. She sits, meeting my gaze with desire as I take my seat across from them.

"This looks incredible," I say, taking in the perfectly cooked chicken-fried steaks, creamy gravy, green beans, and roasted potatoes. "You didn't have to go through all this trouble."

"Trouble? I let Colby choose what he wanted for dinner," she replies with a smile, placing a smaller piece of meat on Colby's plate before scooping generous portions of his chosen sides. "Is that enough?"

He nods enthusiastically, a grin spreading across his face as he eagerly snatches up his fork. "Thank you, Emma. This looks good."

"You're welcome."

I reach over with my knife, cutting his steak into manageable pieces.

"Daddy, I've got it! Give it to me."

"No," I insist gently. "It's too sharp, and I don't want you to hurt yourself."

He pouts, his bottom lip jutting out in disappointment.

"Can you cut mine, too?" Emma asks, blinking up at me with a playful glance, scooting her plate closer to mine. "I'd prefer you do it for me."

My eyes flick in her direction, and Colby's attitude immediately changes. She's a pro at this; her presence always transforms the atmosphere into something lighter.

"After he's finished with mine," Colby informs her calmly, a smirk dancing on his lips. "You can be next."

I grin at him, then cast my gaze back to her. Once his food is in manageable bites, I turn my attention to her. She watches me intently, anticipation gleaming in her eyes as I cut her steak.

"Mm. Good boy," she mutters approvingly as I slice hers into similar, bite-sized pieces. My cock twitches.

"Great job, Daddy." Colby stabs a sliver and pops it into his mouth. "Mm!"

"How is it? Did I do a good job?" Her excitement threads through her words.

"Yes! I want to eat this every day! Tomorrow and the next day and the next day."

She nervously laughs, the sound mingling with the faint clinking of forks against plates. "I've created a monster."

"You have," I say, glancing at their dynamic and noticing how special their relationship is. Emma makes Colby incredibly happy. He wasn't unhappy before, of course, but now he shines with a newfound brightness. She's attentive, genuinely interested, and never once treats him like a baby, which I know he appreciates. My boy is becoming more independent and before I realize it, he'll be driving.

"Did you decide what you wanted for your birthday?" I ask Colby, eager to hear his thoughts.

He puts on his thinking face, furrowing his brow as he counts with his fingers. "LEGOs, a new bike, and a puppy!"

"We'll see," I say, raising an eyebrow. "I heard from Mr. Stinky."

Emma glances in my direction, her brows knitting together. I realize I forgot to explain him.

Colby's eyes widen with excitement. "Yeah? Is he coming to visit me on my birthday?"

"He is!" I confirm, unable to hide my grin.

"We're expecting guests?" she finally asks, glancing between us with a mix of curiosity and uncertainty.

"Oh yes," Colby explains eagerly. "Mr. Stinky is naughty, though. He gets in trouble sometimes."

Emma's eyes flick back and forth between Colby and me.

"He also makes a mess," I add. "One we have to clean up every day."

"Where will he sleep?" she asks, her voice tinged with concern.

"He never sleeps, Emma," I reply, shaking my head as a grin plays at the corners of my mouth. "He's always awake so he can tell Santa what I've been up to. But he's a good elf," Colby explains.

"Elf," she says, slightly relaxing. I smirk at how quickly her anxiety dissipates. No way I'm allowing anyone to fuck up the little time we're guaranteed.

We finish eating dinner and tackle the kitchen cleanup together, our movements synchronized like a well-rehearsed dance. When we're finished, she approaches me. "Today, at the diner, I saw men taking pictures of me and Colby. I left immediately, but…" She pauses. "I know how protective you are of his face not being shown online. I'm so sorry," she urges.

"That's why you left?"

"Yes," she admits.

Alarm bells ring and I'm fucking pissed, but not at her. I

run my fingers across her cheeks. "It's not your fault. You did what you could."

I softly kiss her.

Moments later, Colby stands at the top of the stairs. "Emma! I'm ready!"

She steals another kiss before walking away.

While she helps him during his bath, I shower. I can hear their laughter echoing in the background as the dinosaur capsules hatch.

Afterward, I tuck him in with a bedtime story, the room filled with the warm light of his bedside lamp.

When I click his door shut, Emma meets me in my room. As soon as she enters, I press her back against the door, our mouths crashing together as I devour her lips like she's my lifeline. She sighs against me, the sound both a plea and a declaration.

"I missed you today," she admits desperately, her eyes shimmering with sincerity. "You were on my mind so much."

"Fuck, me too," I reply, feeling the tension and longing between us surge. I gently lead her over to the bed. She climbs under the blankets, and before I join her, I slide open the top drawer of the nightstand.

"What's an O-bill?" she asks, glancing down at the stack of fake dollar bills I place in her hand. She bursts out laughing at my playful attempt to bring some humor into the moment.

"It's payday," I tell her, leaning over to capture her lips again.

Her eyes widen as realization dawns on her. "Orgasm money," she says, her brows lifting in surprise as she counts them out loud. "Thirty?" Her head falls back with infectious laughter. "I'm fucking *rich*. And what if I want to cash them in right now?"

"Dare you," I tease, the temptation flooding my senses. I greedily want to pleasure her until the sun rises. "But you'll be useless tomorrow."

"The only reason I won't is because I can tell you're exhausted," she responds, her voice sultry and laced with desire. "Now, come here. I need you."

Emma casually places her sexy-time cash on the bedside table. The rustle of bills, a reminder of the pleasures that lie ahead. I move closer to her, my hands gliding over her peaked nipples before slipping inside her panties. The heat radiates off her, and she's so fucking wet for me that I can barely handle it. Her mouth falls slightly open, pants escaping as she gently rocks her hips, urging me forward. "Yes. Oh."

But just as my hungry lips meet hers, the door to my room swings open with a suddenness that steals the breath from my lungs. Emma's eyes widen in shock, and she slips off the bed into a crouched position, hiding like a Navy SEAL in the shadows. I instinctively adjust myself, the evidence of my arousal standing at full attention, a reminder of interrupted intentions.

"Daddy," Colby calls, his small voice cutting through the silence like a knife.

"Hey, Bee." I sit up, grabbing a pillow in a frantic attempt to cover myself while masking my surprise. "What's going on?"

"I couldn't sleep. I wanted to talk to you about something," he explains innocently. I scoot over, making space for him to climb onto the bed, my body instinctively positioning itself to shield Emma, who's still hidden on the floor. I glance at her, and to my relief, she's grinning, eyes wide, a mixture of amusement and disbelief dancing in her gaze.

I gently move his brown hair out of his face, and his bright green eyes, filled with curiosity, gaze back at me. "Why can't Emma be my mom?"

The question hits me like a freight train, catching me completely off guard. I try to keep my expression soft.

"Well." I take a steadying breath, searching for the right words.

"Evie said you could marry her and make her my mom. Can you?" he asks, his tone simple, yet the weight of his request is anything but light.

I chuckle, trying to ease the tension. "Son, that's not how it works. I can't just marry Emma. She has to want to marry me back."

His brows knit together, and I can feel his mood dampening, disappointment already churns inside. "But she *likes* you, Dad."

"Maybe you should tell Evie that she needs to mind her own business?" I suggest, trying to inject a bit of humor into the conversation.

"No! What if Emma asks you to marry her? Then will you do it?" he asks, his innocence on full display.

I grin wider, my heart swelling at his unfiltered desire for happiness. "It's grown-up stuff that you don't need to worry about. Emma is your friend and your nanny and Claire's sister. She's returning to New York at the end of December, and it will be us again. Just like before."

"No," he whispers, his voice breaking, and crocodile tears start to stream down his face.

"Bee, please don't cry. She's going to come back and visit you and Aunt CeCe often. Guaranteed." He sits up and hugs me tightly, his small arms wrapping around me. I pull him close, my arm enveloping his tiny frame. I stare blankly at the wall as thoughts spiral through my mind. This is something I've contemplated a million times, but now, it feels overwhelmingly real.

"I don't want her to go, Daddy."

The words catch in my throat, heavy and suffocating. "I know. Can we talk about this later? Come on, let me walk you back to bed."

"Fine," he says, though the bitterness in his tone reveals

his frustration. I follow behind him, his small feet pad against the floor, leading me back to his room. When we arrive, he climbs into bed, and I sit at the edge of the mattress, pulling the blankets up to his chin with gentle care.

"It's not fair," he mutters, clearly still upset, his voice thick with disappointment.

"I know," I tell him, my heart aching for him. "But everything happens just how it's supposed to, okay? Have faith, Bee."

He rolls over and turns away from me, too upset to even look at me. I rub his back in gentle circles, feeling the tension beneath my fingertips until his breathing steadies, lulled into a more peaceful rhythm.

After a deep breath of my own, I finally return to my room, the air thick with unvoiced thoughts. Before I push the door open, I pause outside, steadying my nerves and recomposing myself, as if bracing against a wave of uncertainty.

Emma sits with her legs crisscrossed on my bed, her brown eyes hold an unsettling mix of light and shadow. I notice the underlying sadness that lingers just behind those bright orbs. An expression of worry etches across her face. Our silent conversation flows effortlessly, words unspoken yet understood, as we grasp the gravity of the moment.

We simultaneously open our mouths, caught in the whirlwind of emotions, and try to speak at the same time.

"Emma," I mutter, quietly locking the door behind me. I take a seat beside her on the bed, the mattress sinking slightly under my weight. Gently, I place my finger under her chin, guiding her gaze up to meet mine, forcing her to hold my eyes. "Am I going to have to deal with two meltdowns tonight?"

She fights back a smile, a flicker of hope lighting up her face, but it's short-lived as she leans forward, pulling me into a hug. I breathe her in deeply, nuzzling against her neck, the scent of her sweet skin grounding me amidst the chaos cluttering my mind.

"I'm sorry," she murmurs, the words tinged with vulnerability. "I—"

Carefully, I pull away so I can meet her eyes directly, holding her gaze firm with reassurance. "Don't apologize. He's attached to you, just like everyone else. We'll worry about the future when we're living it, you know?" I try to convey strength through my words, hoping to ease the burden we share.

"He'll be heartbroken," she whispers, searching my face for answers, a flicker of fear flashing in her eyes. "I hope you make the right decision."

"I will," I confirm, allowing a smile to break through the tension. "I'm doing what you said."

My heart beats with resolve, fueling my determination to navigate this unfamiliar terrain together.

With a gentle motion, I lay her back on the bed and kiss her sweetly, feeling the warmth of her skin against my lips. As we lose ourselves in one another, too many emotions float to the surface.

Too many unspoken words linger in the air as we make love beneath the silver glow of the moonlight. I watch her ride me like a fleeting daydream, capturing every moment as if she might slip away.

I can't ever let that fucking happen.

CHAPTER 27

HUDSON

Lucas slumps against the counter after setting down the heavy boxes we were carrying. The gift shop is packed full of people, and navigating the area is challenging, but it's always like this during the season. Tourists zip around with souvenirs, eagerly clutching colorful magnets, quirky coffee cups shaped like sleighs, and delicate handmade ornaments that shimmer under the store's bright lights. The gift-wrapping station has a line that nearly spills out the door. Tomorrow is Thanksgiving, so most are trying to get ahead of the rush, which then creates a bigger rush.

Every person is smiling, their faces alight with the thrill of holiday shopping, except for Lucas, who seems to be lost in his own storm.

"Cheer up; it gets worse," I tell him with a laugh and a hard pat on the shoulder, trying to lighten the mood. "We're almost done."

He groans loudly, a mixture of frustration and fatigue.

"Sometimes, you act just like a five-year-old," I say, shaking my head as he follows behind me, dragging his feet. We have two more boxes to carry to the cramped storage room that smells like cardboard and old wrapping paper.

Mom called in the muscles—us—to move them around like we don't have a million other tasks piling up on our to-do list.

Just then, Jake shows up with messy hair and swollen lips, looking as if he just finished *visiting* Claire.

"Sorry," he says, grabbing the box from my hands with an exaggerated grunt. I narrow my eyes at him, trying to gauge if he's in a mood or not, as well.

"Thanks for the help," Lucas says sarcastically, his tone dripping with annoyance. He grumbles something under his breath.

"I said I was sorry," Jake replies. When Lucas is out of sight, he turns to me. "Did the Grinch shit in his cereal this morning?"

"He's in a mood. I haven't asked why; I don't care," I explain, following behind Jake. We stack the boxes on top of one another.

"Usually, that's how you act," Jake tells me as I follow him outside. Just as the cool air hits my cheeks, my phone vibrates in my pocket. It's a FaceTime call from Emma. Colby is still in school, so I'm not sure what she could need.

Jake catches sight of her name on my phone.

"So...you two?" he asks, his brows arching.

I meet his eyes, silence stretching between us. Not saying a word, I let the truth hang in the air, heavy and undeniable. It's written all over my damn face. I'm not the same person I was before Emma arrived back in town.

"I knew it. Damn." He claps his hands together, happy. "So...about our bet. I want to be paid in all hundreds. Got it? By February 14th."

"Don't piss me off," I reply in a hushed whisper. "I don't have a girlfriend."

Yet.

"You two have done the dirty." He nudges, a teasing smirk spreading across his face. "You're basically playing house right now."

"Shut. *The fuck*. Up," I state, irritation flashing through me. "Anyway, I need to take this call, then I'm on ax sharpening duty for the rest of the afternoon. You need me, holler."

"Mmhm," he responds, smirking even wider. "I knew it."

He lets out a loud yoo-hoo. The sound echoes behind me as I shake my head. I pick up Emma's call as I move toward the truck.

"Hey," she says with the camera close to her face, a glimmer of mischief in her eyes. "Tell me when you're completely alone."

My brows raise in surprise, and I pick up my pace, the anticipation thrumming in my veins. I climb into the cab and shut the door. "Okay."

Emma moves the camera back, and to my shock, she's naked, sprawled temptingly in my bed. She props the phone up on a pillow, revealing her perfect body, and a rush of desire surges through me.

"I was about to start baking cookies, and you were on my mind," she purrs, her voice sultry.

"Fuck," I growl out, cranking the truck, my cock hardening at the sight.

Her fingers slide down her body, teasingly playing with her clit. Her desperate moans, sweet and intoxicating, drive me crazy. I back out of the parking lot, the gravel crunching under the tires as she slips a finger inside, drawing out a breathless sigh.

"Hudson," she whispers, her voice thick with longing. "I wish it were you."

"Don't you dare fucking come," I demand, the primal urge to claim her building within me. "I'm on my way."

I don't know how I make it home so fast, but I park and stalk up the porch steps with a sense of urgency. The door is unlocked, and I climb the stairs two at a time, shedding my clothes as I go. Each piece falls away, a weight lifted from my shoulders until I reach my room. I push open the door, and there, illuminated by the gleam of the morning sunlight, Emma waits.

"What a surprise." Her brow arches. Her nipples perky.

I grab her ankles, pulling her to the edge of the bed. Then I flip her over on her stomach, holding her hips. She arches that plump ass for me, and I slam my cock deep into her tight little pussy. I groan out, feeling like I'm home.

She screams out with pleasure, her fingers gripping the comforter with a tight grasp as our bodies move together in a desperate dance.

"Yes, more. All of you," she gasps out.

"You're a bad fucking girl," I say, palming her perfect ass as her back arches under me. I reach around her body, teasing her clit with my fingers as we get lost in one another. Guttural groans release from her throat. "Oh, my fu—"

Her pussy clenches me so fucking tight I see stars. She rides out her orgasm, and I pound into her harder, faster, making sure to hit that G-spot.

"Who do you belong to?" I growl, my nostrils flaring as the orgasm violently builds.

"You," she screams out between her deep moans. Her voice is a mixture of ecstasy and desperation. "You, Hudson. Only you."

A wave of intensity crashes over me and pulls me under as I empty inside her. She presses against me and hums with satisfaction. The world outside fades away, leaving only the two of us in this intimate moment. We stay connected for a little longer, our ragged breaths mingling as my heart races.

"Nothing else matters when I'm with you," she admits. "Thanks for being my ho, ho, ho this season. You're the gift that keeps on giving."

"Mm. Yes. Merry *fucking* Christmas to me," I respond, a wry grin tugging at the corners of my lips, savoring the unexpected gift of this moment.

Her expression grows serious and quiet. "I can't imagine a life without you," she confesses.

I lean over the bed, kiss her, and whisper in her ear. "I feel the same."

She runs her fingers through my hair, desperately searching my eyes. "Don't break my heart, please."

"Never."

"Happy Birthday to you!" we sing to Claire, our voices blending in cheerful harmony.

She sits in front of a decadent triple chocolate cake, lovingly baked by Mawmaw. The cake is drizzled with velvety white-chocolate ganache and is covered with colorful sprinkles. On top, two large candles form the numbers three and six. Emma stands proudly beside her sister while Colby is close enough for the flickering candlelight to dance across his face, casting a warm, golden glow. With a mischievous grin, he reaches forward, swiping a generous dollop of icing from the side of the cake.

Emma raises an eyebrow at him, shaking her head with amusement. Colby instantly licks the chocolate from his finger. "Shh," he tells her, looking at her innocently.

He pulls her closer to him and whispers something in her ear. Emma raises her brows and shakes her head. I can only imagine what he tried to pull. Their eyes dart toward me, and I lift my brows in a silent question. Colby quickly looks away, a hint of guilt flashing across his face. He knows better than to tempt fate in front of me.

"It's gift time!" Mr. Manchester announces, his voice booming with excitement. "This is for you."

Claire takes the slender box with eager hands and carefully unwraps the delicate paper that shines and sparkles.

"What is this?" She asks with wonder in her tone.

As she opens the box, a gasp escapes her lips, and her eyes widen in awe as she removes a stunning gold chain that shines in the light.

"Mom's necklace," she breathes, happiness lacing her voice.

Emma's expression softens, a warm smile spreading across her face. "This is perfect, Claire," she says with affection.

"Thank you, Daddy," Claire replies, her voice trembling with emotion as Jake helps her fasten the jewelry around her neck. Her fingers brush against the delicate pearls of her mother's necklace; a bittersweet smile on her face.

I catch Emma's eye; she seems genuinely happy, her joy radiating like sunlight. We exchange stolen glances and playful smirks, a secret connection that only we share.

My family gathers around Claire, and their laughter echoes. Mawmaw, with her infectious energy, distracts Colby, and I seize the moment to excuse myself from the room. Thanksgiving had been a whirlwind of food and fun, but despite the joy around us, Emma and I still find ourselves navigating *this* in uncharted territory. So many times today, I wanted to touch, kiss, and whisper in her ear how pretty she is, but I couldn't.

I feel like I'm losing it.

I step onto the back porch of my parents' house, the cool evening air brushing against my skin. I gaze out into the backyard, where the sun begins its slow descent, painting the sky in shades of orange and pink. A sinking feeling grips me as I contemplate the future and the unknown paths ahead of us.

Am I what she really wants?

"You okay?" Emma asks, her voice breaking through my thoughts as she gently shuts the door behind her. She stands next to me, her hand brushing against mine, sending a spark of warmth through me. I instinctively hook my finger with hers, and she smiles, a genuine expression that makes my heart flutter.

"I'm fine," I assure her. "Sometimes, family gatherings feel overwhelming. I just needed some fresh air."

I inhale deeply, savoring the coolness filling my lungs, grounding me in the moment.

"So, this is where you grew up?" she asks, eyes scanning the familiar surroundings.

I nod, nostalgia washing over me. "Yep. My old room is still set up. I'll turn forty in a few months."

Emma laughs, a melodic sound that brightens the dimming day. "Why?"

"That's where Colby stays when he's here. He loves it. I've still got the posters hanging," I reply, a hint of pride in my voice.

"I'd love to see it," she says, her enthusiasm infectious.

"Really?" I ask, keeping my finger interlaced with hers as I lead her back inside. Instead of heading to the kitchen, I guide Emma upstairs, excitement bubbling within me.

"It's pretty much identical to your house," she observes as we ascend the stairs.

With a gentle nudge, I open the door, inviting her inside. It creaks slightly, revealing the time capsule in my parent's house.

"Wow," she says, glancing around at the *Star Wars* posters that plaster the walls, the gleaming sports trophies that stand proudly on shelves, and the framed photos capturing moments frozen in time. Each item tells a story of my past.

"Have you ever had sex in here?" she asks mischievously.

"Absolutely not," I reply, my voice laced with amusement and horror. "My parents would've actually murdered me."

Just as I finish my sentence, she turns and locks the door with a click.

My brows pop up in surprise. "Emma," I whisper urgently,

shaking my head in disbelief. "Everyone is downstairs, including your father."

She lays back on the bed, lifting her skirt, pantiless.

"Fuck," I whisper, the anticipation of getting caught nearly takes hold.

"I want to be the first and last of something in your life," she whispers.

"You already are," I say, knowing she's the first woman I've ever truly loved and she will be the last.

She swallows hard as I move to her. Emma quietly unzips my pants, releasing me, and then she pulls me onto the single bed with her.

I laugh against her smooth skin. "You're getting coal in your stocking."

"I'll make a fire with it," she says in a hushed tone, widening her thighs allowing me entrance. I slide my hand under her ass, lifting her onto me.

She moans out.

I lean over and cover her mouth with my hand as I whisper in her ear as I slam into her. "You can't scream when you come on my cock."

Her breasts rise and fall as she rocks her hips, nodding with a sultry smile. My girl is greedy, and lately, we've become experts at quickies—mastering the art of seizing passion in stolen moments.

In just five minutes flat, we're unwinding, surrendering to the heat of our desires, and losing ourselves in the intoxicating rhythm of the moment. We're breathless, racing toward the end. The orgasm rips through me as Emma pulses around me. I want to scream out, but I nuzzle into her neck and hair. My girl holds back, too. Emma bites my shoulder, a playful mix of pleasure and pain that sends shivers down my spine.

"Good fucking girl," I whisper in her ear. "You do know how to be quiet."

She pants, breasts rising and falling. "Felt so good."

We stand facing each other, the air thick with sex and a thirst for one another that we'll never be able to quench.

I check my phone, noting that we've been gone for just fifteen minutes. With a playful nudge, I help reposition her hair.

"How do I look?" she asks, her voice bright as she gazes up at me, her eyes sparkling.

"Like you're mine," I reply, my heart swelling with pride and desire as I take in her flushed cheeks and the way her lips, still swollen from our kiss, glisten invitingly.

"I am. But do you think they'll know?"

I place my hands firmly on her shoulders, turning her toward the full-length mirror that stands sentinel in the corner, reflecting her in all her stunning glory.

"Probably."

Her mouth falls open in shock as she catches sight of herself. "My lips! Another hickey on my neck! Hudson! I look sex-drunk, and I have just-been-fucked hair." The realization washes over her, a mixture of embarrassment and exhilaration.

I chuckle, unable to hide my amusement. "Sorry? But I'm not."

She hastily rearranges her hair to one side, attempting to cover the mark, her fingers trembling slightly. "Please tell me we're leaving soon?"

I shake my head, relishing the moment just a bit longer. "Not a chance."

"Hudson!" A voice calls from the bottom of the stairs, unmistakably my mom's.

Leaning over, I steal a sweet kiss from Emma, pressing my lips against hers, savoring the moment. "Good luck," I whisper, a teasing grin on my face.

I open the door, adjust myself, and step into the hallway.

"Yeah? What's up?" I call down to her.

"Never mind," Mom replies, her eyes narrowing slightly as

they land on me. I glance at Jake, whose brows lift in curiosity, studying me with amusement and suspicion.

I smile innocently. "What's up?"

Their faces are giddy as they exchange glances, the atmosphere thick with unspoken questions.

"Did you go upstairs and give yourself a hickey?" Lucas asks, his expression is mock disbelief.

Mawmaw's brows lift in surprise, as she sips her spiked eggnog. Her eyes dart toward me with a knowing glint. "Where's Emma?" she asks.

"What's a hickey?" Colby pipes up, his childlike curiosity shining through. "Can I have one?"

"No," I interject firmly, trying to steer the conversation back to safer ground.

Just then, Emma descends the stairs, and every eye in the room swivels to her, captivated. "What?" she asks, a hint of confusion in her tone.

I glance back at her, my admiration swelling as I drink in her beauty and the way her hair cascades over her shoulders. She stops beside me at the bottom of the stairs, and the atmosphere feels electric.

"Are you two dating?" Mr. Manchester asks, the question hanging in the air like a challenge, the one no one else was brave enough to voice.

Emma laughs lightly, brushing off the question with a wave of her hand. "I'm just the nanny. Come on, everyone. Don't be ridiculous."

Jake's laughter bursts forth, cutting through the tension. "Hundred-dollar bills. Thirty of them. In my palm by Valentine's Day," he quips, his grin infectious.

Claire's shocked. I don't think she's said anything, but she's eyeing us.

I suck in a deep breath, redirecting my focus back to Emma, both of us uncomfortably aware of the guilt simmering beneath the surface.

"Want some eggnog?" I offer, hoping it will ease the situation.

"That would be great," she replies, her eyes widening with anticipation. But then, she catches sight of the hickey she left on my neck, and her expression shifts. "Uh."

"Yeah," I say in a hushed whisper, leading her toward the kitchen, acutely aware of the prying eyes still trained on us. A heavy silence forms around us.

"Spiked eggnog?" I announce, my voice louder than necessary, wishing desperately for them to stop scrutinizing us.

"As long as it's Mawmaw's recipe," she says. Then leans in and whispers. "Fuck!"

I can't help but chuckle. I pour us each a glass, our movements awkward and deliberate, knowing that our shared secret hangs heavily between us. We lift our glasses, the tension palpable as we sip, both acutely aware of what we did upstairs.

Did they hear us?

"I'd like to make a toast," I begin, trying to break the ice. Emma lifts her glass, a spark of excitement in her eyes. "To no regrets."

Emma repeats it, smirking. "No regrets and joy to the world."

Mawmaw raises hers with a hearty laugh. "Hear, hear!"

Then we drink, our eyes lock on each other.

"Is anyone going to answer my question?" Mr. Manchester asks.

"Dad, shut up!" Claire snaps.

Everyone takes the hint and returns to their conversations.

The world fades into a blur as Christmas music plays in the background, and it strangely feels like the beginning of a new chapter. The one where every single person in our family, including her father, knows we're fucking. I can't help but laugh.

No regrets, not when it comes to Emma, *ever*.

CHAPTER 28

EMMA

Hudson sets the last plastic bin full of decorations on the floor in the living room. The bin's sound thuds against the hardwood, echoing through the house and reflecting off the tall ceilings.

"How many trees are we putting up?" I ask again, making sure I wasn't imagining it when he told me an hour ago.

"Well, five. No, six if you count the mini ones in the bathrooms. Make it seven," he says with a nonchalant shrug, his eyes sparkling with mischief. "And if you keep making that face, we'll do ten."

"Don't you use your *daddy* voice on me," I retort, arching a brow in playful defiance.

He tries to hold back that sexy smirk, but it slips through and makes my heart flutter. Christmas music plays overhead, filling the air with a cheerful melody as Hudson unboxes the tree.

"Bee," I call, capturing him in my arms as he dashes past me. I pull him back in front of me, and his giggles echo through the large space. The fireplace cracks and pops behind me as I sit on the floor, unraveling a tangled mess of lights. "Did you hear what your dad said?"

Hudson watches us, his smile softening as he takes in our playful moment.

"I was gonna," he says, ripping away from me and moving to the cardboard box with his name written across the side in bold letters. "This one?"

"Whose name's on it?" Hudson asks, and Colby tilts his head, being silly, as if trying to decipher a riddle. "C-o-l-b-y!"

"Great, take it upstairs to your room, please."

"But *Dad*," he whines, his voice tinged with a dramatic flair only a kid can muster. "It's *heavy*."

"It has a handle. You lifted it last year with no problems. You're much stronger now. Don't make me ask again."

He shrugs, momentarily defeated, and returns to running around with the silver tinsel in his hand. It flutters behind him like a kite dancing against the wind, trailing a sparkly shimmer as he zooms through the room.

"Is it hypocritical that you own a tree farm but use plastic ones in your house?" I ask with a teasing tone.

"Colby's allergic," he explains. "When conifers are in a confined space, it gets pretty bad. I hope he grows out of it one day because it might be a hard life working on a farm full of trees."

I snicker. "I'm sure he will. So, have you decided if you're joining my cookie team yet?"

"No," he says, his answer firm yet playful.

"Okay then. Mawmaw said she'd join me if you weren't going to."

His eyes are full of disbelief. "Don't joke with me. I'll call and ask her."

"Go ahead," I challenge, hoping he doesn't follow through. But if I've learned anything from these Jolly boys, they will call my bluff every single time.

As if he reads my mind, Hudson does exactly that. He puts it on speakerphone with a mischievous glint in his eye.

"Hey, Cookie. Calling to tell me you're proposing to Emma?" she asks.

Hudson smirks. "Not yet."

The words hang in the air like a disco ball in the middle of the room, shimmering with potential.

Not yet.

That would be a Christmas wish come true.

"Emma just told me you're joining her cookie-baking team."

There's a pause, and then the playful banter resumes. "Of course I am. She's a winner."

I smile wide, appreciating Mawmaw's unwavering support. She is a girl's girl, always ready to rally behind anyone who can make her grandsons happy. Or at least that's what my sister has told me.

Hudson scoffs, laughter bubbling up. "You're coming out of retirement for her?"

"Aren't you?" she throws back, and her implication is clear; they both know it's not just about cookies.

I fall back, pointing and laughing at him, unable to contain my delight.

"Keep it up," he says to me, shaking his head before returning his attention back to her. "Okay, well, love you, Mawmaw."

"Love you, Cookie."

He ends the call, and the room feels a bit warmer, or maybe my body is on fire. Hudson does that to me.

"She *would* come out of retirement for you if you actually asked her," he tells me, his gaze teasing yet sincere.

"Did you?" I ask, my curiosity piqued. "Dating retirement."

That charming grin illuminates his face. "What do you think?"

Just then, Colby rushes over to me, dangling strands of

tinsel on my face. "Tickle monster is going to get you," he announces.

"Not the tickle monster! Rawr!" I growl, reaching forward to tickle his belly.

"Emma!" His laughter is contagious as he swats me away.

"Colby," Hudson says, more sternly. "The tree. Unbox it and set the branches on the floor, and I'll be right up, okay?"

He huffs and then grabs the box handle, his tiny muscles flexing as he effortlessly lifts it. Still, he gives a dramatic strain, swaggering up the stairs with an exaggerated grunt. The floorboards creak beneath his feet, each step echoing the weight of his playful performance. Once he's out of sight and I hear his door latch shut with a soft click, I stand and move toward Hudson, who's on his knees, carefully arranging the branches on the tree.

I look down at him, my fingers gently running through his tousled hair. His focus is intense, and his brows furrow in concentration. Suddenly, he turns to me and lifts my shirt, his plump lips brushing against my stomach. "Mm. Your skin tastes so good," he murmurs, sending a shiver of delight through me.

"Will you bake your gingerbread cookies for me?" I ask.

A half-grin spreads across his face, and desire dances in his eyes.

"The recipe is top-secret. I can't share it until I slide a ring on your finger," he replies, his tone teasing but underlined with sincerity.

"Until?" My heart won't stop fluttering each time I meet his eyes.

"Did I stutter?"

"No, you did not," I say, wanting to linger on that thought a little longer. I clear my throat. "If we work together, I guarantee we'll win without having to stupidly get the judges drunk before the event," I say enthusiastically.

He bursts into laughter, the sound rich and infectious.

"Mrs. Baxter tried that," he retorts, shaking his head, the memory amusing to him.

My tone shifts slightly as I lean closer. "Give me a chance to prove myself to you."

The words float in the air between us, heavy with unspoken implications, more profound than I'd intended. The moment's charged with possibilities and the weight of what lies ahead.

"Guaranteed?" he questions. "How?"

"After you taste it, you'll know the answer."

Feet running across the floor has me pulling away and creating space.

"The tree is up!" Colby says from the banister. "I did it all by myself. Come see."

After wrapping the final tree with lights, we carefully add the ornaments, each one carrying a story of its own. Some are handmade, crafted with love and care, while others gleam with the sheen of store-bought perfection. It's a delightful hodgepodge of decorations, each unique piece contributing to the charm of our tree. I love it so much.

"Last but not least," Hudson announces, opening a golden box that catches the sparkling light.

Colby rushes to it.

"The angel!" he exclaims, his face lighting up with pure amazement.

With great tenderness, he retrieves the ornament, cradling it like fragile China.

"Ready?" Hudson asks.

Colby nods eagerly, and Hudson lifts him toward the top

of the tree, raising him high so he can carefully set the delicate doll on top. Colby's eyes are level with the topper.

"This thing looks like Emma." Colby points at it. "You're a Christmas angel."

I glance up at the angel and see the likeness—same color hair, bright eyes, rosy-red cheeks, and lips painted a vivid red. She smiles sweetly, a smirk playing on her face as if she's guarding the secrets of the holiday season.

"How?" I ask, glancing at Hudson with surprise in my voice.

"Hm. That is weird," he replies with a shrug. "I picked it out during Colby's first Christmas and thought she was the prettiest of them all."

I continue to stare up at it, pondering its significance, and suddenly, I realize that maybe, just maybe, I *am* Hudson's type after all.

"Time to light it," Hudson says. He bends down next to the tree, glancing at us. Me and Colby take a step back and then he plugs it in, joining us. Collective gasps of awe escape our lips as we admire the tree's full glory, glittering and sparkling like a beacon of holiday cheer.

"It's the best tree ever! Now fill it with presents underneath!" Bee declares, his voice brimming with excitement.

Hudson wraps his arm around me, and I can't help but smile at the joy and love that fills the room. For the first time since my mom passed away, it feels like Christmas.

Emotions bubble and I think I might cry.

"You okay?" Hudson quietly asks.

"Yeah," I tell him, smiling. "It's just the magic of Merryville."

After dinner, bath time, and tucking Colby into bed, Hudson and I settle onto the couch downstairs with tall glasses of wine. Each glass holds half a bottle. The flames dance in the fireplace, and the glow of the Christmas tree lights cast a warm, inviting radiance throughout the room. It wraps us in a cozy ambiance that only appears during this time of year. The scent of pine candle mingles with the faint aroma of woodsmoke, enhancing the atmosphere as we sip our merlot, the rich, velvety liquid warming us from the inside out.

We sit in silence, captivated by the flickering fire, both of us too exhausted to muster the energy for anything more. An ache settles into my lower back, a reminder of how much we did today, and I feel every bit of thirty—the joy of having a kid around is etched into my bones. I wouldn't trade that kid for anything, though, and I find myself growing more attached.

"What did you want to be when you grew up?" Hudson asks, our heads resting on the same cushion. He turns toward me, and our mouths are so close we could kiss. The smell of his soap mingles with the warm air around us.

"A mom," I admit. The fantasy washes over me like a comforting tide. "I used to say I wanted seven kids."

Hudson's eyes widen in genuine surprise. "Seven?"

"And if you keep making that face, we'll make it ten," I tease, echoing his earlier words with a playful smirk.

"Jokes on you, Emma," he whispers, his eyes almost darkening. "I'm into it."

A sly smirk dances across my lips as I glance down, noticing the bulge in his gray joggers. "Mm. Thinking about putting a baby in me, turns you on."

"Fuck yes," he breathes, his voice thick with desire.

"You wanted a big family," I say, connecting the dots and realizing that's why his house is as large as it is. He dreamed of filling the spaces with laughter and love.

"Yes. At this point, I'd settle for what I have, though." He takes a deliberate sip of his wine. "Having kids is a big responsibility, and it's been rewarding. It made me view life differently, but I wouldn't jump into that again without knowing."

"Knowing what?" I urge as curiosity takes over as the fire crackles.

"Until I knew *you* weren't going anywhere," he states matter-of-factly, a seriousness sliding into his gaze. "You could still change your mind on us, Emma. You could wake up one day and realize this life, this house, this town isn't what you want."

I lean forward and kiss him, tasting the dry wine lingering on his lips. "Don't ever doubt the way I feel about you, Hudson. Okay? I'm not *her*."

"I know," he whispers. "I just don't want to be a fool in love again. I'm waiting for the bottom to fall out, for you to tell me you made a big mistake. Emma, you can have *anyone* in the world."

A small smile meets my lips, warm and genuine. "You're not *anyone*."

He breathes in deeply.

"There's something I need to tell you," he says, the seriousness settling back into his tone.

I meet his eyes, my heart races with anticipation. "Okay."

His hand rests gently on my cheek; the flicker of the fire creates a cozy ambiance.

"Emma," a tiny voice calls out from the top of the stairs, breaking the quiet moment we shared.

"Bee? You okay?" Hudson asks.

I turn my full attention back to Hudson, my heart quickening.

"Emma, will you come tell me another story?"

I glance at Hudson, wondering what he was going to say, a mix of regret and urgency bubbling up inside me. "I'm sorry. We'll finish this conversation, okay?"

He nods, his expression softening. "Bee, you sure you don't want me to come tuck you in?"

"I want Emma," he says, his tiny voice cracking.

"I've got it," I reply, forcing a grin as I rise from the cushion.

I take the stairs two at a time, meeting Colby at the top. We slip into his room, where the familiar sight of his plush toys and scattered books brings back sweet memories of earlier. His tree is lit in the corner and full of ornaments he's made.

He slides under his covers, and I gently bring them to his chest, tucking him in snugly. "Now you're like a burrito."

He grins back at me, a glimmer of joy splashing across his sleepy face. "I like burritos."

Exhaustion is etched into his features, his eyelids growing heavier. "Me too. With all the good stuff inside like chicken, rice, beans, and cheese."

"Emma?"

"Yeah?"

"Why can't *you* be my mom?"

My heart rattles in my chest at that innocent question. I keep a gentle demeanor for him as if my heart isn't breaking into a million pieces. "Because I'm your friend, Bee. That's like asking Davidson and Evie to be your mom."

My answer isn't good enough, and I think he might start crying. I move closer to him, leaning my head on his chest as his big, green eyes meet mine, glistening with unshed tears. "If you start that, I'll bring the tickle monster out," I warn.

He kicks his legs under the cozy blanket, but a smile breaks through his frustration with me. "Please no."

"Only because you said please!" I wiggle my fingers playfully at him, teasing him with the idea of the tickle monster lurking, but I know better than to get him worked up before bed. With a little coaxing, I can have him asleep in ten minutes.

All the Jollys might have those enchanting green eyes, but they're also the first thing to give away their emotions.

"I just want you to be my mom though. I even told Santa that's what I want."

I playfully gasp, the surprise almost exaggerated. "You can't ask Santa for *that*."

His innocence is unyielding, leading him to press further. "Where's your mom?"

Emotions start to bubble inside me, a mixture of both sadness and happiness, but it's been a rough day. I take a breath, steadying myself, and reply sweetly, "My mom isn't here anymore."

"Where is she?"

I force a smile, even though it feels strained and heavy on my lips. "My mom is in heaven."

Colby gasps, his eyes widening as if a lightbulb has just gone off in his mind. "She's an angel? Like on top of the tree?"

A choked laugh escapes me. "Yep, like that. Now listen, I want you to know that it's okay not to have a mom. I don't have one anymore. Neither does Aunt CeCe. You're a very, very lucky little boy who has a dad who loves you sooooo much. Plus, all your uncles care so dearly about you."

He giggles, the sound brightening the dim room.

"And your grandparents are a hoot and adore you. What other little boy in this world has Santa as a grandpa? Like, that's the absolute *coolest*! And then there's your great-grandma —lord have mercy! You won the lottery, kid." I gently pat his chest, feeling the warmth radiating from him. "Not having a mom doesn't make you any different. Okay?"

He props his head up on his elbow, tilting it at me with a curious expression, his eyes filled with admiration. "You're an angel too, Emma! Just like your mom."

I nod, a faint blush creeping up my cheeks. "Thanks, Bee."

"Will you tell me a story?" he asks, already finished with this conversation. But I have a feeling he won't forget this.

"Sure. Um. A long time ago, there was a girl who was scared of the dark. She traveled worldwide, searching for *light* to make her heart happy. She looked high and low, exploring far-off places and in hidden corners of her imagination, dreaming about feeling sunshine on her skin. One day, she thought she found it. Her heart glowed so bright for years until she realized it was only temporary."

"The batteries ran out?" he asks, his brows knitting together in contemplation.

I almost whisper, slowing down my words as if weaving a spell. "Yeah. So, for two more years, she continued to search the world. Then she decided to escape her busy life and got on a plane and flew straight to the heart of Texas to visit her sister, who'd captured the light first. The only problem is her sister couldn't share it with her because that's not how it works. But the girl had to see it with her own eyes to make sure the light really existed."

Colby's eyes grow heavy, weighted by sleep, as if my words hypnotize him. "Did it exist?"

"It did. The girl saw how beautiful the light was and how it shone so bright that there was no way in the entire world it would ever dim for her sister. It was all the proof she needed to know it was real. She felt overwhelming joy for her sibling, yet jealousy ate at her heart because it was everything she wanted. But just before the girl turned to leave for her castle in the city, she found the love of her life."

Before I'm finished, he's fast asleep, and I stare at his cute little Christmas tree with dinosaur ornaments and lights, waiting to make sure he stays asleep this time.

"Good night," I whisper, careful not to wake him as I sneak out of his room.

When I gently close the door until it clicks, Hudson stands

in the dimly lit hallway, his silhouette comforting in the shadows.

Without hesitation, he wraps his arms around me, pulling me into a tight embrace. I breathe him in, allowing the warmth of his body to capture me.

As I exhale, I release the emotional weight I've been carrying.

Today has been particularly hard, and my mother's absence weighs heavily on my mind. Christmas has always been challenging for me, but until now, I managed to keep those feelings at bay.

Hudson pets my hair as I cry, and his gentle touch is a comfort I didn't realize I needed. When I've finally poured out my heart, he pulls away slightly, his fingers tracing my cheek tenderly. "I love you, Emma."

"I love you." The words slip from my mouth like a whispered prayer. It's three words I didn't think I'd ever string together again. They carry the weight of my deepest feelings, and I've never meant them more than I do right now.

CHAPTER 29

HUDSON

I t's the morning of December first, and all through the house, not a creature is stirring—except for Mr. Stinky, who shit an entire pile of Tootsie Rolls onto the kitchen counter. His pants are down and he's bent over. Behind him are ten miniature logs stacked high. I personally think it's fucking hilarious. I capture a photo of that dirty little elf so I can have it for the album I'm compiling for Colby. Once Bee no longer believes, I hope he appreciates the trouble I go through every season to make the holidays special. I enjoy it, though; it's why I'll enthusiastically continue this charade until he's grown out of it. I'm always eager to create memories he can look back on fondly.

As Emma and Colby sleep soundly, I make a breakfast fit for my little king—and queen, of course. I've always loved the early mornings when the house is still quiet. It gives me time to think about my life and contemplate the future. The aromas of frying bacon fill the air, mingling delightfully with the rich scent of freshly brewed coffee.

Around here, birthdays are treated like their own holiday, and I always strive to make them as magical as possible. The excitement of the day buzzes beneath the surface, intensifying as I imagine the joy on Colby's face when he sees his cake and gifts.

I plan to leave work around two, ensuring I have plenty of time to mentally prepare myself to host. Large groups aren't my thing, and I typically try to avoid them, except for occasions like this. When it comes to my kid, I'll put on a cheerful facade and mask the urge to escape into the solitude of another room. I'm pro-level at this point.

In less than twelve hours, the house will be a whirlwind of bouncing kids and chatty adults. Colby invited his entire Pre-K class to celebrate with him, and it brings a giddy flutter to my heart knowing my family will be here, adding their own jolly energy to the festivities.

He'd even sweetly begged Mawmaw to bake him a cake just like Claire's, but bigger—with his charm, Mawmaw couldn't say no. It's proof that Bee can wrap any woman around his little finger. All it takes is one look, and their hearts melt.

I chuckle to myself, a soft smile gracing my lips as I reflect on how he undoubtedly inherited this gift from me. I just hope he won't be a heartbreaker like I was in my younger years; those paths often lead to trouble and loveless marriages, something I pray he steers clear of.

After taking a sip of my coffee, I remove the crispy bacon from the skillet—a task I've mastered over countless mornings. As I reach for the eggs, a pair of arms snakes around my waist, pulling me gently back into a warm embrace. Emma presses loving kisses against my back, and I turn around to find her gaze waiting for me. I slide my mouth against hers, savoring the taste of her spearmint toothpaste.

"Good morning, beautiful. How'd you sleep?" I ask, my voice still thick with sleep. I'm exhausted, but I'll catch up after Christmas. As long as it's ho ho ho season, it's go go go for me.

"Good morning. I slept great." She wears a sleepy

expression, her eyes barely open behind her black-framed glasses. "Mm. The bacon smells delicious, but can I have your meat for breakfast instead?"

I hold her close, wrapping my arm around her waist and kissing her forehead tenderly. Her hand slips into my joggers, and I feel her warm grasp.

"Jolly Jr. is fully awake this morning," she teases, grinning cheekily.

I groan out a laugh. "You named my dick Jolly Jr.?"

"Better than tripod," she quips, her laughter dancing through the air as she continues to stroke me long and hard. I slide my hands down into her pajama pants, and I'm greeted by the familiar slickness of her desire. My girl wants me all day, every day. The feeling is mutual.

I adore it when she wakes up with that fiery hunger; it's a surefire sign that I'm going to have a *very* good day. Soft sighs escape her lips, urging me on, and then I slide two fingers into her pretty pussy. As I penetrate her, she clenches around me. A sound of pleasure escapes her as she leans her elbows against the counter, presenting herself to me, eager for more.

Emma spits on her palm, then returns to sliding her hand up and down my length. The saliva adds just the right amount of friction, and my body aches with the desperate need for release. I draw wide circles around her clit, deliberately withholding the direct stimulation she craves. We have plenty of time to play this morning, and I intend to savor every delicious moment.

"Enjoy it, Em," I say, capturing her mouth with mine. She breathes me in deeply, her legs nearly giving out when I graze past her hard nub. I pull my fingers from her panties, tasting her arousal on my tongue before diving back into the game we're playing.

"I want you in my mouth. I need to taste you," she whispers. I can hardly take my eyes off Emma, as she kneels

LYRA PARISH

before me in my kitchen. I place my hand under her chin, and she devilishly smirks up at me.

With precision, Emma takes me into her mouth slowly, working me with her hand, slowing then increasing her pace. She's in complete control as she drives me further into her throat. The sensation is so intoxicating that I feel like I'm dreaming.

The pressure builds rapidly, and I grasp the edge of the counter for stability. My head falls back, exposing my neck.

"Fuck, Emma, I'm so close," I tell her, thrusting my fingers through her hair, encouraging her to take me deeper, but she pulls away.

"Not yet," my greedy girl says, smirking as she slides her tongue up and down me. "What's that you said to me? Enjoy it?"

Her fingers trail up my stomach, and she tweaks my hard nipples. "Mm, my little maneater."

"The only man I'm ever eating again is you," she confesses, returning me to her mouth. She works me up. Guttural groans release from my lips as she brings me to the brink again. My cock throbs, aching with the anticipation of giving her what we desire.

She returns to me, licking the pre-cum that's pooled at my tip, devouring me like I'm her favorite flavor. She moves me in and out of her mouth at a tortious pace.

My muscles tense, the wave of pleasure surges as I fist my fingers through her hair.

Seconds later, I hiss out a warning as I feel the desperate rush surging through me. Emma pulls back, allowing me to watch my silvery cum shoot onto her tongue in an almost surreal cascade. I grunt out my release and she swallows every drop, eager to savor the taste, licking her lips clean of the salty remnants.

Standing, she smirks with that familiar, self-satisfied grin.

"Good *fucking* girl," I say, a husky whisper in the early morning silence. I kiss her, tasting the blend of us on my lips.

"Thank you," she whispers, her smile warm against my mouth. "I'm almost convinced it's my birthday."

"I guess that makes me the present?" I ask, my heart rapidly thumps in my chest, my breathing still ragged.

She chuckles while making herself a cup of coffee, satisfied she has so much fucking control over me. Emma watches me intently from the bar stool, her gaze longing. Before I go back to cooking, I move to her, falling to my knees before her.

She holds my face in her hands, her brown eyes sparkle.

"May I pretty please return the favor?" I ask.

Emma nods, and I peel her pajama pants off her body. She scoots her ass to the edge of the chair, opening her thighs wide for me. I kiss up her thighs, planting my mouth on her clit. Her body instantly responds to my tongue flicking against her. "You taste so good."

A whimper releases from her as she rocks her hips forward, bracing herself on the barstool. Her hair falls back over her shoulders as a breathy moan escapes her. Pleasing her gives me so much pleasure I can barely stand it. I move from her clit to her tight little hole, fucking her with my tongue. She grows breathless and I know if I keep going she'll lose herself.

"Yes," she hisses out, her back arched like she's suspended in air. I smile against her, working her slower as she steadily climbs. I slide two fingers inside, curling upward, tickling her G-spot. Emma mutters something, and I chuckle against her, but keep going.

"You want it so fucking bad, I can taste it," I whisper, sucking her lips into my mouth before returning to that cute little clit.

Her muscles tighten, and I pull away, leaving her suspended in time and space. She fists her fingers through my hair, forcing my face back to her. I give her exactly what she craves. Seconds later, she groans so loud that when she comes, I think she might wake Colby. I lick her clean, not wasting any part of her, loving how sweet she tastes. Then I kiss her thighs before she leans down and slides her mouth against mine.

"I can never get enough of you," she says between breaths.

"I hope you never do." I help slide her pants back onto her body, and she squeezes her thighs together when she stands.

Once we've both come back down to reality, I wash my hands and return to cooking breakfast as she watches me. I chop the bacon and assemble the ham and cheese for the neon green omelets I'm preparing for Bee's birthday breakfast.

"On a scale of one to ten, how mad would you be if I got Colby a Rottweiler puppy?" she asks.

I set down the knife and turn to her, eyes widening in disbelief. "You didn't."

"A ten is the maddest you are on my scale."

I raise my brows.

"Okay, what if it were a Golden Retriever puppy?"

"Ten! Please tell me you didn't."

Her expression is theatrical worry, but she can't hold it very long as I stare at her. "Okay, I didn't. I was testing the waters."

"Please promise me you won't. I've got a puppy plan in place already."

Her eyes light up. "That's all I needed to hear. Just making sure my little bestie gets everything he wants in life."

I raise a brow. "Oh, so you're besties now?"

"Absolutely."

"Happy Birthday to youuuuuuu!" The room bursts into song for Colby, the joyous sound floats through the air. Everyone is happy, and my son is having the time of his life.

I stand across from him with Emma on one side and my brothers on the other.

"Blow out the candles and make a wish," Mawmaw urges, her love radiant as she watches her great-grandson.

Colby looks from me to Emma, excitement bubbling in his eyes. "I wish for—"

"Not out loud," I interrupt, my tone playful. "Or it won't come true."

He closes his eyes, concentrates, and makes his secret wish before blowing out the five candles in one swift breath. My boy is growing up before my eyes; I can nearly see his entire life unfolding in faded memories, snapshots of laughter and joy. On the outside, my demeanor remains steady, but Emma must've sensed something was off and hooks one finger to mine—a hidden gesture, a reminder that she's here, that she sees me. The warmth of her touch makes my smile widen when I glance at her.

"So," I step forward, breaking the brief, beautiful moment. "I guess we should cut this cake."

Every kid, along with Mawmaw, Jake, and Claire, yells excitedly. Their voices merge into a joyful cacophony that fills the air. I pick up the cake slicers, their silver edges glint under the bright lights. I get to work, plopping hefty pieces of five-layer chocolate cake onto colorful plates decorated with playful dinosaurs. The rich aroma of chocolate wafts through the room, heightening the anticipation as the cake makes its way around. Just as the last slice is being served, the doorbell rings. Its chime cuts through the laughter.

"I don't think I've ever heard anyone ring it before," my mother muses, her brow furrowing slightly in curiosity.

Jake and Lucas nod in agreement, their eyes darting toward the door, intrigued.

"I'll get it. Carry on," Emma chirps, her bubbly personality shining like a beacon in the crowd.

"Dad, when can we open presents?" Colby interjects, his voice brimming with eagerness as Emma breaks away. Chocolate is already all over his face, fingers, and shirt.

"After you've finished eating," I explain, trying to keep the distraction from derailing the excitement.

My eyes stay glued to Emma as she moves toward the door, the brightness of her smile lighting up her face as she glances back at me watching her. In a crowded room, I'll always have my gaze planted on her.

As she swings the door open, I notice her entire demeanor shifts, like a cloud passing over a sunny day. My heart rate upticks, and I put down my fork.

When I glance past her, I see a ghost from my past. One that I had hoped would never haunt me again.

Meredith.

CHAPTER 30

EMMA

"Can I help you?" I say, immediately recognizing her. Thank God I flipped through those wedding albums; otherwise, her presence would have completely blindsided me.

She's wearing a fake designer pantsuit, an ill-advised imitation that screams desperation, and she carries herself like she's hot shit. Her confidence is unwavering, yet it feels unwarranted, considering she's unwelcome here. Her ice-blue eyes are as cold as her heart, and her smile doesn't quite reach her eyes. A shiver runs down my spine as I wonder what Hudson saw in her.

I close the door behind me, crossing my arms over my chest, creating a barrier between us. "What do you need?"

"If you could fetch my husband for me, I'd appreciate it," she says impatiently, her tone dripping with condescension.

My nostrils flare.

She's lying.

"Oh, he didn't tell you that we're still married? I'm sorry. He's always been so secretive," she says, attempting to glide past me, but I stand my ground, immovable.

"You're not welcome inside," I say, unamused, my voice steady.

"Not welcome? Sweetheart, half of this place is mine." Her words slice through the air, thick with bravado.

Just then, the door swings open, and Hudson steps out; fury radiates from him.

"Meredith," he spits her name, each syllable laced with venom. And knowing what he's shared about her, it's warranted.

"You didn't tell your little adulteress that you're still married? Shame on you, Hudson. How old is she? Twenty?" Meredith shakes her head in mock disbelief, a smirk dancing on her lips.

"Shut the fuck up," he states, not biting at her taunts. It's as if he's trained himself to withstand the sharp, daggered words she throws his way, and I'm astounded by how effortlessly she wields them.

"What do you want? Because if you don't answer in thirty seconds, I'll call the police and have you escorted off my property."

She shakes her head, dismissive. "Until we're officially divorced, that's a civil matter. You and I both know they won't do anything. I'd like to see my son now," she says, waving her hand like a queen shooing away a servant.

"You'll see him when he asks to see you. And that will never happen," Hudson growls, his voice low and lethal. He's livid; I can tell by his rigid stance, the pulse in his neck thrumming like a war drum.

"I need to go back inside," I say, unease creeping in with each passing second. He didn't deny their marriage.

I feel sick, the punch I drank earlier threatening to come back up.

If the internet finds out about this...

I push the thoughts away, trying to yank my mind out of this doom spiral, fearing I might not survive the descent.

Right now, it doesn't matter what anyone thinks; all that matters is what Hudson has to say.

I want to escape; I want to run when the weight of this situation becomes unbearable, but I won't do that—for Colby's sake. It would make me no better than her.

How could she try to ruin his party like this?

When I return to the festivities, I plaster on a fake grin, hoping it will stave off the questions, but my sister sees right through it.

"Who is that?" she whispers, concern threading through her voice.

"Hudson's wife," I say, meeting Claire's eyes, silently questioning if she knew. If everyone in this house knew but no one had the respect to tell me, I'll leave for New York tonight.

Jake and Lucas are standing in the kitchen, deep in conversation, while everyone else indulges in cake. Laughter rings out and happiness continues to fill the space. The scent of chocolate wafts through the air, making me queasy. Colby is at the coffee table, surrounded by his friends from school, their voices a lively buzz as they eat cake and share excited whispers.

"It doesn't mean anything," Claire eventually says, grabbing my hand and squeezing it tightly, her grip both reassuring and pleading. "Hudson isn't like that."

"But he is. Did you know?" I whisper urgently, fear lacing my words.

"No, I swear I didn't."

"Claire, if the internet gets this information, it will ruin everything," I insist, the weight of the impending disaster pressing heavily on my chest. I won't be able to handle the smear campaigns.

"Will it?" she questions, her brow furrowing slightly. "You don't need the internet to survive, Em. You only need you."

I nod, grounding myself in the truth. I'm the only person who has never let me down.

"You're doing that thing you do," she explains, her tone

softening, but the words pierce me nonetheless. "Where you try to ruin a good thing."

"I don't do that." I protest.

"Are you sure?" she presses, and my heart races, the rhythm echoing in my ears. I think back to various situations in my life that didn't work out, flipping through memories like a worn book, the pages fluttering whimsically yet painfully.

"For once, I did nothing wrong," I tell her, my voice steady.

"You're right. It's how you react when things happen, sis. You run."

Her words stab me in the heart, a reminder that maybe I'm no better than Meredith, after all.

As if summoned by my thoughts, Hudson returns, and his eyes immediately find mine. I quickly look away, my stomach churning. The air in the room is thick with a suffocating cloud of unspoken truths.

"Are we ready to open those presents?" Hudson asks. To everyone else, he's just a happy dad, but I see through it.

I move to the kitchen to pour another glass of punch, the deep blue liquid promising a brief escape as Colby excitedly rips wrapping paper open.

"You okay?" Lucas sidles up beside me, his casual demeanor a stark contrast to my inner turmoil.

"Sure," I tell him, taking a sip, its sweetness momentarily distracts me.

"You're a horrible liar, you know that? The absolute worst." He chuckles lightly, a hint of warmth in his voice.

"Shut up," I retort, rolling my eyes but unable to suppress a smirk.

"It's gonna be okay, Em. Trust me," he says, sincerity in his gaze. I keep my back toward the crowd, but Lucas looks out at them with an amused expression. "Oh, look. My brother is watching you like a hawk right now." He lifts his punch glass. "Probably scared I'm gonna steal you away."

I can't help but laugh, the sound breaking the gloom for a moment. "Can you not do that right now?"

"You're prettier when you smile."

"And now you're flirting with me?" I shake my head, the situation feeling almost absurd. "It's really not the time."

He smirks, unfazed. "Well, if you ever need a knight in shining armor to save you, you've got my number."

I playfully scoff just as Jake walks over, a protective aura surrounding him. "There's my favorite sister. You good?"

Lucas holds out his hand in mock indignation. "Excuse me? We were having a conversation. I was just about to ask Emma out on a date."

Jake glares at him, the tension shifting momentarily as he pours a cup of punch. "Do not start *that* again. It's not the time."

Lucas raises an eyebrow, a playful smirk dancing at the corners of his lips. "There is no greater gift than the present."

He winks at me, and despite everything, I feel a smile push its way onto my face. They stand on either side of me, tall and muscular, their presence both comforting and humorous. I snicker, unable to help myself. Regardless of all the thoughts sliding through my mind, this feels like home. I feel safe.

"What?" Lucas asks, an air of genuine curiosity in his tone.

"You're like my bodyguards," I tease, the absurdity of the moment drawing me from the edge of my worries.

Jake shrugs, the corners of his mouth twitching upward. "I'd fuck someone up if they tried to mess with you."

Lucas gives him a high five.

"Look at Hudson. He's pissed, isn't he?" Lucas says, his voice laced with disbelief and amusement as he leans slightly toward me, gesturing toward Hudson with a nod. "Jesus. I haven't seen him this angry in a very long time. Almost looks like he's going to explode. I bet the sex is great after this."

"Shut up!" I elbow him hard in his side and double over, laughing.

"Hudson will be fine," Jake reassures, though the underlying concern in his tone suggests otherwise. He then glances at me, with a gentle expression. "Will you?"

"Yes," I mutter, but it feels like a lie. "I'll survive."

"Promise me that you'll hear him out," Jake offers, his eyes pleading as if my agreement could somehow mend the rift between us. "Please, Emma."

"I promise." As the words leave my mouth, Colby calls my name. His small voice cuts through the crowd as he enthusiastically waves me over. I glance back at Jake, his worried gaze lingering on me, before moving across the living room.

They do know. All of them.

"Can we put this LEGO together?" he asks, holding up the brightly colored box, his eyes shining eagerly. The children from his classroom gather around him, their laughter mixing with the remnants of wrapping paper strewn across the floor and the tables—evidence of the chaotic joy that filled the room. A stack of opened gifts sits in the middle, their shiny boxes reflecting the warm light of the room.

"Of course," I say, my heart warms at his excitement. It always does.

I lean down to wipe some chocolate icing from his face, and he giggles, turning his head away from me in that playful way only little boys can.

The kids play for thirty more minutes, their shouts of glee filling the air, but as shadows grow longer and darkness settles outside, the adults begin shuffling out, signaling the end of our gathering.

Claire hugs me tightly, her arms wrapping securely around me. "If you need me, text me, okay?" Her voice is a soft murmur against my ear.

314

"I will," I say, appreciating the gesture more than she knows.

"Bee, you wanna come to Grandma's house until dinner?" Hudson's mother asks him, her voice warm and inviting.

"Oh yes! Daddy?" Colby grabs Hudson's shirt, tugging gently as he tries to bring him back from whatever distant place his mind had wandered. He's lost in thought, his gaze distant and unfocused.

He forces a grin, even if it's a weak one. "Sure, if you want. You're the birthday boy."

"Yes!" Colby exclaims, his face lit up with pure joy.

Hudson's mom looks between the two of us and nods, extending her hand for Colby to take.

"Can we watch *Elf*?" he asks her eagerly as they move toward the front door, his little feet patter on the wooden floor.

She chuckles softly, a warm flicker of nostalgia in her eyes. "Of course."

Colby waves goodbye to us, his excitement palpable, and as soon as they leave, a heavy silence settles in the room.

Neither of us speaks.

I find myself staring at the fireplace, aware that more wood needs to be added to keep the flames alive, just as I need something to keep my own heart warm.

"I'm sorry I didn't tell you and—"

"Don't apologize," I say, shaking my head gently, trying to brush away the unspoken hurt lingering in the air. "I just..."

I thought he trusted me. Words escape me, swirling just out of reach, and I swallow down the pain, feeling my throat tighten. His eyes remain locked on me, intense and searching, but I can't bring myself to meet his gaze. Hudson steps closer, the space between us is almost suffocating.

"Emma," he whispers, his voice barely above a breath. When my eyes flick up to his, I see the weight of his pain reflected back at me, raw and real.

"I'm sorry for hurting you." His jaw clenches tight, the muscles taut beneath the surface.

The silence hangs heavy in the air. Hudson sucks in a deep breath, and in that moment, he wraps his arms around me, pulling me tight against him, as if he can shield me from everything outside of this moment.

I inhale him like this might be the last time.

"I filed for divorce the day after I met you back in July. When I saw you, my world changed, Emma. I tried to track Meredith down to discuss it, but couldn't, so my lawyer filed the petition without her. Two days before it was set to be finalized, she contested." He swallows hard, and the harsh reality of his words cuts through me like a knife. "She's trying to take Colby away from me, Em."

I take a step back from him, my heart racing as I search his eyes for some semblance of hope. There is none. "What? No."

"We tried mediation, and she refused to cooperate. Next month, I have a court hearing with evidence proving she hasn't been a part of Colby's life since the beginning. Not to mention the handfuls of addresses she's lived at over the years in different states. Everything will be presented in front of a judge. But..." His voice cracks, his words hanging heavy in the air. "This is Texas, and if her performance is good enough, she could get partial custody. She agreed to everything else I requested in the divorce, except for that."

"So, all she has to do is agree to full custody, and this is over?" I lean forward, urgency coursing through me as I grab his hand, anchoring myself in the moment.

"Yes. But she never will. She's determined to make my life hell for as long as possible."

A fire ignites inside me, a fierce determination rising to the surface as I remember who I truly am. "Consider it taken care of."

"What?" He shakes his head, panic flashing in his eyes. "No, don't get involved."

"Please find out where she's staying while she's here, or I will." The intensity in my voice leaves no room for doubt.

"Emma," he pleads more desperately, gripping my hand tighter as if he could physically pull me away from his troubles.

"We'll figure it out together, okay? *Let me help you.*" I cradle his face in my hands, searching his eyes for that glimmer of hope I want to reignite. Slowly, I see it—the light responding to my touch. I'm not running away from this situation. "I do require one thing."

He nods, his expression steely. "Anything."

I smile, the warmth of our connection filling the space between us. "You're joining my cookie team."

Laughter erupts from him, breaking through the tension like a ray of sunshine on a stormy day. He pulls me closer, and in that moment, he kisses me as if tomorrow will never come. It grows desperate and needy, our lips moving in a passionate dance that speaks volumes. He moans against me, and I feel my emotions bubble over, a heady mix of love and urgency.

"You deserve your freedom, Hudson. No matter what happens between us, I'll fight for you and Colby to get that."

"I don't deserve you," he says, his voice thick with emotion.

"That's where you're wrong," I whisper, letting my breath mingle with his, the promise of a shared future hanging in the air. "I'll burn the world down for you and let the fire light our path. Me and you."

CHAPTER 31

HUDSON

I pull the gingerbread cookie dough from the fridge. I've made enough to last until January. A portion is earmarked for the fierce competition that takes place this weekend. We'll compete against some of Merryville's most notorious cheaters, the Purple Hairs. They are cunning and relentless, doing whatever they can to secure a spot in the Hall of Fame and be crowned as the Cookie Queen or King.

Last night, I promised Emma I'd join her team. Tonight, we're doing a test run.

Together, we'll win this contest and conquer whatever life throws our way.

This morning, I woke up hours earlier than usual, driven by a restless energy that's haunted me since I saw Meredith again. I regret giving her any part of myself, and I was furious to learn she's staying in town with her aunt until our court hearing in January. That means six long weeks of me constantly glancing over my shoulder, checking to confirm she's not lurking in the shadows, especially when I'm with Colby.

I refuse to let that Grinch bitch steal Christmas.

While the house was still asleep, I mixed away my worries

and frustrations, pouring every ounce of care and attention into the preparation. Mawmaw always promised I'd want to bake with the love of my life and often spoke about how truly special sharing our family recipe is—like a family heirloom passed down through generations, cherished and revered.

I've only shared the experience of making these cookies with my son. Each memory is tinged with the joyous chaos of a messy kitchen and the innocent laughter that fills the air, an echo of sweetness that reminds me of how lucky I am. And soon, those moments will expand to include Emma.

The thought brings me happiness, filling me with warmth as I imagine the laughter and mess we'll create together— flour dust swirling like fairy dust around us, our hands sticky with dough while we whimsically cut out each cookie.

I look around the dark house, the shadows stretching across the walls like whispers of the past, secrets held tight in every corner. The only lights on are in the kitchen, softly illuminating the space with a warm glow, and the twinkling Christmas tree stands sentinel, radiating a gentle luminosity that dances across the room.

My eyes drift up to the delicate angel perched at the top of the tree, a porcelain figure that seems to embody all the hopes and dreams I've tucked away. I can't help but notice how much it resembles Emma, with her soft features and radiant spirit—a beacon of light in the reflection of my life.

As if I summoned her, Emma moves gracefully down the stairs, floating toward me like she was plucked from my dreams. I watch every quiet step she takes, how she navigates the wooden boards that creak just a bit too loudly in the hush of the night. She's so breathtakingly gorgeous that she steals my breath away, leaving my heart racing and my thoughts scattered like fallen leaves in the crisp autumn air.

When she glances in my direction, she grins, and I return the gesture. Her bright, shining eyes lock onto mine, sparking a silent question deep inside me: can I be the man who makes her happy?

"He's asleep," she whispers, moving closer toward me. "I made sure."

She pauses, hooking her finger with mine, her soft skin sending tiny electric shocks through me. "Are you okay?"

"I am, now," I say, her simple touch igniting a flutter within me. It's not like anything I've ever felt with anyone before. Every second of her closeness is charged with unspoken possibilities.

"Okay," she replies, her gaze shifting to the counter where the mounds of dough sit, waiting to be brought to life. A smile spreads across her face, deepening the warmth in her kind eyes with a sense of adventure. "Teach me. Show me what it's like to bake for fun for once."

An overwhelming rush of joy floods through me, and I can't help but wonder if this is the very sensation Mawmaw had spoken of. It's a beautiful blend of happiness swirling around us like a festive snowstorm. The feeling fills the kitchen and mixes with the sweet scent of sugar and flour.

"You have goose bumps," Emma observes, her attention caught by the tiny eruptions of sensations that capture me.

"You do that to me," I admit in a hushed tone, the heat of the moment urging me forward. Her finger trails across my skin, a gentle caress that ignites an overwhelming urge to kiss her.

So I do.

Her eyes flutter closed, and my fingers caress the outside of her cheek, feeling her smooth skin beneath my fingertips. A soft, unexpected moan escapes her lips, and I can't help but smile; a light inside my heart glows, a soft flicker in the dark.

"What was that for?" she asks her voice a soft melody that dances between us.

"I wanted to make sure you were real."

"Am I?" she whispers, her breath barely a wisp in the space between us.

"Fuck, I hope so. Because if this is a dream, I never want to wake up."

With a teasing pinch, she giggles—a sound that seems to brighten the room even more. "You're living it with me this Christmas."

"Do you want my answer now?" I inquire, curiosity dancing in my eyes.

She shakes her head; the tree lights reflect in her eyes like shimmering stars. "New Year's Eve."

"Why're you so damn stubborn?" I playfully ask, captivated by her.

"I'm adamant," she states, pausing as if weighing the decision to share her next thoughts. The air thickens with anticipation. "When I was a little girl, my mother told me the man I was meant to be with for the rest of my life would kiss me as the ball dropped in Times Square at midnight. We used to laugh about it, and she said she could envision it as clear as day." Emma's voice softens, and her eyes reflect the distant memories. "For as long as I've been alive, no one has ever kissed me at midnight as the ball dropped. The little girl in me longs to live out my mother's fairy tale. I want to feel that magic so she remains a part of that special moment for me somehow."

A few tears fall, catching the soft light and glistening like diamonds on her cheeks. I immediately move forward, kissing them away, feeling the weight of her unfulfilled dreams settle heavily in the space between us.

"That's why I want your answer then. We have weeks until that moment arrives, and skeletons are falling from closets. You can still change your mind."

I move closer, my fingers brushing lightly against the soft skin of her neck, the warmth that radiates between us drawing me in deeper as I lose myself in the depths of her gaze. It feels as though we're suspended in time—a fragile bubble surrounds us, holding us in place. "You're sure I'm still what you want?"

She looks at me, eyes glistening with so much care and passion that I don't need her words. It's as if I can hear her heart beating just for me—a gentle thrum that resonates in the silence between us.

"Never doubt the way I feel about you."

Our lips crash together, a collision of need and want.

"If we don't stop, we'll never get these cookies baked," I say playfully, pulling away to gather my thoughts and preheat the oven. The comforting scent of the dough warms my spirit as I grab the light-colored baking sheets and the parchment paper. I set them out on the countertop.

"Choose the shape of the cookies," I offer, gesturing towards the drawer brimming with an array of metal cookie cutters I've collected over the years.

Emma swings it open and digs around, and the metal clanks together. Eventually, she pulls one out with a mischievous grin. "This is the one."

I glance over at her, raising a brow in playful protest. "We're not making dick cookies."

She bursts into laughter, her delight bright and infectious. "Come on, at least a few! Why do you even have this?"

A flood of memories washes over me.

"One time, Lucas had the flu, so I baked him cookies to cheer him up," I admit as the silly recollection unfolds in my mind.

"Did it work?" she asks, continuing her search.

"He enjoyed the hell out of it," I reply, laughing like it was yesterday. "He sent me tons of pictures of him with the dick cookies in his mouth. It cheered me up too."

"You're a great big brother," Emma comments, her eyes sparkling with warmth. "And dad."

"Eventually, husband," I say, and she chews on her bottom

lip as she returns to me, holding a traditional gingerbread cutter. She bends down and smells the dough.

"Mm. We're winning this." A flicker of competitiveness ignites behind her eyes, gleaming like a hidden fire ready to blaze.

I take a step back, my heart racing. "You're serious."

She smirks, an expression that holds pure determination. "When I want something, I get it."

"Fuck," I growl, a mix of admiration stirs within me. "Let's win this, then. Do you want them soft or hard?"

Her eyes trail down my chest, my stomach, and to my cock that's ready to play.

"Hard, but if we're talking about cookies soft."

I try to stay focused, but she's making it *hard*. Literally. I adjust myself and clear my throat. "For a softer cookie, we'll keep them thicker and bake them for less time."

I sprinkle flour on the counter, the white powder settles like fresh snow. Suddenly, she flicks some at me, a playful challenge dancing in her eyes.

"Don't start no shit, won't be no shit," I tell her, an amused grin creeping onto my face as I return the favor.

She happily helps me unwrap the dough, its coolness a sharp contrast to the warmth building between us. I plop two mounds in front of us. The sight of the soft, buttery mass makes my mouth water. They're a holiday tradition.

I hand her a rolling pin, while I take the kid-sized one that Colby uses during our baking sessions.

"That thing looks miniature in your hands," she quips, and I take a mental snapshot of how pretty she looks at this moment. She's like the sunlight breaking through clouds.

"What?"

"You're gorgeous," I mutter, taking a few more seconds to drink her in, her laughter ringing like music to my ears. "Now get to rollin' and use those muscles."

"Is that what you tell Colby?"

"Exactly," I reply, thinking about his little hands working the dough. "And he rawrs every time afterward."

Emma slams the rolling pin onto the mound, and with a fluidity that suggests she's done this a million times, she gets to work. I turn on some holiday music, letting the warm melodies fill the kitchen and hug us in a cozy ambiance.

The smile that settles on my face might be permanent as the sweet aroma of spices and sugar begins to bind us together, swirling around us. I show her the correct thickness for the dough, and she matches mine with ease, our movements synchronizing like a well-rehearsed dance.

When the dough is flat, I grab the cutter and hand it to her, my heart swelling with anticipation. "Go ahead."

She presses out the shapes, each gingerbread figure taking form with her careful touches. "Can't forget the dicks," she tells me, her brows raised in jest as she cuts out the cock and balls.

"You're addicting," I say.

"You are too."

We work diligently, not allowing any dough to go to waste. The extra scraps get rolled out again, our laughter mingling with the clatter of rolling pins.

There are too many stolen glances and unspoken words, an electric tension simmering between us as we dance around one another in the kitchen, moving like we've practiced this choreography countless times.

I slide the full trays inside the oven, the warmth rushes us. Emma grabs a mixing bowl and measuring cups, her excitement bubbling over.

"What's all this?"

"We're making gingerbread man sandwiches with my favorite vanilla cream cheese frosting. I stumbled across it a long time ago, and if your cookies are as orgasmic as my sister says, well...we win."

I tilt my head at her, a knowing smile spreading across my face. "It's always been my dream to win this."

"That trophy is ours, babe," Emma declares, her determination shimmering in her eyes as she softens the butter and cream cheese. "Can you sift the powdered sugar, please?"

"Yes, Chef," I reply, winking at her as she lifts the top of the stand mixer. She slowly adds the ingredients, turning the mixer on, the rhythmic whir filling the air. Not rushing, she carefully incorporates everything, dashing in this and splashing in that, her instincts guiding her rather than precise measurements. It's what Mawmaw calls baking with love.

When it's smooth, she swipes her finger inside the bowl, her eyes sparkling.

"Want to taste it?" she asks as the soft notes of "Have Yourself a Merry Little Christmas" plays overhead. It sets the mood perfectly.

I nod, pulling her hand to my mouth, sucking the sweet, rich icing off her finger. The taste is a mini explosion of flavor. Her breath catches in her throat, her eyes full of desire.

"Fuck, tastes so good," I growl, my voice a low rumble that vibrates through the space between us.

"Look what you did to me," she whispers, glancing down at her arm, where goose bumps cover her skin along with the remnants of flour.

"I hope it never fades away," I say, pulling her into me, and we slowly sway barefoot in the kitchen—a dance that feels both intimate and carefree. The soft rhythm of the moment pulls us closer as I spin her around, joy stretches between us.

"Are you happy?" she asks.

"Yes," I admit, just as Frank Sinatra's smooth voice flows through the air, crooning about shining stars and boughs. The last notes of the song fade away, and we step apart, the moment brief yet electric. Emma's cheeks flush a vibrant pink, and she takes a cautious step back, her gaze lowered.

"You make me want to do very bad things to you," she adds, a mischievous edge to her voice.

"Mm. Like what?" A playful smirk dances on my lips.

Before she can respond, the oven dings, slicing through the moment. I quickly grab a mitt and slide the trays onto the top of the oven. Years of practice have taught me to let the cookies rest for about two minutes before transferring them to the cooling rack—patience yields the best results.

Emma leans against the counter, her eyes fixed on me, animated by the infectious cheer of "Jingle Bells" playing. A moment later, she opens the liquor cabinet and retrieves a bottle of whiskey, her movements fluid and confident.

"Oh, we're going there tonight?" I raise an eyebrow, a playful challenge in my tone.

She smirks. "Yes, the icing is made. Now we just have to wait for those cookies to cool."

"Thirty minutes," I remind her, a countdown hanging in the air.

Unfazed, she uncaps the bottle and swallows down two big gulps, the whiskey gliding down her throat. She shakes it off, her cheeks flushing a deeper shade of pink. I take a generous swig, the burn both painful and welcoming. I anticipate the calm it brings.

Emma carefully places the cookies on the wire racks, then takes my hand, leading me to the living room.

The tree lights the space, casting a yellow glow around us, while the cheerful holiday music floats lightly in the background.

"I found out where Meredith is staying," I say, the words thick with unease.

She climbs onto my lap, straddling me. Her weight on me is both grounding and intoxicating.

"I don't want to talk about her," she whispers against my lips. "I can see the stress etched on your face. I want to take your mind away from it all, Hudson."

I lean back, surrendering to her allure, the whiskey swims blissfully through my system. Emma unbuttons her shirt, revealing her beautiful breasts. I lean forward, capturing one peaked nipple in my mouth, then tease the other. She threads her fingers through my hair, the sensation exhilarating and desperate.

"Everything will work out. I promise," she says, her body rocking against me. My body responds instantly, the heat between us undeniable. Her lips trail along my neck, and she places soft kisses just below my ear before nibbling at my lobe.

"I wish I could describe how you make me feel." Her breathless whispers ignite that familiar buzzing only she can evoke in me, and it spreads through my body like wildfire.

With tender care, I slip her shirt off her shoulders, my fingers trailing down her spine, savoring the feel of her skin beneath my touch.

Her mouth meets mine, and our tongues dance in perfect harmony. The sweet scent of her skin captures me, clouding my thoughts, making every worry and stress fade away. When I look up into her eyes, it's like I can see the world differently.

"I ache for you, Hudson," she gasps, rocking against me. I lay her down on the couch, craving her as much as she craves me. Emma wiggles out of her shorts, the fabric slipping to the floor, exposing her body to me in the dim light. I slide off my joggers, the air between us electric.

I say her name so softly as I slide inside her, a whisper filled with longing. With my forehead pressed against hers, she adjusts to me, and I savor the softness of her body below mine. Our kisses and movements grow more intense, a dance of lips and tongues as I drive deeper. There is no rushing or urgency; I want to spend every precious second with her.

The sound of her breathless moans and hushed whispers nearly drives me to the edge. And nothing matters as we make love by the twinkling lights of the Christmas tree.

Nothing but us.

CHAPTER 32

EMMA

"You want me to join you? And do what exactly?" Claire asks, her voice laced with confusion.

"Look. You're the scariest person I know, and I'd like moral support. Please?" I lean against her bedroom doorway, wearing my favorite black heels and a dress that hugs my body like a second skin. I can still feel the remnants of last night with Hudson coursing through my veins. Today's bullshit quickly overshadows my hungover haze.

She huffs, her arms crossing over her chest as her piercing gaze assesses me. Deep down, she knows that I'm a softie. "Pretty, pretty, please?" I add, my tone thick with desperation.

"Fuck. Fine. Let me change. Five minutes?"

"Make it three," I counter, the urgency in my voice creeping up. "If we're late, it will ruin everything."

She groans dramatically. "This is my day off, you know."

"Thank you. I'll owe you big time." I turn and make my way into the living room, where the soft morning light spills through the half-drawn curtains, painting everything in muted gold. My father is seated at the bar, coffee steaming in front of him. The faint scratch of a marker against paper echoes in the stillness as he works on a crossword puzzle. Dressed in plaid pajamas that have seen better days, he looks oddly at home here, his demeanor calm in a way that feels foreign.

"How are you?" he asks, glancing up with mild curiosity. Since he arrived in Merryville, I can count how many times I've seen him on one hand. To say I've avoided him has been an understatement, but I've also been busy having fun with Colby daily. Still, my sister says responsibilities aren't an excuse.

"I'll be better in a few hours." My face is a mask, set in stone, my mind racing with the choices ahead. "I have a lot on my mind."

"Love does that," he mutters, returning to the puzzle.

I don't deny it. I can't.

Standing beside him, I notice a word he hasn't circled yet. I reach over, my fingers brushing the paper as I point at it. "Cashmere."

He circles it absently, then glances back at me. "Do you love him?"

The weight of his question settles heavily in the air. I meet my dad's eyes, and the steady rhythm of my heartbeat pounds in my ears. We've never discussed anything like this before. "Yes," I say, knowing it's the truth.

"It's mutual, Em." He smiles, as if what he said is merely a fact, an everyday truth.

Is it?

I study my father, searching for answers. "How do you know that?"

"Hudson and I have coffee once a week. And have since I arrived," he says nonchalantly, as though it's the most normal thing in the world.

My mouth falls open. "What?"

"Wait, you didn't know?" he asks, bewilderment flaring in his eyes.

"No," I whisper, my heart racing as I process this. Hudson's seen my father more than I have.

"Hm. Well. He just moved up a rank on my respect list. I asked him to keep it between us. He did. Good on him."

My mind races, and I struggle to grasp the idea of them meeting up. When would he have had time for that?

"What do you talk about?"

Dad grins, his tone taking on a reflective air. "Life. Being a father. How hard it is to raise kids without a mother present."

My heart lurches, a combination of sadness and guilt flooding through me.

I realize I never gave my father the same grace I've extended to Hudson. I've watched Colby struggle to understand his mother's absence and have seen what it's done to Hudson. I've never paused to consider my own father and how he navigated losing his true love while raising a pre-teen.

Tears well in the corners of my eyes as the weight of shared grief settles between us.

"Oh, Emma," Dad says, setting down the marker. He opens his arms, and I hug him, inhaling the comforting scent of his familiar aftershave, which carries the faint traces of sandalwood and something distinctly him. "I know I was a shitty dad after losing your mom, and I'll forever regret not being there for you when you needed me the most. There aren't many things in my past that I wish I could change, but that's one of them. There's no way you can begin to understand what it feels like to lose the love of your life, and I hope you never do. It changes you." His voice falters slightly, revealing the raw emotion that he rarely lets surface.

I squeeze him tighter, feeling the weight of the world on my shoulders. Understanding what real love feels like floods my senses and losing that would destroy me. What he and my mom had wasn't fake. "I'm so sorry."

"Uhh," I hear from behind me.

I turn to see Claire, who's dressed in a sharply tailored black pencil skirt and a crisp white shirt that accentuates her figure. Her heels, high and fierce, echo against the wooden floor. She struts forward with a mixture of attitude and urgency.

"Too much?" she asks.

"Perfect. Boss bitch outfit." I smile wide, reveling in her confidence. "You can take the girl out of corporate but..."

Claire flips her hair over her shoulder and grabs her phone. "Dad, watch Tinsel. And please do not let her outside again." Claire's tone suggests there is no room for argument.

He sheepishly smiles at me, a flicker of remorse in his eyes. "Maybe we can have dinner soon?"

I grin back, warmth spreading over me. "I'd like that."

Claire grows impatient. "I don't have all day. You said nine sharp."

"Okay, okay, let's go." Sometimes, I forget that my sister is a psycho about being on time.

As we step outside, my sister stops dead in her tracks when she sees the minivan parked on the pavement. "We aren't driving that."

"Why not? It's cool. It has a TV that flips down," I explain, waving my hand toward the vehicle, hoping to sway her. Colby loves it.

"No. One second." She rushes back inside and returns a moment later, keys jingling with purpose in her hand. Inside the garage sits her sparkling white Mercedes, sunlight glinting off the immaculate surface. The only reason it's so clean is because she hardly ever drives it.

"Aw, it has a full tank of gas," she exclaims, her face lighting up as we climb in. "Jake keeps it full for me."

"I wonder why," I mutter under my breath, a smirk creeping onto my lips, knowing full well she's run out of fuel more times than I can count, leaving her stranded in some inconvenient location, usually on the side of the road outside of Merryville.

"Do you have a plan?" Claire glances at me, her brow arched.

"No," I tell her, my voice steady. "Mawmaw told me to do what I had to do."

Claire makes a face at the mention of Hudson's grandmother. "Mawmaw is unhinged sometimes."

I burst into laughter, the tension of the morning almost dissipates. "I think we might become besties."

We drive to town and park at a cozy little antique shop. The streetlamps are decorated with lit wreaths. They're all wrapped like candy canes, too.

Claire radiates confidence as we get out of the car, and I follow her into the Snowflake Salon. We pass the diner, the air is scented with sweet vanilla and freshly brewed coffee, and if we had time I'd stop.

"Are you sure about this?" Claire asks, her voice tinged with curiosity as we approach the salon.

"Mawmaw told me to be here at nine sharp. I'm trusting her," I explain.

Claire pushes open the door, and I follow behind her. As we step inside, a woman with jet-black hair and bright red lipstick greets us, handing us magazines while gesturing to the waiting area. "Hide your faces."

We do as she says, instinctively lifting the *Southern Living* magazines, shielding ourselves from whatever may come. Claire leans in, whispering with a hint of alarm, "What the fuck?"

"I don't know what's going on," I reply, a mix of anxiety and excitement bubbling within me, grateful for the barrier.

Two minutes later, the high-pitched bells jingling above the door shakes the air. I lower the magazine, my breath hitching as I see *her*. Meredith, a vision from my nightmare, steps into the shop.

"Is Hilary here? I have an appointment at nine," she says, her tone dripping with a condescending edge that cuts through the air like a knife. Instantly, the happy energy that filled the room evaporates, leaving a charged silence in its wake. The chatter and laughter stop.

My mouth slightly falls open. She's an energy vampire who drains joy and replaces it with an oppressive gloom wherever she goes. How did Hudson handle this and come out sane on the other side?

Her heels tap sharply against the polished floor, their sound echoing in the hushed salon. I lower the magazine, helplessly caught in the dark cloud of her presence. Her complaints come relentless and loud, and as the woman who handed out the magazines leads her to the hair washing station, I can only guess she's Hilary.

"Please tell me you thought of a plan," Claire whispers beside me, her voice threaded with impatience. I can sense her annoyance bubbling under the surface—she's a meticulous planner, the type who sketches out her weeks in detail. I, on the other hand, tend to drift through life, embracing spontaneity.

While Hilary washes Meredith's hair, the woman continues to grumble about the traffic, the incessant tourists, and the strange smells she's encountered on the way here. Her complaints fill the air of the salon like an unwelcome fog, thick, heavy, and suffocating. No one is listening to her. I'm afraid Hilary's eyes might get stuck in the back of her head from rolling them so much.

"Can you hurry up today?" Meredith says as she's guided to the stylist's chair after her wash. She crosses her legs as Hilary prepares to cut her hair.

Claire groans beside me, and I set the magazine down and stand.

"What are you doing?" she whispers, her wide eyes.

"Improvising," I reply, a spark of mischief igniting within me as I lock the salon door. Meredith is engrossed in an article, oblivious to the brewing storm around her. I move beside Hilary and take the scissors from her hand. The cold metal glints under the fluorescent lights. Hilary moves toward the front of the shop, pulling the large blinds closed against the world outside.

Two older women with foil in their hair occupy chairs nearby, along with a few stylists, but no one intervenes. Silent spectators to my surprising rebellion.

With a rough grip, I seize a handful of Meredith's blonde hair, jerking her head backward, and she yells in surprise.

"That hurt!" Her eyes dart to meet mine in the mirror, shock etching her features. "You? What the fuck?"

"Hi. It's so nice to see you again," I say, my voice laced with unspoken challenges as I open the scissors, steadying my grip on her hair. "I think it's time for you and me to talk."

Claire strides over, arms crossed tight against her chest, a silent beacon of fury. My sister's gaze could pierce steel.

"Who the fuck are you?" Meredith snaps at her.

"We..." Claire's voice is unwavering. "Are your worst fucking nightmare."

The smirk curling Claire's lips is charged with wickedness.

Meredith shifts, unease swallows her.

"What do you want?" Meredith glares at me through the reflection, her gaze icy and unyielding.

I clutch her hair tighter, drawing her into this moment. "What do *you* want?"

She swallows hard, her mask slipping for just a heartbeat, revealing a flicker of vulnerability—an admission that she's a coward beneath her fierce facade.

"Are you going to answer? We don't have all damn day," Claire states impatiently, her voice steady and firm.

"Well, since you can't seem to find your words, I'm going to settle this bullshit for you right now. You're going to leave Merryville and never show your bitch face in town ever again. You won't fight Hudson for Colby because you were nothing more than a surrogate."

"I'm his *mother*," she hisses, a desperate defiance creeping into her tone.

"Really? What did he want for his birthday? What's his favorite color? Animal? Who's his best friend at school?" I tighten my grip on her hair, the sharpness of it catching my breath in my throat. Thoughts swirl in my mind as blood pulses in my ears. "Do you know he cries himself to sleep because he doesn't have a mom? You do not deserve that title. Also, you do realize if you fight for custody and actually get it, you'll have to act like you give a fuck?"

"You're hurting me," she hisses, yet her body remains frozen, a testament to her fear—or perhaps her stubbornness.

"It's not comparable to what you've done to that little boy. And you're not going to continue to do that."

In a fractured moment, I catch a glimpse of my reflection in the mirror: wild eyes, exuding a volatile energy that rivals the chaos surrounding us. I look just as unhinged as Claire.

"Or what? I'm not afraid of you." She crosses her arms defiantly, a vestige of bravado masking the tremor in her voice.

"I will make every day a living hell for you for the rest of your life." I chuckle dryly, feeling the weight of my words, meaning every single one.

She scoffs, a thin veneer of confidence painted across her face. "I'll tell everyone."

"Hmm." I glance at Claire, who stands resolutely beside me, and then at the older ladies in the room, absorbed in their magazines, acting blissfully unaware. "Who's your witness?"

Claire seizes a hair clipper from its dock, the sleek device humming to life with a menacing buzz. Meredith's eyes widen in horror as the realization dawns. "You wouldn't."

"Try me," Claire retorts, taking a defiant step forward, her gaze locked onto Meredith.

Before my sister gets too close, I clear my throat. "You're

going to call your lawyer right now and tell them you agree with the terms Hudson laid out for you."

"No," she barks back.

"Okay." I shrug nonchalantly, then snip a small section of her hair, the delicate blonde strands cascading to the floor.

"You're fucking crazy!" she screams, her voice rising with panic as she picks up her phone. Her fingers fly over the screen, dialing a nine and a one.

I quickly move the scissors to her chin, the point digging in ever so slightly. Instantly, she freezes, the fear palpable in her expression.

"Call your lawyer," I say, my patience waning.

"Okay," she whispers, reluctantly conceding. She opens her contact list, her fingers trembling as she selects the number.

"Speakerphone," I urge. The shiny scissors glint menacingly under the overhead light, amplifying the stakes. I won't hurt her, but I want to. "I need to hear the conversation."

"Stone and Wolfe legal group," a woman states.

Meredith clears her throat. "Yes, I need to speak to Morgan."

An agonizing moment of silence stretches, and then a man's voice breaks through, tinged with disinterest.

"Hey Morgan. This is Meredith Jolly."

The moment I hear her use Hudson's last name, a wave of rage washes over me, and I grip the scissors tighter, almost as if I could physically drive the point home.

"Yes, Mrs. Jolly." His tone is flat, lacking enthusiasm. "Please tell me you had a come-to-Jesus moment and decided to end this custody battle before it starts?"

My eyes narrow at her, waiting.

"Wow," Claire states flatly, her incredulity echoing my own.

A VERY MERRY NANNY

"Actually," Meredith responds, her voice softer and edged with uncertainty. "Yes. I am."

He exhales a breath of relief that sounds overly dramatic. "It's a Christmas miracle."

"More like a Christmas maniac," she mutters, the tip of the scissors still in place, her hair entwined in an unforgiving grip.

"I'll get the paperwork filed. Expect finalization soon."

"Great," she mutters through clenched teeth, her pride hanging by a thread.

"Anything else?"

"No," she states, and the call ends abruptly, leaving an unsettling silence in the air.

I stare her down, an intensity in my gaze that feels electrifying. "Why would you move forward with that, when your lawyer advised against it?"

"The truth?" Her tone is laced with skepticism.

"Are you even capable of that?" Claire asks, piercing the moment with her incredulity.

"Because I hated seeing him happy with *you*."

My teeth clench, and Claire notices my shift. I've never wanted to physically hurt anyone in my life, except her. Colby and Hudson deserved so much more.

Meredith continues, knowing she got under my skin, and smirks like it gives her energy. "And I need money. Hudson is *refusing* to give me what's rightfully mine. Half of the house. The property. The bank account. His savings. I was miserable with him for five fucking years of my life. Then he knocked me up, and I resent him for it. I always will."

My anger bubbles just beneath the surface, and I remove the scissors from her chin before I do something I regret. She lets out an easy breath, but we stare one another down.

"I will give you enough money to live a comfortable life. But I never want to see your face in this town again unless Colby asks to see you directly. Then, you'll drop everything to

337

meet him." My words hang in the air, heavy with consequences.

She doesn't break eye contact, a flicker of defiance sparking in her gaze. "How much?"

"You do realize a verbal agreement is legally binding in Texas, right?" I state, my voice steady, looking for any chink in her armor.

"*How much?*" she urges between her teeth, revealing her desperation.

I glance at Claire, her negotiating prowess well known. She shoots me a knowing look, ready to take charge.

"Half a million," my sister declares firmly.

"Fuck no. What Hudson owes me is more than that." Frustration clouds my thoughts as I cross my arms, posture tightening.

"How much does he *owe* you?" Claire asks, unamused.

"Two million."

"Consider it done," I say, not realizing Hudson was worth so much.

An evil smirk spreads across her lips, momentarily disarming me.

I jerk her head back, eliciting a grunt of surprise. I force her to look into my eyes, unwavering and fierce. "Do you agree to my terms?"

"Yes," she whispers, the word escaping her lips like a reluctant agreement. "Yes. I agree."

"You leave town today, and you never speak about this to anyone," Claire tells her, her voice brokering no argument. "And you'll ensure our lawyer knows where you are at all times just in case you need to be found."

"Fine," she says, the fight seemingly drained from her. "When do I get my money?"

"I'll request a wire transfer today," I reply.

"Call this number. Give them your information," Claire says, businesslike, as Meredith captures the details.

I let her go, reluctantly releasing her hair, my fingers brushing the wisp of damp strands that fell at the back of her scalp. Hilary walks over to us, and I hand her the sharp scissors.

"You and Hudson are meant for each other. You're fucking crazy," Meredith remarks, shaking her head.

"At least I'm not a selfish bitch," I retort, grabbing the strand of hair from the floor. "I don't ever want to see you again."

"Feeling is mutual," she says, and I stare her down, knowing I've made a deal with the devil. The jingle bells crash against each other, and it pulls me back to reality.

I meet Claire outside, and the sounds of laughter and chatter contrast the silence in the salon. The blinds inside flutter open, and it's like nothing happened.

My sister turns to me, her brow raised in amusement and disbelief. "Way to keep it together."

"No fucks given," I say, a smile breaking across my lips, the adrenaline still coursing through me. "You're still as scary as I remember."

She scoffs, the sound light but edged with truth. "Speak for yourself. Everyone in town is going to be afraid of you. The scissors, Em?"

"I watch too much TV," I say with a teasing glint. She grabs my hand and squeezes it.

Once we're in the car, I let out a sigh of relief. This is over.

The familiar landscape of the farm coming into view, Claire turns to me, her expression serious. "How's everything? I guess he had a good reason as to why they were still married."

My brows furrow as I process her question. "She was planning to fight Hudson for custody of Colby."

Claire's face tightens with determination as she abruptly pulls over and slams on the brakes, the sudden stop jolting us both.

"What are you doing?"

"I'm going back to kick her ass," she declares, fire igniting in her eyes.

"Claire, no. Seriously. That's a bad idea." I plead, knowing well the potential consequences of her impulsive actions.

She's breathing heavily, her protective instincts surging to the surface. "You're giving me some of her hair."

I give her a dirty look. "For what?"

"To curse her!" Claire says, and I break into a fit of laughter. She does too.

My sister's carefree demeanor contrasts with the tension that had hung in the air moments before. She pulls back onto the road, tires crunching over gravel as the scenery shifts from dusty trails to the fields of trees that surround our farm.

"I'm seriously pissed about this. And I thought you lost control. You handled it better than I ever would've."

"Yay! We're not going to prison."

Claire shakes her head. "She deserves *nothing* as Hudson intended."

"I'm going to leave it to karma to handle her," I say. The thought of her draining presence makes my stomach churn. "I don't know how he stayed with her that long."

"Hudson's a pleaser," Claire replies. "And a peacemaker."

We turn into the farm and take the employee entrance. When we finally reach Claire's house, I marvel at how busy the farm is. Each day is busier and busier.

She parks by my van and lets me out, her eyes serious as she turns to me.

"You can never tell anyone what we did," I say.

"Oh, I'm telling Jake. You make negotiations like that beforehand, not after," she says, and I know there's no convincing her otherwise.

I look up at the sky, feeling the invigorating chill of the breeze brush against my cheeks. I breathe in the fresh air, closing my eyes for a moment, allowing the scents of the earth to fill my senses. A smile creeps across my face because I did it. I fixed this for Hudson.

"Oh my God. You're in love *love*," Claire says.

The truth registers in my expression.

She squeals. "I'm so glad! When are you moving here? When are you getting married?"

Her enthusiasm is infectious, but she's too caught up in the excitement.

"Not yet. My one requirement hasn't been met," I reply, trying to keep my tone light, but my mind races with uncertainty.

"Not the kiss at midnight thing, Em. You're not going back to New York for that?" Claire raises an eyebrow.

"I promised Billie I'd be at her party and I won't ditch my friends—hoes before bros and all that. It's a friendship promise," I assert, recalling all the nights spent laughing and confiding in them. That's why I'm so particular about what I agree to; things change so quickly now. I used to crave change, but now I want time to slow down to savor these precious moments.

I clear my throat. "I asked Hudson to meet me in New York if he wanted to give us a real chance."

My sister studies me, her brow furrowed with concern. "I'm not trying to be pessimistic, but what if he doesn't show?"

"He will." I breathe in deeply, the air feeling heavier at the thought. "But if he doesn't, I'll pretend he doesn't exist until I believe it."

CHAPTER 33

HUDSON

I stand at the kitchen counter, munching on the cookies we made last night before I need to head back to work. I might rage if one more person tells me Meredith is back in town. I'm already tired of the whispers and the rumors that have started spreading around town.

I love Merryville, but sometimes people need to stay the fuck out of my business.

Meredith Jolly's return has already spread around town. Hearing my last name attached to her still makes me fucking sick. While in the office, I overheard a few staff members talking about it. It triggered me, just like it used to. I came home before I spiraled.

The door swings open, and Emma walks in, her presence instantly known. She shines like a beacon and shields me from my dark thoughts.

"You're home," she says, surprised to see me.

"I was starving," I explain, lifting the half-eaten gingerbread man cookie sandwich. It's soon to be award-winning.

With this recipe, there's no way we'll lose. It's fucking incredible—rich and decadent, with a soft, chewy texture that melts in my mouth. I'm addicted to both Emma and her icing. It's the perfect touch to a Jolly family holiday staple.

As my eyes slide down her body, I realize she's dressed in crisp business attire that hugs her curves. Since she arrived, I don't think I've ever seen her look this polished and professional.

"Where were you?" I ask, and I notice she's holding something in her hand, her fingers delicately wrapped around it.

Emma lifts a lock of golden blonde hair that glimmers under the light.

It catches my breath.

I swallow down the bite in my mouth before I choke on it. Somehow, I manage to hold onto my cookie sandwich in my trembling hand. "Please, for the love of old St. Nick, tell me you don't need help burying a body."

She bursts out laughing, the sound rich and melodic. "The fact that you'd help."

Her heels tick across the wooden floor, contrasting sharply to the quiet I was drowning in before she arrived. Emma sets the hair on the counter casually, sending my heart racing.

"She was *handled*," she confirms, going to the pantry and grabbing a storage bag. She tucks the strands inside of it, sealing it.

I stare at her, jaw to the floor, trying to process this. My mind races, a flurry of chaotic thoughts colliding with each other like storm clouds.

"She did say I was meant for you because we're both unhinged. That's gotta count for something, right?" Her laughter dances in the air, carefree.

I shake my head, struggling to find words as if caught in a dream. Every possible scenario runs through my mind, but none makes sense. I open my mouth to say something, then close it again, the weight of her words pressing down on me.

This woman is my everything, confirmed by *Satan* herself.

"You cut her hair?" My voice is barely above a whisper as I stare at it in disbelief.

"Yep. Proof the conversation happened. If I ever legally need it." Her tone is casual.

My phone rings, jolting me from my spiraling thoughts. I glance at the screen and see it's my lawyer, Chris Frost. My brows furrow, a mix of anticipation and dread whirlpool in my stomach.

"Hudson? This is Chris Frost. I received a call from your soon-to-be ex-wife's attorney. She agreed to your terms with no changes. As soon as Judge Pine signs the divorce decree, it will be filed with the county clerk. I'm calling in a family favor so we can finish this today."

"Excuse me?"

"Oh and she's legally required to change her last name after she receives the divorce certificate from the state. I gotta say, I don't know what made her change her mind, nor does her lawyer, but it saved us from a lengthy and expensive custody battle. Consider it a Christmas miracle. Seems you got your wish after all."

My phone slips from my hand, crashing against the counter with a clatter that's like thunder in the stillness. Emma's brows raise in curiosity, her eyes sparkling with intrigue.

She did handle her.

Without a second thought, I move toward her, sliding my lips across hers, tasting the sweetness of freedom and a hint of the cookie I was eating. The kiss ignites a fire within me, an electric jolt that drowns out all doubt and fear about who I'm supposed to be with.

I hear my lawyer saying something, but I'm too lost in the moment to care as the world dissolves around us. The realization that this is finally over sends a rush of exhilaration coursing through me, and I can't help but chuckle at the unexpected turn my life has taken.

"How?" I whisper between desperate kisses, cradling her cheeks in my hands, feeling the warmth of her skin.

"Threats and money go a long way," she replies, a teasing glint in her eyes.

My eyes widen in disbelief. "You little *mobster*. I didn't know you had it in you."

She wraps her arms around my waist, pulling me closer. "No one messes with you or Colby. Ever."

"I don't need you fighting my fights for me, Em," I say.

"I know, but sometimes it's nice to have a little help, isn't it?"

I fall into her gaze, not believing this woman *actually* exists.

"Hudson? Hudson?" Chris's voice echoes through the receiver, pulling me back to reality.

I pick up the phone, trying to shake off the haze of emotion surrounding me like a fog. "Sorry. I'm sorry. I'm in a state of shock."

He chuckles lightly, a sound that feels oddly comforting. "It's fine. Do you have any questions for me?"

"Yeah," I say, stopping to glance back at Emma. "How long do I have to wait before I can remarry?" I ask, my heart racing at the thought of a new beginning—a future entwined with Emma and Colby. The idea wraps tightly around my heart.

"Thirty days unless we file a waiver, but there aren't any special circumstances. It's easier to wait, considering it's December, and people are out of the office. Anything else?" he asks, his tone professional.

Emma watches me intently. The weight of anticipation teeters like a top.

"Merry Christmas," I offer, the words feeling more significant than ever, laced with gratitude and hope. He returns the sentiment, and the call ends with a soft click.

Emma stares at me, her expression a complex mosaic of

concern and hope. I move toward her, returning my arms to her.

"Do you want to know details of what happened?" she asks, her voice soft and almost hesitant.

"No. I trust you handled it the way you felt was right," I say, kissing her forehead, inhaling the sweet scent of her hair —a comforting blend of her blue bubble bath and flowers.

"You and Colby are finally free, Hudson," she murmurs as she runs her nails through the back of my hair.

"Thank you," I whisper, holding her a little tighter as relief surges through me—washing over the anxiety I've had since yesterday— like a gentle tide. "You're my Christmas miracle, Emma. You saved me."

"And I'd do it again and again and again if it gives you closure and helps you and your son heal."

I kiss her softly, smiling against her lips as we dance in the living room. "That won't happen until you're my wife."

"Meet me in New York," she whispers, her voice tinged with excitement.

"I'll do whatever makes you happy," I reply, the weight of how I feel about her evident in my words.

Emma's brows raise. "You've been having coffee with my father."

She states it like it's a fact, a known truth rather than a question, something undeniable in the fabric of our current reality.

"Since he arrived," I say. "Please don't be upset."

"I'm not," she admits.

"It was important to me. Your family, whether good or bad, shapes the fabric of who we are, and why we do the things we do. Sometimes, if you pay attention, it can tell a story about a person. And I know so much more about you after spending time with your dad and your sister," I say. "Things that you could never share."

The corners of her mouth lift slightly. "No one has ever made an effort. Only you."

"I give a fuck, Em. And I will always make time for the things I care about."

She looks at me like she sees me, her eyes soften at the edges. "We're having dinner soon. I'd love it if you joined us."

"I will," I admit. "I have a suit I need to pull out of the closet."

"Mm. I'm going to have to fight women off of you." Her alarm goes off, piercing through our moment. Emma kisses me softly, pushing away with a hint of reluctance. "I have to pick up Colby. Sorry. Can't be late. He gets grumpy like his daddy."

I pull her back to me, running my fingers through her hair, cherishing this fleeting moment. "Thank you for saving me."

"I could say the same to you." She kisses my cheek. "Bye. Hope you have a better day. Also, that looks *really* fucking good on you."

"What does?"

"Your *real* smile."

DAYS LATER

Emma and I drive to the Community Center, where we must submit our cookie entry for the competition.

"Nervous?" I ask as we park, glancing at the long line of people holding desserts that snakes out the door and down the sidewalk.

"No," she replies, her eyes still sparkling with determination. "I know we have the best recipe. Even

Mawmaw said it was a winner when she tasted it. If we lose, I'm hiring a team to investigate them."

"Is it that serious?" I chuckle, raising an eyebrow.

"We deserve that trophy, dammit." Her red, plump lips turn upward.

I lean over and kiss her, shielded by the truck's tinted windows. "A kiss for good luck."

"I'll take another one of those, please," she says, and I savor her, temporarily losing myself in the moment.

"Mm. Let's go win this," she mutters, breathlessly.

This morning, Emma woke up extra early to decorate the tops of our cookies with royal icing, her meticulous artistry transforming each cookie into a small masterpiece. The presentation is a dazzling array of colors and intricate designs that would catch the eye of any judge. We both know it.

I open Emma's door for her, and she steps out, her festive red and white holiday dress hugging her waist and accentuates her figure. The fabric flutters lightly in the brisk air, and my eyes slide down to admire her. Her red hair is curled perfectly, catching the sunlight and reflecting it.

"Fucking gorgeous," I whisper, my voice barely more than a breath as she grabs the containers filled with our carefully crafted cookies.

Suddenly, I hear someone yelling her name, snapping out of my daydream. Then several others chime in. A group of people with cameras surround us, like a swarm of bees buzzing in an intrusive frenzy. Overwhelm immediately sets in, and my fist clenches instinctively. I don't like being crowded like this; it makes me feel cornered.

Emma notices my discomfort and hooks her finger with mine, grounding me. "Pretend they don't exist. Just me and you. Okay?"

The smile that was there has faded, replaced with a flicker of anger.

"Are you two dating?" someone asks, the question slicing through the din like a knife.

"Emma, are you still single?"

One guy gets a little too close for comfort, and I shove a shoulder into him, instinctively shielding her from the barrage.

The line of entrants watches the commotion, their expressions a mix of curiosity and concern. I quickly rush Emma inside.

She leans against the wall, shaking her head, but still holds our cookies tightly.

"What the fuck?" I whisper, my tone low but urgent. "You deal with that everywhere you go?"

"Except here. But I guess that's over," she says, closing her eyes as if she can make it all disappear. I can hear the pain in her voice, a tinge of vulnerability that makes my heart ache. "I'm sorry, Hudson. I thought I could do *normal* things."

"Don't be sorry." I shake my head firmly. "It's not your fault."

Moments later, Mawmaw moves toward us like a force of nature, her presence commanding the room. She pushes through the double doors and hollers at the photographers like they're standing on her lawn. Her voice booms with authority.

"Go on, now. Get," she says, her eyes fierce. "We don't want none of that trouble here. I'll call the sheriff!"

One of them says something rude, and she takes a step toward him, her stance unyielding. I'm halfway convinced she'll take her shoe off and swing it like a weapon. Emma's eyes widen with admiration and disbelief.

"Sorry, Mawmaw can be a bit... *unhinged*?" I quip, a slight smirk tugging at my lips.

Her pretty face relaxes.

The door slams shut behind Mawmaw, and she returns to us.

"You two okay?" Concern is etched across her face, and her brow furrows.

"Yes," Emma replies, her voice steady.

Turning to the gathered crowd, Mawmaw raises her voice. "Anyone have any objections to letting them move to the front of the line?" Her words hang in the air, bold and commanding.

The crowd, a mix of familiar faces and strangers, and no one objects.

"Come on," Mawmaw tells Emma, and we move to the front of the line, escaping chaos. I grab her free hand and squeeze it gently, feeling the warmth of her palm against mine as we're called forward to place our entry on the competition platter.

Emma carefully pulls each cookie out of the container, her smile radiating joy. I take a mental snapshot of her happiness, wanting to hold on to this moment forever.

We're given a number, a small piece of paper that feels like a ticket to something special, and we set our entry in place, carefully aligning it with pride.

"Oh, can we take a picture?" Emma exclaims. She pulls out her phone with excitement. We lean in close for a selfie, fingers pointing enthusiastically at the cookies behind us. "Perfect," she says, her eyes twinkling. "I think this is the only picture I have of us."

"We'll have to change that," I say, my heart swelling with hope and anticipation as we leave the busy judging floor together.

"Good luck," a woman at the door says. "Come back tonight at eight for the award ceremony, where the winner will be announced."

I wrap my arm around Emma, drawing her in close. The sweet scents of cookies linger in the air around us.

"We've got this," I whisper, infused with confidence. "No matter what happens, we still won."

"Yes," she replies with a perfect smile that meets her eyes. "We did."

I feel that flutter again and can't help but wonder how *I* got so lucky.

CHAPTER 34

EMMA

"Now, are you nervous?" Hudson asks as we stand in the bustling auditorium of the Community Center, surrounded by a sea of faces from every corner of Merryville. The vibrant energy in the air is palpable, and I think the entire community has gathered for this momentous occasion. Excitement twists through the room.

"Yes, I'd say I am. But it's a good nervous," I reply. He hooks his finger with mine, a gesture both reassuring and electrifying. I find strength and adoration in his simple touch.

Off to the side, Hudson's entire family is gathered with Colby, their faces illuminated with pure joy. Mawmaw, with her twinkling eyes, watches us proudly, and I'm convinced she's already planning our wedding. She gives me a thumbs-up, and I chuckle.

The judges stride onto the stage, clad in crisp culinary jackets. As they take their positions, the room grows quiet. Their footsteps echo eerily in the silence, amplifying the tension that hangs in the air like a thick fog.

Leaning in, Hudson whispers into my ear, his breath warm against my skin. "No matter what happens, you'll *always* be my Cookie Queen."

His words send a rush of warmth to my cheeks, igniting an unexpected blush.

"Welcome to the Ninetieth Annual Community Cookie Contest," the head judge announces, their voice booming with authority. "This year we had 382 entries, and every cookie was meticulously judged by professional chefs across several categories, including presentation, freshness, taste, and texture. Yes, every single cookie was eaten and rated."

Hudson interlocks his hand with mine, an intimate connection that feels daring and new, especially in front of so many people. The sensation of his fingers entwined with mine sends goosebumps racing up and down my arms. A mix of excitement and euphoria rushes over me. I'm in my own little world, lost in thoughts of what could be. Hudson smiles at me, his eyes sparkling with hope, the same hope I have tucked deep inside my heart.

Suddenly, Hudson turns to me, placing his hands firmly on my shoulders, his eyes wide with enthusiasm. His excitement mirrors Colby's infectious spirit. "Emma!"

"What? What is it?" I respond, shaking off my daydream, only to find the crowd erupting in cheers, all eyes fixated squarely on us. "We won!"

His arms swoop me into a warm embrace, and our lips connect in a kiss that suspends us in time. In that moment, the crowd dissolves, leaving the two of us in a private bubble of elation. I can't help but laugh against him, knowing we could do this...*together*.

"Oh my God! We won!" I say, realizing what's happening.

"I knew we could do it," he beams, gripping my hand tightly as we bounce toward the front of the room, our hearts racing in tandem. A large screen showcases images of our cookies, and the crowd's applause showers us in approval.

"We thought pairing a soft, traditional gingerbread cookie with a more modern icing and a delicate dusting of cinnamon was pure genius. It melted in your mouth like ice cream. Best cookie of the day by far," the judges praise. "My new favorite cookie."

"Thank you," Hudson replies, his grin infectious as they hand us the trophy. An elaborate sash is draped across both of our shoulders, and he wraps his arm around me, pulling me close as we pose for a photo that captures this monumental moment.

He tilts my chin gently with his fingers, his eyes sparkling with determination. "We did it. Going in the Hall of Fame together. No one else I'd rather share the title of Cookie Champion with."

"Me and you," I affirm, my heart swelling with joy, my smile wide and uncontrollable.

Our family rushes us. Hudson holds Colby in his arms, and I don't think I've felt this happy in all my life.

"You did it!" Claire exclaims, pulling me into a tight hug. "I knew you would."

"I guess all that practice wasn't wasted," I say, not talking about my depression baking, but all the men I dated to prepare me for *The One*.

"I'd say so," she says.

"Holy hell! You did it!" Jake says, pulling me into a hug and effortlessly swinging me around in a circle.

Hudson laughs and so does Colby. "She's not a rag doll. Put her down."

Lucas gives me a high five, then leans in and whispers in my ear. "When's the wedding?"

"Shut up!" I tell him, playfully shaking my head.

Hudson sets Colby down and meets him at eye level. "You're going with Mimi tonight. Be good, okay?"

"I am! Mimi made pumpkin pie! Mmhmm!" Colby nods, moving back to Hudson's mother who is having a proud mama moment.

We're met with congratulations, people wanting to take pictures with us. The next hour is a whirlwind.

After the ceremony ends, Hudson and I step back into the world outside. We're immediately bombarded by cameras and people yelling and jostling for our attention. The chaos is overwhelming and intrusive, and it snaps me back to my reality.

It's nearly too much for me to bear, and I can see that Hudson's similarly affected. "I'm sorry," I murmur, looking up at him, wishing I could shield him from this.

"It's not your fault, Em," he says, giving me an encouraging smile that reaches his eyes. "Now, can we please get the fuck out of here?"

"Yes, please." I laugh, knowing crowds aren't his thing and probably won't ever be. And I love that about him.

Traffic leaving Merryville is a nightmare, but somehow we manage it. The truck's headlights illuminate the road ahead, casting long shadows that dance across the landscape.

"We'll never be able to do normal things without being watched or followed. Are you ready for that?" I ask, my voice trembling slightly as I search his face for assurance.

"What is normal, anyway?" he asks, his tone firm yet soothing. "There's nothing normal about you, Em, and that's okay. I've accepted who you are and everything that comes with being with you. I don't always like all the outside bullshit, but it's out of our control." He glances in my direction, reaching for my hand. Our fingers interlock, and he kisses my knuckles. "I *still* choose *you*."

"Thank you," I say, strangely aware that I have only a little over two weeks left in Merryville before I must return to New York.

When we arrive home, the soft glow of the Christmas tree fills the living room with warmth and cheer. Hudson carefully places the trophy on the mantel, a symbol of our triumph, and I can't help but smile as I look up at it.

"Do you think we can beat Mawmaw's record?" I ask.

"We can try. Only twenty-one more to go." He picks up

his book—the one he and Jake are still buddy reading—and joins me on the couch, settling beside me. After the day we've had, the quiet soothes my soul.

I pull out my phone and text my best friends a picture of Hudson and me accepting first place. The moment is officially frozen in time, and it's something I'll cherish for eternity.

HARPER

Does he have another brother?

I laugh at the text, and Hudson glances up, curiosity flickering in his eyes. I try to ignore the way his gaze makes my heart flutter and focus on the conversation, but I can't resist stealing a glance at him. His brow quirks up, a playful challenge, and I feel like I'm in actual heaven—at least, my version of it.

EMMA

Actually, yes! Not your type though. The paps have followed me to Texas. What's being said about me right now?

They only follow me like this when a spotlight is directly on me.

BILLIE

How are things in Texas?

I know she's sidestepping my question, but I see right through it. The last thing I want is to go online and type my name into a search bar. It would drag me into a place I haven't visited in a long time. I'm heavy on protecting my peace and staying shielded from it all, but knowing what's being said allows me to defend myself and protect Hudson.

My old life has been out of sight and out of mind. It will stay like that until I return to New York and face it head-on. When I think about the city, it doesn't feel like home. I'm not sure it ever has.

EMMA

> Please tell me what's going on.

HARPER

> Sigh. I'm sorry, Emma.

Both of their text bubbles pop up simultaneously. Billie's disappears, but Harper's continues, and seconds later her text appears.

BILLIE

> Maddox broke up with that woman he was engaged to and did an exclusive interview. He told the world he realized he's still in love with you. And might always be.

HARPER

> There are pictures of you and Colby going in and out of his school. Everyone knows that Hudson is divorced. They're saying he left his wife for you after you infiltrated his life and pretended to be a nanny.

BILLIE

> It's a dumpster fire. But there's nothing to worry about. The speculation is ridiculous. Everyone's invested, though.

HARPER

> The rumors are better than reality TV. But a lot of people are rooting for you, Emma. Do not worry about this, okay? Enjoy the holidays.

BILLIE

> You're still attending my party, right?

Suddenly, adrenaline courses through my body like a shockwave, and I drop my phone onto the plush couch. Hudson immediately sets his book down. Concern is etched across his face. "Em?"

I check my heart rate, feeling like I might slide into a panic attack. Closing my eyes, I take a deep breath, desperately

LYRA PARISH

trying to stop the rising tide of anxiety. He sits up and wraps his arms around me, holding me tight, anchoring me to this reality—the one where it's us against the world. "What's wrong? Talk to me."

I cling to him, fearing that this life with him will slip through my fingers like sand. My trauma whispers that it's too good to be true, but my heart screams that it's the real deal.

"You're worrying me," Hudson murmurs, his voice low and filled with concern.

With trembling hands, I pass him my phone, letting him read the messages. I watch his face closely. His jaw clenches, and his nostrils flare in a way that betrays his growing frustration. I can see the bricks of the protective wall he builds around his heart being constructed carefully, each one a response to the harsh reality of our situation.

He hands it back to me with a perplexed look in his eyes. Then he unlocks his phone and opens his web browser, the soft click of the keys echoing in the silence.

"Don't," I say urgently, latching onto his wrist, my heart pounding hard. "You might not like what you find."

He exhales slowly, a cloud of uncertainty hanging between us. "Do you want him back?"

"I don't do second chances, Hudson. Except with you. And *only* you," I admit, my voice barely above a whisper. The weight of my confession hangs heavy in the air.

Gently, he brushes his thumb against my cheek, a tender touch that sends warmth coursing through me, and I can see his shoulders relaxing. The tension vanishes. "Okay."

"I'll do whatever I can to get the pictures of Colby removed," I promise him, my heart aching with sincerity. "I'm so sorry."

"Don't apologize. We'll navigate it together. Me and you, Em." His voice is steady, a life jacket in the constant current that tries to sweep me under and away from him.

He leans forward, painting his lips across mine. I pour

every bit of who I am and who I'll ever be into the kiss. It's a fusion of gratitude and yearning, a moment of pure connection. I cherish this man who adores me for who I am, the real me, flaws and all.

My thoughts still tug at me, and I'm so overwhelmed that a few tears spill from my eyes.

"Oh, please don't do that," he says, wiping my cheeks with gentle fingers.

"It almost feels like the end." My voice trembles.

"No, Em. This is only the beginning. And it's already so fucking beautiful." His reassurance protects me like a shield, protecting me from the storm.

Hudson stands, his presence commanding as he holds out his hand. "Come on."

In one swift motion, he lifts me and carries me over his shoulder, smacking my ass playfully.

"Mine. Always mine," he declares. The possessiveness in his tone isn't lost as he effortlessly takes the stairs two at a time. He nudges open the door to his bedroom, and with a fluid motion, he lays me down on the bed. My hair spills around me, and he looks at me with pure admiration.

The moonlight splashes through the big windows, casting silver shadows across the room. His smile is so warm it could melt ice.

After a few heartbeats, Hudson joins me on the bed, the space between us shrinking into nothingness. Our mouths slowly magnetize toward one another, pulled by an invisible thread of passion, want, and raw desire that fuels the inferno burning between us.

In that moment, I feel like I'm twirling, falling, and dancing into the abyss with him, losing myself in the depths of our connection. As we make love, our hearts braid together so tightly and meticulously. The sharpest blade can't destroy what we've built, a soul bond. Each heartbeat echoes the rhythm as we move together, surrendering to the intoxicating pull of desire and affection. His moans in my ear send me to a different dimension.

"I'll always choose you," I say, surrendering myself in this sliver of time and space with him, wanting an eternity more.

We make love until we're breathless, until we're absolutely nothing without the other. Then we do it all over again. Every caress and kiss deepens our bond. A life without Hudson just doesn't exist. This man has my heart, body, and soul in a chokehold. I want this to last forever.

"I love you, Emma," he says, kissing and holding me tight against him. His voice is a gentle whisper, yet it carries the weight of a future with him.

"I love you," I whisper into the night. My heart swells.

He holds me as he falls asleep, and I stay awake, lost in my thoughts of wishes coming true. The quiet of the night captures me. As his breathing becomes steady and rhythmic, I drift closer, listening to his heartbeat as he sleeps.

I want to be a better woman, lover, and friend because *of* him and *for* him. His presence encourages me to live and love more than I ever thought was possible. I smile, knowing a perfect human does exist, and surrender to the tranquility surrounding us. I drift away, knowing I'm already living in a dream.

CHAPTER 35

HUDSON

CHRISTMAS MORNING

I wake up super early, knowing I need to beat Colby downstairs. As soon as my foot hits the top step, I freeze, and my mouth falls open. The entire house has been transformed into what looks like Santa's workshop overnight. Twinkling lights dance along the banister, and the scent of pine wafts through the air, a warm reminder of the holiday season. The sight is so surreal that I don't know how to react.

Emma's hands wrap around my waist from behind, a tender gesture that momentarily brings me back to reality. I step aside, and her reaction mirrors my own, which throws me off because she's notoriously bad at hiding things. This girl wears her emotions and heart on her sleeve like a badge of honor, and yet, here we are, both utterly baffled by the transformation around us.

"When did you find the time?" she asks, her eyes wide with disbelief. "We fell asleep together."

"I thought you did this," I whisper, scanning the room.

"No," she states, her brows knitting together in confusion. My eyes continue to roam over the massive sea of presents.

Gifts line up and down the stairs, their vibrant colors creating a festive rainbow, and additional boxes spill into the kitchen, turning the space into a treasure trove of wrapped surprises.

"Must've been Santa," I laugh, my mind racing but offering no logical explanation.

"You serious, Clark?" she replies, incredulously.

I chuckle lightly. "We're watching that movie tonight. It's next on my list."

"One of my favorites," she says, yet her expression reveals that she's just as confused by our holiday miracle as I am. She reaches down and grabs a package wrapped in shimmering silver paper, and I catch sight of her name emblazoned on the front in elegant script. I glance over and notice a gift with my name, the same handwriting unfamiliar yet neat, as if written by someone who truly cares.

"Who has the code to your house?" Emma's eyes widen with realization. "*The code!*"

I smirk, fully aware of its significance.

"0704. The day we met," she whispers, her voice full of wonder.

"The day my life changed," I reply, pulling her close, my heart swelling with emotion. "Best day of my life after my son was born."

"I'll happily take second place to him. But also know you're my number two as well," she adds, the sincerity in her voice makes my chest swell. She loves Colby so damn much.

"Welp," I say, unable to contain my grin, "I'm officially jealous of a five-year-old. Unless there's something else in your number one spot."

"Just your son," she says softly, pulling me even closer.

I steal a spearmint-flavored kiss, the taste of her toothpaste is on my tongue. "You promise you didn't do this?"

She lifts her brows. "I swear."

"It must've taken them hours," I say, unable to keep the awe out of my voice. This is impossible.

I place a gentle kiss on her forehead before she skips down the stairs, her face lit up with amazement as she moves towards the Christmas tree, which glows in the dim light of the early morning.

I slowly descend the stairs behind her, an electric energy coursing through the air, making the moment feel even more magical.

"They're almost too pretty to tear," she whispers, her hand brushing delicately across the glittery red paper, tied with big silk ribbons. Every gift seems meticulously wrapped, a labor of love.

My face softens as I memorize every tiny freckle on her pretty face, wanting to etch this moment into my memory.

"Coffee?" I ask, eager for some caffeine before the festivities fully begin.

"Thought you'd never ask," she replies, her eyes sparkling with joy, and we make our way to the kitchen. There, an espresso machine like Jake's sits gleaming on the countertop, accented by a big red bow.

"Okay," I say, noting a new stand mixer beside it. I turn to Emma, and a question forms in my mind. "Do you think Claire did this?"

"No," Emma says. "My sister would've given me a warning."

The coffee brews, filling the kitchen with its rich scent. We pour ourselves mugs, savoring the warmth of the ceramic in our hands.

After several gulps, Colby's excited screams pierce the air from the top of the stairs.

"Santa! He listened!" Colby skips toward us, his eyes wide with the magic of the season, and he spots a gift with a bright green bow—his name elegantly scrawled across it in gleaming gold letters. "Daddy, can I open this?"

"What do you think, Em?" I glance over at her, catching the spark of joy reflected in her eyes.

She places a finger against the pout of her lips, her brow furrowing in contemplation. "Hmm."

"Pretty, pretty please?" His tiny voice squeezes my heart a little tighter.

"YES!" she exclaims, her eyes twinkle like the lights on the tree. "But only if I can open one with you."

"You can!" he replies giddily, bouncing on his feet, nodding furiously.

I watch as Emma moves to him, her hand gently resting on his back, a soft connection of warmth and love. He glances up at her, and she beams back at him with a smile that radiates comfort. The sight of them together almost makes me choke up, a swell of emotion rising within me. As they tear through the colorful wrappers, the sound of paper crinkling fills the air.

I preheat the oven for the cinnamon rolls I prepared the night before. As the rolls bake, the sweet, bubbling smells of cinnamon and sugar waft through the house. I sink into the couch with my steaming coffee and watch Emma and Colby whirl around the living room, plucking presents from the floor. Their laughter dances around me, and I know this is true happiness.

I eventually join in on the gift opening, something I haven't done in far too long.

"This is an exclusive stay in the presidential suite in Paris," I announce, holding the reservation.

"It's one of my favorite hotels," she continues, as if memories are flooding back. "You can see the Eiffel Tower from the balcony. I haven't been there in a long time."

"We'll go together," I promise.

Colby watches us intently, his eyes sparkling with curiosity. "You like each other."

Emma leans forward, her fingers dancing along his sides as she tickles him. "I like you too."

I graze along her back with my hand, and I can see the

chill bumps racing up her arms as her body responds to the gentle touch.

The oven beeps, pulling me from the moment, and I dash to grab the cinnamon rolls, their golden tops glistening as I place them on the counter. While they continue ripping through paper, I allow them to cool then add sugary icing on top. They smell incredible.

"Time to take a break and eat."

"Aww, Dad," Colby whines, his excitement momentarily dashed.

Emma, ever the negotiator, coaxes him into the kitchen, her playful demeanor a testament to their close bond. I'm pretty sure she has him wrapped around her little finger, just like every other person in his life.

"Milk?" I ask, and he eagerly nods. I pour a glass and set it in front of him before placing a big, fluffy cinnamon roll on his plate.

"It's hot," I caution, but Emma is already helping him cut it open. Steam rises from the freshly baked rolls. I hand Emma one, and we sit at the bar top in matching pajamas.

This is family in its purest form.

After eating, we return to the joyous chaos of gift opening. It stretches on for hours, each present eliciting squeals from Colby as he swims through the sea of wrapping paper.

"Daddy! I told you the house was gonna be full of presents to the sky! Santa actually listens. I was a very good boy!" His enthusiasm is contagious.

"You were," I respond proudly, still trying to wrap my head around how this happened and who was responsible. Every gift was like it was chosen by someone who knew us, personally. I feel an overwhelming sense of gratitude; it transformed this day into something truly unforgettable for Colby. I just don't know who to thank.

Suddenly, Emma gasps as she looks at the mantle.

Mr. Stinky, the mischievous elf, is bent over, mooning us. His tiny hand clutches a small note.

"It has your name on it," she offers, eyes wide with curiosity.

I take the note from that dirty little elf and unfold it. My heart races as I read the message:

Thank you for making my daughter happy. I look forward to calling you son.

I swallow hard, realization washing over me. *Mr. Manchester.*

"What is it?" she asks.

I hand the paper to her, and her eyes flick across the handwriting, absorbing each carefully formed letter as if they were precious artifacts.

"*My father,*" she whispers, a hint of disbelief tinging her voice.

"Yes," I say, smiling as I recall all the beautiful memories he's shared with me—private thoughts, tender moments from years gone by. We've become friends over the past six weeks, forming a bond that feels as natural as breathing.

"He didn't have to do this," I whisper, glancing over at Colby, who is too occupied by a truck with hydraulic arms to notice our conversation.

"No, he didn't," she explains, her tone softening. "My holidays were always spent away. I'd wished for home. *This.*" She smiles wide, and I see appreciation etched on her face.

"Seems like he's trying to make up for that, Em."

"This is a start. I'm trying to give him a chance." There's hope in her voice.

"Merry Christmas," I say, leaning forward to steal a quick kiss.

A pretty grin touches her lips. "Merry Christmas, Hudson. I hope all your wishes and dreams came true this season."

"Almost," I say, sneaking another kiss when Colby isn't looking. "There's still one more thing on my list. Actually, two, and then my life will be complete. I could die a happy man." The corner of her mouth quirks up in a way that tells me she's holding back questions, her curiosity piqued.

She swallows hard, and for a moment, we're lost in unspoken words and future possibilities, a shared dream hanging tantalizingly close.

Colby kicks paper around the house. "That's all, Daddy!"

He runs over to me, wrapping his tiny arms around my waist in a hug that feels both grounding and joyful. "I love you."

"I love you, Bee." My heart swells at his affection.

"I love you, Emma," he adds, his sincerity melting my heart.

She bends down, opening her arms to him, pulling him close. "Love you, Bee. You're such a good little boy."

He squeezes her tight, burying his face in her shoulder. "Do you still have to leave?"

She nods gently, the sadness evident in her eyes. "Yes. But it's not goodbye. Just taking a short trip."

"Can I go with you? I will be really, really good." He blinks up at her with wide, pleading eyes.

Emma boops his nose with a soft smile. "Not this time. But maybe one day."

Before he gets upset, I speak up, my tone brightening the mood. "Change out of your pajamas. Time to go to Mimi's for lunch."

He bolts up the stairs, energetic and eager, doing exactly what I say without any protest. He's still riding the high from all the presents he received from me, Emma, and her dad. Tonight, he'll open all the gifts from my brothers, grandma, and mom. By then, he'll likely be cranky, and we'll have to leave early.

When I hear his door close, I shift closer to Emma, the air between us thick with unfulfilled longing.

"I wish we had time for each other," she says, her voice a blend of frustration and desire. "I want you so bad."

"Maybe a few minutes." With a playful smirk, I slide my hand into her panties, feeling her breath hitch as my fingers flutter over her clit. She holds on to me for dear life, her body responding instinctively as I give her exactly what she needs. I have her body memorized, every curve and contour, knowing precisely how she likes to be touched.

Leaning in, I whisper in her ear, relishing the way her skin shivers under my breath. "Love hearing those little moans."

"Feels so good," she mutters breathlessly, her voice laced with pleasure as I wrap my free hand around her to steady her shaky legs. Her mouth falls open, a soft gasp escaping as my fingers sink deeper. A few more circles against her clit, and she's crumbling under my touch.

"Good fucking girl," I say, savoring the moment, allowing her to ride out her orgasm, wanting her to enjoy every jolt of pleasure coursing through her. I place my fingers into my mouth to taste her. "I want some more of that later."

"Yes," she breathes, pulling me closer and kissing me with a fervor that ignites something deep within me. "We should probably get ready, too?"

"Yeah," I reply, and as she walks past me, I can't resist giving her a playful slap on the butt. "Sexy."

"You are," she says over her shoulder, her voice drifting back to me like a whisper as she gracefully ascends the stairs. I can't help but admire her, captivated by the way her hair catches the light and the effortless sway of her hips as she makes her way to the top.

Once we're dressed, we hop into the truck, the cold air surrounds us.

"I have one more thing for you," I tell Emma, the excitement bubbling beneath my words.

"Oh?" she replies, her eyebrows arching in curiosity as we turn off the main road, the familiar landscape becoming a backdrop to our little adventure. "Where are we going?"

Colby, lost in the world of his tablet, pays no attention to us as the screen's glow reflects in his eyes. His focus is unwavering.

"You'll see," I say, trying to keep the smile from spreading too widely on my face. As soon as the barn comes into view, she glances at me.

"Colby, stay here, okay?" I say, ensuring the heat stays on for him as I step out. "I'll be right back."

He gives me a thumbs up, immersed in his game.

Emma steps out of the truck, her hand slipping into mine, warm and trusting. We walk into the first stable, the scent of hay and fresh straw filling my lungs, and stop in front of a beautiful chestnut-colored quarter horse the same color as her hair.

"Is this Thor?" she asks, tilting her head in confusion.

"It's Aphrodite," I say, a grin breaks across my face. "She's yours."

Her mouth falls open, disbelief washing over her features like a sudden rush of wind.

"You're kidding."

"No," I assure her, the joy in my heart overflowing. "She's a rescue, too. I got her so you can ride with us this summer."

"You're planning for the future?" she asks, her gaze searching mine for sincerity, the weight of her question settling between us.

"Our future," I reply, my words filled with promise.

She hugs me tight, her body shaking with happiness. "Thank you. She's beautiful."

"A pretty horse for a pretty girl," I say, kissing her forehead softly, savoring the moment.

I hold on to her tight, excited for all the adventures we're going to share. She shivers and I pull away.

"Let's go eat," I say, and we drive to my parents' house.

Emma smiles, stealing glances at me like I'm the best surprise of all.

When I park, Colby hops out and races inside, eager to join the festivities.

As we enter my parents' house, we're greeted by a round of applause when they see the containers of cookies. Today, we brought our winning recipe—Gingerbread man sandwiches—and there won't be any leftovers.

Emma hugs my parents and says hello. Her genuine affection is evident as she squeezes Mawmaw tightly. She's effortlessly woven herself into the fabric of my life, becoming a part of my every day.

"Remember, I wanna be paid in hundreds," Jake says from beside me, watching me. Lucas smirks with his arms crossed over his chest. I try to ignore my brothers, but they already know I'm so fucking in love with this woman, it's almost unreal.

Emma glances at me, grinning as she says something playful to Colby, who has remained by her side since this morning.

I tilt my head at her, admiring how stunning she is and how lucky I am that she's mine.

I just have to seal it with a kiss at midnight on New Year's Eve.

CHAPTER 36

EMMA

L eaving Hudson and Colby was one of the hardest things I've ever had to do, but I can do hard things. I've told myself over and over that it's just temporary. Hudson will come for me. I know, deep down in my heart, he will.

Throughout the day, I spent countless hours at various brokerage offices, signing stacks of paperwork to sell every piece of property I own in the city. The pungent smell of fresh ink and the sterile atmosphere left me feeling drained yet liberated as I detached myself from the familiar that's been ingrained in me since I was a kid.

As I walk into my high-rise that overlooks Central Park, an unsettling foreignness stops me. The space feels cold, void of warmth and life. Echoes of laughter and warmth that lived in Texas are nowhere to be found. Here, there's only a haunting silence.

This penthouse, once a sanctuary, will be placed on the market at the end of the month. As I look around, I feel a weight lifting off my chest; it feels good to let it go. It no longer serves me. If I ever need to visit the city, Claire and my father have homes for me to crash. I'm just over it. I want no ties to this place any longer.

A part of me thought I'd feel a tinge of sadness as I stand in the center of the living room, but all I feel is pure excitement. A new beginning is just on the horizon.

I still haven't returned to social media, and for once, I feel like I have real control over my life. The rumors swirling around me are just that—whispers in the wind—and I'm thankful that Hudson was the anchor in my storm. Now that the fog has cleared, I realize how right my sister was—I don't need the internet; it needs me.

As I take in the view, my phone buzzes, breaking the stillness of the apartment.

I don't expect it to be Hudson; I know he's busy with after-season farm cleanup for the next four weeks. Yet, a flicker of hope ignites within me.

UNKNOWN

> Sorry for texting you from a different number.
> First, hi. Second, I have something of yours
> that I'd like to return.

EMMA

> Who is this?

Attached is a picture of Maddox—his carefree smile juxtaposed with a necklace of my mother's. I'd lost it years ago. My heart drops, and a gasp escapes my lips as memories flood me.

EMMA

> When can I meet you?

MADDOX

> I'm downtown at The Monarch.

I glance at the time, quickly calculating how long it would take me to arrive. Dread of seeing him again runs through my veins.

EMMA

I'll be there.

I turn and walk into my bedroom, where everything remains exactly as I left it two months ago. It feels like a time capsule from a different lifetime. Photos of laughter and carefree days with my friends are taped on the mirror, vibrant reminders of joy. My closet is filled with clothes in every color, garments that shift with the seasons.

I hurriedly change out of the business attire I've worn all day, trading it for something more comfortable.

Fifteen minutes later, as I climb into the car, I'm blinded by camera flashes. The chaos captures me, and I haven't missed being tracked. If I could click my heels and be transported back to Texas, I'd do it in a heartbeat.

The car door closes behind me, soundproofing me from the world outside. I close my eyes, replaying the last two months with Hudson and his family. As my heart fills with warmth, it's almost as if I'm back there again, surrounded by the love and laughter that had become like home.

As we sit in the slow crawl of traffic, the world outside blurs into a haze of red brake lights and muffled sounds. I pull my phone from my bag, fingers trembling slightly, and open my text messages, hoping to find a text from Hudson.

EMMA

Thinking about you.

HUDSON

You're always on my mind.

A lump forms in my throat because I never asked if he was meeting me. It's a question I left unspoken. Now, uncertainty hangs heavy in the air around me.

After my initial meltdown over the rumors, I asked Billie and Harper not to tell me anything unless my safety was jeopardized. So far, there have been only short conversations here and there—nothing out of the ordinary.

As the car finally slows to a halt outside The Monarch, my heart starts to race. The dimly lit facade of the lounge beckons me inside, and I take a deep breath to steady myself to move forward. Photographers lounge outside, their cameras poised as I enter. The familiar scents of aged whiskey mix with the faint trace of cigar smoke, and memories flood me.

It feels like a lifetime has passed since I've walked these floors, a place once filled with laughter and unguarded moments. Maddox loved this hangout more than any other in the city, and I diligently avoided the places he frequented, priding myself on my resilience.

Once inside, my gaze lands on him. He sits at the bar alone, striking in a tailored navy blue suit and brown shoes that balance sophistication with casual flair. Our eyes meet, and I feel his gaze sweep over me, lingering, weighing, taking inventory of what he once held. But when I look back at him, I feel nothing—an echo of indifference washes over me. It's as if I'm staring at one of the countless billionaires who have tried to win my affection, just another attractive man in a tailored suit.

"Emma," he says, a smile stretching across his face as he pulls out the stool beside him.

"I'm not joining you," I state decisively, my voice cold, even harsh.

"Please. I need to talk to you," he pleads, his tone softening, laced with desperation. "Just give me ten minutes of your time, and I'll never contact you again. I need closure, Em."

I cross my arms over my chest, and a bitter laugh escapes me. "You need closure? It's been two years. That's plenty of time."

"Please?" His brows knit together, and I feel a fleeting twinge of sympathy.

I huff softly and slide onto the stool next to him. His familiar scent is strangely foreign now. I pull out my phone and set a timer so he can watch every second tick by.

"Ten minutes," I say, my voice firm.

"I know how I treated you in the past was wrong," he begins, his tone shifting as he looks me straight in the eyes. "I didn't realize what I had until it was too late. I owe you an apology for being selfish when we were together. In my mind, I thought you'd always be there, waiting for me, for when I was ready for you. But I realize now how much of a mistake that was. You're the only person who ever loved me with your entire heart, and I'm so in love with you, Emma. I know you don't give second chances, and I also recognize you've moved on; I'm not trying to win you back."

"You couldn't even if you tried," I say, the words slipping out easier than I expected.

"I know. I've seen the pictures. What is it about him?" he asks, curiosity etched across his face.

A sweet smile creeps onto my lips. "He's not afraid to show his heart, and he loves me so fiercely—the way I've always deserved. Hudson treats me like a queen."

His Cookie Queen.

Maddox nods, a look of resigned understanding washing over him. "I respect that. You'll always be the one who got away, Em."

"I know," I reply simply, an edge of finality in my voice.

Standing up, he reaches into his pocket and pulls out my mother's old necklace. The silver glints softly under the dim bar lights as he slides it around my neck. I glance down at the sterling silver heart charm, its weight familiar yet distant.

"I can tell you're in love with him," he continues, his voice tinged with sadness. "I thought, maybe, everything I've said would have you running back to me."

"I'm in love with him. Also, I don't know what you've been saying. I'm on hiatus from the internet indefinitely. It doesn't control me anymore. And a tip for the future: only desperate girls drop their lives to run back, Maddox. I know my worth."

"You always have," he tells me, the weight of his words heavy in the air between us. "Losing you will always be my biggest regret."

"I was all in with you, and you took that for granted," I confess, my voice trembling with emotion. "And I can't thank you enough for making me realize I deserved so much better. Without you, I wouldn't be *this* happy."

The shrill sound of my phone alarm breaks the charged moment we share.

He glances down at it, the reality of the situation creeping back in, and I stand. I place my hand on his shoulder, feeling the warmth radiate from him. "Good luck. I wish you the best."

"Will I see you again?" he asks, his eyes searching mine.

"No," I say, the finality of the word echoes in my ears. "I'm leaving New York. I hope you got the closure you were searching for and you find someone who makes you happy."

As I walk away, I hold the heart charm in my grasp, feeling it's reassuring weight. It almost feels like a sign from my mom, a gentle reminder of her love, a sign.

Cameras flash in my face, mercilessly capturing the bittersweet moment as happy tears stream down my cheeks. I'm ready for a new beginning, filled with the promise of love. I'm excited to live with Hudson and Colby and the magic of Merryville.

As I walk inside my penthouse, my phone buzzes insistently in my pocket.

BILLIE

Emma! You did not meet up with Maddox!

HARPER

> The pictures. Why did he give you jewelry?
> They're saying you're cheating on Hudson
> with your ex. Already.

My mouth falls open in disbelief. The truth was spun so quickly.

EMMA

> That's ridiculous. It's my mother's necklace
> that I thought I lost. He was returning it to me!

I feel a knot of unease tightening in my stomach as I immediately text Hudson.

EMMA

> Many things are being said right now, and it's
> not what it looks like, I swear.

He doesn't reply immediately, and an anxious flutter starts in my chest.

I call him, and it goes straight to voicemail. The monotone beep feels like a finality I'm not ready to accept. Instead of spiraling into panic, I take a deep breath, reminding myself everything will be okay. Because it will, won't it?

"Countdown is in five minutes!" Billie calls out, her voice cutting through the crowd as I stand by the large windows overlooking Times Square. The vibrant lights of the city glitter like a sea of stars, pulsing with life, and every face in the crowd glows with excitement. The world is celebrating, engulfed in a joyous atmosphere.

But he's not here.

I thought we were on the same page...
It felt like destiny...

I told him I loved him and meant it with every fiber of my being.

Harper glides toward me in her silver poofy dress, which looks like it was plucked straight from an '80s prom photo, all shimmering sequins and satin fabric. She holds two glasses of champagne and offers me one with a determined look as if trying to instill hope. I crave the cold bubbles fizzing against my lips.

"He should be here by now." As the glass touches my hand, I take two big gulps, hoping it will ease the anxiety tightening in my chest.

I pull my phone from my pocket, my heart pounding as I read the last text I sent him again. Still no reply.

I scan for notifications that aren't there, a pit of dread opening up inside me.

"I don't understand, Harp."

"Don't get upset yet," she replies softly, wrapping her arm around me in a comforting embrace. The warmth of her presence seeps into my skin, momentarily pushing back the chill of disappointment. She pushes away, meeting my eyes with a soft gaze. "The night isn't over."

"I didn't expect the internet to take a lie and run with it." My voice cracks, the weight of my disappointment crashing down like a heavy wave. I shake my head and drink more champagne as the crystal glass shimmers in the dim light.

"That's what the internet does. Rumors aren't truths. It means nothing. And Hudson doesn't seem like the type of man to care about anything other than you," Harper insists, giving me a small, encouraging smile. Her eyes drift toward the door, and so does mine, but it's not him who enters. "Also, being single isn't so bad. You make it seem like a curse."

"Pfft. You have no idea what I experienced, Harp. I'll never be the same after Hudson." I take a deep breath, swallowing hard against the rising tide of emotion that threatens to overflow. "I'll search for that feeling for the rest of my life."

She nods, determination glimmering in her eyes. "I know that it's all going to work out. It always does."

"I think I need some fresh air," I tell her, finishing the glass of champagne, the bubbles dancing on my tongue before evaporating into the void of my thoughts. I crave solitude, and a moment to wallow in my sorrows.

Maybe I'll adopt a cat. The thought has me thinking about Tinsel, and a knot tightens in my chest. I texted Claire earlier, asking if Hudson was still in Texas, but she told me she wasn't sure—a truth that gnaws at me.

When I step onto the balcony, the cold wind swirls around me like a brisk embrace, invigorating yet painfully reminiscent of what I've lost. The icy chills are the only thing that makes me feel alive right now, cutting through my despair.

I glance over at several couples wrapped in their own worlds, sharing whispered secrets and passionate kisses. I can't help but roll my eyes, the bitterness takes hold.

That should be me.

No matter what decision Hudson made, I promised I'd respect it. I wouldn't ask questions, and I won't. Maybe he changed his mind, realizing I might be a bit too much—too loud, too fiery, too complicated.

The seconds pass too quickly, ticking away my hope and resolve.

A tight knot forms in my chest as the reality sinks in. The very thing I feared has come to life. Maybe Hudson Jolly was my karma, a reckoning for my past mistakes. The thought spirals me deeper into despair.

Nothing will erase the memories we made together; they are etched in my mind—vivid, beautiful, and painfully bittersweet. He's burned into the very essence of who I am.

Before I upset myself further, I try to focus on the crowd

of people below, many of whom have waited in the biting cold all day to witness one of the most iconic moments in the world —the Times Square ball drop.

He made me believe he'd come for me.

I breathe in the crisp New York air, wishing it could soothe my soul in the same way Merryville did. The air in Texas was tinged with sweet nostalgia, familiar warmth, and most of all, love. For the first time in my thirty years, I understood what home felt like, a feeling I desperately miss.

The gigantic clock strikes one minute, and time slips between my fingers like it has since Halloween. It's elusive and mocking.

I slam my eyes shut, trying to hold back tears, knowing this isn't how I wished I'd ring in the New Year. I'd imagined he'd be right here with me, together—our laughter mingling with our desperate kisses, our dreams interwoven with the promise of what could have been.

With each passing second, my heart hardens like stone.

Twenty seconds.

I want to disappear; the ache in my body is almost unbearable. My eyes unfocus as I stare into the bustling street, a blur of faces and voices. My thoughts continually drift back to Hudson, the warmth of his smile and the softness of his laugh.

If given the chance, I would turn back time and live it all over again with him.

The energy pulsates through the street, laughter and cheers washing over me like waves, but I can't bear to engage. The thought of enduring the year ahead without him would be my own personal hell.

Before I completely drown in my sorrow, strong arms snake around me—a lifeline when I least expect it. I breathe in deeply, and the familiar scent of him takes hold of me, igniting a flicker of warmth amidst my despair.

"You're way too damn pretty to look so fucking sad," he

says, his voice warm and rich as his lips brush against my neck.

I turn to face him, and my breath catches in my throat.

He stands before me in a tuxedo that fits him perfectly, exactly as I'd always imagined. He's rugged and effortlessly handsome with dark hair that's a wild mess, lending him an air of untamed charm. Hudson's green eyes sparkle like emeralds catching the sunlight. He breathes me in, and I laugh, nearly crying simultaneously.

"You're here," my voice cracks, and tears well in my eyes.

He gently kisses them away, wrapping me in an embrace that feels like home. "You didn't warn me about the checkpoints. It took me nine hours to navigate the city alone," he says, urgency threading his tone. "I'm so sorry for worrying you."

"I texted and called you," I remind him, my heart pounding.

"I left my phone on the plane," he admits, regret shadowing his features. "I'm so fucking sorry."

As I glance around, I realize the people surrounding us are beginning the ten-second countdown. I lock eyes with him, and the chaotic world around us blurs into insignificance.

Ten. Nine. Eight.

"I love you, Emma. I choose you. I'll always choose you, no matter what," he whispers, sincerity coating his voice.

"I love you," I say, my voice barely more than a whisper.

Five. Four. Three.

In a moment that catches me entirely off guard, Hudson drops to one knee, pulling a ring from his pocket. My heart races wildly as he looks up at me, vulnerability etched across his handsome face. "Emma. Will you do me the honor and spend forever with me?"

Two. One.

As "Auld Lang Syne" plays, the music fills the air around us, wrapping us in its sweet melody. Overcome with emotion, I nearly knock him over as I throw my arms around him, the words catching in my throat as tears stream down my cheeks —joy and disbelief washes over me.

"Yes, a million times over," I confess, my heart bursting with love. "You were my Christmas wish, Hudson. You, this, us."

"You and me. I'm so in love with you, Emma. You're my other half, my everything. You saved me, and I'll always save you," he whispers fiercely, his eyes burning with intensity. "You've had me since the moment we met. And for the first time, my life feels complete. I'll protect you, love you, care for you. I'm deeply, madly, obsessively in love with you, Cookie Queen. My heart is yours if you want it."

"Yes, please. I want all of you. I love you so much, Hudson. I'm so stupidly in love with you. And I love Colby with every inch of my heart too," I say, tears streaming down my face. He wipes them away gently, his touch electric against my skin, and I can't kiss him enough.

Each swipe of his lips against mine is a promise, a testament to the connection that bound us together from the first time we kissed in July. When I finally pull away, I'm so happy I feel drunk, completely high on life, on him, my future husband.

He slides the ring onto my finger, and my eyes widen in disbelief. "Hudson. This is…"

"Your mother's ring. One of them, at least," he replies, his voice steady.

I study him. "My dad knew."

"Asking him was the Southern thing to do. Em, the entire family knows what I came here to do," Hudson responds, his hands reaching out to hold mine. "Will you dance with me?"

A smile flutters across my lips, widening.

"You know how to dance?" I question, and suddenly I'm transported back to Halloween, the memories swirling like snow flurries in the wind.

"Only with you," he replies, his hands resting confidently at my waist, warmth radiating from his touch. His eyes lock onto mine with an intensity that makes my heart race. "You're so fucking beautiful."

"You're a dream come true," I breathe, my face hurting from the overwhelming happiness surging through me, each moment amplifying the joy until it feels almost unbearable.

"I wished on stars for love like this. All it took was finding you," he says with absolute certainty. We sway together to the pulsating rhythm of the music as colorful confetti cascades down from the heavens, transforming the city around us into a whimsical scene from a fairytale. My world becomes a mesmerizing kaleidoscope of vibrant colors, and everything sparkles with newfound hope.

I think about our future and Colby and the radiant happiness of us being a family.

This is everything I've ever wanted and more. I never thought I'd get this chance, a golden opportunity to embrace a life full of love and laughter.

"You really didn't think I'd show?" His brow lifts, a playful challenge glinting in his eyes, lighting up his handsome face.

"I—"

"Never doubt my love for you, Emma. It's unwavering. I'd travel to fucking space if that's what you wanted," he declares, spinning me around in a whirl of laughter and adrenaline. "And I don't give a fuck about the necklace. Claire told me it was your mother's. Explanation not needed. The more they try to tear us apart, the harder I'm hanging on. I'll only let you go if you stop loving me."

"Never. As long as I can breathe, I'll love you. I can't imagine my life without you or Colby in it. Trying to return to who I was before you is impossible. The old Emma no longer exists," I confess breathlessly.

I need him as desperately as I need air itself, an essential lifeline that I cannot live without.

Our lips collide with intensity, and butterflies erupt in my stomach, a dizzying wave of emotion that fans out to every inch of me. Our tongues intertwine, and I moan softly against him, the sound mingling with the distant throb of music from the party surrounding us.

"I've missed you. The last two days have been torture."

I haven't been myself since I left Texas; every second away felt excruciating, as if a part of my soul was missing.

"Do you want to get out of here?" Hudson asks, his hand resting possessively on my waist, fingers brushing against my skin, sending electric shivers coursing through me.

I reach inside the pocket of my dress, feeling the familiar crinkle of bills—the comforting weight of them bringing me a sense of purpose.

"What's this?" he asks, glancing down at the stack of O-bills I place in his hand.

His eyes widen in surprise before he bursts into laughter—a sound that warms my heart and makes me feel light as air.

"That smile looks good on you," I say. He leans over and playfully nibbles on my neck, setting my body on fire with each teasing bite.

His eyes roam over my face, then slide down my body, taking in every curve with a gaze that feels both appreciative and possessive. I grab his hand, and we rush out of the party without saying goodbye.

As soon as we enter the elevator, my mouth crashes against his, a rush of passion that feels as though it could ignite the walls around us. The air is thick with a forever promise and unspoken desires.

"What are you thinking about?" he asks, as we step out into the chaotic lobby. People are bustling in and out, each one trying to return to their homes in the city now that the celebration is over.

His bow tie is crooked—a charming imperfection that

makes my heart flutter—and I turn to adjust it with tender care. I brush my finger against his cheek and smile.

"You. Us. Being your wife," I confess, interlocking my fingers with his. "No more hiding."

We walk out of the building, and flashing cameras momentarily blind us, a shimmering haze of light and noise. Hudson holds me tight against him, his body a shield, protecting me from the onslaught of paparazzi.

"Back the fuck off," he warns, protectiveness lacing his tone. His fierce and possessive growl sends a thrill through me.

"Emma!" one photographer calls out as we hurry toward my car, parked in the valet. The driver has been waiting since he dropped me off two hours ago, and my stomach flips at the sight of the sleek vehicle waiting for us.

"Is that an engagement ring on your finger?" a guy shouts, snapping a thousand photos per second.

Hudson allows me to climb inside first, then follows me, the door clicking shut behind him, sealing us away from the chaos outside.

As soon as we're alone, I turn to him, searching his eyes for reassurance. "You sure you're okay with this?"

"Absolutely. And no one is ever going to rush you like that again." His voice is full of determination.

"God, I missed you," I admit, moving closer, my lips grazing against his, the world outside fading away as I lose myself in him.

He cradles my face in his hands, his eyes searching mine, filled with admiration and devotion that makes me feel cherished. "My fiancée is gorgeous."

"Thank you for being my Mr. Forever, Hudson. I love you," I murmur, my eyes fluttering closed as we get lost in the beauty of the moment, one that feels timeless and electric. One that we will one day share with our children and grandchildren.

"I love you more." Hudson swipes loose hair from my face, tucking it behind my ear. "I love you so fucking much."

CHAPTER 37

HUDSON

I wait on the couch for my mother to return with Colby. The air hangs thick with tension, and I can feel the anticipation in my chest as I watch the door. When it finally swings open, Colby strides in, his arms crossed defiantly over his chest, his expression a storm cloud of anger. I've never seen him this mad before. His little face is twisted in frustration, and for a moment, I wonder if I act the same when I'm upset. *Probably.*

He attempts to give me the silent treatment as he walks toward the couch.

"How was your weekend with Mimi?" I ask, my tone light, hoping to break through the wall he's building.

"Blah." His response drips with disinterest as he plops down.

My mother stands in the doorway and casts a knowing smile in my direction. "That's your son. Love you, Bee."

"What do you say?" I prod gently, nudging him towards a response.

"Love you, Mimi," he mutters, his voice devoid of enthusiasm.

"Good luck," she tells me with a wink.

387

"Won't need it," I retort, trying to keep my spirits high.

With a sharp snap, the door shuts behind my mother. I interlock my fingers and stare at my son knowing he's growing up in front of my eyes, attitude and all. Colby stands his ground, arms still folded tightly across his chest, refusing to meet my gaze.

I sigh. "What's wrong?"

He shakes his head, and I hope this isn't a taste of what I'll be dealing with when he's a rebellious teenager struggling with hormones. I almost groan, but then I'm reminded of how much peace Emma has brought into our home. She's pure sunshine and brought light into my dark world.

"Do you remember when you asked me about marrying Emma?" I ask.

He rolls his eyes, irritation dancing in his expression. "You let her leave, Dad! I didn't get to say bye! It's dumb."

"Why would you need to say bye?" Emma's voice drifts down from the top of the stairs, a hint of amusement in her tone.

Instantaneously, Colby's frown reverses. His face lights up as he races halfway up the staircase to meet her, wrapping his arms around her tightly.

"Emma! You're really here?" he exclaims with a quiver in his small voice. Tears flow down his cheeks.

"Yeah, of course. I told you it was temporary, just a little weekend getaway." She stops and kneels down in front of him. "I'm not ever leaving you, Bee. I promise you I will always come back unless I physically can't," she assures him.

He hugs her neck, and they stay like that for what feels like an eternity. She eventually breaks hold, then gently guides him to the couch where he had been moments ago. Her presence instantly soothes him. Me too.

"I want to show you something," Emma says, squeezing between us. Her eyes sparkling with excitement as she reaches into her pocket and pulls out a small T-Rex wearing high heels. The hot pink shines bright, and it matches the one she gifted him on Halloween.

"Aww! Can I give this to Evie?" Colby beams, and my heart lurches forward. That little girl is going to break this kid's heart; I can already see it.

"You can do whatever you want with it," Emma says. "You have its match."

"Thank you!" Happiness bursts from him as he bounces eagerly on the cushion with the toy clutched in his hand.

The afternoon sunlight cascades through the windows and illuminates Emma's dark red hair, and I take a moment to admire her. I place my hand on her thigh, and she squeezes my fingers.

Fuck, I love her touch. I love *her*. Every little thing about her. This is how love should feel—easy.

"That's not all I wanted to show you," Emma continues, then stretches her left hand toward him. The diamonds of her ring glint with a dazzling brilliance, catching the light perfectly and scattering sparkles like starlight across the room. Being with her is like magic.

"Oh, wow!" Colby exclaims, spinning the ring around her finger, his eyes wide with wonder. "That's so pretty and shiny."

I drape my arm around Emma, my heart swelling with pride and affection. "Bee. I asked Emma to marry me," I announce, my voice steady yet laced with excitement.

His eyes grow even wider, a mixture of shock and joy illuminating his face. "Does that mean you're staying here?" Hope vibrates in his question.

Emma's laugh is pure and contagious. "Yes. Forever and ever."

She glances over at me, and in that moment, I lean down to kiss her softly on the cheek.

"I asked Santa for you!" Colby proclaims, jumping up and down in elation. "Woohoo!"

"Seems like you and him have something in common,"

Emma says, a playful glint in her eye as she looks at me. She was at the top of my Christmas list.

"You're going to be my mom?" Colby asks, his voice filled with uncertainty yet longing.

"I'll try my best," she admits, her tone sincere and reassuring.

"And I can have brothers and sisters?" he adds. A bigger family is something we all want.

"Eventually," she replies with a smile. "But I kinda want to enjoy hanging out with you for a little while first. And we have a wedding to plan. Sometime after that."

I'm filled with excitement, as we embrace this new chapter of our lives together.

"Okay," he says. "But I want like five brothers and sisters."

She chuckles softly. "We'll see what happens."

Colby wraps his tiny arms around her neck, the warmth of their embrace radiating love and innocence. She holds him tight, her eyes sparkling with affection as he runs his fingers through her long hair, a gesture both tender and playful. He looks at me, his round face beaming brightly. This might be the happiest I've ever seen him.

"Do you forgive me?" I ask.

He shifts away from her and pulls me into a hug that feels like home. "I love you, Daddy."

"Love you too, Bee. Always. Hold that thought," I say and head upstairs to the bedroom.

Just as I push open the door, a golden retriever puppy comes trotting toward me.

"Ready, little lady?" I ask, crouching to meet her big brown eyes.

As Emma and Colby share a few words downstairs, the sense of anticipation swells within me.

Suddenly, Colby's expression shifts; his mouth falls open in shock, and more tears spill from his eyes.

"Is...is..."

"She's yours," I say gently, handing the squirming puppy over to him.

"We picked her out just for you," Emma adds.

"But you get to name her," I offer, grinning widely. "Anything you want, Bee."

He sobs, but somehow manages to set the puppy down, plopping onto the floor beside her.

"Goldie!" he declares.

The puppy's tail wags furiously as if she loves it. I'm just glad he chose something normal because he named Mr. Stinky the Elf.

"That's perfect for her," Emma says, watching them happily.

"Goldie, welcome to your new home. This is my mom and dad," he introduces, beaming with pride as the puppy rushes toward him and licks his face enthusiastically. He rolls around on the floor, hugging her close while laughter tumbles from his lips. I settle closer to Emma, a sense of peace washing over me.

I lean into her side, my fingertips brushing against the smooth skin of her back. "I love you."

It's more than three words; it's a forever promise.

She steals a kiss and I notice goose bumps form along her arm. "I love you. I love us. Thanks for bringing me home."

"This is where you belong."

The three of us walk into my parent's house, where the entire family eagerly awaits our arrival, the atmosphere vibrant with warmth and excitement. Jake, Claire, Mr. Manchester, Lucas, my parents, and Mawmaw are gathered around the kitchen table, playing dice. As we enter the dining room, we're bombarded with congratulations and enthusiastic hugs.

"I was worried you'd say no," Lucas teases Emma.

"Shut up. You knew I'd never," she retorts playfully, and he instantly bursts into laughter, wrapping an arm around her shoulders. "Glad you're gonna be my little sister. Happy to not be the youngest. Damn."

"Daaaaamn," Colby exclaims, mimicking Lucas's tone with youthful exuberance.

"I knew he wasn't hearing *that* from me," I state, a smirk stretching across my face as I glare at him. "Was wondering which of you needed your mouths washed with soap."

"Not me. I'm the best Uncle," Jake says, holding up his hands in protest.

We move to the table, and Colby eagerly asks my mother for something to drink before settling in the living room with his tablet. The screen's glow illuminates his face as intrigue takes over. He's enjoyed the math and word games we loaded onto it. My son is a smart cookie, too.

"I have an announcement." Emma clears her throat, capturing everyone's attention.

"You're pregnant?" Mawmaw exclaims, her eyes sparkling with delight at the mere idea.

"Not yet," Emma clarifies, her gaze softening at the edges as she glances at me. I'm filled with a sense of hope and anticipation. "We're opening a cookie shop!"

Excitement ripples through the room like a giddy wave, met with a chorus of congratulations that fills the air with joy. "Were you the ones who bought that building in town?" my dad inquires, his curiosity evident.

Emma and I exchange a knowing glance. The connection between us isn't like anything I've ever experienced. We can have an entire conversation with just one look.

"Something else is going there," I say, realizing my cousin

must not have shared her good news about Sugar & Spine with everyone just yet.

"Actually, we'd like to build it on the property," I continue, my voice steady. "If I can get approval from the family, I'll move forward with the plans. We think it would bring more business to the farm and increase the bottom line."

"As long as I get free cookies, you have my approval," Mawmaw asserts, a twinkle in her eye.

"We have no issues with it," Dad tells me, glancing at Mom, who nods enthusiastically in agreement.

"I want free cookies, too," Lucas chimes in, his playful grin infectious.

"Okay, so unlimited cookies to the Jolly family. Consider it done," Emma says with a laugh. "A cookie shop seemed right. We love baking, and our cookies are a hit. Of course, I'll have to hire a few employees, but I think it'll be great. Hudson and I will make the gingerbread dough every week," she confesses, her voice tinged with excitement.

I can't wait to share the secret recipe with her, but she's insistent on figuring it out on her own first. My girl is stubborn, but I love her for it.

"Have you come up with a name yet?" Claire asks, curiosity evident in her tone.

Emma's face lights up as she nods enthusiastically. "I think it will be called Jolly Good Cookies unless something better comes along." The name dances on her lips.

"I love it. It's perfect," Mawmaw says with a smile.

"So when's the wedding?" Lucas asks.

"Soon," we both say at the same time.

"What does that mean?" Mawmaw's interest piques, which is never a good thing. She's never one to shy away from getting direct answers.

"Well." Emma's eyes meet mine. "Next weekend."

I smile. "Are y'all busy?"

Everyone gasps, the sound echoing with disbelief and anticipation.

"We don't want to wait," I explain, my heart racing. "No reason to." The spontaneity of it all feels intoxicating, a sweet promise of our forever just around the corner.

"Oh goodness, so we're getting a wedding soon?" Mawmaw is so damn excited that it brings a smile to my lips.

"That's right," I confirm as Emma asks her dad if they can talk alone. They step away, and I listen to Mawmaw chat about weddings and babies.

I glance at Emma, knowing what she's saying to her dad. It was important for her to thank him in person for everything he's done for us, from the presents to the engagement ring. I have given him my gratitude countless times, and I know how important it is for him to be involved. He desperately wants to make up for lost time with his daughters and has a kind heart. He's trying to be a good dad.

Emma hugs him for a long time, and I see her wipe away happy tears. Claire notices and gives me a sweet smile. This is a new beginning for everyone.

As Jake stands to grab more eggnog, I join him, pulling an envelope from my pocket.

I hand it to him, and he sees the crisp one-hundred dollar bills inside.

"Count it. There are thirty, just like you requested," I say.

His smile widens. "You should've never made that bet."

"I never thought, in my wildest dreams, I'd actually find love. You won fair and square. We're even."

Jake pulls me into a tight hug. "So fucking happy for you."

"Thanks. Me too."

"Now we just need to find Lucas a woman and we're set," he says with a snicker.

I look at our little brother. "Might be impossible. He's too picky."

"So were you," Jake quips. "Christmas miracles happen every year."

After an hour of being with family, Colby grows tired, and we return home. The day has been full of excitement and emotions, and I look forward to relaxing. The first thing I do when I walk in is let Goldie outside. When she's finished, she rushes Colby, and he runs around giggling. He sprints up the stairs, and Goldie struggles to follow him.

"Carry her to your room with you," I tell him. "With both hands in your arms, like she's a baby. Carefully, okay?"

He bends down and picks her up, placing sweet kisses on her head. Slowly, he takes the stairs, and I can't hear what he's saying to her.

"He's going to be the best big brother. Just like his daddy," Emma says, interlocking her fingers with mine as we go upstairs. The day has been full of emotion and the three of us are tired. After Colby is tucked in with Goldie, I climb into bed with Emma.

She's researching recipes and shop ideas. When I'm settled, she rests her head on my chest, listening to my heartbeat as I draw gentle circles on her skin. Randomly, she moves toward me, capturing my lips.

I meet her kind eyes. "Are you happy?"

"I'm *Jolly*," she whispers.

I kiss her again, grateful that she's mine and we get to live our forever together.

EPILOGUE

EMMA

EARLY SEPTEMBER

"Hudson," I say, rushing into the living room, my heart racing with anxiety. "I can't find my wedding rings."

"What?" he replies, sitting straight up on the couch, his brow furrowed in concern.

I frantically search around, peering under cushions and glancing behind the furniture. "I know I took the welded rings off in the bathroom before my shower because they felt tight on my finger, and I'm freaking out a little bit. What if it's a sign?"

He chuckles softly, trying to ease my tension. "I have no doubt you'll find them. Rings don't just walk off. But," he pulls me in close to him, "you better make sure that if any men try to hit on you while you're ringless, they know you're taken."

"Oh, you don't have to worry about that. No one else will put up with my sass," I say with a playful shrug, trying to mask my worry. "You're stuck with me. Also, who wants a pregnant woman?"

He kisses me, a tender connection that sets my heart at ease. "I love being stuck with you, to you, *in* you. Oh, and I fucking love seeing you pregnant. I want you however you come." He waggles his brows.

"If you don't stop, I'll have to take you upstairs and be *very* late to my interviews."

"Nope, you can wait," he says.

"I know. I have to hire a manager today," I sigh, wanting him, needing him, even. I thought maybe the newness of us would wear off, but every single day I've been with Hudson, I've wanted him more.

The babies are being delivered in the second week of December, so I have to get someone trained immediately. I look down at my bump, still amazed by the life growing inside me.

Twins—two tiny lives to nurture and love—sometimes the thought still freaks me out. "We probably should've planned this better."

"It's planned perfectly," he insists, his voice steady and reassuring. "I love this adventure with you. I'll be with you in December, Em. By your side the entire time. Lucas has really stepped up and we hired more people so it will be possible. This Christmas is ours."

"Thank you. I love you so much," I say, capturing his lips again. My need for him lingers between us. "Now, I gotta go, or you'll make me change my mind. Then I'll look like a hot mess mama who can't arrive anywhere on time. Then no one is going to work for us, and this season will be the best one yet."

"Okay, okay. It's going to be fine," he says. "Relax, Em. No stress, remember?" His calm words ground me in place. There is so much to do, and so little time, per usual. "Don't forget I'm picking Colby up from school today. His teacher called this morning and said she wanted to talk to me about something."

"Uh-oh," I say, an amused smile creeping onto my face. "We're going to have our hands full."

"We'll survive," he replies, kissing me again, his lips lingering against mine. Then he falls to his knees, peeling my shirt up, and kisses my belly. "I'll see you soon, my little chocolate chips."

I sit through interviews for three hours, feeling the weariness tug at me, but then the woman in front of me now is *The One*. I feel it in my bones—the connection between us is undeniable. We shared laughs and exchanged silly stories during the interview. The synergy between us feels like we're meant to be friends. She's a dream come true, bursting with culinary talent and pastry chef experience.

"You're incredible. I love your attitude. You remind me a lot of my sister and I admire her so much," I say as the interview comes to a close. Excitement bubbles inside me. "I know this is a little wild, but you have the job if you want it. You've baked with some of the best, and you used to live here. It feels like it's meant to be, and I think you could help us level up when we're ready to expand."

Her bright blue eyes light up with excitement, reflecting the dreams and ambitions we both carry.

"Really? Oh my God. Thank you, Emma. I promise I will not let you down," she says, just as excited as me. She stands up and pulls me into a hug, smiling. "After being away for so long, I realized this is home. This job just gave me a reason to come back for good."

We both return to our stools.

"Home sweet home. This Christmas already feels like it's going to be magical," I say, my hand instinctively resting on my belly, feeling the gentle flutter of anticipation. The magic of Merryville always seems to dance in the air, as Christmas is celebrated every day of the year.

The bell above the door jingles open, announcing the arrival of Colby. Following closely behind him is Hudson, whose hand rests possessively on his shoulder. Lucas falls in line, laughter spilling from his lips like music, carefree and bright. But the look on my husband's face contrasts sharply with the joyful atmosphere. He's pissed.

"Stop giggling," Hudson snaps at Lucas, his tone stern. However, Lucas, in his usual fashion, ignores him entirely.

When Hudson notices I'm not alone, he halts in his tracks. "I'm sorry, I thought you were done for the day."

"Oh we are. Come on in," I reply, gesturing for them to step into the baking area of the shop. An inviting aroma of freshly baked pumpkin cookies fills the air, mixing with the autumn chill outside.

Hudson keeps pushing Colby towards me, and I can see the guilt effortlessly etched across his tiny face.

As Colby shuffles closer, Hudson clears his throat, prompting him with a gentle nudge. "Go on."

Colby's expression shifts, contorting with hesitation as he holds his hand toward me. I instinctively reach for whatever it is, my pulse quickening as I feel the weight of something solid resting in my palm.

I glance down and see my wedding ring nestled there, a glimmer of light-catching its surface. My eyes widen in disbelief as I flick between Colby and Hudson, searching for answers.

Lucas's laughter fades the moment Holiday looks at him over her shoulder. And I notice something there, sizzling between them. My gaze snaps back to Colby.

"I'm really sorry," he says, his voice trembling.

Hudson clears his throat again, the tension growing.

"I'm really sorry for taking your ring. But I wanted to give it to Evie," he explains, his eyes burdened with guilt.

"Oh my God. That's adorable. But please don't ever take my things without asking first. We can go pick out a ring for you to give to Evie. One that's special to you, because this one is really special to me. Okay?"

Colby lowers his eyes, the weight of my words pressing down on him.

"Like your rubber ducky?" he mumbles.

My cheeks heat as Hudson chuckles beside me. "Yes, exactly like that."

I slide my ring back onto my finger, a wave of relief washing over me, knowing I didn't lose something so precious. I'd already faced that once with my necklace. I reach for it, rubbing the heart pendant between my fingers. Everything feels right, the way it was always meant to be.

"Oh, I'm so rude. Hudson, Lucas, this is Holiday Patterson," I say, my voice laced with excitement for my new manager.

"Hi, Holiday," Hudson responds politely, his smile warm and inviting.

"Lucas, come here. Don't be rude," I urge, though the tension is thick enough to cut with a knife.

He steps forward, and I notice his eyes darken. I recognize that grimace, it's the same for all the Jolly brothers.

A quick glance at Holiday reveals she has gone stone cold as well.

"Why is she here? Is this a joke?" Lucas crosses his arms over his chest defensively.

I study him closely, trying to understand if he's playing a prank on me.

"Excuse me? This is the new manager of the shop. I just offered her the job," I clarify, my heart racing.

"What the fuck, Emma!" Lucas erupts, his fury palpable. I've never seen this side of him, and it leaves me confused.

My brows furrow, and he groans in frustration, turning and storming out of the shop. The door slams behind him.

"I'm really sorry," I explain softly, my heart heavy. "I've never seen him like this."

She forces a smile. "It's fine. Thank you for the opportunity. Like I said, I promise I won't let you down. Nice seeing you again, Hudson."

The bells above the door jingle softly as she leaves, creating a gentle chime that lingers.

"Go wait outside the door, please," Hudson tells Colby, his tone firm but tempered with patience. Colby remains rooted to the spot, an air of defiance around him. "*Now.*"

Colby groans dramatically, the sound reverberating through the building, before stomping away.

"I love your dad voice," I whisper, watching Hudson's stern demeanor transform into a smirk.

"When you're grumpy, it's hot."

He turns to me, placing his fingers on my cheek. "You're adorable."

My heart flutters at his compliment. "Can you explain what the hell is going on, please?"

A moment of hesitation flickers across his face before he responds. "Oh. Right, about that. Holiday is the person Lucas has been in love with since he was a kid. Kinda like Colby and Evie. I wonder if he said her name; each time he does, she shows up like Beetlejuice."

I burst into laughter, picturing the absurdity of the situation. "They don't seem to like each other. Like, at all."

When Lucas saw her, his body tensed, and the color drained from his face. He looked as if he'd seen a ghost.

"Oh, it's more than that. They *hate* each other—public enemy number one. Lucas wouldn't piss on her if she were on fire," Hudson says, lifting my finger and kissing my ring with a tenderness that sends a shiver down my spine.

"What happened?" I ask.

"No one knows." He shrugs, "He doesn't talk about it."

I sigh, realizing this is going to be difficult.

Hudson brings me back to the rings, "When Colby's teacher told me what he'd done, I nearly shit a brick," he explains. "He knew he was in big trouble."

"And you said rings don't walk off," I reply teasingly, leaning closer until our lips nearly touch.

He stops, his eyes tracing the scattered freckles on my nose, admiring me with an intensity that sends warmth cascading through me.

"I hope you never stop looking at me like that," I whisper.

"Never," he replies, capturing my lips in a delicate kiss. "You and me forever, Cookie Queen."

THE END

Not ready to say goodbye to Hudson and Emma? (Me either!) I wrote an **exclusive bonus scene** just for you!

Download here: bit.ly/verymerrynannybonus

Need to know what happens between Lucas Jolly and Holiday Patterson?

Find out in *A Very Merry Enemy*
books2read.com/averymerryenemy

WHAT'S NEXT?

❤A VERY MERRY ENEMY❤

A *Very Merry Enemy* is an enemy to lovers, best friend's twin sister, holiday romcom. If you're searching for a small-town, hate to love you romance set in a small Southern town, this book is for you! Each book in the *Very Merry Series* can be read as a standalone and ends with a sweet as gingerbread happily ever after.

https://books2read.com/averymerryenemy

ACKNOWLEDGMENTS

Wow, here we are again! First of all, thank you so much to my readers—old and new. I will forever be grateful for you and appreciative of the time you give my words. You're the reason I'm allowed to do this. I adore you so freakin' much.

Thank you to my ARC team. You're all amazing and I'm so thankful that so many of you want my words before release. Thank you for the incredible compliments and for hyping me up. It always eases my nervous excitement that bubbles before the book goes live.

To my Beta Bishes (Thorunn, Mindy, Lakshmi, Brittany) seriously thank you for being the best hype squad out there. I can never say thank you enough. Your comments (while sometimes completely unhinged…bwahaha) and support keep me going when I'm elbow deep in the writing cave. You make this so much fun! Who does Hudson belong to?

Big thank you to Erica Rogers for helping me with *everything* with this release—super assistant/editor. It's kinda what authors dream of having in their life and I'm so lucky to have you. Thank you to Erin Branscom for stepping up to the plate last minute and for being such a huge support of me and my work. I'm so honored to call you a friend and I can't wait until we go see Taylor Swift. *Manifesting it*. I also have to give a shoutout to JS Cooper because we always seem to be racing against deadlines together. It's nice to have someone who "gets" it.

Thank you to my proofreaders: Ali Joi, Mama Debra, and

Jess Hodge. You did an amazing job and I'm appreciative that you helped me with this book.

Thanks to Dee Garcia with Black Widow Designs for designing such a cute cover. Thank you to Qamber Illustrations for making sure my character illustrations were absolutely perfect.

Big thank you to all the writers who joined me on 4thewords while I finished this book.

Writing is a lonely job and I'm one of the lucky ones who never feels that alone in the process. I have the best readers in the world and the greatest team of people.

Gigantic thank you to my hubby Will (deepskydude) for always being there for me and encouraging me when I need it the most. You're the only one who really knows the emotional rollercoaster I ride on when I'm drafting these books and how much of my life I dedicate to this career. You're the love of my life and I'm so happy to be living happily ever after with you.

KEEP IN TOUCH

**Want to stay up to date with all things Lyra Parish?
Join her newsletter!
lyraparish.com/newsletter**

**Let's be friends on social media:
TikTok 🖤 Instagram 🖤 Facebook
@lyraparish everywhere**

**Searching for the Lyra Parish hangout?
Join Lyra Parish's Reader Lounge on Facebook:
https://bit.ly/lyrareadergroup**

**You can find signed paperbacks in the shop:
https://bit.ly/lyraparishshop**

ABOUT LYRA PARISH

Lyra Parish is a hopeless romantic obsessed with writing spicy Hallmark-like romcoms. When she isn't immersed in fictional worlds, you can find her pretending to be a Vanlifer with her hubby. Lyra's a self-proclaimed 'fall queen' who loves coffee, authentic people, and living her best life.

Made in United States
Orlando, FL
07 December 2024

55096283R00250